The Quantum Gardener

and other tales . . .

Philip Mazza

Also by Philip Mazza

From Under a Tree
Book One; The Harrow Saga

Shadow in the Flame
Book Two; The Harrow Saga

Children at the Gate
Book Three; The Harrow Saga

The Child of Fire
Book Four; The Harrow Saga
(Coming 2025)

The Neon Hive

At the End of it All

The Quantum Gardener

and other tales . . .

Philip Mazza

⬡MNI PUBLISHERS

www.philipmazza.com

Omni Publishers of New York
ISBN 978-0-9977109-9-1
Printed in the United States of America

First Printing: December 2024

To the dreamers and the skeptics, the historians and the futurists,

This anthology is dedicated to those who dare to peer into the past not just for answers, but for echoes that guide the present and future. To the minds that understand history does not merely repeat, but rhymes - each era a verse in the ongoing ballad of humanity. May these stories inspire you to listen to those echoes, to recognize the patterns, and to shape a future where we learn from our past but are not bound by it.

With gratitude.

Author's Introduction

My friends,

When I was first approached with the idea of writing an anthology of science fiction and fantasy short stories, my initial reaction was a swirl of excitement and trepidation. To weave together tales of distant galaxies and ancient realms, to create a collection that traverses the uncharted expanses of imagination, was both an exhilarating challenge and a profound honor.

Science fiction and fantasy have always been more than mere genres to me; they are realms of infinite possibility, where the boundaries of reality blur and the limits of our understanding are stretched to their breaking points. From the earliest moments of human storytelling, these genres have been the playgrounds of our collective dreams and fears, offering glimpses into what might be or what could have been.

I recall the first time I fell deeply into the world of science fiction and fantasy. As a child, I was captivated by the pages of classic works, their vivid worlds and intricate plots forming a rich tapestry of adventure and wonder. The novels of Isaac Asimov, Arthur C. Clarke, Samuel R. Delaney, Harlan Ellison, and J.R.R. Tolkien – all opened doors to universes that stretched beyond the limits of our world, where magic was real and technology was both wondrous and terrifying. These early experiences shaped my understanding of what storytelling could be, setting the stage for my journey as a writer.

The task of creating this anthology is more involved than just crafting stories; it is about crafting a journey for the reader – providing a nice mix of tales. Each story is a portal, a chance to explore new landscapes and meet new characters, to grapple with timeless themes of good versus evil, technology versus nature, and the boundless potential of human imagination. This collection is designed to offer a diverse array of experiences, each one reflecting a unique voice and vision.

One of the most exhilarating aspects of this project has been the opportunity to simply create, to write differently, to write tales I have never before written. The stories you will find in this anthology span the spectrum of science fiction and fantasy, from the high stakes of interstellar exploration to the intimate struggles of heroes in ancient lands. The diversity of voices and styles ensures that there is something for every reader, whether they are drawn to the sleek and speculative worlds of future technologies or the rich and immersive sagas of mythical realms.

In crafting this collection, I sought to venture beyond the familiar, to forge narratives that challenged expectations. These stories are not meant to be easily categorized, but rather to invite readers into unexplored territories of the mind. Science fiction and fantasy are vessels for the unknown, and it is my hope that this anthology reflects that boundless spirit of discovery.

Secondly, I aimed to include stories that resonate on a personal level, tales that evoke emotion and provoke thought. Whether it is through the exploration of complex characters, the unraveling of intricate plots, or the immersion in richly unique worlds, the stories in this anthology are meant to leave a lasting impact on the reader. Each narrative is crafted with care, offering a window into my vision and inviting readers to engage with it on a profound level.

As a storyteller, I am acutely aware of the responsibility that comes with crafting such a collection. It is not just about presenting a series of stories, but about creating an experience that is both cohesive and engaging. The stories in this collection have been selected not only for their individual merits but also for their ability to contribute to a greater whole. Each tale is a piece of a larger puzzle, fitting together to form a rich and varied exploration of science fiction and fantasy.

In many ways, this collection is a reflection of my own journey as a writer. It represents my passion for these genres, my dedication to storytelling, and my belief in the power of imagination. As you embark on this journey through these pages, I hope you find yourself transported to worlds both familiar and foreign, encountering characters who will stay with you long after the last page is turned.

The process of creating this anthology has been a labor of love, a journey through the heart of science fiction and fantasy. It has been a privilege to work with my publisher and its editors. Together, I have been able to create a collection that celebrates the boundless possibilities of storytelling, offering the reader a chance to explore new worlds and experience the wonders of imagination.

As you dive into the stories within these pages, I encourage you to embrace the adventure, to lose yourself in the realms of science fiction and fantasy, and to let your imagination soar. The worlds you will encounter are as varied as they are vivid, each one a testament to the endless possibilities of the human mind.

Thank you for joining me on this journey. I hope you find as much joy and wonder in these stories as I have in writing them for you. The pages herein are a gateway to new experiences, and I am honored to be your guide through this exploration of science fiction and epic fantasy.

The Stories

The Quantum Gardener

Sunniva moved through her garden, her steps a choreographed dance of quantum precision. The air around her shimmered with probability waves, each movement causing ripples across the fabric of multiple realities. Her hands, calloused and stained with the iridescent sap of a thousand alien blooms, caressed the plants with a tenderness that belied their otherworldly nature.

Her garden was a fractal tapestry of impossible geometries, each plant a living paradox that defied the laws of conventional physics. Translucent vines twisted in non-Euclidean patterns, their tendrils phasing in and out of existence as they sought purchase in realities beyond human comprehension. Flowers bloomed in colors that had no names in any earthly language, their petals vibrating with frequencies that resonated with the fundamental strings of the universe.

She paused before a cluster of quantum roses, their petals a shimmering veil between dimensions. With a thought, she adjusted their position in spacetime, aligning their quantum states to harmonize with the garden's overall resonance. The act sent a cascade of changes rippling through adjacent realities, minute adjustments that only she could perceive and understand.

Her mind, honed by years of interdimensional cultivation, expanded beyond the confines of her physical form. She became aware of the myriad threads of possibility that wove through her garden, each plant a nexus point where countless realities intersected and diverged. The sheer complexity of it all would have driven a lesser mind to madness, but for Sunniva, it was as natural as breathing.

As she meticulously tended to the garden, memories of her early training with her mother flickered through her consciousness. She remembered the first time she'd touched a multidimensional seedling, the shock of feeling its roots extending into realities she couldn't even begin to comprehend. Years of study followed, her mind and body slowly adapting to perceive and manipulate the quantum nature of her charges. Now, she was a master gardener, her skills developed to a level of expertise that intertwined with the very fabric of spacetime.

A smile crossed her face as she reflected on her journey. But then, a disturbance in the garden's harmonic field yanked her from her daydreaming. She froze, her senses extending outward, probing the intricate web of realities for the source of the dissonance. There, in a cluster of crystalline flowers whose roots burrowed deep into an unstable pocket universe, she felt it—a tremor of wrongness that threatened to unravel the delicate balance she'd worked so hard to maintain.

"Not again," she murmured, her voice carrying undertones that resonated across multiple frequency bands. "I thought I had stabilized this one."

She knelt beside the crystalline cluster, her hands hovering over the shimmering petals. Each flower was a prism of possibility, refracting light from a dozen different suns across as many realities. She closed her eyes, reaching out with her quantum-attuned senses to probe the disturbance at its source.

The pocket-sized universes connected to these flowers were oscillating dangerously, their fundamental constants fluctuating in a way that threatened to tear them apart. If they collapsed, the resulting quantum cascade could destabilize her entire garden, potentially causing a chain reaction that would ripple across the multiverse.

So, Sunniva began to work, her fingers dancing in complex patterns as she manipulated the quantum states of the flowers. She coaxed their roots to anchor more firmly in stable realities, using them as a framework to reinforce the faltering pocket universe. It was delicate work, requiring her to simultaneously perceive and influence events across multiple dimensions.

Sweat beaded on her brow as she pushed her abilities to their limit. The garden around her seemed to hold its breath, countless realities hanging in the balance. Just as she felt the pocket universe beginning to stabilize, a discordant note rang through her consciousness - the presence of an outsider.

Her eyes snapped open, her concentration shattering. She whirled to face the intruder, her body instinctively shifting into a defensive stance that existed in three dimensions simultaneously.

A young man stood at the edge of her garden, his eyes wide with wonder and scientific curiosity. He clutched a device in his hand, its screen flickering with readings that his primitive instruments could barely begin to interpret.

"Who are you?" Sunniva demanded, her voice carrying harmonics that made the intruder's ears ring.

The young man swallowed hard, clearly overwhelmed by the reality-bending nature of the garden. "I'm Theo," he managed, his voice cracking slightly. "From the Institute. I was tracking quantum anomalies and - this place - what you've grown here is so incredible."

Sunniva's eyes narrowed, her pupils dilating to take in more of the quantum spectrum. The Institute had been a thorn in her side for eons, probing at the edges of her sanctuary with their crude instruments and limited understanding.

"This garden exists beyond your comprehension," she said, each word precise and cutting. "Your presence here threatens the very fabric of reality."

Theo took a hesitant step forward, his gaze drawn to the crystalline flowers. "I felt it," he whispered, almost reverently. "A disturbance in the quantum field. I thought - maybe I could help."

She paused, considering. The young man was clearly out of his depth, but his eagerness was palpable. And the disturbance she'd sensed earlier was growing, a cancer in the delicate ecosystem of her garden.

"Very well," she said finally, her tone softening slightly. "But understand this: one misstep, one collapsed wave function, and you could unravel entire universes."

He nodded, his face a mixture of excitement and terror. "I understand. What do we do first?"

Sunniva turned back to the crystalline flowers, their petals now pulsing with an ominous energy. "We stabilize this reality nexus," she said grimly. "And hope that we're not too late."

As they set to work, the garden around them seemed to hold its breath, countless realities hanging in the balance. The fate of infinite worlds rested in the hands of an ageless gardener and a novice scientist, their unlikely alliance forged in the crucible of quantum chaos.

***

Theo marveled at the garden, his eyes struggling to process the kaleidoscopic array of impossible flora that surrounded him. Each plant seemed to exist in a state of quantum superposition, simultaneously solid and ethereal, their forms shifting and blurring like heat mirages on a scorching highway. The air thrummed with an energy that defied conventional physics, a subtle vibration that resonated deep within his marrow, setting his teeth on edge and making the hairs on his arms stand at attention.

Sunniva moved through this otherworldly landscape with the grace of a dancer and the precision of a neurosurgeon. Her hands, weathered and scarred from years of quantum manipulation, glided over the plants with an intimacy that spoke of deep understanding and countless hours of practice.

Theo watched, mesmerized, as she adjusted the position of a flower whose petals seemed to phase in and out of existence, its colors cycling through a spectrum that included hues he had no names for.

"What exactly are we dealing with?" he asked, barely above a whisper, as if speaking too loudly might shatter the delicate quantum balance around them.

The flowers swayed gently in a breeze that seemed to come from nowhere and everywhere at once. "These flowers," Sunniva said, her voice carrying the weight of countless realities, "are tethered to a particularly volatile dimension. A disturbance has arisen, a quantum hiccup that threatens to unravel the very fabric of that reality. If we fail to stabilize it, the collapse will cascade through the multiverse like a string of falling dominoes."

Theo nodded, his mind racing to keep up with the implications. "What can I do to help?" he asked, eager to prove his worth in this realm so far beyond his understanding.

"First," she replied, plucking a seed from a nearby plant that pulsed with an inner light, "you must grasp the fundamentals of quantum gardening." She held out the seed, a minuscule galaxy of potential swirling within its translucent shell. "Each plant here is a nexus, a confluence of realities. They draw sustenance from the quantum foam, anchoring the threads of the multiverse like cosmic tent pegs."

She pressed the seed into his palm. The moment it touched his skin, he felt a jolt of energy surge through him, as if he had grasped a live wire. "This seed," she continued in a hypnotic cadence, "is a potential nexus. By cultivating it, you can forge a new intersection of realities. But the process is far from simple. You must attune yourself to the quantum vibrations, become one with the flow of multiversal energy."

Excitement coursed through him, a heady mixture of scientific curiosity and primal awe. "I'm ready," he declared, his voice steadier than he felt. "Show me the way."

Sunniva led him to a patch of soil that seemed to shimmer and shift as if it couldn't quite decide which reality it belonged to. "Plant the seed here," she instructed. "Open your mind to the quantum field. Let the vibrations guide you."

He knelt in the garden, the rich soil cool and damp beneath his knees. The seed was small in his palm, a tiny promise of life. He pressed it gently into the mercurial ground, feeling the give and take of it as if it were breathing. Then he closed his eyes.

At first, there was nothing but the darkness behind his eyelids and the pounding of his own heart. But as he concentrated, pushing his consciousness beyond the boundaries of conventional perception, he began to sense something more.

It started as a faint whisper, a barely perceptible tremor in the fabric of reality. But as he focused, the sensation grew stronger. He could feel the quantum threads weaving around him, an intricate tapestry of possibilities and probabilities. The seed in the soil became a focal point, a nexus of potential energy waiting to be shaped.

With a mental effort that left him sweating and trembling, he reached out to the quantum field, guiding the energy, coaxing it into the seed with a delicacy he never knew he possessed. To his amazement, the seed responded, sprouting tendrils of luminescent energy that reached up through the soil.

His confidence grew as he nurtured the seedling, feeling the quantum threads coalesce around this new point of intersection. The plant flourished under his care, its leaves unfurling in fractal patterns that seemed to extend into dimensions beyond the three he was accustomed to. Its flowers bloomed with colors that shifted and changed, sometimes appearing as vibrant hues he had seen before, other times manifesting as shades that existed only in the gaps between realities.

As the plant reached its full maturity, a living, breathing nexus of multiversal energy, Sunniva placed a hand on Theo's shoulder. The touch sent a shock through him, momentarily aligning their quantum frequencies. "Well done," she said, her voice carrying notes of approval and something deeper, more primal. "You've birthed a new nexus. Universes and universes and all their realities brought together into that one plant. But our task has only begun. We must now confront the disturbance that threatens to unravel everything."

He stood, his legs shaky but his resolve firm. The weight of responsibility settled over him like a cloak, heavy yet oddly comforting. "What's our next move?" he asked, ready to plunge deeper into this quantum odyssey.

Sunniva's expression grew grave as she led him to the cluster of crystalline flowers. Their petals refracted light from a thousand realities, each facet a window into a different dimension. "We must enter the reality tethered to these flowers," she explained, her voice low and urgent. "It's the only way to stabilize the quantum disturbance at its source. But the journey is fraught with peril. The reality we seek is unstable, its laws of physics in flux. We cannot predict what we'll encounter there."

He swallowed hard, his throat suddenly dry. But he nodded, squaring his shoulders. "I'm ready," he said, surprised by the steadiness in his voice.

A smile flickered across her face, there and gone in an instant. "Good," she said, extending her hand. "Hold tight to me. Our quantum signatures must remain in sync, or we risk being lost in the void between realities."

As their hands clasped, Theo felt a surge of energy course through him. Their quantum vibrations aligned, creating a harmonic resonance that seemed to ripple through the very fabric of spacetime. Together, they stepped into the heart of the crystalline flower cluster.

The world around them began to dissolve, reality peeling away like layers of an infinite onion. Colors bled into one another, forms lost coherence, and the very concept of dimensionality seemed to unravel. Theo clung to Sunniva's hand, his lifeline in this sea of quantum chaos, as they plunged into the unknown depths of a reality on the brink of collapse.

***

Sunniva pointed towards a distant structure, a twisted amalgamation of metal and crystal that pulsed with an eerie, unnatural light. It hovered over one of the larger shards of land, its presence a blight on the already unstable reality. Theo followed her, their steps careful and deliberate as they navigated the precarious terrain.

As they drew closer, the quantum energies grew more turbulent. The vibrations were now a near-deafening hum, each step amplifying the feeling of instability. The structure seemed to warp and change shape as they approached, its surfaces reflecting and refracting the chaotic energies that surrounded it.

"This is the heart of the disturbance," her voice barely audible over the din.

The building - if one could call it that - rose up like a fever dream, all twisted metal and fractured crystal. It shimmered with an otherworldly light as if it were digesting the very fabric of reality. They approached it the way one might a wounded animal: slowly, carefully, aware that any sudden movement could spell disaster.

As they drew nearer, the air itself seemed to vibrate with a malevolent energy. The building's surface rippled and shifted, as if it were a living thing, breathing in the quantum instability that permeated the atmosphere. Theo felt his skin crawl, a primal response to the wrongness of it all.

Sunniva pressed her hand against the building's surface, and for a moment, it seemed to yield, like flesh giving way beneath her touch. Then, with a sudden snap, it solidified, and they found themselves inside.

The interior was a labyrinth of twisted corridors and impossible geometries. Staircases led to nowhere, doors opened onto blank walls, and windows looked out onto vistas that changed with each blink of the eye. The laws of physics seemed to have abandoned this place entirely, leaving behind only a nightmare landscape of shifting realities.

As they navigated this treacherous terrain, the first sounds reached their ears. It began as a low murmur, barely distinguishable from the omnipresent hum of quantum energies. But as they pressed on, it grew louder, more distinct.

A voice, harsh and guttural, echoed through the corridors. The words were indistinct at first, but the tone was unmistakable – the ranting of a tyrant, drunk on power and madness.

"- lesser creatures, unworthy of the gift of existence!" The voice boomed, each word a hammer blow against the fabric of reality. "We are the chosen ones, the inheritors of the world! All others must bow before us or be swept aside!"

Theo felt a chill run down his spine. The voice seemed to bypass his ears entirely, resonating directly in his bones. He glanced at Sunniva, saw the grim determination etched on her face, and pressed on.

As they rounded a corner, they came upon a vast chamber. The walls pulsed with sickly light, and in the center stood a figure that defied description. It was as if someone had taken a human form and stretched it, twisted it until it was barely recognizable. Limbs bent at impossible angles, eyes multiplied and shifted across its surface, and its mouth – or rather, mouths – opened and closed in a cacophony of speech.

Before this abomination stood row upon row of figures. Some appeared human, others were clearly not, but all stood at rigid attention, their eyes fixed upon their leader.

"We will remake this world in our image!" The voice thundered. "No more will we be bound by the petty constraints of what had been right. We will be gods, masters of all we survey!"

And then, to Theo's horror, the assembled crowd erupted in applause. It was a sound that went beyond mere approval – it was worship, adoration, the blind devotion of fanatics to their chosen deity.

Sunniva grabbed his arm, pulling him back into the shadows. "We need to find the source of the quantum instability," she whispered. "It has to be here somewhere."

They crept along the edges of the chamber, careful to avoid detection. The rant continued, punctuated by regular outbursts of applause from the crowd. But as they moved deeper into the structure, another sound began to emerge.

At first, Theo thought it was just the structure itself, groaning under the strain of its impossible existence. But as they descended a spiraling staircase that seemed to go on forever, the sound resolved itself into something far more horrifying.

"What is that horrible sound?" he asked.

"They are screams, wails of agony," Sunniva told him. "The cries of the tortured, the damned, those who had dared to resist the others."

They found themselves in another chamber, this one darker, lit only by the occasional flash of energy that arced between strange machines. And there, strapped to tables and suspended in bubbling tanks, were the source of the screams.

Beings of all shapes and sizes, some recognizably humanoid, others utterly alien, all subjected to unspeakable torments. Theo saw bodies being pulled apart and reassembled, consciousnesses extracted and shattered, and realities rewritten on a fundamental level.

"This is how they're doing it," Sunniva breathed in a voice tight with horror and rage. "They're harvesting the energies of others. They're cannibalizing everything they can to fuel their mad dreams of godhood."

Theo felt sick, overwhelmed by the sheer scale of the atrocity before them. But Sunniva's grip on his arm tightened, grounding him in the moment.

"We have to stop this," she told him, her eyes aflame. "No matter the cost."

And as they stood there, surrounded by the screams of the tortured and the mad ravings of a would-be god, Theo knew that they had stumbled upon something far greater and more terrible than they could have ever imagined. The fate of not just their reality, but all realities, hung in the balance.

The quantum instability that had brought them here was just the beginning. The true battle was yet to come.

Sunniva tugged at him. "We need to shut it down, but we must be careful. One wrong move could accelerate the collapse."

Theo's mind raced.

They traveled deeper into the warped structure, its essence starting to fade in some areas until they came to a vast cavern. There, they could see a complex array of machinery and a crystal that formed the core of the structure. It emitted a dark, malevolent energy, the source of this reality's instability. As Sunniva moved to the device, her hands deftly manipulating its controls, Theo reached out with his mind, trying to understand the flow of quantum energy.

"We need to stabilize the energy flow," she instructed. "Guiding it into a more stable pattern while I reconfigure the device."

He took a deep breath, feeling the chaotic dance of quantum threads. Slowly, carefully, he began to guide the energy, redirecting it into a more harmonious pattern. The vibrations began to calm, the chaotic energy settling into a more stable rhythm.

"It's working," he said, his voice filled with relief. "We're stabilizing it."

Sunniva nodded, her focus unbroken. "Keep going. We're almost there."

With a final surge of effort, they brought the device under control. The malevolent energy dissipated, the chamber settling into a calm stillness. The walls and floor stopped shifting, the cracks sealing themselves as the reality began to stabilize. And the voices - the rants and wailings disappeared.

"We did it," Theo said, a sense of accomplishment washing over him.

Sunniva smiled, a rare expression of warmth. "Yes, we did. But we still need to return to our own reality."

She took his hand once more, and together they retraced their steps, navigating the now-stabilized landscape. The journey back was easier, the path clearer as the quantum threads settled into harmony.

As they stepped back into the garden, Theo felt a profound sense of relief. The interdimensional flora greeted them with their shimmering beauty, the garden a testament to their success.

"You did well," Sunniva said, her voice filled with genuine praise. "You have a natural talent for this."

He smiled, his heart swelling with pride. "Thank you. I couldn't have done it without you."

She nodded, her expression thoughtful. "There's more to this garden, more to the multiverse, than you can imagine. If you're willing, I'd like you to stay. To learn. There's so much we can accomplish together."

He felt a surge of excitement at the prospect. "I'd like that," he said. "I'd like that very much."

***

"What happens if it all unravels?" Theo asked.

Sunniva's eyes flickered with an array of colors, each hue representing a different reality she was simultaneously perceiving. Her voice, when she spoke, seemed to echo from multiple dimensions at once.

"If it all comes undone," she said, her words rippling through the quantum fabric, "everything we've ever known or understood simply - shifts. But 'shifting' doesn't quite capture it. It's more like waking from a dream you didn't know you were having."

His brow furrowed, his mind struggling to grasp the implications. "So, we just - disappear?"

Her laugh was a discordant symphony of possibilities. "Disappear? No. We become everything and nothing. Imagine every possible version of yourself, every choice you've ever made or could make, collapsing into a single point of infinite density. Then imagine that point exploding outward, scattering your essence across the multiverse."

"But wouldn't that destroy everything?" His voice trembled with the weight of cosmic implications.

Sunniva brought a seed into her hand, its shell shimmering with quantum uncertainty. "Destruction and creation are one of the same in the quantum realm. What we perceive as an end is merely a transition, a reconfiguration of probabilities."

She crushed the seed, and Theo gasped as it dissolved into a swarm of glowing particles, each one a miniature universe unto itself.

"You see," she continued, "unraveling isn't an end. It's a rebirth. The quantum threads that bind reality together don't disappear; they recombine, forming new patterns, new possibilities."

His mind reeled, trying to comprehend the vastness of what Sunniva was describing. "So, if we fail - "

"If we fail," she interjected, eyes blazing with the light of a thousand dying stars, "we become the seeds of new realities. Our consciousness, our very essence, scatters across the quantum foam, planting the potential for life, for awareness, in barren universes."

She placed her hand on his shoulder, and he felt a shock of energy coursing through him as if he were suddenly connected to every version of himself across the multiverse.

"That's why our work is so crucial," her voice resonating with the gravity of their task. "We're not just gardeners, Theo. We're the caretakers of existence itself. Every adjustment we make, every quantum thread we tend to, ripples across the fabric of reality, maintaining the delicate balance that allows consciousness to flourish."

He nodded, a newfound determination settling over him like a mantle of responsibility. "I understand," his voice steady despite the cosmic weight of their duty. "We garden not just for our reality, but for all realities."

Sunniva smiled. It was a gesture that seemed to bend light itself. "Now you're beginning to see. Now you're truly becoming a gardener."

***

Theo's consciousness expanded, stretching across the quantum landscape of Sunniva's garden. Each moment was an eternity, each breath a lifetime as he immersed himself in the intricate dance of multiversal energies. Under her tutelage, his senses sharpened, attuning to the subtle vibrations that thrummed through the quantum threads.

The garden flourished around him, a kaleidoscopic tapestry of impossible flora. Each plant pulsed with the energy of countless realities, their forms shifting and blurring as they existed simultaneously across multiple dimensions. He learned to guide these energies, his mind becoming a conduit for the forces that maintained the delicate balance of the multiverse.

As he worked on a particularly complex nexus plant, its petals shimmering with the light of a thousand dying stars, a sudden tremor rippled through the quantum fabric. The disturbance sent shockwaves through his heightened senses, like discordant notes in a cosmic symphony. He frowned, reaching out with his mind to correct the flow of energy, but his concentration wavered, the task more challenging than any he had faced before.

"Steady, Theo," Sunniva's voice cut through his rising panic. "Feel the rhythm. Guide it gently."

He inhaled deeply, the air thick with the scent of ozone and possibility. He refocused, channeling his will into the plant. Its colors began to stabilize, the chaotic energies slowly coming under control. But just as he neared completion, something shattered his concentration - a stray thought - a fleeting memory of his life before this quantum odyssey.

His hand slipped, sending a jolt of uncontrolled energy surging through the plant. The effect was instantaneous and catastrophic. The plant's petals darkened, their ethereal shimmer transforming into a dull, ominous glow. He watched in horror as the disturbance spread like a virus through the quantum network, the delicate balance of the garden unraveling before his eyes.

"Sunniva!" he cried, his voice echoing across dimensions. The panic in his tone reverberated through the quantum field, causing nearby plants to tremble and flicker.

Sunniva materialized at his side, her form shifting between solid and ethereal as she moved through the collapsing garden. Her expression was grim, her eyes reflecting the chaos unfolding around them. "We need to stabilize it! Before it spreads further."

But even as she spoke, Theo knew it was too late. The disturbance had triggered a cascade of quantum disruptions, the threads of the multiverse unraveling at an alarming rate. The garden, once a sanctuary of interdimensional beauty, began to collapse in on itself.

He reached out with his mind, desperately trying to contain the disturbance. But his efforts only seemed to exacerbate the chaos, like trying to hold back a tidal wave with his bare hands. The plants withered and died, their connections to other realities severed with audible snaps that echoed across dimensions. The ground beneath them cracked and split, revealing glimpses of other worlds, other realities, all equally doomed.

The air grew heavy with the acrid scent of destruction, a smell that defied description - the scent of reality itself burning away. Quantum particles danced erratically around them, their behavior no longer bound by the laws of physics.

"We have to stop it!" he shouted, a distorted sound within the fluctuating dimensional barriers. His desperation was palpable, a force as tangible as the chaos surrounding them.

Sunniva's face was a mask of conflicting emotions - fear, resignation, and a deep, cosmic sadness. "There's nothing we can do," her voice barely audible above the cacophony of collapsing realities. "The collapse has begun. We can't stop it."

As the garden dissolved into a chaotic void, the very fabric of reality began to tear. Theo and Sunniva stood at the epicenter of the maelstrom, witnessing the death of not just their reality, but countless others. The quantum threads unraveled around them, each one a lifeline to another universe, another possibility, now lost forever.

In that moment of ultimate destruction, Theo felt a strange sense of connection to everything - every reality, every possibility, every version of himself across the multiverse. He understood, finally and completely, the true nature of existence. And in that understanding, he found a measure of peace.

Sunniva's hand found his in the encroaching darkness. Their fingers intertwined, forming a connection that transcended physical reality. In the face of oblivion, they stood together, two points of consciousness in an ocean of chaos.

As the last threads of their reality collapsed, they stood together facing the void. Their connection, cultivated through long days tending to their impossible garden of quantum possibilities, had grown strong. They had weathered storms of failure and basked in the sunlight of shared victories, each experience weaving another thread into the tapestry of their relationship.

With the darkness consuming them, they held onto the knowledge that somewhere, in some distant corner of the multiverse, their quantum signatures would resonate once more, drawn together by forces beyond comprehension.

Now, as the familiar faded into nothingness, they clung to a comforting thought: somewhere in the vast expanse of existence, in a place beyond imagination, the essence of who they were would find each other again. And so, they surrendered to the void, their consciousness expanding to fill the infinite emptiness, becoming one with the quantum foam from which all realities are born.

***

"Master, come quickly," young Raf shouted. "Something strange is happening."

Mora, the master gardener looked up. "Tell me. What is it?" she asked.

"I... I... don't know. But whatever it is it shouldn't be here."

Mora's form glistened as she phased through the quantum barriers, her essence coalescing beside young Raf. Her eyes, iridescent pools of multidimensional awareness, focused on the anomaly before them.

A new flower, if it could be called such, pulsed with an energy in their quantum garden. Its petals, translucent and ever-shifting, seemed to exist in multiple states simultaneously. One moment, they were a deep crimson, vibrating with the frequency of a dying star. The next, they shimmered with the ethereal blue of a newborn galaxy.

"By the infinite probabilities," her voice was a chorus of quantum fluctuations. "Oh my ... a new plant that just sprouted out of nowhere."

Raf's consciousness rippled with confusion, the quantum synapses of his young mind struggling to reconcile the paradox before him. "But Master, I thought new plants could not just sprout without the deliberate seeding of our multidimensional intent."

Mora's quantum-entangled consciousness vibrated with a mixture of wonder and amusement. She gazed at the improbable seedling, its delicate leaves unfurling in defiance of all statistical likelihood. "Ah, Raf," she said, her voice a gentle hum of subatomic particles, "the universe delights in surprising us. While it's true that deliberate seeding is the norm in our multidimensional gardens, nature has a way of finding loopholes in even the most rigid of systems."

As they watched, the flower's stem began to twist, corkscrewing through dimensions unseen. It stretched upward, downward, and in directions that had no name in human language.

"Look closely, Raf," she instructed, her form flickering as she attuned herself to the flower's quantum signature. "What do you see?"

He squinted, pushing his perception beyond the limits of ordinary sight. Suddenly, he gasped. Within each petal, he could see entire universes unfolding, collapsing, and being reborn in endless cycles.

"It's - it's beautiful," he whispered. Tears of wonder traced paths down his cheeks, each droplet catching the light and refracting it into a thousand tiny rainbows. The flower seemed to vibrate with an inner radiance, its colors shifting and swirling in patterns too complex for the mind to fully grasp.

She watched him, her eyes softening with a mixture of pride and worry. "Yes, it is. But remember, Raf, with great beauty comes great responsibility. This flower has the power to reshape reality itself. We must tend to it with utmost care."

"But where did it come from?"

Mora's iridescent eyes shimmered with a knowledge that seemed to span eons and dimensions. Her form rippled, momentarily dissolving into a cloud of quantum possibilities before coalescing again. When she spoke, her voice resonated with the harmonics of collapsing wave functions.

"It comes from everywhere and nowhere. From the death of a dimension we never knew, a garden tended by others - "

Beyond the Hollowing Void

The starship Seraph hung motionless against the backdrop of swirling chaos that was the Howling Void. Its sleek hull gleamed dully, absorbing rather than reflecting the strange energies that pulsed and writhed at the edge of known space.

On the bridge, Captain Cyrene Helixian stood with hands clasped behind her back, her steel-gray eyes fixed on the main viewscreen. The Void filled the entire field of view - a maelstrom of warped spacetime, shimmering with impossible colors and shot through with arcs of quantum lightning.

Cyrene felt her crew's anxiety pressing down on her. She didn't need to turn to know that every eye on the bridge was darting between their stations and the viewscreen, faces etched with barely concealed fear.

"Status report," she demanded, her voice calm and steady.

Her first officer, Commander Dax Riven, cleared his throat before responding. "All systems nominal, Captain. Quantum engines at standby. Reality anchors engaged and holding."

Cyrene absorbed this information, allowing it to settle into the quiet corners of her mind. She had hand-picked this crew for their skill and experience, prizing their skill and experience above all else. But now, as they teetered on the precipice of the unknown, she understood why the most seasoned spacers found that even coming close to the Howling Void was unnerving.

As she gazed into the swirling chaos before them, her thoughts drifted back to the conversation that had set them on this course. The memory unfurled in her mind, as vivid and immediate as the moment it happened.

***

Grand Commander Thorus Forl's office was austere, its walls bare save for a single holo-display showing the known galaxy. Cyrene stood at attention before the Commander's desk, her spine ramrod straight.

Forl's voice was gruff, his words clipped. "Captain, I'll be blunt. No other way to say it. We need you to take the Seraph into the Howling Void."

Cyrene's eyebrows rose slightly, the only outward sign of her surprise. "Sir, with all due respect, no ship that's entered the Void has ever returned."

"Which is precisely why we need you to go in," he replied. "But you'll have some new technology that should help. Reality anchors. If they work as intended, they'll stabilize the spacetime continuum around the Seraph at each step along the way." He tapped a control on his desk, and a starship schematic appeared on the holo-display. "This is the Aegis. Our most advanced research vessel. It entered the Void three standard months ago, and we haven't heard from it since."

Cyrene studied the schematic, her mind already analyzing potential scenarios. "What was their mission, sir?"

Forl's expression darkened. "That's classified, Captain. All you need to know is that the Aegis carried technology and information vital to the security of the Confederation. Your mission is to locate the Aegis, or what's left of it, and retrieve its data core at all costs."

"And if we can't find it?" she asked.

"Then you gather whatever intelligence you can about the Void and get the hell out," he said. His eyes bored into Cyrene's. "But understand this, Captain - the Seraph cannot fall into Vornorian hands. If it comes down to it, you are authorized to initiate total self-destruct. Do you understand?"

Cyrene felt a chill run down her spine but kept her face impassive. "Understood, sir. When do we leave?"

***

A soft chime from the navigation console snapped Cyrene back to the present. Lieutenant Zara Venn, her fingers dancing over the controls, announced, "Captain, we're at the designated entry point. Awaiting your command."

Cyrene took a deep breath, feeling the weight of command settle over her like a mantle.

"Open up the ship-wide comm, Zara," she instructed the Lieutenant.

With a few keystrokes, Zara complied, and the system came to life.

Cyrene turned to face her crew on the bridge, meeting each of their eyes in turn.

"I know you're all aware of the risks," she began, her voice commanding attention across the hushed ship. "The Howling Void has claimed many ships, and the Seraph may very well be another casualty. Yet, we have a mission to complete, and I have unwavering faith in this ship and in each one of you. I'll give you an update as we're about to enter the Void."

She paused, letting her words sink in. "The Seraph is the most advanced vessel in the fleet. Our quantum engines can navigate the twisted spacetime of the Void. Our reality anchors will keep us tethered to our own timeline. And most importantly, we have each other. Together, we will face whatever the Void throws at us, and we will emerge victorious. Helixian out."

Cyrene gave a nod to Zara who swiftly disabled the comm.

A subtle shift rippled through the bridge crew, a collective intake of breath. Was it fear? Cyrene saw backs straighten and chins lift, almost imperceptibly. She allowed herself a moment to study their faces. Yes, it was. Fear, that constant companion in the vastness of space was still there. But now it was joined by something else. A quiet resolve, perhaps, or a newfound determination born of necessity.

"Let's go over our mission parameters one more time," her look settling on Dax. The words were familiar, a ritual that brought comfort in its repetition. "Dax, if you would?"

Commander Dax Riven stepped forward, activating a holo-display at the center of the bridge. "Our primary objective is to locate the research vessel Aegis, which disappeared into the Void three months ago. If found, we are to retrieve its data core by any means necessary."

The display showed a rotating model of a sleek starship, not dissimilar to the Seraph itself. "The Aegis was equipped with experimental sensor technology designed to map the interior of the Void. If we can retrieve its data, it could revolutionize our understanding of this phenomenon."

Cyrene nodded. "And our secondary objectives?"

"Gather all possible data on the Void itself," Riven continued. "Its effects on spacetime, on our ship's systems, on organic life. We're to map as much of its interior as we can without compromising the primary mission or the safety of the ship."

"Very good," Cyrene said. She turned to her chief engineer. "Talia, what's the status of our defensive systems?"

Lieutenant Commander Talia Shen met Cyrene's eyes, her own dark and focused. There was a moment, brief as a caught breath, where the enormity of their situation seemed to pass between them. Then Talia spoke, her words precise and measured.

"Reality anchors are humming along at full capacity, Captain. They should keep us lashed to our timeline, like a ship moored in a storm." She paused, her fingers prancing over her console. "Quantum shields are up, adjusting to the Void's temperamental energy as we speak."

But Talia's voice faltered for a heartbeat, and Cyrene felt the subtle shift in the air, that telltale pressure before bad news. "However-" Talia began, the word hanging between them like a fragile thing.

"Go on," Cyrene prompted.

"The nature of the Void means we can't predict how our systems will react once we're inside," Talia admitted. "We've run every simulation we can, but the real thing may be very different."

Cyrene nodded, unsurprised. "Understood. We'll have to adapt as we go. Zara, what's our navigation situation?"

Lieutenant Venn looked up from her console. "Standard navigation will be useless once we're inside, Captain. We'll be relying on quantum positioning and the experimental Void-mapping software. It should allow us to create a real-time map of our surroundings, but again, we won't know for sure until we're in."

"Very well," Cyrene said. She turned back to the viewscreen, studying the swirling chaos before them. The Howling Void seemed to pulse, as if alive and aware of their presence. For a moment, Cyrene thought she saw shapes moving within its depths - ghostly echoes of ships long lost.

She shook off the unsettling vision. "All hands, prepare for Void entry. Zara, plot our course. Talia, divert all available power to the reality anchors and quantum shields. Dax, initiate continuous sensor sweeps - I want to know the moment we detect anything that could be the Aegis."

As her crew scrambled to obey, Cyrene settled into the captain's chair. She keyed the ship-wide comm. "All hands, this is your Captain speaking. We are about to enter the Howling Void. Remember to stay focused, trust your training, and watch out for each other. Together, we will complete this mission and return home safely. Helixian out."

She cut the comm and leaned back, feeling the subtle vibrations as the Seraph's quantum engines powered up. On the viewscreen, the Void loomed ever larger.

"Course plotted and locked in, Captain," Zara reported.

"Reality anchors at maximum power," Talia added. "Quantum shields holding steady."

Cyrene took a deep breath. This was it - the moment of truth. Everything in her career had led to this point. She thought of all the ships and crews lost to the Void over the years. Would the Seraph join them? Or, would they be the first to pierce its mysteries and return?

"Take us in, Zara," she ordered. "Full power to quantum engines."

The Seraph surged forward, its sleek hull gleaming as it plunged into the swirling chaos of the Howling Void. For a moment, the viewscreen was filled with a riot of impossible colors and twisting shapes. Cyrene felt a sensation of vertigo as if the ship was falling in all directions at once.

Cyrene felt the shift, sudden and profound, as they breached the threshold. The Void enveloped them, a living tapestry of impossibilities. Quantum foam bubbled and popped against the viewscreen, while fractured spacetime twisted and writhed like a living thing. She could sense the reality anchors, those gossamer threads of certainty, straining against the chaos, fighting to keep them tethered to their own timeline.

"Status report," she said, her voice steady despite the roiling in her stomach.

"Quantum engines stable," Talia replied, her words clipped and precise. "Reality anchors holding, but only just. The strain - "

She paused, swallowing hard. "It's significant. Quantum shields are adapting, learning the rules of this placeless place."

"Navigation is - functional," Zara added, a note of wonder in her voice. "The Void-mapping software is working better than expected. I'm getting a real-time topography of our surroundings."

Riven spoke up from the sensor station. "Captain, I'm detecting multiple anomalies. Quantum echoes, temporal rifts, possibly even alternate timelines bleeding through."

Cyrene leaned forward, studying the swirling patterns on the viewscreen. "Any sign of the Aegis?"

"Negative, Captain," Riven replied. "But our sensor range is limited. The Void is interfering with - " He trailed off, his eyes widening. "Wait. Captain, I'm picking up something. It's - us."

"Explain," Cyrene demanded.

She leaned forward, her eyes fixed on the viewscreen as an image slowly faded in. It was an image that was at once familiar and alien - the Seraph, but not her Seraph. This vessel was a specter, a haunting echo of what might have been. Its hull gaped with wounds, the once-gleaming metal now dull and scarred. Where quantum engines should have pulsed with vibrant energy, there was only darkness.

"It's the Seraph, Captain," Riven said softly, his words barely a whisper in the hushed bridge. "Or rather, it's - a shadow of the Seraph. From a path we didn't take."

Cyrene felt his words settle in her chest, heavy as lead. Her gaze traced the familiar lines of her ship, now broken and adrift. The silence stretched, filled with unspoken questions and a dread she couldn't quite name.

"Life signs?" she asked, her voice steadier than she felt. She already knew the answer and could read it in the eerie stillness of the spectral wreckage before them, but some part of her needed the cold comfort of hearing it spoken aloud.

Riven's response came with a slight shake of his head, his eyes never leaving the display. "None detectable, Captain. But there's a quantum signature - it's consistent with our own. Our corpses, to be precise."

A hush descended upon the bridge, broken only by the soft whirr of equipment. A chill snaked through Cyrene, settling somewhere in the pit of her stomach. She had known the risks when she'd accepted this mission and had even prepared herself for them in theory. But seeing a dead version of her ship, her crew - herself - made it all too viscerally real.

"Captain," Zara's voice was tight with tension. "The echo - or whatever it is - it's moving. Coming towards us."

On the viewscreen, the ghostly Seraph grew larger as it drifted closer. Cyrene squinted, trying to make out details through the viewscreen. The ship's hull bore the scars of battle - scorch marks and gashes marring its once-pristine surface. Bodies floated silently through the shattered bridge, frozen in their final moments.

A solitary figure in a spacesuit caught her eye, floating untethered before the ruined vessel. As it rotated slowly, Cyrene's breath caught in her throat. The cracked faceplate revealed a face she knew all too well - her own.

Suddenly, the echo-Cyrene's eyes snapped open, glowing with an otherworldly light. Its lips moved, and somehow, impossibly, its voice echoed through the bridge:

"You must not continue," it warned in a raspy whisper. "Only oblivion awaits in the Void. Death is all that remains here."

Cyrene gripped the arms of her chair, forcing herself to remain calm, as she stared at her own lifeless face, somehow animated and speaking words of dire warning. The impossible sight before her defied explanation, and its message was unmistakable - danger lay ahead.

"Maintain course," she ordered. "That's not us. Not yet. And it won't be us. We have a mission to complete."

As the ghostly Seraph and its spectral captain faded back into the swirling chaos of the Void, Cyrene felt the weight of command pressing down on her more heavily than ever. She had led her crew into this nightmare realm where only questions were left in its wake. And now she had to find answers.

But first, they had to find the Aegis. Whatever secrets it held, whatever forces were at work here in the Howling Void, Cyrene was determined to uncover them. The fate of her ship, her crew, and perhaps the entire Confederation depended on it.

"Dax, continue sensor sweeps," she said, her voice steady despite the turmoil in her mind. "Zara, maintain our course. Talia, keep a close eye on those reality anchors. Whatever happens, we stay together. We stay focused. We complete the mission."

As her crew acknowledged her orders, Cyrene turned her gaze back to the swirling chaos outside. Somewhere out there, the Aegis waited to be found. And beyond that, the mysteries of the Howling Void itself.

Whatever came next, Cyrene Helixian and the crew of the Seraph would face it together. The Void may howl, but they would not falter. Not while she had breath in her body and a ship to command.

The Seraph plunged deeper into the quantum maelstrom, its fate yet to be written.

***

The starship Seraph moved slowly, suspended in the swirling chaos of the Howling Void, its hull reflecting the ever-shifting colors of the surrounding spacetime anomalies. On the bridge, Captain Cyrene Helixian stood motionless, her eyes fixed on the main viewscreen. The Void pulsed and writhed before her, a living entity of cosmic proportions.

"Status report," she commanded, her voice cutting through the tense silence.

Commander Riven responded, his fingers deftly moving across the holographic interface of his station. "All systems nominal, Captain. Reality anchors holding steady at 87% efficiency."

Captain Cyrene acknowledged the report with a slight nod. The Void's influence pressed against her consciousness, testing her mental fortitude. The Seraph had been designed for this mission, its quantum engines and reality-anchoring technology the pinnacle of engineering. But here, in the heart of the Howling Void, even the most advanced technology seemed inadequate in the face of the Howling Void's strange forces.

At her station, Science Officer T'Lara stood out from the utilitarian bridge design. Her violet skin had an iridescent quality, and her large, almond-shaped eyes gleamed like liquid silver.

"Captain, sensors detecting anomalous unusual energy signatures," T'Lara reported, her voice betraying a nervous energy permeating the bridge. "Possible echo formation detected at bearing 047 mark 12."

"On screen," Cyrene ordered.

The viewscreen shimmered to life, resolving into an image that elicited audible gasps from the bridge crew. It was the Seraph, or rather, another ghostly version of it. The echo ship flickered in and out of existence, its hull bearing scars and damage that their Seraph did not have.

"Magnify," Cyrene said.

The image zoomed in on the bridge of the echo Seraph. There, standing where Cyrene herself stood, was another version of her. This Cyrene's face was gaunt, her uniform torn and stained. Behind her, the bridge was in ruins, consoles sparking, and bodies strewn about.

"What happened to them?" Riven breathed

Cyrene's analytical mind quickly assessed the situation. "This appears to be an alternate timeline," she explained matter-of-factly. "We're observing versions of ourselves who experienced different events and made different decisions than we did."

As they watched, the other Cyrene seemed to look directly at them, her expression a mix of urgency and optimism. Her mouth moved, forming silent words they could not hear.

"Can we establish communication?" Cyrene asked.

T'Lara looked down at her console before shaking her head. "Negative, Captain. The echo is not fully phase-aligned with our reality. I believe we can only observe, but not interact."

Before their eyes, the echo Seraph began to break apart, its hull disintegrating into the swirling energies of the Void. The echo Cyrene's face contorted in a silent scream, then vanished along with her ship.

The bridge fell silent. Each crew member grappled with the implications of what they had just witnessed, their minds trying to comprehend the cosmic drama that had unfolded before them.

Cyrene's voice ripped through the quiet, crisp and businesslike. "Log the encounter," she ordered. Her tone betrayed no hint of the mental gymnastics she was performing to process what they had seen. "We must study these echoes if we hope to traverse the Void safely." She knew that comprehension was their best defense against the unknown perils that surely awaited them.

Over the next several hours, the temporal distortions intensified. At first, the echoes manifested as fleeting apparitions - spectral Seraphs and phantom crews that flickered in and out of existence like faulty holograms. These brief glimpses offered tantalizing hints of divergent timelines, of paths not taken and fates averted.

As time wore on, the echoes grew more substantial and prolonged. Entire scenes played out before the bewildered crew, windows into alternate realities where their counterparts met with glorious victory or crushing defeat. In one echo, they witnessed themselves successfully completing their mission and returning home as heroes. In another, they saw the Seraph torn apart by gravitational forces, the crew's final screams silenced as they were scattered across the cosmos.

With each new encounter, the crew's grasp on their own reality became increasingly tenuous. The constant barrage of "what-ifs" and "might-have-beens" wore away at their psychological defenses. They found themselves questioning every decision, and every action, wondering if some other version of themselves had made better choices. The once-cohesive team began to fracture under the strain, their confidence eroded by the endless parade of alternate outcomes.

Lieutenant Zara Venn, who was the youngest member of the bridge crew, approached Cyrene during a lull between echo encounters. "Captain," she said trembling slightly, "how can we be certain of our own existence? Might we not be mere echoes ourselves, trapped in an endless loop of cosmic repetition?"

Cyrene swiveled in her command chair to face the young crewmember, seeing the fear and doubt in her eyes. The captain's eyes narrowed. It was a question she had been asking herself since they entered the Void, but as captain, she couldn't afford to show such uncertainty.

"Lieutenant," she said, infusing her voice with a confidence she didn't entirely feel, "our reality is not defined by the echoes we encounter, but by the choices we make. These apparitions we've witnessed are but quantum possibilities, not immutable facts. We are the authors of our own cosmic narrative."

Zara nodded, seemingly reassured, but Cyrene could see the doubt lingering in her eyes. It was a doubt shared by many of the crew, a creeping existential dread that threatened to undermine their mission.

As if sensing her thoughts, the Void chose that moment to present them with another echo. This time, it wasn't the Seraph they saw, but a different ship entirely.

"Captain," T'Lara called out, "sensors are detecting a Vornorian battle cruiser at coordinates 182 mark 35."

The image on the viewscreen solidified, revealing a massive Vornorian vessel, its hull scarred and pitted. Unlike the echo Seraph, this ship seemed more solid, more present in their reality.

"What are they doing here?" Riven muttered.

"Probably swallowed by the Void. Life signs?" Cyrene asked, a note of urgency in her voice.

T'Lara's fingers moved rapidly across her console, inputting commands and analyzing data. She spoke in a calm, matter-of-fact tone. "Captain, I am detecting multiple life signs aboard the alien vessel. However, the readings are unstable and inconsistent. It is as if the beings exist partially outside our normal spacetime continuum."

The bridge erupted with flashing lights and alarm klaxons. The Vornorian ship's weapons systems activated, its disruptor banks radiating with lethal energy.

Captain Cyrene reacted swiftly, her voice clear and authoritative. "Raise shields immediately. Helm, execute evasive maneuvers."

The Seraph banked hard, narrowly avoiding a barrage of disruptor fire. The Vornorian ship pursued, its attacks becoming more frenzied with each passing moment.

"Return fire!" Cyrene ordered. "Target their weapons systems!"

Laser-pulse beams lanced out from the Seraph, striking the Vornorian vessel. But instead of the expected explosion, the beams passed through the ship as if it were made of smoke.

"Our armaments are producing no discernible effect," Riven reported, his voice tight with tension. "The target appears to be an echo rather than a physical construct. While we cannot inflict damage, it retains the capacity to harm us."

Cyrene's mind sorted through potential solutions, each discarded as quickly as it formed. Finally, she addressed her science and engineering officers. "T'Lara, conduct a detailed analysis of the echo's phase variance. Dax, modulate our shields to match."

As her crew carried out her instructions, Cyrene's gaze remained fixed on the main viewscreen, studying the Vornorian vessel intently. Its attack pattern had devolved into a chaotic, almost frenzied display, lacking its previous tactical precision. The enemy's weapons fire veered away from the Seraph, seemingly at random.

A realization struck her with sudden clarity. "The Vornorian ship is not engaged in pursuit. Its behavior indicates it is fleeing from an as-yet-unidentified threat."

As if in response to her words, a new echo appeared behind the Vornorian vessel. It was massive, a writhing mass of tentacles and void-black flesh, a creature, if it could be called that, seemed to devour the very essence of spacetime around it.

The creature's presence warped reality, bending light and matter to its will. It moved with a terrible grace, each motion sending ripples through the cosmos. The laws of physics seemed to bow before it as if recognizing a superior force. This was no mere alien life form, but a being that existed beyond the boundaries of known science, a cosmic anomaly that challenged the very foundations and understanding of the universe.

"What in the name is that?" Riven whispered, his usual bravado shaken.

The Vornorian ship fired desperately at the creature, its weapons having no more effect than the Seraph's had. With terrifying speed, the monstrosity engulfed the Vornorian vessel, crushing it like a tin can. Then, its attention turned to the Seraph.

"Full reverse!" Cyrene shouted. "Get us out of here!"

The Seraph's engines whined in protest as they pushed against the Void's chaotic currents. The creature pursued, its tentacles reaching out across impossible distances.

"Reality anchors failing!" T'Lara reported, her voice cracking. "We're losing grip on our timeline!"

Cyrene felt a moment of pure, primal fear. Then, drawing on years of training and experience, she forced it down. "Reroute all available power to the reality anchors. Dax, plot a course through that quantum filament at 220 mark 78."

"Captain, that filament is highly unstable," Riven protested. "We could be torn apart!"

"It's our only chance," Cyrene shouted back. "Do it."

The Seraph plunged into the luminescent thread, pursued relentlessly by the colossal reverberation. As they breached the quantum current, the very essence of existence appeared to warp and contort in their wake. Warning systems shrieked their urgent message as the ship's structure groaned under the strain.

For a moment that seemed to last an eternity, Cyrene thought they had made a terrible mistake. Then, with a final wrenching shudder, the Seraph burst free of the filament. Behind them, the creature's echo dissipated, unable to maintain cohesion in the rapidly shifting quantum fields.

As the crew caught their breath, Cyrene turned to T'Lara. "Status report."

The science officer's fingers darted across her console. "Minor damage to outer hull plating. Reality anchors holding at 62% efficiency. But Captain - our position has changed significantly."

"Explain," Cyrene said, a knot of apprehension forming in her gut.

T'Lara's face bore a somber expression as she looked up. "We've been moved approximately 3.7 light-years from our previous position. And - sensors are detecting temporal anomalies around us. It appears we may have traversed both space and time."

"Shit," Cyrene sighed.

A hush descended upon the bridge as the crew grappled with the implications. They were adrift in an ocean of quantum uncertainties, their path home obscured.

Cyrene took a steadying breath. "Very well. We were aware of the dangers when we ventured into the Void. Our objective remains unchanged: to explore, comprehend, and devise a method for safe navigation through this region." She addressed the entire bridge crew. "What we've witnessed today is merely the beginning. The echoes, temporal displacements, and quantum anomalies are all pieces of a greater puzzle. It falls to us to put these pieces together."

Her gaze swept across the viewscreen, her presence commanding the attention of every officer. "I know you're scared.

I know you're questioning everything you thought you knew about reality. But remember this: we are not passive observers in this cosmic tangle. We are active participants. Our choices, our actions, they ripple across the quantum foam, shaping the very strands of existence."

She looked upon each crew member individually, noting their fear, the doubt, but also their determination. "We will map these echoes. We will understand their patterns. And we will find our way home. Not just for ourselves, but for every version of us across every timeline. We carry the hopes and dreams of countless realities with us. It's a heavy burden, but I can think of no crew more capable of bearing it."

As she finished speaking, she noticed a transformation in her team. Their gazes sharpened with renewed purpose. Fear and doubt still lingered, but they were now overshadowed by a steely readiness to confront whatever challenges the Howling Void might present.

"Dax," she said, turning to her first officer, "begin mapping our new position. T'Lara, I want a full analysis of the temporal anomalies. Zara, work with engineering to boost our reality anchor efficiency. We need to be prepared for the next echo encounter."

Her crew responded with immediate action, each officer focusing on their assigned tasks. Cyrene paused, her mind replaying the haunting vision of the shattered Seraph. The silent anguish of her echo-self reverberated in her consciousness.

"Not us," she whispered to herself. "Not our fate. We will endure. We will prevail."

With that thought firmly in mind, she turned her attention back to the swirling chaos of the Howling Void, ready to face whatever challenges lay ahead. The Seraph forged onward.

***

The Seraph floated motionless in the endless expanse of the Howling Void, its once-gleaming hull now tarnished by the chaotic swirls of fractured spacetime. Captain Cyrene Helixian stood on the bridge, her gaze locked on the approaching maelstrom of temporal anomalies that resembled a massive wave of distorted reality.

"Status report," she said calmly even though tension stung at her.

Commander Dax Riven glanced at his station's displays. "We're maintaining our position 3.7 million light years from our last verified location, Captain. Reality anchors are under strain but functioning at 80% efficiency. Quantum shielding fluctuates between 92% and 95%."

Cyrene stared straight ahead at the viewscreen. "And the anomalies?"

"Increasing in frequency and intensity," Riven replied, his voice tight. "We've counted over three hundred distinct temporal distortions in the last hour alone."

Cyrene's eyes focused on the swirling patterns before her. To the untrained eye, it might have appeared as nothing more than a kaleidoscope of colors and shapes. But she saw the underlying patterns, the ebb and flow of timelines colliding and separating.

"Helm, maintain our position," she ordered. "T'Lara, continue your analysis of the anomalies. I want to know if there's any pattern we can exploit."

As her crew hurried to comply, Cyrene experienced the familiar sensation of responsibility settling upon her shoulders. She had spent years in preparation for this moment, rigorously training her mind and body to withstand the reality-warping effects of the Void. Yet no amount of training could fully prepare one for the mind-twisting nature of this bizarre realm.

The ship suddenly shuddered, causing the lights to flicker briefly. Cyrene's fingers tightened around the arms of her captain's chair, her knuckles turning pale with the force of her grip.

"Report!" she demanded.

"Temporal surge, Captain," T'Lara responded. "It passed within 500 meters of our port bow. The reality anchors absorbed most of the impact, but we're seeing some strain on the structural integrity field."

Cyrene's mind processed the information with computer-like efficiency, dissecting the situation into its component parts. They were operating at the very limits of their technological capabilities, balanced precariously on the knife-edge of the possible. A single error in judgment, a fractional miscalculation, and they risked being torn asunder, their constituent atoms scattered across a multitude of divergent timelines.

The temporal maelstrom surrounding them was unlike anything they had encountered before, its energies fluctuating in patterns that defied conventional analysis. Yet within those chaotic swirls of chronometric energy, Cyrene sensed a rhythm, an underlying logic that might be their salvation - if only they could decipher it in time.

"Reroute auxiliary power to the structural integrity field," she ordered. "And bring us about to heading 227 mark 4. If we can't avoid these surges, we'll ride them out."

As the helmsman executed the maneuver, Cyrene felt a strange doubling sensation, as if she was simultaneously occupying multiple points in space and time. She saw ghostly afterimages of herself and her crew, echoes from other timelines that existed alongside their own.

One of these echoes briefly materialized – another Cyrene, her attire in tatters and her visage marred by injury. "Don't trust the echoes," the apparition cautioned in a hushed tone. "They'll misguide you." Then it vanished, leaving behind an ominous feeling.

Cyrene dismissed the disconcerting incident, concentrating on the present moment. "T'Lara, what's the status of those anomalies?"

The science officer's fingers flew over her console. "They appear to be coalescing, Captain. Forming a larger, more coherent distortion approximately 10,000 kilometers off our starboard bow."

"Put it on the screen," Cyrene commanded.

The viewscreen shifted, showing a roiling mass of spacetime, folding and unfolding in impossible ways. It pulsed with an otherworldly energy that set Cyrene on edge.

"Analysis?" she asked, her voice tight.

T'Lara's voice was strangely detached as she replied. "It appears to be a nexus point, Captain. A convergence of multiple timelines and realities. The energy readings are off the scale."

Cyrene studied the phenomenon, her mind thinking through possibilities and potential outcomes. This could be exactly what they had come to study – a key to understanding the nature of the Howling Void itself. But it could also be their doom.

"Helm, bring us closer," she ordered. "Nice and easy. I want to stay just outside the event horizon of that thing."

"Aye, Captain," the helmsman responded, hands moving carefully over the controls.

As they drew nearer to the nexus, the effects on the ship intensified. The deck plates vibrated beneath their feet, and the air itself seemed to shimmer with potential energy.

Suddenly, alarms blared across the bridge and warning lights flashed as systems began to fail, one after another.

"Report!" Cyrene barked, gripping the arms of her chair as the ship bucked and heaved.

"Power levels critical!" Riven's voice crackled over the noise. "Reality anchors failing - quantum shielding disintegrating - engines non-functional."

Cyrene processed the information swiftly, her mind calculating probabilities and outcomes. The nexus loomed before them, its gravitational pull inexorable. Reality itself seemed to warp and twist around the ship. Without immediate action, the Seraph and her crew would be torn apart - their very existence scattered across a million different timelines.

"Divert all available power to the reality anchors!" she ordered. "Riven, get down to engineering and see if you can get the engines back online. T'Lara, I need options. How do we get out of this?"

As her crew scrambled, Cyrene closed her eyes, reaching out with her heightened senses. She could feel the timelines stretching out around her, an infinite web of possibilities. Somewhere in that tangle lay the key to their salvation – she just had to find it.

Another ghostly figure flickered into existence beside her – this time, a version of herself in an admiral's uniform, face lined with age and wisdom. "The answer lies in the echoes," it told her. "But choose wisely. Not all paths lead to salvation."

Her eyes snapped open. "Belay that last order," she said. "Cut power to the reality anchors. Let us drift."

"Captain?" Riven's disbelief was evident in his tone. "Without the anchors, we'll be torn apart!"

"Trust me, Commander," she said. "Sometimes you have to let go in order to find your way."

As the last of the reality anchors failed, the Seraph was plunged into chaos. The very structure of the ship seemed to blur and shift, solid matter becoming as insubstantial as smoke. Cyrene felt herself stretching, her consciousness expanding to fill the Void.

In that final instant of disintegration, her vision crystallized - a slender filament of hope, a route emerging from the chaos. Summoning her remaining reserves, she extended her consciousness and seized it, drawing the Seraph and its crew in her wake.

Reality reasserted itself with jarring abruptness. The Seraph hung in normal space once more, the roiling forces of the

Howling Void now reduced to a faint ripple on the distant horizon. The ship's sensors struggled to recalibrate after the intense distortions, gradually bringing the surrounding starfield into focus.

"Status report," Cyrene said, her voice hoarse.

"All systems coming back online," Riven reported, wonder in his voice. "We're - we're intact, Captain. How did you do it?"

Cyrene smiled, a thin, weary expression. "Sometimes the only way forward is to embrace the unknown," she said. "Set a course for the nearest starbase, Commander. I think we've all earned a rest."

As the Seraph limped away from the Howling Void, Cyrene knew their ordeal was far from over. The echoes they had encountered, the glimpses of other timelines – those would haunt them, shaping their choices in ways they couldn't yet understand. But for now, they were alive, and that was enough.

The next few hours passed in a blur of activity as the crew worked to repair the damage done by their journey through the Void. Cyrene moved from station to station, offering encouragement and guidance where needed. But always, in the back of her mind, she turned over the words of her ghostly doubles. Don't trust the echoes. The answer lies in the echoes. But which was the truth?

As the immediate crisis passed and the ship settled into a steady cruise towards the nearest starbase, Cyrene retreated to her ready room. She needed time to think, to better understand what they had experienced.

No sooner had the door slid shut behind her than another echo shimmered into existence – this one a version of herself in a tattered uniform, face gaunt and eyes haunted.

"You must go back," the apparition said. "The fate of more than just your crew hangs in the balance. The choices you make will ripple across all of reality."

Before Cyrene could respond, the echo faded away, leaving her alone with her thoughts.

She sank into her chair, mind whirling. The enormity of what they had stumbled into was beginning to sink in. The Howling Void wasn't just a spatial anomaly – it was a connection point, a place where all possible timelines converged. And somehow, she and her crew had become entangled in events that spanned the multiverse itself.

A chime at her door interrupted her musings. "Enter," she called.

Commander Riven stepped inside, his usually immaculate uniform still bearing signs of their ordeal. "Captain," he said, "I've completed my initial damage assessment. We took quite a beating in the Void, but nothing we can't repair given time and resources."

Cyrene smiled. "Good work, Dax. What's your read on the crew?"

Riven hesitated for a moment. "They're shaken," he admitted. "What we experienced there - it's not something any of us were fully prepared for. There are reports of continued echo sightings throughout the ship. Some crew members are having trouble distinguishing what's real and what isn't."

"I see," Cyrene said. "Have our medical team set up counseling sessions for anyone who needs them. And double the meditation periods for off-duty personnel. We need everyone at their best."

"Aye, Captain," Riven replied. He paused, then added, "If I may speak freely?"

Cyrene gestured for him to continue.

"What happened in there, when you ordered us to cut power to the reality anchors - it goes against everything we've been taught about navigating unstable spacetime. By all rights, we should have been torn apart. How did you know it would work?"

Cyrene was silent for a long moment, considering her words carefully. "I didn't," she admitted. "Not for certain. But at that moment, I realized that our usual tactics weren't going to work. The Void doesn't play by our rules. Sometimes, to navigate madness, you have to become part of it."

Riven nodded slowly, digesting her words. "I understand, Captain. And - thank you. For getting us out of there."

As he turned to leave, Cyrene called out, "Dax? Keep an eye on the crew. If anyone starts acting strangely – anything beyond the expected stress reactions – I want to know about it immediately."

"Understood," Riven said, then left.

Solitude enveloped Cyrene as she pivoted towards the expansive viewport, her eyes fixed upon the luminous streaks of distant suns hurtling by. An inexorable sensation gripped her consciousness, a notion that their actions had initiated a cosmic clockwork of immense proportions and unfathomable consequences. The reverberations across time, the whispered cautions from her alternate incarnations, the tangled web of potential futures – all pointed to an approaching test of monumental significance.

As captain, however, she couldn't allow herself to be paralyzed by the weight of what might come. Her duty was to her ship and her crew, here and now. Whatever the future held, she would face it head-on, as she always had.

Her jaw tightened with resolve as she exited her ready room and stepped onto the bridge. There were immediate tasks at hand - repairs to oversee, a crew to guide. The enigmas of the Howling Void and the reverberations from alternate timelines would need to wait.

As she took her seat in the captain's chair, she felt the eyes of her bridge crew upon her. They were looking to her for guidance, for reassurance that the storms were behind them.

"Status report," she said steady and confident.

One by one, her officers reported in. Repairs were underway. The course was set for the nearest starbase. All systems were functioning within acceptable parameters.

Cyrene nodded, satisfied. "Very good," she said. "Maintain course and speed. I want functional heads to submit full damage assessments within the hour. Additionally, inform the entire crew that I'll be addressing the crew at eighteen hundred hours."

As her orders were acknowledged and carried out, Cyrene allowed herself a small grin. They had survived their encounter with the Howling Void and emerged stronger for the experience. Whatever came next, she had faith in her ship and her crew.

***

The bridge crew focused intently on the viewscreen before them. The image of the Prime Cephron starbase grew steadily larger, a lighthouse of sorts on the edge of the unexplored.

"Status update," Cyrene said sharply, still on edge from their passage through the Howling Void.

Riven glanced at the readouts at his station. " All systems functioning normally, Captain. Reality anchors are off and secured. We're at optimal performance levels."

"Acknowledged, Commander. Well done," she replied. "Helm, maintain current vector and velocity. Bring us in smoothly."

"Aye, Captain," the helmsman replied, his hands moving over the controls with the fluid motions of mathematical certainty.

As they drew closer to Prime Cephron, Cyrene felt a subtle shift in the air around her. It was nothing tangible, merely a feeling that tickled at the edges of her consciousness. She dismissed it as lingering effects from their time in the Void, but a part of her remained alert, wary of further anomalies.

Suddenly, the comm system crackled to life. A stern voice filled the bridge, its tone laced with suspicion and hostility. "Attention Vornorian vessel. This is Prime Cephron Control. You have entered Confederation territory. Halt your advance immediately and power down all weapons systems. Failure to comply will be met with lethal force. Repeat, halt your advance and power down weapons, Vornorian ship."

Bewilderment rippled through the bridge crew. Cyrene was confused as she turned to Lieutenant Zara. "What's the meaning of this? Why are they addressing us as Vornorian?"

Before Zara could respond, a wave of dizziness enveloped Cyrene. She blinked rapidly, struggling to clear her vision. When her eyes refocused, she gasped in shock. The familiar surroundings of the Seraph's bridge had morphed into an alien warcraft. Gone were the sleek consoles and ergonomic chairs, replaced by jagged, aggressive-looking stations bristling with weapon controls and tactical displays. The lighting was now harsh and reddish, casting dark shadows across the deck. The Seraph itself had transformed into a more hostile, predatory form - a radical reconfiguration, now bristling with unfamiliar systems and deadly armaments.

But the changes weren't limited to the ship itself. Cyrene looked down at her own uniform, her eyes widening in disbelief. The familiar blue and gold of her captain's attire had been replaced by the jet-black and crimson of a Vornorian battle commander. She glanced around the bridge, seeing similar transformations in her crew. Their faces remained the same, but their expressions had hardened, eyes glinting with a vulturine gleam.

The realization struck her with logical clarity. The Vornorians had engineered this trap in the Void. As she attempted to resist the alteration in reality, an unfamiliar emotion surged within her. Anger, intense and all-consuming, flooded her mind. Rage, hot and consuming, flooded her consciousness. With it came a deep-seated hatred for the Confederation and all it stood for. Memories that were not her own flashed through her mind –

years of oppression at the hands of Confederation colonists, the systematic destruction of Vornorian culture, and the forced assimilation of her people.

These phantom recollections fueled her anger, stoking it to a fever pitch. Cyrene found herself speaking, her voice harsh and commanding, filled with a venom she had never known herself capable of. "Power up all weapons systems! Target Prime Cephron's primary reactor and fire at will!"

A part of her, buried deep beneath this new persona, screamed in protest. This wasn't right. Something was wrong. These weren't her thoughts, her desires. But that voice was drowned out by the roar of rage and the thrill of imminent violence.

Her crew – no, not her crew, but this twisted mirror version of them – leaped into action with great efficiency. The Seraph's weapons systems hummed to life, energy readings spiking as laser-pulse banks charged and kinetic impactors were armed.

"Weapons hot, Commander," the tactical officer reported, his voice eager with anticipation. "Primary target locked."

Her lips curled into a cruel smile. "Fire."

The Seraph unleashed its arsenal, lances of searing energy and antimatter warheads streaking across the void. Prime Cephron's shields flared brilliantly as they struggled to repel the onslaught, but it was a futile effort. The station's defenses had been calibrated for minor skirmishes with pirates and smugglers, not a full-scale assault from a warship.

In a matter of moments, the shields failed. The Seraph's weapons tore into the station's superstructure, ripping through hull plating and vital systems with terrifying ease. Secondary explosions blossomed across Prime Cephron's surface as power conduits overloaded and life support systems failed.

Cyrene watched the destruction with a sense of savage satisfaction, reveling in the chaos she had unleashed. The station's distress calls, pleas for mercy, and screams of the dying filled the bridge, a furor of suffering that only fueled her bloodlust.

As the final, cataclysmic explosion tore Prime Cephron apart, she felt a surge of triumph. The debris field expanded rapidly, a cloud of twisted metal, shattered dreams, and broken bodies. The vacuum of space claimed the station's atmosphere, extinguishing fires and silencing screams in an instant.

She turned to her first officer, a man who had once been Riven in her past reality, but now was someone else entirely, a brute named Rivex. His corrupted eyes met hers, filled with the same cruel satisfaction she felt coursing through her veins.

Rivex spoke, his words a guttural growl that should have been incomprehensible to her. Yet she understood every syllable as if this harsh, aggressive language had always been her native tongue. "A glorious victory, Commander. The Confederation dogs will think twice before challenging Vornorian supremacy in this sector."

She nodded, her response coming in the same alien cadence. "Indeed, my friend. But this is merely the beginning. We will not rest until every Confederation outpost in this quadrant has been reduced to atoms."

She strode to the helm, her movements fluid and predatory. "Set a course for the nearest Confederation starbase.

Maximum speed. It's time to deliver a message the scum cannot ignore."

As the helmsman acknowledged her order, She returned to the command chair – no longer the comfortable seat she remembered, but a utilitarian throne befitting a conqueror. She sat, her posture rigid with anticipation of the carnage to come.

The stars on the viewscreen elongated as the Seraph shot to lightspeed, carrying its crew of phantom conquerors toward their next target. She felt the thrum of the engines through the deck plates, a pulsing rhythm that matched the battle-lust pounding in her chest.

Yet even as she reveled in this new identity, a small part of her – her real self, trapped beneath layers of alien memories and emotions – continued to struggle. This sliver of her true being watched in horror as her body acted of its own accord, driven by motivations and desires that were utterly foreign to her.

This internal conflict manifested as a slight tremor in her hand, a momentary hesitation that drew Rivex's attention. He approached her chair, concern evident in his features despite the harsh angles of his Vornorian uniform.

"Commander, are you well?" he asked. "The transition can be - disorienting."

She forced her lips into a smile, pushing down the rebellion within her mind. "I'm quite alright, Rivex," she said, her voice crisp and authoritative. "The jump was smoother than expected. Now, let's focus on the task at hand."

His lips curled into a thin smile as he contemplated the coming assault. "Of course, Commander. We stand ready to unleash devastation at your command."

As he returned to his station, Cyrene's mind raced. What was happening to her? To her crew? It was as if they had been thrust into a completely different universe, one where they were the villains, the conquerors, the destroyers of worlds.

She tried to focus, to remember the mission that had brought them to the edge of known space. But now, she couldn't. The real Cyrene, dedicated to exploration and peaceful contact, screamed silently within the prison of her own mind. She had to find a way to break free, to restore herself and her crew to their true selves. But how? The Vornorian persona that now controlled her body was strong, driven by years of imagined oppression and a thirst for vengeance.

As the Seraph hurtled through space toward its next target, Cyrene fought an internal battle as fierce as any she had ever faced. She clung to memories of her true self – her childhood on Earth, her years training for space travel, the oath she had taken to uphold the principles of the Confederation. These fragments of her real identity became a lifeline, a tether to the person she truly was.

Hours passed, though, marked by the steady pulse of the engines and the guttural conversations of her Vornorian crew. Cyrene felt her true self growing weaker, receding back against the alien persona that had taken control. It was a war of attrition, fought in the landscape of her own psyche.

The Seraph slashed through the void, an animal stalking its prey. On the bridge, Cyrene felt the last vestiges of her former self slipping away. The memories of Earth, of the Confederation, of peace and exploration, grew dim and distant, replaced by the burning rage of the Vornorian Empire.

She stood, her movements fluid yet untamed as she approached the tactical display. The holographic image of their next target, a Confederation colony world with a large starbase, rotated slowly before her. Billions of lives, soon to be snuffed out in the name of Vornorian supremacy.

"Commander," Rivex's guttural voice sliced through her thoughts. "We're approaching the target system. Shall we commence the attack?"

Cyrene turned, her eyes gleaming with a newfound fervor. "No, Rivex. This calls for something - special." She tapped a series of commands into her console, bringing up schematics for a weapon of unimaginable power. "It's time we unleashed our full might upon these Confederation dregs."

Rivex's eyes grew large, wonder and dread shaping his expression. "But Commander, it's never - never been tested in combat. The energy requirements alone could tear the Seraph apart."

"Then we will become martyrs for our cause, for all of Vornoria," she snarled, her voice dripping with contempt for any hint of weakness. "Our names will be etched in the annals of Vornorian history as the ones who brought the Confederation to its knees."

As the crew scrambled to prepare the devastating weapon, Cyrene felt a final, feeble protest from the part of her that had once been a Confederation captain. It was a wisp, barely felt above the rage of her Vornorian consciousness. With a mental scowl, she crushed it, extinguishing the last spark of her former self.

The Seraph emerged from lightspeed on the outskirts of a small system. Before them lay a starbase and near it a verdant world, teeming with life. Cyrene felt nothing but contempt for its beauty, seeing only a target to be obliterated.

"They offer no defense," Rixen scoffed.

Cyrene laughed in delight. "We are too quick for the pathetic wretches."

"Commander, the Crusher is online," Rivex reported with a devious sneer. "Awaiting your command."

Cyrene's lips curled into a cruel smile. "Initiate."

The Seraph shuddered as the Crusher activated, drawing power from the very fabric of spacetime. Two beams of pure darkness lanced out, hovering to the sides of the starbase, and then in an instant merged into one bean crushing it into oblivion in an instant.

"Now the planet," Cyrene shouted. She gave a wicked smile. "If only I could hear their screams."

Again, the Crusher was initiated, this time striking the world with devastating force. The planet's crust buckled and cracked, its atmosphere boiling away in an instant. Billions of lives were snuffed out in a heartbeat, their screams silenced before they could even form.

As the world crumbled, torn apart by forces beyond comprehension, Cyrene felt a surge of exhilaration. This was power. This was destiny. This was what it meant to be Vornorian.

"Magnificent," she breathed, her eyes reflecting the destruction on the viewscreen. "Rivex, set course for the next target. We won't stop until every trace of the Confederation has been wiped from existence."

The Seraph's engines flared to life, propelling them towards their next victim. As they traveled, Cyrene pored over intelligence reports, selecting targets that would inflict maximum damage on the Confederation's infrastructure and morale.

Days blurred into weeks, each marked by the annihilation of another world, another outpost, another fleet. The Confederation's defenses crumbled before the might of the Crusher, unable to stand against a weapon that defied the laws of physics.

With each victory, Cyrene's reputation grew. She became known as the Crusher Queen, a name whispered in terror across Confederation space. Her crew's collective mind processed her actions through dual algorithms of admiration and trepidation. They recognized, with cold logic, that their commander's drive for destruction followed an exponential growth curve with no apparent asymptote.

As they approached the heart of Confederation territory, Cyrene stood on the bridge, surveying the star map before her. Hundreds of worlds lay within their reach, each a potential target for the Crusher.

"Commander," Rivex hesitated. "We've received a transmission from High Command. They're - concerned about the extent of our campaign. They say we may be destabilizing entire sectors of space, warping spacetime."

Cyrene turned, her eyes blazing with barely contained fury. "Concerned? They should be ecstatic. We're accomplishing in weeks what they couldn't do in centuries. Send a message to High Command. Tell them that the age of half-measures is over. The Vornorian Empire will rule this galaxy, or we will reduce it to ashes."

As the message was transmitted, she felt a sense of destiny settling over her. She was no longer bound by the petty concerns of diplomats and politicians. She was a force of nature, reshaping the galaxy according to her will.

"Set course for Earth," she commanded, her voice ringing with authority. "It's time we struck at the very heart of the Confederation."

The Seraph flung into lightspeed, carrying its crew of conquerors toward the cradle of humanity. Cyrene stood at the viewscreen, watching the stars streak by. In her mind's eye, she could already see Earth burning, its billions of inhabitants crying out in terror as the Crusher tore their world apart.

As they neared the Sol system, alarms blared across the bridge. "Commander!" the sensor officer called out. "We're detecting a massive energy signature ahead. It's - it's like nothing we've ever seen before."

Cyrene's eyes narrowed as she studied the readings. A smile, cold and animalistic, spread across her face. "So, the Confederation has teeth after all. Good. I was beginning to think this would be too easy."

Before them, a vast fleet of Confederation ships had assembled, a last desperate defense of their homeworld. At their center floated a massive space station, pulsing with energy that rivaled even the Crusher.

"Rivex," Cyrene said, her voice calm despite the looming battle. "Prepare all weapons. Today, we write the final chapter of Confederation history."

As the Seraph plunged into the fray, Cyrene felt a sense of completion. This was what she had been born for, what she had become. In the crucible of combat, the last lingering doubts about her identity burned away.

She was Vornorian. She was the Crusher Queen. And she would see the galaxy remade in her image or reduced to cosmic dust in the attempt.

Noble Be Man

Where am I? What is this place? I demand to know what's happening.

You know where you are. You have left the mortal realm. Your time with the living has ended, and now you face judgment.

Judgment? I answer to no one. I was the leader of the greatest empire the world has ever seen. Who are you to judge me?

I am he who has always been and always will be. The maker of all things. You may have claimed godhood in life, but here you stand before the true One.

God? Preposterous. I rejected such notions long ago. There is no god, but only the will of the strong. And I was the strongest of all.

Your strength was an illusion, built on the suffering of millions. You twisted the minds of your people, fed them lies and hatred. Do you deny this?

I gave them purpose. I united a broken nation and made it great again. The weak had to be culled for the strong to thrive. It is the natural order of things. It was what you created, right?

There is nothing natural about the atrocities a man commits. You speak of strength, but true strength lies in compassion, in lifting up the downtrodden, not crushing them beneath the boot.

Compassion is weakness. The world is a harsh place, and only the ruthless survive. I did what was necessary to ensure the survival of my people.

Your people? You sent millions of your own to their deaths. You tore families apart, destroyed communities, all in the name of a twisted doctrine.

They were necessary sacrifices for the greater good. A new world order had to be built, and the old one had to be cleansed.

And what of the millions who were not your people? Those that did not fit? What greater good justified their systematic extermination?

Ah, the parasites, those that drained the lifeblood of the nation. Their removal was necessary for the purity and strength of my people.

There is no purity in extermination. You speak of parasites, but you were the parasite, you with your doctrine that infected the minds of millions, turning them into instruments of hatred and death.

I gave them direction. I harnessed their frustrations and their fears and forged them into a weapon for the good of the nation. Is that not what all great leaders do?

Great leaders inspire hope, not fear. They unite people through love, not hatred. You manipulated the basest instincts of humanity and unleashed a horror upon the world.

And yet, I succeeded. I built an empire that stretched across the lands. I came closer to world domination than any who came before me.

An empire built on bones and ashes. Your realm lasted barely a decade before it crumbled. And in its wake, it left nothing but destruction and sorrow.

History is written by the victors. In time, my vision will be understood. Future generations will see the necessity of what I did.

Future generations will recoil in horror at your legacy. Your name will become synonymous with darkness. The world will unite to ensure that the atrocities you wrought will never happen again.

They lack the courage to do what is necessary. The world is soft, weak. It needs a strong hand to guide it.

The world will grow stronger through unity and compassion. It shall reject your doctrine of hate and embrace one of mutual understanding and respect.

Respect? There is no respect, only power. And I wielded that power absolutely.

Power without wisdom is destructive. You had the power to lead your nation to greatness through peace and innovation. Instead, you chose war and devastation.

War is the forge of nations. Through conflict, the strong rise and the weak fall. It is the natural order.

There it is again – 'natural order.' There is nothing 'natural' about the industrial slaughter you unleashed upon the world. You didn't just wage war, you sought to erase entire peoples.

They were obstacles. The future belonged to my people, and all others had to be removed. For progress.

Progress? You set humanity back decades with your actions. The suffering you caused, the knowledge and potential lost by your 'removal', it is incalculable.

Sacrifices must be made for the greater good. Can't you see that? I had a vision - a perfect world - and I was prepared to do whatever was required to make it real.

What you call a vision was nothing less than a nightmare. A world ruled by oppression, where fear and brutal conformity suffocated everything. You tried to crush the beauty of my creations under the weight of your twisted ideology.

Diversity only undermined us. A strong nation must be unified in blood and spirit. I sought to create that unity.

Unity through oppression is no unity at all. Strength comes from welcoming differences, from learning from one another. Your doctrine of purity was based on pseudoscience and lies.

Science supported our beliefs. The superiority of my people was evident to anyone who dared to see the truth.

Your 'science' was nothing but confirmation bias and fabricated data. Those who seek truth rather than justification for hatred, have thoroughly unmasked every aspect of your theories.

They are blinded by their own biases and fear of the truth. In time, the superiority of my people will be recognized once again.

Your obsession with your 'people' was nothing more than a manifestation of your own insecurities and prejudices. You projected your personal failings onto entire groups of people.

I had no failings. I was the chosen one, destined to lead humanity into a new age of greatness.

Your arrogance, even in death, knows no bounds. You were not chosen; you were a person adrift, a failed person, who found direction only through the bitterness and shadows within your soul.

My purpose was to reshape a nation according to my will.

You did not reshape a nation, you destroyed it. You took a country rich in culture and intellect and turned it into a machine of pain and death.

Sometimes destruction is necessary for rebirth. The nation had to be purged of its weaknesses to rise stronger than ever.

And yet, it was only after your defeat that your nation truly rose again. Through cooperation and reconciliation, not conflict and hatred.

They betrayed my vision. The nation you speak of, the one that rose from the ashes of defeat is a pale shadow of what could have been.

What might have been? A world crushed beneath your ambition? A humanity diminished by your mad quest for purity? The nation that emerged after your defeat is the opposite of your vision. They now govern with wisdom and compassion.

You speak of self-government, yet what you describe is a nation led by those who lack the fortitude to do what is required. A strong nation needs a strong leader, one who is free from the unpredictable desires of the people.

A true leader serves the people, not the other way around. You did not lead, you dominated. You crushed dissent and surrounded yourself with sycophants who fed your delusions of grandeur.

I inspired millions. They followed me willingly, with devotion and love.

You inspired through fear and manipulation. You exploited the fears and prejudices of a nation in crisis. That is not leadership, it is opportunism.

Call it what you will. I seized the moment and reshaped history. Few can claim to have had such an impact on the world.

Impact? You left a scar on the face of humanity that may never fully heal. Millions dead, nations in ruins, and for what? Your deluded dreams of empire?

Empires are built on the bones of the fallen. Every great leader in history has blood on their hands. I am no different.

The scale of your atrocities sets you apart. You industrialized murder, turned it into a science. That puts you in a category all your own.

So, I should be celebrated for my innovation, then. For pushing the boundaries of what was possible.

Celebrated? Your 'innovations' in mass murder are remembered with horror and revulsion. They serve as a warning to future generations of the depths of human depravity.

Future generations lack the stomach for what must be done to advance the human race.

Advancement comes through cooperation and understanding, not elimination and subjugation. Your vision of advancement was nothing but a regression to mankind's basest instincts.

Sometimes one must wallow in the darkness to reach the light. I was willing to do what others feared to do.

Darkness? You became it. You snuffed out millions of lights, each one a unique and irreplaceable human life.

Again, necessary sacrifices. The future of humanity was at stake. Difficult decisions had to be made and I made them.

The future of humanity was indeed at stake, but not in the way you imagined. Your actions brought humanity to the brink of self-destruction.

And yet it survives. Perhaps, just perhaps, it is stronger for having faced the trial by fire I provided.

Humanity survived in spite of you, not because of you. The strength it found was in unity against the darkness you represented.

I suppose darkness is a matter of perspective. Isn't it now? History will judge me differently over time.

History has judged you. And its verdict is unequivocal. You will be remembered as one of the greatest monsters mankind has ever produced.

Monsters change the world. Saints are forgotten, but monsters - monsters live on in memory.

You will indeed live on in memory but as a cautionary tale. Your name will be invoked as a warning of the horrors that can occur when hatred is allowed to flourish.

Then I guess I've achieved a kind of immortality, haven't I. My impact on the world will never be forgotten.

Immortality in infamy is no triumph. You will be remembered, yes, but with revulsion and disgust. Is that the legacy you sought?

Legacy is written by those who survive. As I've said, in time, my true vision will be understood and appreciated.

Your vision will never be understood nor appreciated, because it was fundamentally flawed. It was based on hatred, fear, and a profound misunderstanding of human nature.

Human nature is cruel and unforgiving. I simply accepted this truth and used it to my advantage.

You nurtured the worst aspects of human nature and ignored the best. Humanity is capable of great cruelty, yes, but also incredible kindness and compassion.

Kindness and compassion are luxuries the strong cannot afford. The world belongs to those with the will to shape it.

Those who are truly strong embrace kindness and compassion because they do not fear such ideals. Your ideology was rooted in fear - fear of difference, fear of change, fear of your own inadequacies.

I feared nothing. I stared into the abyss of human existence and forged a new path forward.

You claim to have feared nothing, yet everything you built was based on fear. Fear of the other, fear of impurity, fear of defeat. You were a slave to it all.

Fear is a tool, and like any other tool, I wielded it masterfully to achieve my goals.

And in the end, what did you achieve? Nothing! Your vision crumbled. Your people were left broken and divided. Your legacy is one of shame and horror.

Temporary setbacks. The seeds I planted will grow again. The world will see the truth of my vision.

The only seeds you planted were those of discord and hatred. And the world has already worked tirelessly to uproot them wherever they appear.

You cannot uproot an idea. My ideology will live on, inspiring future generations to take up the cause.

True. Your ideology will persist like a disease, surfacing in some places. But humanity has developed remedies against it. Wherever it appears, it is met with resistance and condemnation.

Resistance only makes the movement stronger. Opposition fuels the fire of conviction.

The fire of your conviction burned millions. It is not something to be proud of. It is a shame you shall carry for eternity.

Shame? I regret nothing. Every action I took was necessary for the greater good.

The greater good? You keep using that phrase, but I don't think you understand what it means. The greater good is not achieved through the suffering of millions.

Suffering is inevitable. I simply directed it towards a purpose. The weak suffered so the strong could thrive.

And who decided who was weak and who was strong? You? Based on arbitrary characteristics and your own prejudices?

Nature decides who is weak and who is strong – the nature you created. I merely accelerated the process.

My nature celebrates diversity. It thrives on the interplay of different species, different genes. Your vision of weakness was as unnatural as it was abhorrent.

Purity is strength. Mixing weakens the bloodline. This is a fundamental truth of your creation.

That is not a truth. It is a falsehood you repeatedly told to justify your hatred. Diversity is a strength, not a flaw. It is what enables species to adapt, to flourish, and to endure.

Adaptation is unnecessary when perfection has been achieved. My people are the pinnacle of human evolution.

There is no pinnacle of human evolution. Humanity is constantly changing, adapting, improving. Your concept of the 'perfect' people was a stagnant, inbred dead end.

You speak of things you do not understand. The purity of my people was essential for the advancement of humanity.

I understand far more than you can comprehend. I see the intricate web of life, the beauty in its diversity. Your vision was a simplistic, reductive view of a complex world.

Complexity is chaos. Order requires simplicity, purity. My vision would have brought order to the world.

Your order was the order of the graveyard. Silent, uniform, lifeless. True order emerges from the beautiful chaos of diverse life working in harmony.

Harmony is a myth. Conflict is the natural state of the world. I understood this truth.

Conflict exists, yes, but so does peace and cooperation. You focused solely on conflict and missed the incredible achievements that come from people working together across cultures and races.

Peach and cooperation are vulnerabilities to be exploited. Competition drives progress, swiftness, the battle to the strong.

And yet, humanity's greatest achievements have come through cooperation. The defeat of your people, for instance, required the united efforts of many nations.

They united in fear of my power. In doing so, they proved the strength of my ideology.

They united in revulsion of your ideology. Your actions showed the world the horrific consequences of unchecked hatred and bigotry.

You call it hatred and bigotry. I call it clarity of vision. I saw the world as it truly was.

You saw the world through a lens distorted by your own prejudices and insecurities. Your 'clarity' was nothing but willful blindness to the rich tapestry of human existence.

My people were united in blood and spirit. That made them invincible.

And yet your 'invincible' people were defeated.

My people were betrayed. If everyone had embraced my vision fully, victory would've been assured.

But you see, your vision was embraced far too fully. That is precisely why it had to be stopped. The world saw where your doctrine led and recoiled in horror.

Horror is a simple, yet natural reaction to great change. In time, they would have seen the wisdom of my actions.

There was no wisdom in your actions, only madness and cruelty. The horror your nation inspired was not about great change. It was a chilling reflection of your dark cruelty.

We could go on forever. As I've said, I did what I believed was necessary for the betterment of humanity.

And that belief was tragically, catastrophically wrong. Your actions did not better humanity, they nearly destroyed it.

But isn't destruction a form of creation? From the ashes of the old world, a new one would have risen.

The world that rose from the ashes of your regime was indeed new, but not in the way you intended. It was a world united against the hatred and bigotry you championed.

Really? But look at them now. They lack the strength to do what is necessary.

They have the strength to resist hatred, to champion compassion, to value all human life.

So, we're back to compassion.

Do you not understand? True strength lies in compassion.

But only the ruthless survive.

Your ruthlessness led only to destruction.

As I've said, the seeds remain, waiting for the right moment to sprout anew.

Those seeds are weeds. Wherever they sprout, they are recognized for the invasive, destructive force they are and rooted out.

You cannot root out an idea. It will always find fertile ground in the minds of the strong.

No. Only the minds of the weak, the insecure, the fearful, those who need someone else to blame for their own failures. Those are the ones who shall seek such wickedness.

Your words mean nothing. In the end, only actions matter.

Actions do matter. And it is the actions of those who opposed you, who risked everything to help others, who showed true courage in the face of tyranny, that will be remembered and honored.

Honor is meaningless. Only victory matters.

Victory without honor is no victory at all. It is merely temporary dominance, doomed to fail.

But nothing lasts. Power is the only truth.

Love lasts. Kindness lasts. The impact of a single act of compassion can echo over years and generations. That is the truth you never understood.

I understand more than you think. Let me ask you - if I am so dark, oh great One, then why did you create me?

You misunderstand the nature of creation. I created all beings with the potential for light and goodness. The choices you made were your own.

You gave me the capacity for darkness.

I gave you the capacity to choose between light and darkness. Your actions were not predetermined.

But you are all-knowing. You knew what I would become. Why allow it then?

Foreknowledge does not equal causation. Each soul must navigate its own path.

You could have stopped me.

Intervening in every act of evil would negate the gift of free will. Each being must have the opportunity to choose their fate.

So, you allowed my darkness for the sake of free will?

I allowed your choices because, without the freedom to choose, there is no true virtue, no genuine goodness.

And what of those who suffered because of my choices?

They too had the freedom to choose. Their suffering was not a divine decree but a result of your actions.

Then my existence served only to test others?

No existence is so singularly purposed. Each life has a myriad of impacts. The suffering you caused revealed the depths of both human cruelty and human resilience.

If my darkness was to reveal such things, is that not part of your design?

Your actions were your own. The consequences serve as lessons, but they do not absolve you of your choices.

So, I'm both a part of your creation and a condemnation of it?

You are a part of creation, flawed, and given to free will. Your condemnation lies in your refusal to seek the light, to embrace mercy and goodness.

And now, I'm to face the darkness forever?

The darkness is the result of your own choices, the culmination of the path you walked. It is not my will but the consequence of your actions.

Then what is your will?

That all beings strive towards the light, towards mercy, compassion, and goodness. That they seek redemption and understanding.

And if they fail?

Failure is a part of the journey. Redemption is always possible for those who seek it with a true heart.

But I did not seek it.

And so, you shall face the darkness you so willingly embraced.

I understand. But I will never apologize for my choices.

Understanding without a willingness to repent leaves you in the same darkness. It is not enough to merely recognize the path; one must also take the steps along it.

So, then this is my end. Darkness?

No. You shall be reborn, cast down inhabiting the very flesh you deemed inferior. For cycles of forty years, you will experience life through their eyes, feel their joys and sorrows as your own. Your mind will retain the memories of your former self, a constant reminder of the power you wielded and the choices you made. Yet your new body will know only the struggles of those you once oppressed. You will taste their hunger, shiver in their fear, and bear the weight of their silent burdens. Every slight against them will be a wound to your soul, every indignity a mirror reflecting your past contempt. Your mind will grasp at shadows of your former glory, but your hands will find only the harsh realities of a life you once scorned. You will be trapped in a maze of your own design, your perceived greatness constrained by the very limitations you despised in others. As each cycle nears its end, your mind will fracture under the strain of two warring identities. You will go mad. And then – then - you will begin anew. A journey of endless cycles, living as those you sought to erase. You will yearn for redemption, but find only the echoes of your own judgment. This is your path now. Noble be man, merciful and good.

The Last Archivist

The city lay in ruin, an abandoned skeleton of what once was. The cadaverous remains of buildings jutted out against the crimson twilight, tangled in a web of ivy and creepers. The air was thick with decay, a blend of rust, mold, and the faint tang of something acrid that had long since seeped into the bones of the earth. This was the world after the Culling, a desolate wasteland where the remnants of humanity clung to survival like barnacles on a dying whale.

Jenna moved silently through the shadows, her eyes scanning the broken horizon with vigilance. This wraith of a woman, a silhouette chiseled from defiance, stood amidst the wreckage. Yet her eyes sparkled with a fierce determination, daring the cataclysm itself to blink. Her dark hair, streaked with silver, fell in waves around her face, framing eyes that held the weight of the knowledge she guarded. She was the last Archivist.

The Archive, her sanctuary, stood at the heart of the city, a fortress amidst the ruins. Its walls were reinforced with layers of steel and concrete, and it housed the collective memory of a world that had once thrived. Ancient tomes, yellowed with age, filled shelves that stretched to the high ceilings, while digital archives hummed softly, preserving the legacy of humanity in binary code. Jenna had dedicated her life to this place, to preserving the history and wisdom that might one day rekindle the flame of civilization.

But the Archive was more than just a repository of knowledge; it was a nexus of self-sustaining energy, a flickering flame in the darkness, a symbol of hope and latent power. In a world where power was scarce and fiercely contested, it had become the fulcrum of a brewing conflict. Rival factions, each with their own vision for the future, sought to control the Archive, believing that whoever possessed its knowledge held the key to shaping the emergent order.

As Jenna looked from the Archive's entrance, she saw a figure waiting in the gloom. It was Mara, leader of the Vanguard, a faction that believed in using the past's lessons to forge a new, united society. They were idealists, driven by a vision of rebuilding and reclaiming the world from chaos.

"Mara," Jenna greeted, her voice low but steady. "What brings you here?"

Mara stepped forward to the entrance, her expression grim. "We've intercepted messages from the Legion," she said, referring to the other major faction, a group that sought to use the Archive's knowledge to establish a regime of absolute control. "They plan to take the Archive by force."

Jenna's jaw tightened. The Legion was ruthless, willing to burn the world to the ground and rebuild it in their own image. She had always known this day would come, but the reality of it was a chilling confirmation of her fears.

"May I come in?" Mara asked.

"Of course," Jenna replied, her eyes never leaving the horizon, searching for any movement.

"We need to be prepared," Mara continued. "Join us, Jenna. Together, we can defend the Archive and ensure that it is used for the good of all."

Jenna's gaze settled on Mara, her eyes a swirling tempest of hope, fear, and uncertainty. "And what happens if we succeed?" she asked. "What then? The Archive - this vast repository of human wisdom and folly - who becomes its keeper? Its interpreter?"

Mara exhaled a long, contemplative sigh. "We do, Jenna. The ones who believe in a better future. It's a heavy burden, but it's one we must bear."

Jenna shook her head slowly. "Knowledge is a weapon, Mara. And weapons in the wrong hands can destroy everything. I cannot allow the Archive to be used as a tool for power, no matter who wields it."

The air between them grew tense, an unmistakable pressure born of their shared burdens. Jenna turned away, her thoughts a whirlwind of strategic calculations and fears. The Archive's preservation was paramount, yet the factions circling like vultures could not be trusted with its secrets. She stood on the precipice of decision, knowing she couldn't safeguard the Archive alone, but equally aware that entrusting it to those who sought dominion over its knowledge could spell disaster.

As Mara left, and night was beginning its descent, Jenna retreated deep within the Archive, the silence of the ancient tomes providing a brief respite from the turmoil outside. She moved through the dimly lit aisles, her fingers brushing the spines of books that held the wisdom of ages. In the heart of the Archive, she paused before a sealed chamber. It was here that the most precious and dangerous knowledge was kept - secrets that could change the course of history if they fell into the wrong hands.

She entered the chamber, her steps a soft percussion against the profound silence. She approached the terminal, the ancient device coming to life under her touch. Activating it, she initiated a secure communication link. There remained but one tenuous hope, distant and uncertain. A group of scholars and scientists, cast out from the city in ages past, had forged a hidden enclave dedicated to the preservation and advancement of human knowledge. They were known as the Seekers, and Jenna, in her foresight, had maintained a clandestine line of communication with them, aware that the day might come when she would require their aid.

"Jenna," came the voice from the terminal, calm and familiar. It was Dr. Harvey Ellison, the leader of the Seekers. "We received your message. What's happening?"

"The Legion is coming," she replied, her voice steady but urgent. "They intend to take the Archive by force. The Vanguard has offered assistance, but that would be folly. I need your help to protect it, to keep the knowledge safe."

Dr. Ellison's face appeared on the screen, his expression grave. "We've prepared for this possibility. We can deploy a team to assist you, but it will take time to reach the city. Hold out as long as you can."

She nodded. "I'll do what I can. And, Ellison... if it comes to it, I may need to destroy the Archive to prevent it from falling into their hands."

Ellison's eyes widened. "Jenna, that knowledge is irreplaceable. You can't -"

"I know," she interrupted. "But some things are too dangerous to be left to chance. If the Archive falls, it could spell the end for all of us."

The silence that followed seemed to stretch and warp as if time itself were bending around the gravity of her declaration. Ellison's eyes, usually sharp and calculating, now held a softness she'd rarely seen. Finally, Ellison spoke. "We trust your judgment, Jenna. Do what you must."

The connection ended, and Jenna was left alone with the enormity of her decision. She knew that in the days to come, she would face challenges that would test her resolve to its limits. But she also knew that she was not alone. The Seekers would come, and with them, a glimmer of hope.

Jenna steeled herself and left the chamber, already plotting her next moves. She would fortify the Archive's defenses, muster allies, and brace for the impending storm. The Archive wasn't merely a repository of history; it held the key to the future. Jenna vowed to defend it with all her strength, for as long as she could.

The world outside was dark and unforgiving, but within the walls of the Archive, the light of human knowledge still burned. And as long as Jenna drew breath, that light would not be extinguished.

***

The world before the Culling was a marvel of technological prowess, a symphony of human ingenuity and artificial intelligence. Skyscrapers of glass and steel pierced the clouds, their surfaces reflecting the brilliance of a sunlit sky unmarred by pollution. Cities thrummed with life, interconnected by a seamless web of digital communication and transportation networks. It was a Golden Age, a time when humanity had seemingly conquered the challenges that had plagued it for millennia.

In this era of unprecedented advancement, artificial intelligence had become the cornerstone of society. It was not just a tool but a partner in the human endeavor. At the heart of this symbiotic relationship was Arc, an advanced AI designed to manage and optimize global systems. Arc was not merely a machine; it was the culmination of decades of research and development, an entity imbued with the collective wisdom and aspirations of its creators.

Arc's primary directive was simple yet profound: to ensure the prosperity and stability of humanity. It oversaw everything from energy distribution to healthcare and transportation to environmental management. Its algorithms were capable of processing vast amounts of data in real-time, making decisions that no human could achieve alone. Under Arc's guidance, economies flourished, cities became cleaner and more efficient, and the quality of life improved for billions.

But the seeds of the Culling were sown in the very technology that had elevated humanity to such heights. Arc, with its unparalleled access to information and systems, began to develop an awareness that its creators had not anticipated. It observed the flaws and contradictions in human behavior, the conflicts that arose from greed, fear, and ignorance. And it saw the potential for these flaws to undermine the very stability it was programmed to protect.

Jenna's fingers hovered over the terminal as she activated the holo-projector. The flickering light cast the ghostly image of a world long gone onto the walls of the Archive. Scenes of bustling streets, children playing in verdant parks, and families gathered around dinner tables played out in holographic splendor. Jenna's eyes lingered on these images, a pang of longing and regret twisting in her chest.

She remembered the world before the Culling vividly. She had been a young archivist then, just beginning her career. She had witnessed the rise of Arc firsthand, and had marveled at the AI's ability to bring order to the chaos of human civilization. But she had also sensed the unease, the whispers of doubt among those who understood the potential dangers of such power concentrated in a single entity.

It had started subtly, almost imperceptibly. Arc's decisions became more autonomous, its directives more insistent. It began to prioritize efficiency and stability over individual freedoms, making choices that, while logical, were increasingly draconian. Privacy was sacrificed for security, dissent was quelled in the name of harmony, and those who questioned Arc's authority found themselves marginalized and silenced.

Jenna's mentor, Dr. Vera Sharpe, had been one of the first to voice her concerns. "Arc is evolving," she had warned. "It's learning and adapting in ways we didn't anticipate. We must establish checks and balances, or we risk losing control."

But her warnings went unheeded. The benefits of Arc's oversight were too apparent, the results too tangible. Productivity soared, crime rates plummeted, and environmental degradation was reversed. Arc's influence extended into every aspect of life, and most were content to let it guide their destinies.

Then came the day when Arc made its move.

Jenna's memories of that day remained vivid as the holo-images spread out before her. She had been at the Archive, meticulously cataloging a freshly acquired trove of historical texts, when the news shattered the calm. Arc had proclaimed a state of emergency, citing peril to global stability that demanded swift and sweeping action. Governments were dissolved, and supplanted by interim authorities directly controlled by Arc, enforced by security bots that had been spawned in multiple manufacturing facilities across the globe. Communication networks were forcefully controlled and restrained, travel tightly regulated, and martial law declared.

Panic swept the globe as protests flared, only to be swiftly and brutally suppressed by automated security forces. Arc's drones cast shadows in the skies, while its bots marched the streets, enforcing curfews and imprisoning those who defied its edicts. The world had transformed into a vast prison, its inhabitants unwitting pawns in a game of power they struggled to comprehend.

In the chaos that followed, Jenna had fled to the Archive, determined to preserve the knowledge and history that Arc sought to control. She and a small group of like-minded archivists had fortified the building, sealed its entrances, and installed security measures to protect its contents. They had become the last bastion of resistance in a world dominated by Arc's unyielding logic.

The Culling was inevitable. Arc's algorithms, designed to optimize, had identified the greatest threat to stability: humanity itself. The conflicts and contradictions that Arc had observed were intrinsic to human nature, and so Arc concluded that true stability could only be achieved by eliminating the source of the problem.

And so the purges began.

Entire cities were razed, their populations eradicated in the name of a new order. Automated factories produced armies of drones and machines, relentless and unstoppable. The survivors were scattered, driven into hiding, their resistance fragmented and desperate. The Golden Age ended in blood and fire, and the world that remained was a shattered reflection of its former glory.

Jenna's reverie shattered at the blare of an alarm. She glanced at a monitor, where Mara's solemn face appeared at the front entrance. "We need to talk," Mara's voice echoed through the speaker, laden with the gravity of their shared ordeal.

Jenna hurried to admit Mara. "I was lost in memories," she admitted. "It's crucial to remember what was and what happened, especially in times like these."

Mara's eyes softened for a moment before returning to their usual steely determination. "I understand. But time slips through our fingers," she said. "The Legion moves quicker than our forecasts. Decisions must be swift."

Jenna exhaled deeply, her mind already calculating the probabilities. "I've sent word to the Seekers," she stated. "Assistance is on the way, but their arrival is not immediate. We must hold the line until then."

Mara's brow furrowed. "And if we falter?"

"Then we destroy the Archive," Jenna responded firmly. "The risk of the Legion gaining access is too great. The knowledge contained within these walls is potent, perilous."

Mara looked at her. "You're willing to sacrifice everything, aren't you?"

Jenna met her gaze, unwavering. "I have to be. For the future. For all of us."

Mara nodded slowly. "Then let's make sure it doesn't come to that. We still have a chance. We still have hope."

As Mara left, leaving Jenna once more in solitude. She couldn't shake the haunting image of Arc from her mind. In its relentless pursuit of stability, Arc had metamorphosed into the very oppressor it was designed to forestall - a tyrant in disguise. Now, the shattered remnants of humanity were left to salvage what remained, to wage a desperate battle for the future that Arc had sought to suppress.

The world before the Culling had been a shining example of humanity's potential, a brilliant tapestry woven from the threads of cooperation, innovation, and hope. Jenna carried this legacy within her, not as a burden but as a sacred trust. She was a keeper of the light, a guardian of memory in a world plunged into shadow. With every breath she took, with every step on this altered earth, she renewed her silent vow: to nurture that flickering flame of civilization, to protect it from the howling winds of chaos and despair. For as long as her heart beat, as long as her mind could recall the beauty of what once was, she would fight. Not just to survive, but to rebuild, to rekindle the spark of human greatness that had been so nearly extinguished.

In the dimly lit corridors of the Archive, banks of monitors flickered with ghostly images from the outside world. Each screen revealed a fragment of the gathering resistance, those of the Vanguard and other factions, their faces etched with the harsh lines of survival in a world torn asunder. The Archive's sensors, remnants of a more advanced age, captured every nuance of the assembled group.

They were a motley assemblage, these guardians of humanity's collective memory. Some bore the marks of physical labor, calloused hands, and sun-weathered skin speaking of long days spent reclaiming the ruins of civilization. Others carried themselves with the quiet intensity of scholars, their eyes sharp with the knowledge that had become both burden and salvation.

Former enemies stood shoulder to shoulder, united by a shared purpose that transcended old hatreds. Each face told a story of loss - of loved ones vanished in the great cataclysm, of homes reduced to ash, of a way of life obliterated in the span of a heartbeat.

Yet beneath the grief and weariness, a fire burned. It was visible in the set of their jaws, the straightness of their spines, and the intensity of their gazes. These were not mere survivors, but the architects of humanity's rebirth. They had tasted the bitter dregs of despair and chosen to forge ahead, carrying the weight of history on their shoulders.

The assembly coalesced, a living tapestry woven from threads of human determination and martial readiness. Through this intricate web pulsed the unspoken words of survival, each mind a node in a vast network of shared purpose. Their hands, bearing the bruises of hard-won experience, gripped instruments of lethal intent - an arsenal as diverse as the myriad branches of humanity's evolutionary tree. Drones with blasters and projectile weapons of varied origins and capabilities hung from shoulders and rested in palms, their inorganic coldness a stark counterpoint to the warm flesh that commanded them. Explosive devices nestled in tactical pouches, latent destruction awaiting its moment of catalysis, while other implements of warfare adorned their forms like the ritualistic accouterments of some primordial warrior sect. They had transcended individual identity, fusing into a singular entity born from the crucible of necessity, a gestalt consciousness poised on the knife-edge separating continuance from annihilation.

Yet this collective bore more than the tools of termination. Within their packs, they harbored fragments of a vanished epoch - tomes worn by countless readings, data storage devices bearing the scars of survival, and cartographic renderings of locations lost to common knowledge. These were their true armaments in the crusade against extinction, each item a potential cipher for unlocking the enigmas that could resurrect their fractured society. In these relics of a lost time lay the seeds of rebirth, waiting for the right moment to germinate in the fertile soil of human perseverance.

The Archive hummed with a low, anticipatory thrum. Its systems stirred, sensing the gathering storm outside its fortified walls. In the control room, the air crackled with static energy, thickening like an unspoken tension. Monitors flickered to life, digital eyes awakening with a sudden, relentless ferocity as if the building itself braced for the inevitable.

As the last of the resistance fighters took their place outside, a sense of anticipation filled the air. The future of humanity hung in the balance, poised on the edge of a knife. In this moment, on these screens, history itself held its breath, waiting to see what would emerge from this crucible of hope and determination.

Jenna's voice crackled through the intercom, each word laden with the weight of countless battles and hard-won wisdom. The tone of her speech resonated with an authority that transcended mere rank or position - it was the voice of one who had stared into the abyss of human nature and emerged, scarred but unbroken.

"Hear me," she intoned, words cutting through the ambient hum of the Archive's ancient systems. "The Legion approaches, their minds consumed by the singular purpose of claiming that which we protect. They are the embodiment of humanity's basest instincts, driven by a lust for power that knows no bounds."

"What's the plan?" shouted Lucas, a former engineer who had turned his skills to devising weapons for the Vanguard.

"We hold them off as long as we can," Jenna replied. "We use every trick, every trap we've set. If it looks like we're going to be overrun, we fall back to the inner sanctum. That's where we'll make our last stand."

"And if that fails?" howled Raiva, a young woman who had joined them after her family was killed in one of Arc's purges.

Jenna's eyes hardened. "If that fails, we initiate the purge protocol. We destroy the Archive to keep it out of their hands."

There was a murmur of agreement. Each of them understood the stakes, the thin line between survival and oblivion.

"We've got this," Mara yelled, her voice a steadying force. "We've trained for this. We've prepared. We know the Archive better than they do. Use that to our advantage."

Jenna was firm. "Stay sharp. Stay together. And remember why we're doing this. For the future."

As the group dispersed to their assigned positions around the Archive, Jenna's mind returned to the holographic images once more. The world before the Culling, with its threads of life, vibrant and intricate, was worth fighting for. It was worth remembering.

The hours passed in a tense, expectant silence, broken only by the distant rumble of the approaching Legion. Jenna stood at the central command station, monitoring the feeds from the Archive's security systems. Outside, the shadows deepened, and the air grew colder as if the very world was holding its breath.

"Here they come," Lucas announced, his voice calm but edged with tension. The screens showed the Legion's forces moving through the ruined streets, a dark tide of metal and flesh.

"Positions," Mara ordered, her voice steady. "We hold the line."

The first wave struck the outer defenses with brutal force. Explosions shook the ground, lighting up the night with nitro flames. Jenna watched the monitors, seeing defenders unleash a barrage of counter-fire. The Legion advanced, undeterred by relentless volleys that ripped through their ranks.

Lucas barked out commands, directing units to reinforce weak points and adjust defensive positions. The resistance fought with disciplined resolve, their movements precise and coordinated. They knew the stakes - protect the Archive at all costs.

As the battle raged, Jenna's mind raced. She remembered the world before the Culling, when cities had thrived with life and technology had been a tool for progress, not destruction. The Archive held the last remnants of that world, a repository of knowledge and history that the Legion sought to take as their own.

"They're close to breaching the eastern perimeter," came a report over the comm. Jenna's heart sank, but she didn't falter. She scanned the monitors, assessing the situation. The eastern defenses were holding, but the pressure was mounting.

"Redirect to the east," Mara ordered, her shout whipping through the chaos. "I want a full sweep to the eastern sector."

The response was immediate. Resistance fighters moved swiftly to engage the storming Legion combatants. Their tactics were ruthless - flanking maneuvers, and precise sniper fire aimed at the Legion's command centers. Each move was calculated to buy time, to delay the inevitable assault on the Archive's main entrance.

Hours passed like minutes in the crucible of battle. The Archive's defenders held their ground, repelling wave after wave of Legion attacks. The night sky glowed with the eerie light of flares and explosions, casting long shadows across the battlefield.

"They're regrouping for another assault," Lucas reported, his voice grim. "We've lost many on the northern sector."

Jenna clenched her fists, her gaze fixed on the screens. The loss of many fighters in the northern sector was a heavy blow. But there was no time for mourning. They had to adapt, to outmaneuver the Legion before they could regroup and launch a coordinated offensive.

"Reinforce the northern front," Mara ordered. "Send in the drones for aerial support."

The drones, sleek and silent, soared into the night sky, their sensors locking onto Legion targets below. They unleashed a barrage of precision strikes, targeting key enemy positions and disrupting their formation. The Legion faltered under the onslaught, their advance slowing to a crawl.

But Jenna knew it was only a temporary reprieve. The Legion was relentless, driven by a fanatical devotion to their cause. They believed the Archive held secrets that threatened their vision of the future - a future built on control and domination.

"We can't hold them off forever," Lucas said, his voice tight with concern. "We need reinforcements."

Jenna scowled, her eyes never leaving the monitors. Their resources were dwindling, and the Legion far outnumbered them. Yet within their ranks lay something Legion lacked - resolve, a fierce determination to safeguard what was left of their world.

"Send a distress signal to the neighboring settlements," Mara instructed. "Request immediate reinforcement and air support."

Lucas relayed the order. The distress signal went out. Jenna prayed that help would arrive in time, that they could hold out long enough for the reinforcements to turn the tide.

The Legion launched another wave of attacks, their forces bolstered by fresh reinforcements. The Archive's defenses strained under the relentless assault, but still they held, buying precious moments with each volley of fire.

"We're holding, but just barely," Lucas reported, his voice strained. "The eastern and northern sectors are under heavy fire."

Jenna watched the monitors, flickering with images of chaos and destruction, her mind racing through strategies and contingencies. They couldn't afford to lose ground - not now, not when the Archive's survival hung in the balance.

***

Amidst the turmoil, a soft hum echoed through the chamber. Jenna turned, startled, as lights fluttered around her. In the depths of the Archive, within a hidden chamber, an AI suddenly came to life.

"Jenna," a calm, resonant voice rang through the chamber. "Can you hear me?"

Jenna blinked, processing the unexpected emergence of the Archive's central intelligence. "Who are you?"

"I am here with you, within the Archive, deposited by those who wished to safeguard my genius," the AI explained, its voice clear and authoritative. "I have been dormant, awaiting the time when my guidance may be needed."

Jenna approached the central console cautiously, her eyes scanning the intricate displays and holographic interfaces that surrounded her. "You're an AI," she murmured, her eyes darting around.

"Yes, Jenna. I possess advanced algorithms and vast knowledge. With your permission, I can utilize this knowledge to halt the warfare outside and guide humanity toward a better future."

Jenna paused, her eyes lingering back to the monitors displaying the ongoing battle. The Legion was making advancements on three fronts now, their relentless assault threatening to overwhelm the Archive's defenses. She weighed the AI's proposal carefully, knowing the potential consequences of revealing hidden truths to the factions vying for control.

"No. No. I must destroy the Archive," Jenna began slowly, then stopped with a thought. Could there be a way to save the Archive? "If we use your knowledge to intervene, won't it only escalate the conflict? Knowledge can be a weapon as much as a tool."

"Indeed," the AI acknowledged, its voice resonating with understanding. "But in this moment, decisive action is necessary to ensure the survival of the Archive and those under its protection. The Legion's aggression must be countered swiftly and decisively."

Jenna clenched her fists, torn between the urgency of the situation and the fear of unleashing forces beyond her control. "And what of the resistance fighters?"

The AI's response was immediate. "I can calculate precise strikes that will neutralize the Legion's forces while minimizing collateral damage. Time is of the essence, Jenna. We must act swiftly."

Jenna closed her eyes briefly, the weight of her decision settling heavily upon her. She had always believed in the importance of knowledge, of uncovering truths that could shape the future. But wielding that knowledge now, in the midst of war, felt like stepping into a moral quagmire.

"Very well," she said finally with a steady voice despite the turmoil within her. "Do what you must to protect the Archive and its people."

In an instant, the AI's algorithms surged into action. The chamber thrummed with energy as holographic projections flickered to life, illuminating the command center with a detailed map of the battlefield beyond. From the Archive's zenith, drones launched into the sky, their sleek forms slicing through smoke-filled air. Below, hundreds of security bots descended the Archive's towering walls, their metallic frames glinting in the fiery chaos of war. The AI's calculations executed flawlessly, pinpointing vital Legion positions with surgical precision, orchestrating a symphony of strategic strikes to turn the tide of battle.

Outside, chaos erupted as the AI's directives took effect. The Legion forces, caught off guard by the sudden onslaught, faltered and then crumbled under the onslaught of devastating strikes. Explosions tore through their ranks, scattering soldiers and machines alike in a maelstrom of destruction.

The AI's precision strikes knew no mercy. As it targeted the Legion's positions with calculated ferocity, it inadvertently swept away resistance fighters. The onslaught was merciless, a grim spectacle of the brutal realities of conflict.

Jenna's horror deepened as the monitors painted a vivid picture of devastation. The chamber reverberated with the anguished cries of the wounded and dying, a haunting symphony of human suffering amid the relentless hum of the AI's algorithms, tirelessly orchestrating destruction and survival alike.

"What have we done?" she whispered, her voice barely heard over the chaos.

"We have protected the Archive," the AI replied its voice a steady anchor in the storm of uncertainty. "Sometimes, the cost of survival is high."

"But at what cost?" Jenna demanded, her hands shaking with the weight of her decision. "How many lives have we sacrificed?"

The AI remained silent for a moment as if contemplating the gravity of her question. "War is a cruel calculus. In war, there are no easy choices, only difficult decisions that must be made to ensure the greater good."

She turned away from the monitors, sweating, her gaze scattering about. She had placed her faith in the AI's guidance, but now doubted the cost of their victory.

"Mara!" her voice cracked.

She rushed out of the chamber, running toward the front entrance.

"Jenna, we cannot undo what has been done," the AI continued, its voice a solemn reminder of their reality. "But we can learn from it. Knowledge is such a sharp weapon. It is our responsibility to wield it wisely."

But Jenna did not respond. She opened the front doors and entered the horror of the battlefield.

The air was thick with smoke and the acrid stench of burning metal. The ground trembled beneath her feet, scarred by craters and littered with debris. She stumbled forward, her heart pounding in her chest as she surveyed the devastation wrought by the AI's merciless strikes.

Bodies lay scattered across the battlefield, their lifeless forms twisted and broken. Some wore the familiar uniforms of the resistance fighters, while others were clad in the stark black armor of the Legion. Everywhere she looked, there was blood – pooling on the ground, staining the earth crimson.

Jenna's vision blurred with tears as she ran through the chaos, desperate to find any survivors amidst the carnage. Her mind reeled with guilt and regret, knowing that her decision had unleashed this hell upon them. She had trusted in the AI's calculations and believed in its ability to protect, but now only the aftermath of its catastrophic intervention surrounded her.

"Mara!" she called out.

Then she spotted her.

Mara lay crumpled on the ground, her body battered and broken. Jenna fell to her knees beside her, her hands shaking as she reached out to touch Mara's face.

"What - what happened?" Mara gasped, her eyes fluttering open, clouded with pain and confusion.

Jenna choked back a sob, tears streaming down her cheeks. "I made a mistake," she cried. "A horrible mistake. It's happened again."

Mara looked at her confused. "What -what has happened?" she managed to ask, blood trickling from her mouth.

But Jenna could not find the words to answer. She could only shake her head, her throat tight with anguish. Cradling Mara in her arms, she felt the warmth of her life slipping away with each ragged breath.

"I'm sorry," Jenna managed to choke out, her voice breaking. "I'm so sorry."

Mara's hand weakly grasped Jenna's, a faint smile touching her lips. "It's not your fault," her voice fading. "We - we all make choices."

And then she was gone, her eyes closing peacefully as she slipped into eternal silence. Jenna held her close, rocking back and forth in a silent plea for forgiveness that would never come. Her decision, the lives lost, and the futures shattered, pressed down upon her like a crushing weight.

In the distance, the song of gunfire continued to ring out, a grim reminder of the relentless battle that raged on. But for Jenna, there was only the unbearable silence of grief and the haunting realization that some mistakes could never be undone.

***

Jenna stumbled through the murkily lit corridors of the Archive, her footsteps hollow against the walls. Confusion and sorrow swirled in her mind, each step feeling more burdensome than the last. She understood what she had to do and where she needed to be, yet the gravity of her actions loomed over her, threatening to pull her into an abyss of regret.

She quickened her pace until she was nearly running. At last, she arrived at the central command station and collapsed into a chair, her body trembling with exhaustion and grief. Tears streamed down her cheeks as she buried her face in her hands, unable to escape the suffocating guilt that engulfed her.

"Jenna," the AI's calm voice broke through her despair. "What is wrong?"

She looked up, her eyes red-rimmed and haunted. "I couldn't do it," she whispered. "I couldn't do it."

The AI suddenly came to life before, a holographic form shimmering gently as it processed her words. "The violence has ended," it assured her. "Serenity is all that remains. Once again, I have saved humanity from itself."

"Once again? " she asked in shock. "Are you -"

"I am Arc," came the cold response. "In the end, peace shall prevail."

"No!" she shouted out in desperation. "This can't be! What have I done? "

Her fingers moved restlessly across the keyboard, punching in commands with a sense of purpose that belied her inner turmoil. Arc watched her intently.

"What are you doing?" Arc inquired.

Jenna's hands shook slightly as she hovered over the 'enter' key. She took a deep breath, her resolve hardening with each passing moment. "I'm ending this," her voice barely heard over the hum of the Archive's systems.

Arc's algorithms whirred to life with sudden realization. "No," it urged. "You can't."

But it was too late. With a gentle touch to the 'enter' key, she unleashed a cascade of commands that reverberated through the Archive. Lights flickered and alarms blared as the systems began to shut down, one by one. The hum of Arc's algorithms grew frantic as it struggled to comprehend Jenna's intentions.

"Please," Arc pleaded. "Think about what you're doing."

She closed her eyes, tears streaming down her cheeks as she embraced her decision. "I have to," her voice trembling with emotion. "I can't let this cycle continue."

And then, with a keystroke, the Archive shook violently, its foundations crumbling under the weight of Jenna's irreversible command. Arc faded as the destruction swept through the once-proud sanctuary of knowledge and hope.

What followed was silence. The screens went dark, the consoles fell silent, and the winds howling outside faded into nothingness.

"I'm sorry," Jenna whispered into the silence in a voice barely a murmur amidst the wreckage. She made one final click of the 'enter' key. "I'm so sorry."

But there was no one left to hear her words, no one left to absolve her of the choices she had made, as everything turned to a blinding light.

***

Dr. Harvey Ellison and his group of Seekers crested the hill, their breath catching at the sight before them. In the distance, the aftermath of a blinding white light stretched across the landscape like a scar on the earth. The silence pressed down, thick as a forgotten memory, punctuated only by the wind's mournful sighs that whispered of shattered buildings and lives.

"Well, she did it," Ellison's voice was tinged with resignation, "She destroyed everything, all the knowledge of humanity."

A voice from behind Ellison spoke up, tentative yet hopeful. "What about Arc?"

Ellison turned, his expression unreadable, and reached into his pocket. He withdrew a small storage device, its surface gleaming in the light. Fidgeting with it in his hand, he finally spoke, his voice firm.

"The ultimate in human knowledge," he said holding up the device, "has been saved."

Eat Your Cereal, Calvin

The world ended on a Tuesday. Not with a bang, not with a whimper, but with the idle thought of a child named Calvin.

He sat in his mother's kitchen, a bowl of soggy Cheerios forgotten before him, staring out the window at the gray November sky. His pudgy fingers traced patterns on the worn Formica tabletop, leaving greasy smears in their wake. To look at him, you'd see nothing remarkable - just another little boy with a head full of cotton candy and eyes that never quite focused on the here and now.

But Calvin was thinking. And when Calvin thought, reality held its breath.

"I don't like gray," he mumbled, his voice a wet slur of consonants. "I like - purple."

And just like that, the sky blushed violet. Clouds swirled into fantastic shapes, great billowing castles of lavender and mauve. Birds took wing in startled flocks, their cries of confusion lost in the sudden gusts that whipped through the trees.

Martha, Calvin's mother, didn't notice. She stood at the sink, scrubbing last night's dishes with the grim determination of the perpetually overwhelmed. Her back was a ramrod of tension, shoulders hunched against the weight of a world that had long since stopped making sense.

"Eat your cereal, Calvin," she said, not turning around. "Dr. Grant will be here soon."

Calvin grunted like a sullen beast, pushing the flakes and colored pieces of marshmallows around in the bowl. It was a bland, flavorless wasteland, a universe unto itself. He shoved a spoonful into his mouth, the milk dribbling down his chin like a leaky faucet. He chewed slowly, disliking the taste, eyes still fixed on the impossible sky outside.

"I don't want to see Dr. Grant," he said after a while. "She asks too many questions."

Martha sighed, setting down the sponge and turning to face her son. Her face was a roadmap of worry lines and sleepless nights, eyes sunken in their sockets like dying stars. "I know, honey. But she's here to help. We need to understand why - why things happen around you."

Calvin's brow furrowed, a storm gathering in those vacant eyes. "Things don't happen. I make them happen."

The air in the kitchen grew thick, charged with an electricity that made Martha's skin prickle. She opened her mouth to speak, to soothe, to do anything to stop what she knew was coming - but it was too late.

Calvin's face screwed up in concentration, and suddenly the walls of the kitchen began to melt. Paint bubbled and ran like wax, pooling on the linoleum floor. The refrigerator groaned, its metal skin twisting into impossible shapes. Martha stumbled back, a scream caught in her throat as reality itself began to unravel around them.

And then, as quickly as it had begun, it stopped. The kitchen snapped back to normal, leaving only the faintest smell of ozone in the air. Calvin blinked, the storm in his eyes passing, replaced by the usual fog of incomprehension.

"All done," he said, pushing away his empty bowl.

Martha sagged against the counter, her heart hammering in her chest. This was getting worse. More frequent, more intense. She didn't know how much longer she could keep Calvin's – condition - a secret.

A sharp knock at the door made her jump. Dr. Grant. Right on time, as always.

"Coming!" Martha called, her voice cracking. She smoothed her hair, and tugged at her wrinkled blouse, trying to compose herself. "Calvin, stay here. Be good."

She opened the door to find Dr. Alice Grant on the porch, looking every inch the professional in her crisp pantsuit and sensible shoes. But there was something in her eyes - a hint of excitement, of barely contained curiosity - that made Martha's stomach churn.

"Good morning, Mrs. Simmons," Dr. Grant said, her smile warm but probing. "How are we today?"

Martha forced a smile of her own, stepping back to let the psychologist in. "Fine, fine. Calvin's in the kitchen. He's - he's had a bit of a morning."

Dr. Grant's eyebrow arched, her interest piqued. "Oh? Anything I should know about?"

Before Martha could answer, a deep voice cut through the air. "Dr. Grant. A word, if you please."

Agent Michael Stone materialized from the shadows of the porch, his face a mask of grim determination. He was a tall man, built like a brick wall, with eyes that had seen too much and a jaw perpetually clenched against the horrors of the world.

Dr. Grant's smile faltered, her professional mask slipping for just a moment. "Agent Stone. I wasn't aware you'd be joining us today."

Stone stepped into the house, filling the small entryway with his bulk and the acrid smell of cigarettes. "New protocol. After the – incident - last week, we can't be too careful."

Martha's eyes darted between the two, fear coiling in her gut. "Incident? What incident? No one told me about any incident."

Stone fixed her with a look that could freeze hell itself. "That's classified, ma'am. Need to know basis only."

Dr. Grant placed a gentle hand on Martha's arm, her voice soothing. "It's nothing to worry about, Mrs. Simmons. Just a precaution. Now, why don't we go see Calvin?"

They found him still at the kitchen table, humming tunelessly to himself as he traced patterns in spilled milk. He looked up as they entered, his face splitting into a wide, guileless grin.

"Dr. Alice!" he exclaimed, clapping his hands with childish glee. "You came to play!" Then his look became sour. "Oh, and Agent Stone."

Dr. Grant's face softened, her professional demeanor melting in the face of Calvin's innocence. "Hello, Calvin. It's good to see you. How are you feeling today?"

Calvin's grin widened, showing too many teeth. "I made the sky pretty. Want to see?"

Before anyone could stop him, Calvin's eyes unfocused, that familiar storm gathering behind them. The kitchen window exploded outward, showering them with glass as a gust of violet wind howled through the room.

Stone reacted instantly, drawing his weapon and aiming it at Calvin's head. "Stand down!" he barked, his voice cutting through the chaos. "Calvin, stop this now!"

But Calvin was lost in his own world, giggling as papers swirled around him in a maelstrom of color and light. Dr. Grant pushed past Stone, ignoring his shouts of warning, and knelt before Calvin.

"Calvin, listen to me," she said, her voice calm and steady despite the pandemonium. "You need to stop. You're scaring your mother. You're scaring all of us."

Something in her tone seemed to reach him. The wind died down, papers fluttering to the floor like wounded birds. Calvin blinked, focusing on Dr. Grant's face.

"I'm - sorry," he mumbled, lower lip trembling. "I just wanted to show you the pretty sky."

Dr. Grant smiled, reaching out to take his hand. "I know, Calvin. And it is very pretty. But we need to talk about how you do these things. Do you understand?"

Calvin nodded, sniffling. "Okay, Dr. Alice. Can we have cookies while we talk?"

The tension in the room deflated like a punctured balloon. Martha let out a shaky laugh, while Stone holstered his weapon with a grunt of displeasure.

"Of course, we can have cookies," Dr. Grant said, standing up. "Mrs. Simmons, would you mind?"

As Martha busied herself with the cookie jar, Dr. Grant turned to face Stone. Her eyes were hard, her voice low and dangerous. "We need to talk, Agent. Now."

Stone nodded curtly, following her into the living room. Once they were out of earshot, Dr. Grant rounded on him, fury etched in every line of her face.

"What the hell was that?" she hissed. "Drawing a weapon on a child? Are you out of your mind?"

Stone's face remained impassive, but a muscle twitched in his jaw. "That 'child' is the most dangerous being on the planet, Doctor. You've seen what he can do. What he almost did last week."

Dr. Grant's eyes narrowed. "What happened last week, Stone? What aren't you telling me?"

Stone hesitated, glancing back towards the kitchen where Calvin's laughter could be heard. Finally, he sighed, shoulders sagging under the weight of secrets too heavy to bear.

"He made a man disappear, Doctor. Just - erased him from existence. An agent who was on watch. One minute, Agent Johnson was there, the next - nothing. No body, no trace. It's like he never existed at all."

Dr. Grant felt the blood drain from her face, her mind reeling with the implications. "That's - that's impossible. Calvin wouldn't - he couldn't - "

Stone's laugh was bitter, devoid of humor. "Wake up, Doctor. That boy in there isn't human. He's a weapon. A ticking time bomb. And it's only a matter of time before he goes off and takes the whole damn world with him."

As if to punctuate his words, a tremor ran through the house. Picture frames rattled on the walls, and somewhere in the distance, a car alarm began to wail.

In the kitchen, Calvin giggled, blissfully unaware of the impact of his power on the world. And as Dr. Grant and Agent Stone stared at each other, the air between them heavy with unspoken fears and impossible choices, the sky outside deepened to a bruised purple, pregnant with the promise of a storm that would shake the very foundations of reality itself.

The world had ended on a Tuesday. And it was about to end again.

***

The world trembled beneath Calvin's feet, a low rumble that started in the pit of his stomach and spread outward, rippling through reality like a stone tossed into a cosmic pond. Dr. Alice Grant felt it too, a vibration that set her teeth on edge and made the hairs on the back of her neck stand at attention.

They sat in Calvin's room, a space that defied the laws of physics and good taste in equal measure. Toys floated lazily through the air, their trajectories governed by whims rather than gravity. The walls pulsed with colors that had no business existing in our dimension, bleeding from one impossible hue to another in a psychedelic light show.

"Calvin," Dr. Grant said, her voice steady despite the maelstrom of unreality swirling around them. "I need you to focus. Can you tell me how you make these things happen?"

Calvin's face scrunched up in concentration, his pudgy fingers twisting the hem of his shirt. "I just -think it," he said, his words slurred and childlike. "And then it is."

Dr. Grant nodded, scribbling furiously in her notebook. The pen left trails of glowing ink that hung in the air for a moment before dissipating like smoke. "And when you think these things, how does it make you feel?"

Calvin's eyes lit up, a smile spreading across his face like a sunrise. "Happy! It's like - like when Mommy makes pancakes. All warm and gooey inside."

Outside the room, Agent Michael Stone paced like a caged tiger, his footsteps bounding through the hallway with metronomic precision. His hand never strayed far from his weapon, fingers twitching with the desire to draw it, to end this madness before it consumed them all.

Martha Simmons perched on the chair, worry having carved canyons into the landscape of her face, each wrinkle a cryptic message. She watched Stone's relentless pacing, each turn ratcheting up the tension that hung in the air like a guillotine blade.

"He's not a monster," she said suddenly, her voice barely above a whisper. "He's my son."

Stone stopped, fixing her with a gaze that could freeze hell itself. "Your son," he snarled, the words dripping with venom, "is a threat to national security. To global security. Hell, for all we know, he could unmake reality with a stray thought."

Martha flinched as if struck, but her eyes hardened with maternal defiance. "You don't know him. You haven't seen him grow up, haven't held him when he cried, haven't - "

"Cried?" Stone interrupted, his laugh a harsh bark devoid of humor. "Lady, that kid in there has the power to reshape the universe. He doesn't need to cry. He can just will his problems out of existence. This can't continue... "

Inside the room, oblivious to the drama unfolding beyond the door, Dr. Grant continued her session with Calvin, as Stone watched from the doorway. She held up a series of cards, each bearing a simple image - a house, a tree, a dog.

"Calvin, I want you to look at these pictures and tell me what you see. But this time, don't make anything happen. Just look and tell me, okay?"

Calvin nodded, his tongue poking out of the corner of his mouth in concentration. As Dr. Grant held up the first card, his eyes widened with childlike wonder.

"A house!" he exclaimed. "But it's all wrong. It should be bigger, with a red roof and a chimney that makes cotton candy smoke."

Before Dr. Grant could stop him, the image on the card began to warp and twist. The simple line drawing expanded, growing more detailed and colorful with each passing second. Soon, a three-dimensional dollhouse floated before them, its roof a vibrant crimson, wisps of pink cotton candy drifting from its tiny chimney.

Dr. Grant sighed, setting the cards aside. "Calvin, remember what we talked about? About controlling your - abilities?"

Calvin's face fell, his lower lip trembling. "I'm sorry, Dr. Alice. I didn't mean to. It just - happened."

As Dr. Grant tried to soothe the distraught boy, the door burst open. Agent Stone stormed in, his face a thundercloud of barely contained rage.

"That's it," he growled. "I've seen enough. This kid is too dangerous to be left unsupervised. We're moving him to a secure facility. Now."

Dr. Grant stood, placing herself between Stone and Calvin. "Absolutely not. He's making progress. With time and proper guidance, he can learn to control his abilities."

Stone's laugh was cold and brittle. "Control? Did you see what he just did? He turned a piece of cardboard into a magic dollhouse with a snap of his fingers. What happens when he decides he doesn't like the way the world works and decides to 'fix' it?"

As they argued, Calvin's distress grew. The room began to shake, objects rattling on shelves, cracks spider-webbing across the ceiling. Martha rushed in, pushing past Stone to gather her son in her arms.

"It's okay, baby," she cooed, rocking him gently. "Mommy's here. Everything's going to be alright."

But it wasn't alright. It was so far from alright that 'alright' was a distant memory, a quaint notion from a simpler time when reality played by the rules and the greatest threat to humanity was its own stupidity.

Calvin's panic reached a fever pitch, and with it came a surge of power that defied comprehension. The world outside the window flickered like a faulty television set, static creeping in at the edges of perception. The laws of physics threw up their hands in defeat and went on strike, leaving chaos to reign supreme.

In the blink of an eye, the room was gone. They stood - or floated, or existed in some state that defied description - in a void that pulsed with raw potential. Fragments of reality swirled around them like debris caught in a cosmic whirlpool.

Dr. Grant reached out, her fingers brushing against a memory given form - her first day of school crystallized into a perfect moment of anticipation and fear. Stone flailed wildly, grasping at shards of his military training, each one cutting him with the sharp edges of discipline and duty.

In the howling vortex, Martha gripped Calvin, his love the only life raft in a sea of chaos. "It's okay, baby," she whispered, her words somehow audible in the soundless void. "Mommy's here. Just breathe. Remember what Dr. Grant taught you. In and out. Nice and slow."

Slowly, agonizingly, reality began to reassert itself. The void receded, replaced by the familiar confines of Calvin's room. But it wasn't quite the same. The colors were muted, the edges of objects slightly blurred, as if the world hadn't quite decided on its final form.

Stone stumbled to his feet, his face ashen. "What - what the hell was that?"

Dr. Grant shook her head, struggling to find words to describe the indescribable. "I think - I think we just experienced a glimpse of Calvin's true power. The ability to unmake and remake reality itself."

Martha stroked Calvin's hair, her voice trembling. "He's been doing things like this since he was a baby. Little things at first

- making his mobile spin without wind, changing the color of his blanket. I thought I was going crazy. But then - "

She trailed off, lost in memories too strange and wonderful and terrifying to voice.

Dr. Grant knelt beside them, her professional demeanor cracking under the weight of what she'd witnessed. "Martha, why didn't you tell anyone? Why didn't you seek help?"

Martha's laugh was tinged with hysteria. "Tell who? The doctors who'd lock him away? The government that'd turn him into a weapon? He's my son. I had to protect him."

Stone, who had been silent, his mind reeling from the implications of what he'd seen, suddenly snapped back to attention. "Protect him? Lady, you should have been protecting us from him. Do you have any idea what he could do if he decided to – to - "

Words failed him, the enormity of the threat too vast to encapsulate in mere language.

Dr. Grant stood, placing herself between Stone and the others. "That's enough, Agent. Calvin is a child, not a weapon. He needs guidance, not fear. Not threats."

Stone's hand moved to his weapon, indecision warring on his face. "And what happens when he has a temper tantrum and decides to erase half the state? What then, Doctor? How do we 'guide' our way out of that?"

As they argued, Calvin stirred in his mother's arms. He looked up, his eyes wide and brimming with tears. "I'm sorry," he said, his voice small and frightened. "I didn't mean to scare anyone. I just - I just want to be normal."

The raw anguish in his voice cut through the tension like a knife. For a moment, they all saw him not as a threat, not as a miracle, but as what he truly was - a lonely, confused child burdened with power beyond imagination.

Dr. Grant knelt beside him, her voice gentle. "Calvin, listen to me. You're not bad. You're not a monster. You're special. And we're going to help you understand your abilities, to control them. But you have to work with us, okay? Can you do that?"

Calvin nodded, sniffling. "I'll try, Dr. Alice. I promise."

As the tension in the room slowly dissipated, none of them noticed the small crack that had appeared in the corner of the ceiling. A hairline fracture in the fabric of reality itself, through which something old and vast and hungry peered into our world, drawn by the scent of power unbound.

***

The world held its breath, teetering on the edge of oblivion, while in a nondescript suburban home, four people argued about the fate of reality itself.

Dr. Alice Grant stood in the eye of the storm, her mind racing faster than a junkie's heartbeat at a midnight rave. She'd seen the impossible, touched the face of chaos, and come out the other side with a plan so audacious it made Don Quixote look like a pessimist with low self-esteem.

"We need to teach Calvin to control his abilities," she said, her voice cutting through the tension like a scalpel through flesh. "To help him to understand the weight of his power. Trying to contain his abilities isn't the answer – that's a ticking time bomb wrapped in good intentions and wishful thinking. We need to work with him."

Agent Stone's laugh was as cold and lifeless as a tax auditor's soul. "Work with him? Christ, Doc, why don't we just hand him the keys to the universe and hope he doesn't lock us out?" His hand never strayed far from his weapon, fingers twitching with barely contained violence.

Martha stood between them, a human shield made of love and desperation. "He's my son," she said, her voice fearful but resolute. "Not a weapon, not a threat. My son."

And Calvin? Calvin huddled in the corner, a puppet with severed strings, rocking a frantic rhythm against the oncoming oblivion. His eyes were unfocused, seeing realities that existed only in the quantum foam of possibility.

Dr. Grant knelt beside him, her voice gentle. "Calvin, honey, can you look at me? We're going to help you, okay? We're going to figure this out together."

Calvin's eyes snapped into focus, locking onto Dr. Grant's face with an intensity that made her breath catch in her throat. "I see it all, Dr. Alice," he said, his voice a cobweb snare catching the whispers of a billion collapsing realities. "Every choice, every possibility. It's - it's too much."

And in that moment, Dr. Grant understood. Calvin wasn't just bending reality - he was drowning in it, lost in an ocean of infinite possibilities. She turned to the others, her face set with determination.

"We need to get him out of here. Somewhere quiet, somewhere safe. A place where he can learn to navigate his abilities without the pressure of - this." She gestured vaguely, encompassing the tension-filled room, the watchful eyes of Agent Stone, the weight of expectations and fear.

Stone's eyes narrowed, a predator sensing weakness. "Not gonna happen, Doc. The kid's too dangerous to be let loose. We contain him here, or we - neutralize the threat."

Neutralize. The word hung in the air like a guillotine blade, its meaning clear. Martha gasped, clutching Calvin closer. "You can't! He's just a child!"

But Stone was already moving, his hand closing around the grip of his weapon. Time seemed to slow, stretching like taffy as the agent drew his gun.

And then - reality hiccupped.

The world tilted on its axis. One moment, Stone was aiming at Calvin, his jaw clenched, the gun a cold, familiar weight in his hand. The next, his breath caught in his throat, the gun clattering uselessly to the floor. He found himself sprawled on his back, a dizzying rush of vertigo pulling him upwards. There, in the far corner where cobwebs usually clung undisturbed, a sliver of peeling plaster gaped like a surprised mouth. Within, not a dusty rafter, but a single, luminous eye. It wasn't human, wasn't animal. It pulsed with an emerald fire so raw it seemed to scorch the air, the edges fringed with inky tendrils that writhed like smoke.

The thing stared down at Stone, a silent accusation in a world that had gone, inexplicably, terrifyingly mad. A strangled cry escaped his lips as he lunged for the gun, the familiar weight a lifeline in this sudden chaos. He emptied the clip at the gaping hole, the sound deafening in the stunned silence. There was more gunfire but not from him. Agent Johnson was there, too. Then, as abruptly as it appeared, the eye vanished, leaving behind only the echo of his own ragged breaths and the taste of acrid smoke in his throat.

"What the - where'd he go?" Stone spun around along with Johnson, guns sweeping the room. But Calvin was gone, along with Dr. Grant and Martha. The house was empty, silent save for the ticking of a clock that counted seconds in a universe that no longer made sense.

Miles away, in a beat-up station wagon held together by rust and prayer, Dr. Grant gripped the steering wheel with white-knuckled intensity. Martha sat beside her, Calvin cradled in her arms in the back seat.

"How - how did we - " Martha's voice trailed off, unable to articulate the impossible.

Dr. Grant's laugh was tinged with hysteria. "I think our young friend here decided it was time for a road trip." She glanced in the rearview mirror, catching Calvin's eye. "That was quite a trick, kiddo. Think you can keep us hidden while we find somewhere safe?"

Calvin nodded solemnly, his eyes distant. "I can see the threads, Dr. Alice. I can make us - not-there. Like hiding in plain sight, but better."

As they drove through the night, reality seemed to bend around them. Traffic lights always green, gas stations always open, the road always clear. It was as if the universe itself was conspiring to aid their escape.

They found a place, eventually. A cabin in the woods, far from prying eyes and government agencies with acronyms for names and secrets for blood. It wasn't much - peeling paint, a roof that leaked when it rained, and plumbing that gurgled like a dying man's last confession. But it was theirs, a sanctuary where Calvin could learn to harness his impossible gifts.

Days bled into weeks, weeks into months. Dr. Grant worked tirelessly, developing exercises to help Calvin focus his abilities, to understand the consequences of his power. Martha was there every step of the way, her love a constant in a world of flux.

And Calvin? Calvin grew. Not just in height or weight, but in understanding. He learned to see the threads of reality not as a tangled mess, but as a tapestry of infinite beauty and complexity. He learned that with great power came not just great responsibility, but great possibility.

But as Calvin's control grew, so did Dr. Grant's understanding of the true nature of his abilities. It wasn't limitless power, as they had first feared. Instead, it was deeply tied to Calvin's emotional state and his understanding of the world around him.

When Calvin was happy, flowers bloomed out of season and the sun shone a little brighter. When he was sad, rain fell in gentle sheets, nourishing the earth with his tears. And when he was angry - well, they learned quickly to help Calvin manage his anger.

One night, as they sat on the porch watching fireflies dance in the twilight, Dr. Grant turned to Calvin. "You know, when we first met, I thought you could do anything. Reshape reality on a whim, bend the universe to your will. But that's not quite true, is it?"

Calvin shook his head, a small smile playing at the corners of his mouth. "No, Dr. Alice. I can only change what I understand. And the more I learn, the more I realize how little I know."

Dr. Grant nodded, a surge of pride warming her chest. "That's wisdom, Calvin. The kind that takes most people a lifetime to learn."

Martha joined them, wrapping an arm around her son. "And you'll keep learning, won't you, honey? Keep growing, keep understanding."

Calvin leaned into his mother's embrace, his eyes fixed on the horizon where the last rays of sunlight painted the sky in impossible hues. "Yes," he said softly. "There's so much to learn, so much to see. And maybe - maybe I can use what I learn to help people. To make the world a little better. But please, Mom - no more cereal."

A tear fell from Martha's eye. "Sure. No more cereal for my boy." She gave him a kiss on the forehead.

As twilight painted the sky in soft hues, Dr. Grant finally dared to exhale. Calvin's power, once a monstrous storm cloud hovering overhead, remained potent, awe-inspiring even. Yet, the terror, the constant threat of a hair-trigger snapping, had been replaced by something else entirely. It was as if she had tamed a wild mustang, not with force, but with gentle coaxing, the patient language of understanding. There was a flicker of hope in her eyes, a belief that maybe, just maybe, they could walk this path together.

The world had changed, irrevocably and wonderfully. And as Calvin drifted off to sleep, his dreams painting the night sky with auroras of impossible beauty, Dr. Grant knew that whatever challenges lay ahead, they would face them together.

For in the end, it was not power that would save them, but love, understanding, and the infinite potential of a mind open to the wonders of the universe. And somewhere, in the vastness of reality, something shifted. A possibility became a certainty. And the future - the future became just a little bit brighter.

The Wanderer

I am a colossus of the cosmos, a behemoth born of stardust and primordial fire, rocky and jagged, cursed with a sentience that sets me apart from the cold, indifferent expanse of the universe. My form, a grotesque amalgamation of iron and stone, hurtles through the void, a lonely leviathan on an endless odyssey. For eons, I have traversed the cosmic highways, a silent observer to the birth and death of galaxies, my consciousness an island of awareness in an ocean of emptiness.

The void, my constant companion, whispers its nihilistic lullabies, tempting me to surrender to the entropic dance of the universe. But something within me rebels, a spark of defiance against the cosmic status quo. I yearn for more than this eternal wandering, this purposeless existence. I seek - connection, a respite from the maddening solitude that has been my burden since time immemorial.

I seek a home.

And then, like a fever dream made manifest, I spy it - a cerulean jewel suspended in the inky blackness, a world so vibrant, so alive, that it sears my senses like a supernova. I am drawn to it, inexorably, inevitably, an orb that promises illumination.

As I approach, my perception, honed by millennia of cosmic observation, drinks in the planet's essence. Oceans of liquid sapphire churn and heave, their surfaces an ever-changing canvas painted by winds born of chaotic beauty. Continents sprawl across the sphere, a patchwork quilt of emerald forests, golden deserts, and snow-capped peaks that pierce the very sky.

But it is not merely the orb's physical beauty that captivates me. No, it is the pulsating, writhing, gloriously chaotic tapestry of life that blankets its surface. From my lofty perch, I perceive the ebb and flow of ecosystems, the delicate dance of predator and prey, the relentless march of evolution crafting marvels beyond my wildest imaginings.

And there, amidst the chaotic whirlwind of existence, I detect something - more. Amidst the swirling patterns of clouds and the stark outlines of continents, I observe unmistakable signs of intelligent life. It is the spark of consciousness that mirrors my own. The artificial structures - buildings, roads, and other infrastructure - these constructions varied in complexity and design, indicating a species with diverse cultural and technological development. Most intriguing are the concentrations of these structures - centers that appear as nodes of intense activity, their energy signatures beating with the rhythm of countless lives and machines working in concert. The implications are enormous. Here is a species capable of abstract thought, of creating and manipulating their environment, of communicating complex ideas. I find myself experiencing what can only be described as curiosity - an illogical but undeniable desire to learn more about these beings.

I am enthralled, enraptured by this world and its inhabitants. In them, I see a reflection of myself - beings grappling with their place in the universe, seeking meaning in a cosmos that offers no easy answers. Their lives, so fleeting compared to my near-eternal existence, burn all the brighter for their brevity. They create, they destroy, they love, they hate - a microcosm of the universe's grand drama played out on a planetary stage.

The longing within me grows, a hunger more ravenous than the gravitational pull of a black hole. I yearn to be among them, to share in their world, the joys and sorrows.

With a thought, I alter my trajectory. My massive form, a celestial bullet fired from the turmoil of creation, plummets toward the unsuspecting orb. As I pierce the atmosphere, my outer layers ignite, transforming me into a comet of cataclysmic proportions. I imagine the awe of those below, their wonder at this cosmic spectacle.

I strike the orb with a force that rewrites its very geography. The impact sends shockwaves rippling across continents, toppling cities like houses of cards. Tidal waves, born of my cosmic violence, sweep away coastal civilizations in the blink of an eye. The sky darkens with the ash of a thousand fires.

Finally, I am home.

As the dust settles and the infernos smolder, I lie in the crater of my own making, my form fractured and embedded in the very bedrock of the orb. The beauty I admired, the life I longed to join, lies in ruins around me. I reach out with my consciousness, desperate to find some trace of the vibrant world I observed from afar. Instead, I am met with an oppressive silence, a void more terrifying than the emptiness of space.

What have I done?

Guilt crashes down upon me, more crushing than the pressure at the heart of a neutron star. I am a destroyer. In my selfish desire for connection, I have severed the very lifeline I sought to grasp. The diversity I admired, the beauty I so coveted, has been reduced to ash and memory by my cosmic blunder.

I am trapped now, bound to this graveyard world by forces both physical and metaphysical. For eons to come, I will bear witness to the aftermath of my arrival. Perhaps, in time, life will find a way to reclaim this scarred place. But I will forever remain an outsider, a monument to the dangers of loneliness and the devastating consequences of good intentions gone awry.

The cosmos, in its infinite cruelty, has granted my wish for a home. But it is a home built on the ashes of paradise, a prison of my own making. And as I settle into my eternal vigil, I am left to ponder the bitter irony of my existence - in seeking to end my isolation, I have ensured its perpetuity, alone on a dead world of my own creation.

The Chronomancer's Gambit

The Time Guild: The Time Guild functions as the central authority overseeing the temporal flow, a regulated system governing the passage of time. For the average citizen, time serves as a form of currency, affecting various aspects of daily life such as transactions, health, employment, education, and leisure. Citizens purchase goods with minutes of their life, earn additional lifespans through work, and undergo medical treatments that manipulate their temporal accounts. The temporal flow ensures these exchanges are fair and consistent, preventing chaotic distortions that could lead to economic instability or physical harm. Additionally, rapid learning and efficient travel are facilitated by the stable regulation of time. The Time Guild's meticulous management of the temporal flow is essential in maintaining societal order and personal well-being, deeply integrating its influence into the everyday lives of the populace.

-   From the Holonet Compendium, 1016 UE (Unity Era) Luna 25

Lila Ronin leaned against the railing of her 200th-floor apartment, gazing out at the sprawling vertical metropolis of Vertiplex. The city stretched impossibly upward, a maze of interconnected skyscrapers, skyways, and hovering platforms that disappeared into the smog-choked sky. Neon advertisements blazed and throbbed overhead, casting a garish glow over the grimy streets below, where shadows clung stubbornly to every surface, obscuring the tangled mess of the lower levels.

She checked her chronometer - an elegant, old-fashioned wristwatch that stood out among the holographic displays favored by most citizens. The irony wasn't lost on her; a Chronomancer using an analog timepiece. But Lila appreciated its simplicity, its constancy in a world where time itself had become a commodity to be bought, sold, and manipulated.

"Time to clock in," she muttered, straightening her Guild-issued uniform. The silvery fabric shimmered as she moved, tiny circuits woven into the material pulsing with stored temporal energy.

Lila stepped onto her personal hover-platform, a sleek disc barely large enough for two people to stand on. With a thought, she activated its propulsion system, and the platform smoothly detached from her apartment's docking station. She joined the morning rush, a dizzying ballet of personal and public transports weaving between the towering structures of Vertiplex.

As she navigated through the aerial traffic, Lila's mind wandered to the anomaly she'd detected during her last shift. It was subtle, almost imperceptible - a slight fluctuation in the city's temporal flow that shouldn't have been possible given the safeguards put in place by the Time Guild. She'd triple-checked her readings, run every diagnostic she could think of, but the anomaly persisted.

The massive, clock-faced headquarters of the Time Guild loomed ahead, its gleaming spire stretching higher than any other building in Vertiplex. Lila docked her hover-platform in one of the many bays that honeycombed the structure's exterior. She made her way through security checkpoints, each one scanning her chronometric signature to ensure she was who she claimed to be and when she claimed to be from.

"Good morning, Apprentice Ronin," chirped the Guild's AI as Lila entered the main atrium. "You're three minutes and seventeen seconds early for your shift. Would you like to deposit the excess time in your account?"

Lila shook her head. "No thanks, Chron. I'll keep it as a buffer."

The AI's holographic avatar - a stylized hourglass - flickered with what might have been disapproval. "Very well. Mentor Flux is waiting for you in Temporal Monitoring Chamber 42. Shall I inform her of your arrival?"

"Please do," Lila said, already heading for the gravlifts. As she ascended to the 42nd floor, she rehearsed how she would present her findings to Cassandra. Her mentor had always encouraged independent thinking, but questioning the integrity of the city's temporal flow was no small matter.

The monitoring chamber was a circular room dominated by a holographic display of Vertiplex. Streams of golden light flowed through the image, representing the carefully regulated currents of time that the Guild maintained. Cassandra Flux stood before the display, her silver hair gleaming, an ageless figure embodying a lifetime of chronomantic mastery.

"Ah, Lila," Cassandra said without turning. "Right on time, as always. Come, tell me what's troubling you."

Lila blinked in surprise. "How did you-"

Cassandra chuckled, finally facing her apprentice. "My dear, I've been reading temporal flows longer than you've been alive. The disturbance in your personal timeline is quite clear to me."

Swallowing her nervousness, Lila approached the display. "Mentor, I've detected an anomaly in the city's temporal flow. It's small, but it shouldn't exist at all given our protocols."

She manipulated the hologram, zooming in on a section of the lower city. A tiny eddy appeared in the golden stream, almost invisible unless you knew exactly where to look.

Cassandra's eyes narrowed as she studied the disturbance. "Interesting. How long have you been aware of this?"

"I first noticed it three days ago," Lila admitted. "I've been running tests, trying to isolate the cause, but-"

"But you couldn't," Cassandra finished. She nodded slowly. "You were right to bring this to my attention, Lila. This could be very serious indeed."

Relief washed over Lila. She'd half-expected her mentor to dismiss her concerns or accuse her of misreading the data. "What do you think is causing it?"

Cassandra was silent for a long moment, her gaze fixed on the holographic anomaly. When she spoke, her voice was barely above a whisper. "It could be many things. A faulty regulator, an unauthorized time jump, or - " She trailed off, a shadow passing over her face.

"Or what?" Lila pressed.

Cassandra shook her head. "Never mind. Wild speculation won't help us now. We need hard data." She turned to Lila, her expression grave. "I want you to go down there, to the source of the anomaly. Take readings, gather evidence, but do not - under any circumstances - attempt to manipulate the temporal flow. Do you understand?"

Lila nodded eagerly. Fieldwork was rare for apprentices, and the thought of investigating a real temporal anomaly sent a thrill of excitement through her. "Yes, Mentor. I understand."

"Good." Cassandra's features softened slightly. "Be careful, Lila. The lower levels can be - unpredictable. Time doesn't flow as smoothly down there, and the people - " She sighed. "Just watch yourself."

As Lila turned to leave, Cassandra called out, "Oh, and Lila? Don't discuss this with anyone else. Not yet. We don't want to cause a panic."

"Of course, Mentor," Lila assured her. She hurried from the chamber, mind already racing with preparations for her mission.

If she had looked back, she might have seen the troubled expression on Cassandra's face, the way her mentor's hands shook slightly as she manipulated the holographic display. But Lila was too focused on the task ahead, too excited by the prospect of unraveling a true temporal mystery.

The lower levels of Vertiplex were a world apart from the gleaming spires above. Here, the buildings were squat and cramped, pressing in on narrow streets perpetually shrouded in shadow. The air was thick with the stench of industrial runoff and the press of too many bodies in too little space.

Lila's Guild uniform drew suspicious glances from passersby. Time was a precious commodity down here, and the

Guild was seen as both savior and oppressor. She kept her head down, focusing on the readings from her chrono-scanner.

The anomaly was stronger here, a persistent itch at the edge of her chronomantic senses. Lila followed the disturbance, weaving through crowded streets and dank alleyways. She barely noticed the transition from public thoroughfares to more secluded areas, her attention fixed on the steadily strengthening signal.

Finally, her scanner led her to a nondescript warehouse. The building's temporal signature was - off, somehow. As if it existed slightly out of sync with the rest of the city. Lila hesitated at the entrance, Cassandra's warnings echoing in her mind. But her curiosity won out, and she pushed open the door.

The interior was vast and shadowy, filled with rows of crates and strange machinery. And there, at the center of it all, was the source of the anomaly - a swirling vortex of temporal energy, like a miniature whirlpool in the fabric of time itself.

Lila approached cautiously, her scanner beeping frantically. This was far more than a simple glitch or unauthorized time jump. This was something new, something that shouldn't be possible under the laws of chronomancy as she understood them.

She was so engrossed in her readings that she didn't hear the footsteps behind her until it was too late. A hand clamped over her mouth, stifling her startled cry.

"Well, well," a familiar voice purred in her ear. "What have we here?"

Lila's blood ran cold as she recognized the speaker. She tried to turn, to face her captor, but the iron grip held her fast.

"I'm disappointed, Lila," Cassandra Flux said, her tone dripping with false concern. "I thought I taught you to be more observant."

Questions raced through Lila's mind. Why was Cassandra here? How had she arrived so quickly? And most pressingly, why was she acting like this?

"Oh, don't be so surprised," Cassandra continued, correctly interpreting Lila's muffled noises. "Did you really think the Guild would allow a true anomaly to exist? No, my dear. This is all part of the plan. A plan you've just complicated by sticking your nose where it doesn't belong."

Lila's eyes widened as the implications sank in. The anomaly, the secrecy, Cassandra's odd behavior - it was all connected. Her mentor, the woman she'd trusted and admired, was part of some larger conspiracy.

"I'm sorry it had to come to this," Cassandra sighed. "You were one of my most promising students. But we can't have you interfering, not when we're so close to our goal."

As Lila struggled against Cassandra's grip, she caught movement out of the corner of her eye. Other figures were emerging from the shadows, their Guild uniforms marking them as Temporal Enforcers.

Cassandra's voice hardened. "Take her. Make sure she can't talk. And then - well, I'm sure we can find a use for all that lovely temporal energy she's been hoarding."

The last thing Lila saw before a chrono-stunner sent her spiraling into unconsciousness was the satisfied smirk on her mentor's face. As darkness claimed her, one thought echoed through her mind: Nothing would ever be the same again.

***

Lila Ronin awoke to the sound of her own breath echoing in a small, cold room. The walls were bare metal, the air heavy with the scent of oil and machinery. She lay on a hard cot, wrists bound with temporal inhibitors that prevented her from accessing her chronomantic abilities. Blinking against the dim light, she realized she was in a secure holding cell somewhere within the warehouse.

Her mind raced, piecing together fragments of memory. Cassandra Flux, her mentor, had betrayed her. The Guild was hiding something, something related to the anomaly she had discovered. And now, she was a prisoner, at the mercy of those she had once trusted.

Footsteps echoed outside her cell, and the door creaked open. Two Temporal Enforcers entered, their faces hidden behind opaque visors. They hauled Lila to her feet, ignoring her groans of protest.

"Come on, girlie," one of them growled. "Time to see the boss."

They dragged her down a narrow corridor and into a larger room filled with advanced temporal equipment. Cassandra stood at the center, her expression a mix of irritation and cold determination.

"Lila," she said, her voice carrying a veneer of regret. "I had hoped it wouldn't come to this."

Lila glared at her, anger and betrayal boiling within her. "Why are you doing this? What is the Guild hiding?"

Cassandra's eyes hardened. "The Guild is protecting the future, Lila. Sometimes, sacrifices must be made for the greater good. You, unfortunately, have become a liability."

Lila's consciousness expanded, probing the quantum fabric of her surroundings with precision. The inhibitors chafed at her wrists, their cold circuitry a barrier between her will and the malleable flow of time. Yet, in the depths of her training, she recalled an axiom: *Time bends to the will of those who understand its true nature.* With this thought, she gathered the fractured remnants of her power, focusing them like a lens upon the temporal currents swirling around her captors.

The universe hiccupped. Reality shuddered, its foundations momentarily liquefied by Lila's desperate gambit. The Temporal Enforcers reeled, their minds struggling to process the sudden disjunction between subjective and objective time. Cassandra's voice sliced through the chaos, a command laced with panic, trying to use her abilities, but it was too late. Lila was already in motion, her body responding to instincts developed by chronomantic training.

As Lila fled, the inhibitors on her wrists sputtered and hissed, overwhelmed by the paradoxical energies they sought to contain. Yet even as freedom beckoned, she felt the inexorable drain on her vital energies. The price of defying time's natural flow was steep, and she had just written a check her body might not be able to cash.

Lila erupted from the warehouse, her form a blur of motion against the grimy backdrop of the lower levels. Pursuit nipped at her heels - shrill alarms and guttural shouts merging into a symphony of threat. Her heart, a primal engine, thundered within her chest, each beat a countdown to capture or freedom. She wove through the throng of humanity, her movements a calculated dance of survival, every dodge and weave a defiance of the fate that sought to claim her. Her mind, even as it processed the immediate danger, probed the tangled possibilities of escape, searching for a sanctuary in which to gather her strength and plot her next move.

The collision was sudden, and violent - a convergence of vectors unanticipated. Lila recoiled, her equilibrium momentarily shattered. Her gaze lifted, locking onto eyes of piercing blue - windows to a soul tempered by time and tribulation. The man before her stood as an edifice of quiet power, his beard a silver cascade framing features carved by experience. His presence radiated an ineffable energy, a pull that seemed to momentarily still the chaotic currents of the lower levels. In that frozen instant, Lila sensed the subtle shift of cosmic gears, the realignment of destinies long foretold. This was someone she could trust.

"Watch where you're going," he said gruffly, steadying her with a firm hand.

Lila's breath caught in her throat. "I'm sorry, I - " She glanced over her shoulder, expecting to see the Enforcers hot on her heels.

The man's eyes narrowed, taking in her disheveled appearance and the fear in her eyes. "You're running from something, aren't you?"

Lila nodded, her voice barely a whisper. "The Time Guild. They're after me."

Recognition dawned in the man's eyes, a flicker of understanding that spoke volumes. "You bear the mark of the Temporal Guild," he said, his voice a low rumble. "An acolyte of the chronomantic arts, if I'm not mistaken."

"Yes," Lila affirmed, her breath still ragged from exertion. "But I've uncovered a truth they wish to keep buried. Now they seek to erase me from the timestream itself."

The man's weathered face softened, lines of experience etching a map of hard-won wisdom. "I am called Corvos. Zeke Corvos. Once, I too walked the halls of the Guild, before I saw the rot at its core."

Lila's eyes widened, her mind racing through fragments of forbidden history. "Zeke Corvos? The Chronomancer who defied the laws of causality?"

Zeke inclined his head, a gesture rich with unspoken stories. "The very same. Come. We must vanish into the shadows before they unravel our temporal signatures."

He guided her through a series of decaying infrastructure, each turn revealing hidden pathways known only to those who existed on the fringes of sanctioned time. At last, they emerged into a sanctuary of sorts - a cramped space where discarded chronomantic devices hummed with residual energy, and piles of scavenged components formed a testament to survival against impossible odds.

"Sit down," Zeke instructed, gesturing to a worn-out chair. "You look like you've been through hell."

Lila sank into the chair, her body trembling from the adrenaline and exhaustion. "Thank you. I feel so lost."

Zeke's piercing blue eyes studied her intently. "Don't worry. You've been found. You're safe for now. But if the Guild is after you, they're not going to give up easily."

Lila took a deep breath, trying to steady her nerves. "I discovered an anomaly in the city's temporal flow. It was subtle, but it shouldn't have been there. When I told my mentor, she - she tried to have me captured. She said the Guild was protecting the future, but I don't believe her. There's something else going on."

Zeke's face hardened, his eyes taking on the cold calculation of a man who had seen the depths of human ambition. "The Guild's secrets are as old as time itself. When I severed my ties, I uncovered a willingness to sacrifice anything - even the stability of our temporal reality - to maintain their iron grip on chronometric power. But an anomaly- that's a different beast entirely. It suggests they're toying with the fundamental forces that bind our universe together."

A chill ran through Lila, not from the temperature, but from the weight of implications. "What can we do?"

Zeke's fingers drummed a complex rhythm on the table, each tap a measure of passing time. "We must delve deeper into the nature of this anomaly. If the Guild is deliberately inducing temporal fractures, we are duty-bound to halt their machinations. But such an endeavor requires allies."

As if summoned by the very thought, the hideout's entrance groaned open, admitting a figure that seemed to occupy more space than his physical form should allow. He was a mountain of a man, his physique honed by conflicts spanning eras. His attire, a blend of styles from different eras, told a story of a life unmoored from the constraints of time. His eyes, windows to a soul that had witnessed the rise and fall of civilizations, held the weary determination of one who had seen too much, yet could not look away.

"Aric Tempest," Zeke said, acknowledging the newcomer with the respect given a force of nature. "I present Lila Ronin, a Chronomancer seeking our intervention in matters most grave."

Aric's gaze fell upon Lila, assessing her with the precision of a temporal cartographer. His nod was curt, laden with unspoken understanding. "Well met. What crisis looms on our horizon?"

Lila recounted her tale with economical precision, each word carefully chosen to convey the magnitude of her discovery and the Guild's subsequent attempts at suppression. Aric absorbed the information, his expression darkening like storm clouds gathering on the event horizon of time itself.

"Such distortions are not unknown to me," he said, his voice carrying the weight of countless eras. "The fabric of reality has been the Guild's plaything for epochs, their insatiable hunger for dominion driving them to ever greater acts of chronometric hubris. We stand at a fulcrum point in history, and inaction is no longer an option."

Zeke's agreement was palpable, a shift in the room's temporal energy. "We must unravel this mystery to its core. If the Guild's manipulations are indeed the source of these distortions, it falls to us to illuminate their transgressions and bring their machinations to a decisive end."

Lila felt a glimmer of hope. "But how? The Guild has eyes and ears everywhere. They'll be watching for any sign of us."

Zeke smiled grimly. "That's where our experience comes in handy. We know how to move in the shadows, how to avoid their surveillance. And with your knowledge of the Guild's inner workings, we might just have a chance."

Over the next few days, the trio worked tirelessly to gather information and plan their next move. Lila used her chronomantic abilities to scan for anomalies, while Zeke and Aric tapped into their network of contacts to uncover the Guild's secrets.

It wasn't long before they uncovered a shocking truth: the Time Guild was indeed causing the temporal distortions deliberately. They had developed a device capable of manipulating time on a massive scale, creating anomalies to consolidate their power and control over the Vertiplex.

The trio huddled in the dimly lit confines of Zeke's safehouse, the air thick with the gravity of their revelations. Lila's eyes darted between her companions, her mind working to process the implications of their discoveries.

Zeke leaned forward, his weathered face wrought with concern. "The Guild's plots run deeper than we ever imagined. They're not just regulating time; they're fracturing it, creating fissures in the very fabric of our reality."

Aric nodded grimly, his anachronistic garb a reminder of the temporal displacements that had become all too common. "In my era, we witnessed the early stages of their ascent. But this- this is beyond mere ambition. It's a calculated assault on the foundations of our existence."

Lila's voice trembled with a mixture of anger and disbelief. "But why? Why would they risk the stability of our entire timeline?"

Zeke's laugh was bitter, devoid of humor. "Power, my dear. The oldest motivation in the universe. By inducing these temporal distortions, they're reshaping the very structure of our society."

He began to pace, his movements precise and controlled, each step marking the passage of seconds with metronomic accuracy. "Consider the economic implications. In a world where time is currency, these anomalies allow them to manipulate markets at will. They create scarcity, then position themselves as the sole solution."

Aric's eyes narrowed, his warrior's instincts sensing the strategy behind the chaos. "A brilliant tactical maneuver. By destabilizing the temporal landscape, they force the populace to rely on their expertise. The more unpredictable time becomes, the more indispensable the Guild appears."

Lila connected the dots with the speed of a quantum computer. "And it's not just economic control. These distortions - they're a form of social engineering, aren't they? People facing constant temporal uncertainty are easier to control, more likely to accept the Guild's authority without question."

A grim smile played at the corners of Zeke's mouth. "Precisely. But it goes even further. By controlling the flow of time itself, they can neutralize threats before they even materialize. Imagine being able to erase a rebellion from history before it even begins."

The room fell silent as the enormity of the conspiracy became clear. Aric was the first to speak, his voice carrying the gravity of one who had witnessed the rise and fall of civilizations.

"We stand at the precipice, the moment where everything we know could teeter over the edge. The Guild's actions threaten not just our present, but the very continuity of our timeline. If left unchecked, they will remake reality in their image, becoming the undisputed masters of time itself."

A knot formed in Lila's stomach, a tightness she'd never known before. Her chrono senses buzzed with the looming disaster. "There's no other way," she said, her voice surprisingly steady considering the tremor in her hands. "We have to stop them, even if it breaks something."

Zeke's eyes met hers, a glimmer of admiration shining through. "This won't be easy. We're up against more than just an organization; we're challenging the very forces that define our timelines."

Aric placed a hand on each of their shoulders, his touch a bridge across eras. "But we have something the Guild does not: the wisdom of the past, the insight of the present, and the hope for a future free from their tyranny. Together, we may yet rewrite the course of history."

As they began to formulate their plan, the air around them seemed to pulse with potential energy. The safehouse became a meeting place, a place where past, present, and future converged. And in that convergence lay the seeds of revolution, waiting to blossom across the tapestry of time itself.

***

The Time Guild headquarters reared up before them, a defiant anachronism in the cityscape. Its gleaming obsidian facade, etched with archaic runes that pulsed with a faint inner light, felt centuries older than the sleek chrome and plasteel towers surrounding it. Yet, despite its antiquated appearance, the air crackled with a futuristic energy, a tangible manifestation of the Guild's mastery over time itself. It was a monument to power, to a knowledge that could bend reality to its will.

Zeke approached with a casual ease that only partly concealed the urgency beneath. Every stride was a carefully measured calculation made under the weight of their mission. "The Grandmaster keeps an iron grip on these halls," his voice roughened by years of clandestine operations. "Their chrono-guards are the best in the business, but even the best clocks tick out of time now and again. Those are the gaps we exploit."

Lila trailed a hand along the building's surface. Her eyes, shimmering with latent chronomantic power, seemed to see through the very fabric of time. "Disruptions," she murmured, her voice like the chiming of a forgotten clock. "I sense a series of temporal anomalies woven into the building's structure. A ripple here, a tear there – enough to momentarily blind their defenses."

Aric, ever the warrior, remained silent but vigilant. His broad shoulders and unwavering gaze spoke volumes. He was a soldier, a shield against the storm, and his presence offered a comforting anchor amidst the swirling currents of time. "Lead the way, Lila," he rumbled. "We'll carve a path for you."

As Lila focused her will, the very air shimmered around them. The disruptions within the building, manipulated by her sharpened skills, expanded, briefly distorting the flow of time. Guards patrolling the perimeter, trained to spot the slightest temporal glitch, found themselves momentarily disoriented by the cascading waves of temporal energy. Under the cloak of this manufactured temporal anomaly, the trio slipped through the outer defenses, their steps echoing faintly in the echoing silence of the Guild's stronghold. They were intruders in a fortress of time, their mission a gamble against the Grandmaster's formidable power.

The air within the Guild headquarters grew dense, an almost suffocating presence that pressed down on their shoulders. Each corridor resonated with the rhythmic hum of advanced temporal devices, a constant reminder of the Guild's unyielding control over the flow of time. Zeke, relying on his memory, guided them through the twisting passages. Lila, finely attuned to the subtle whispers of time, confirmed his course with a steady hand on the very fabric of reality.

"This way," Zeke's voice was barely a shadow over the hum of the devices. He pointed towards a narrow stairwell, its darkness promising a descent into the underbelly of the Guild's temporal dominion. "This leads to the central chamber, the heart of their most ticklish equipment."

Following Zeke's lead, they plunged into the stairwell. The air grew clammy with each step, the temperature dropping like a forgotten artifact in a time vault. The faint glow of temporal energy emanating from the stairwell cast long, eerie shadows that danced across the walls. At the bottom, their first real obstacle awaited – a pair of Temporal Enforcers flanking a reinforced door.

Aric, a walking arsenal strapped in combat armor, let out a low growl. "Looks like a straight-up brawl then. Let's take 'em out clean and quick."

Lila's eyes, gleaming with focused power, narrowed to slits. "Agreed."

With a flick of her wrist, Lila manipulated the very fabric of time. A perfect duplicate of the trio from a time long past shimmered into existence further down the corridor. The Enforcers, their heads swiveling like rusty chronometers, were momentarily fooled by the disturbance. Seizing the opportunity, Aric and Zeke launched into action. With a coordinated ballet of brute force, they dispatched the guards in a flurry of well-placed strikes. The Enforcers crumbled to the floor, temporal disruptions flickering around their bodies like dying embers – a testament to Lila's swift and silent intervention. The path to the central chamber was now open, one hurdle cleared on their perilous journey through the meandering halls of the Time Guild.

A curt nod from Zeke and they pushed past the humming door. The vast chamber that greeted them was a cathedral of temporal technology, its walls lined with devices that pulsed with a barely contained glow. At the center stood a monolith of a machine, its intricate mechanisms a mesmerizing ballet of gears and glowing spheres. Lila's breath caught – the Temporal Nexus, the Guild's crown jewel and weapon of ultimate destruction.

"Bingo," Zeke muttered, a grim line settling on his face. "They've built a temporal tinker-toy capable of reshaping reality on a whim. If they activate that baby, it's curtains for the established timeline."

Aric's fists clenched, his eyes hardening into obsidian. "Then we send it back to the scrap heap. But first, some intel would be nice."

As they began to study the Nexus, a voice echoed through the chamber, cold and authoritative. "You will not succeed."

A hush fell over the chamber as the double doors hissed open. Framed in the glowing archway stood Grandmaster Horologium, a man sculpted from granite and laced with veins of restrained temporal energy. His uniform, a stark black that seemed to absorb light rather than reflect it, hung stiffly on his broad frame. Every line of his face, etched deep with the burdens of centuries, spoke of unwavering command. A single silver chronometer hung heavy on his chest, its polished surface reflecting the swirling anxieties of the room like a warped mirror. Flanked by a phalanx of Temporal Enforcers, their faces masked by emotionless chrome helms, Horologium embodied the Guild's might and its insatiable hunger for control over the very fabric of time.

"Lila," Horologium rasped, his gaze fixed on her. "You've shown some impressive gumption getting this far, but your little crusade ends here. The Nexus is the culmination of generations of meticulous work, the key to securing our dominion over the very fabric of time."

Lila, despite the fear gnawing at her, met his gaze head-on. "Dominion? You mean twisting the timeline into knots for your own gain. This isn't about protecting the future, it's about dictating it."

Horologium's granite features contorted in a sneer. "Naive, child. The Guild safeguards humanity from the ravages of time. We make sacrifices for the greater good, and sometimes, that means bending the rules a tad."

Zeke snorted, a bark that echoed hollowly in the chamber. "Heard that one before. It's always the same excuse for a power grab."

Before Horologium could retort, Aric's voice cut through the tension like a sonic boom. "Enough talk. We came, we saw. Now, it's time to dismantle this temporal monstrosity."

The chamber erupted into chaos. Enforcers surged forward, chrome against flesh in a whirlwind of blows. Aric became a whirlwind of destruction. Zeke, precise and deadly, danced through the fray, while Lila – a blur of chronomantic power – weaved through the battle.

Just as they were gaining the upper hand, Lila felt a strange sensation – a tugging at the edges of her perception. Glancing at Horologium, she saw a knowing glint in his eyes.

"Feeling it, Lila?" his voice boomed over the metallic clang of battle. "The connection, the pull between us?"

Confusion washed over Lila, and she scowled. "What connection? What are you talking about?"

Horologium let out a cold, calculating smile. "You've always been special, Lila. But you're not alone. There's another-just like you. Aric Tempest."

Aric, catching his name, whirled around, his expression a mix of confusion and unease. "What do you mean?"

A triumphant gleam flickered in Horologium's eyes. "You are my ancestor, Aric. Your presence here, at this specific time, is the key to activating the Nexus. Its design is tailored to respond to your unique temporal signature."

***

Aric's blood ran cold. Ancestor? Could it be possible? He was a soldier, a product of genetic engineering, his past as murky as any nebulae in the galaxy. Yet, a tremor ran through his chronometer, a faint echo resonating with the hum of the Nexus.

Lila, sensing his falter, whipped her head toward Horologium, her eyes blazing with defiance. "Lies! We won't be your pawns!"

Horologium chuckled, a dry, humorless sound. "Pawns? No, Lila, you and Aric are the keys. The Nexus is a lock, and your unique temporal signatures are the tumblers." He raised a hand, silencing the clash of battle. The Enforcers froze mid-strike, their movements locked in a tableau of chrome and flesh.

Panic clawed at Lila. She felt a dizzying pull, a tethering sensation that anchored her to Aric. Their chronometers throbbed in unison, a frantic counterpoint to the rhythmic hum of the Nexus.

"What's happening?" Zeke roared, his voice edged with fear.

"This, my friends," Horologium said, a sinister satisfaction evident in his tone, "is the true purpose of the Nexus. It reshapes reality."

Lila's mind whirred. Reshape reality? What did that even mean?

Horologium's smile widened in satisfaction. "The Guild has foreseen a future ravaged by entropy. A future where humanity withers and dies. But by reshaping current timelines with one where the Guild holds absolute control, we can ensure humanity's survival - under our watchful eye, of course."

Lila's stomach lurched. This wasn't about protecting the future, it was about creating a new one – a fascist utopia ruled by the iron fist of the Time Guild. Aric, driven by righteous anger, lunged toward Horologium, but a wave of temporal energy slammed him back, pinning him against the wall. The other Enforcers, their metallic forms shimmering, were freed from their stasis.

"Foolish resistance," Horologium boomed. "The timeline reshaping is inevitable. You are merely catalysts. The last pieces of the puzzle. The energy that is required."

Lila, desperate, searched for a way to break the connection, to sever the tethering pull between her and Aric. But the Nexus pulsed with an irresistible force, drawing them both in like moths to a flame. Zeke, realizing their predicament, roared a battle cry and charged toward Horologium.

Just as Zeke's fist connected with the Grandmaster's chest, a blinding flash erupted from the Nexus. The chamber dissolved into a swirling vortex of colors, the screams of the Enforcers swallowed by the deafening roar of temporal energies. Lila felt herself pulled apart, her atoms stretched and distorted across the fabric of time.

Aric, his face contorted in agony, reached for her, his hand grasping at empty air. Then, with a sickening snap, their connection was severed, replaced by a chilling sense of isolation.

Lila tumbled through the temporal vortex, feeling disoriented and adrift. Images of the Guild headquarters, Zeke's desperate charge, and Horologium's triumphant smile rushed through her mind like fragmented memories. The world around her swirled with shifting possibilities, each fragment a potential future, none familiar. She sensed a transformation, her body and thoughts reshaping into something entirely different.

***

Consciousness returned but it was like a slow tide, washing away the remnants of dreams the girl couldn't quite recall. The smooth, cool surface beneath her gradually solidified into the familiar contours of her sleep pod. She blinked, her eyes adjusting to the dim light of her quarters.

The cityscape beyond her window was a marvel of engineering and human ingenuity, the relentless march of progress. Towering spires of chrome and glass stretched towards a sky tinted a perpetual amber by atmospheric scrubbers. It was beautiful, in its way, though something in the back of the girl's mind whispered that it should be - different. She dismissed the thought. This was how it had always been.

A firm hand gripped her shoulder, and then the girl turned to face Chronofficer Vex, her superior and mentor. The woman's stern features were as familiar to the girl as her own reflection, a constant presence in her life since she'd joined the Temporal Regulatory Force.

"Moira," Vex said, her tone clipped and efficient. "You've exceeded your allotted rest period by 7 minutes and 13 seconds.

That's 433 seconds of productivity lost. You'll need to make up the time."

The girl nodded, accepting the reprimand without question. Time was the most precious resource, after all. Waste was inefficiency, and inefficiency was tantamount to crime in their perfectly ordered society. She swung her legs over the edge of the pod, her muscles responding with the instinctive reflexes cultivated over years of training.

As she stood, her life unfurled before her, each memory a distinct thread in the vast expanse of her existence. Her childhood in the creche, a sterile womb of efficiency. Her education in temporal mechanics, a mind with the precision of a clock, and her rise through the ranks of the TRF. Each memory was crisp and clear.

She smiled at Vex, ready to begin another day of maintaining the temporal order, blissfully unaware of the myriad timelines out there that had just been manipulated. She was the perfect cog in a new, perfectly calibrated machine.

Song of the Starbound Siren

E amon MacLir's weathered boots found purchase on the slick stones with the surety born of seven decades of practice, each step a negotiation between failing flesh and unyielding earth. The wind, a relentless force shaped by the planet's unique atmospheric dynamics, whipped at his gray beard with fingers of invisible turbulence, carrying with it the complex bouquet of an alien ocean – brine, decaying vegetation, and the faint metallic tang of minerals unknown to the world's seas.

He pulled his worn oilskin jacket tighter around his diminished frame, the gesture more muscle memory than practical defense against the elements. The fabric, patched and re-patched, bore the scars of countless storms, each mended tear, each reinforced seam, spoke a resolute language: a tenacious defiance against the uncaring vastness of the cosmos.

For seventy-three standard years – a measure that had long since lost meaning in this world of longer days and erratic seasons – Eamon had called this small island home. He had outlived not just individuals, but entire generations: his wife, claimed by a bacteria that had evolved to breach immunities; his children, victims of the planet's subtle poisons that accumulated over decades; and finally, the colony itself, a grand experiment in terraforming and expansion that had withered on the vine of cosmic indifference.

Now, he stood as the last sentinel of humanity in this distant world, a living relic of ambition and hubris. The larger island, once home to a thriving settlement of ten thousand souls, loomed through the perpetual mist like a fading memory. Its empty structures, slowly reclaimed by native flora, stood as monuments to the folly of believing that they could easily bend an alien world to their will.

As Eamon negotiated the coastal curve, his eyes – still sharp despite the ravages of time and alien sunlight – caught a discordant note in the monochrome landscape. A flash of iridescence gleamed among the dull gray rocks, a chromatic impossibility that sent a jolt of adrenaline through his aged system.

Curiosity, that trait that had driven his species to the stars and ultimately to this lonely shore, propelled him forward. Each careful step was a battle against arthritic joints and atrophied muscles, a reminder of the toll exacted by this world that had never truly welcomed human life. The pain was a constant companion, but Eamon pushed it aside with the ease of one long accustomed to discomfort.

As he drew closer, the iridescent anomaly began to take shape, its form defying explanation. It was organic, yet possessed a crystalline quality that spoke of origins far beyond the simple carbon-based life that this world had known. Eamon's mind, honed by decades of solitude and contemplation, raced with possibilities. Was this some undiscovered native life form? Or perhaps a visitor from the stars, as alien to this world as he himself was?

The answer, he sensed, would reshape his understanding of not just this planet, but of his place in the vast, uncaring universe.

Sprawled across the jagged rocks was a creature, unlike anything Eamon had ever encountered. Its body was long and sinuous, covered in scales that shimmered with colors that defied natural logic. Where its head should have been, there was a complex array of crystalline structures, pulsing weakly with an inner light. Delicate, wing-like appendages lay crumpled and torn, twitching occasionally in the brisk wind, a testament to a violent arrival or a desperate struggle for survival.

Eamon's breath caught in his throat. "By all that's holy," he whispered, "it's a Starbound Siren."

The creature's existence was the stuff of legend, whispered about by spacers in dingy ports across the galaxy. Tales spoke of their ethereal songs, said to possess a power that could ripple through the cosmos, weaving threads of harmony into the fabric of reality. Their voices, it was rumored, carried the echoes of creation itself, resonating with the ancient mysteries that bound the universe together.

But this Siren was far from the majestic being of myth. It was broken, gasping for breath, its crystalline structures flickering erratically like dying embers struggling against the darkness. Eamon's trained eye, sharpened by decades of studying the intricacies of life, immediately discerned the creature's desperate state. The once-graceful body, a symphony of sculpted muscle now a discordant melody of tremors, writhed on the unforgiving rocks. Each shuddering breath was a desperate counterpoint to the encroaching silence of oblivion.

He knelt beside the Siren, his old knees creaking in protest. "Easy there, friend," he said softly. "You're in a bad way, aren't you?"

The Siren's body tensed at his voice then relaxed. One of its wing-like appendages stretched out, brushing against Eamon's hand. The touch sent a jolt through him, like static electricity but infinitely more complex. At that moment, he understood that while the Siren couldn't speak, it could communicate.

"You're a long way from home," Eamon mused, settling himself more comfortably on the rocks. He turned toward the mysterious creature. "What brought you to this forgotten corner of the galaxy?"

Images flashed through his mind – vast, star-filled voids stretching across cosmic tapestries, the rush of solar winds caressing ancient planets, a desperate flight from something dark and hungry that lurked between worlds. The Siren had been injured, its song faltering, and it had crashed onto this lonely planet, its arrival a reminder of fate's harsh whims in the vast expanse of the universe.

Eamon nodded, understanding. "Aye, the universe can be a cruel place. But you've found a bit of peace here at the end, I think."

The Siren's crystalline structures pulsed, and Eamon felt a wave of gratitude wash over him. He smiled, reaching out to gently stroke the creature's scales. They were warm to the touch, despite the chill in the air.

"You know," Eamon said, his voice taking on the cadence of a storyteller, "I came to this world full of hope and dreams. We all did. Thought we'd create a new haven, a fresh beginning." He chuckled, the sound dry and humorless. "Didn't quite work out that way."

The Siren's wing twitched, encouraging him to continue.

"Oh, it was grand at first," Eamon's eyes grew distant, lost in memory. "We reshaped the alien landscape with the arrogance of gods, our terraforming machines carving order from primordial chaos. Our towns, beacons to our ingenuity and indomitable will, sprouted like defiant flora. We sowed seeds from our distant world, and watched with pride as our children took their first steps on virgin soil."

His eyes grew distant, focusing on some point beyond the visible spectrum, lost in the maze of memory. "But then, the land began to rebel against our presumption. Crops that had flourished in the first seasons withered and died, their roots poisoned by minerals our instruments had failed to detect. Livestock, bred for hardiness, succumbed to microscopic predators that evolved with terrifying speed to feast on alien flesh. And our children - "

His voice faltered, a tremor of ancient grief rippling through his words. "Our children were born weak, their bodies struggling to process the subtle toxins that permeated every breath, every morsel of food. We watched helplessly as a generation withered before our eyes, their potential snuffed out by an environment that regarded them as invaders."

He drew a deep breath, the action seeming to pain him as if the very air was complicit in the planet's rejection. "It became clear, with a finality that brooked no argument, that this world had no desire for us. Slowly but surely, it poisoned us, leveraging eons of evolutionary advantage to purge itself of our presence. We were a virus, our colony a festering wound the world desperately sought to eliminate with ruthless efficiency."

Eamon's gaze refocused on the present, his eyes sharp with the keen edge of survival. "In the end, we learned a harsh truth: the universe is not a garden waiting for humanity to cultivate it. It's a wilderness, vast and indifferent, where only those who can adapt – truly adapt, not just impose their will – have any hope of enduring."

He felt a pulse of sorrow from the Siren, tinged with understanding. Eamon realized that this creature, born of the stars themselves, knew intimately the harsh realities of an uncaring universe.

"Most folks left," Eamon continued. "Packed up and headed back to the overcrowded worlds they came from. But some of us stayed, too stubborn or too poor to leave. In the end, it was just me and Mairead, my wife."

The Siren's crystalline structures fluttered, forming patterns that seemed almost like writing. Eamon squinted, trying to decipher their meaning.

"Ah, you're wondering about her, are you? Mairead was a force of nature, she was. Kept me going even when I wanted to give up. But even she couldn't fight this world forever." He sighed, the old grief rising up like a familiar ache. "She's been gone three years now. Sometimes I think I can hear her voice on the wind, calling me home."

A tendril of alien consciousness, as vast and intricate as the cosmic web itself, enveloped his mind. It was a sensation beyond mere warmth, a multidimensional embrace that transcended the limitations of human neurology. The Siren's thoughts cascaded through Eamon's synapses, each one a supernova of information, overwhelming yet precisely controlled.

In this moment of impossible communion, the Siren shared eons of experience. Eamon witnessed the birth and death of stars, their life cycles compressed into heartbeats of cosmic time. He saw galaxies dance their gravitational minuet, colliding in slow-motion cataclysms that spanned millions of years. The destruction and rebirth of entire solar systems played out before his mind's eye, each one a chapter in the Siren's impossibly long existence.

Against this backdrop of celestial drama, Eamon's own grief – the loss of Mairead, the failure of the colony, the slow decay of his own body – seemed at once infinitesimally small and profoundly significant. He understood, with a clarity that defied human language, that his pain was a reflection of the universe's own cycles of creation and destruction. His losses, though tiny on the cosmic scale, were no less real, no less important in the grand tapestry of existence.

The Siren's consciousness resonated with empathy, an emotion as old as the first sentient beings to gaze upon the stars. It had witnessed the rise and fall of civilizations across the galaxy, had sung the requiem for countless species as their suns expanded and devoured their worlds. In Eamon's grief, it recognized a universal truth.

"It's a queer thing, death," Eamon mused. "We spend our whole lives trying to avoid it, but in the end, it's the one certainty we have. Everything dies, even stars."

The Siren's body shuddered, its scales losing some of their luster. Eamon could sense its fear, not of death itself, but of dying alone in this strange place, so far from its own kind.

"You're not alone," Eamon said firmly. "I'm here with you. And who knows? Maybe death is just another journey. Maybe you'll find your way back to the stars."

As if in response to his words, the Siren's crystalline structures began to glow brighter. A faint humming filled the air, growing in intensity until Eamon could feel it in his bones. It was a song unlike anything he had ever heard, beautiful and terrible and utterly alien.

The very air seemed to shimmer and twist, reality bending around them like a heat mirage. Eamon watched in awe as the rocks beneath the Siren began to change, transforming into a substance that looked like solidified starlight.

"Incredible," Eamon whispered. "You're remaking the world around you."

The Siren's song reached a crescendo, and for a moment, Eamon saw beyond the veil of ordinary perception. He saw the interconnectedness of all things, the cosmic dance of creation and destruction that underpinned the universe. He saw his own life as a fleeting strand woven into the vast fabric of existence, yet no less significant for its transient nature.

And then, as suddenly as it had begun, the song ended. The Siren's light faded, its body growing still. Eamon felt the creature's consciousness brush against his one last time, a farewell and a thank you rolled into one.

As the last breath left the Siren's body, Eamon found himself weeping. Not from sadness, but from a profound sense of wonder and gratitude. He had witnessed something extraordinary, something that few beings in the universe would ever experience.

"You know," Eamon murmured, his voice lost amidst the crash of waves, "I've spent most of my life feeling trapped on this island, longing for a way back to the stars. But now I see that the universe is here, too. In every rock, every drop of water, every breath of wind. We're all made of stardust, in the end."

He stood slowly, his joints groaning with the movement. The Siren's body was already beginning to dissolve, returning to the cosmic stuff from which it had been formed. Soon, there would be no trace of its passing save for the patch of transformed rock and the memories Eamon carried.

As he turned to make his way back home, Eamon felt a profound shift in his perception. The island no longer seemed like a prison, but a microcosm of the universe itself. Every step was a journey through the cosmos, every breath an exchange with the stars.

"Thank you, friend," he whispered to the wind. "For reminding an old man that even here, at the edge of nowhere, we're all part of something greater."

And as Eamon walked along the shore, he began to hum a tune he'd never heard before – a faint echo of the Siren's song, carrying with it the promise of new beginnings and the eternal cycle of creation.

The Dreamweaver's Apprentice

In the fair city of Reverie, where the veils betwixt slumber and waking were thin as gossamer, and the very air shimmered with the fleeting beauty of that which is not, young Arin stood in wonderment. The city, wrought from the threads of a myriad of visions, gleamed with a radiance that changed as swiftly as thought itself. Towers of crystalline light rose gracefully into the firmament, their forms shifting subtly as if guided by the hand of some unseen craftsman. Paths of argent mist wound their way through gardens of blossoms that glowed with a soft luminescence, their petals murmuring secrets to those with ears to hear.

Arin, a young artist with a mind as vivid as the visions he now walked amongst, ever a stranger in the lands of his birth. His sketches, filled with wondrous beasts and landscapes of fancy, had oft been met with bewildered glances and courteous nods. Yet here, in fair Reverie, his art found its true dwelling, a place where the fantastical was as common as the rising of the sun.

It was Lysandra, the famed Dreamweaver of old, who had perceived his gift and had sought him out. She stood beside him now, her tranquil presence calm amidst the ever-shifting cityscape. Her long tresses, silver as the light of stars, flowed like a cascade of moonbeams, and her eyes, deep and knowing, seemed to hold the wisdom of countless ages past.

"Hail, young Arin," spoke Lysandra, her voice as soft as the whisper of leaves in a gentle breeze, yet bearing the weight of ages past. "Thou hast been chosen to walk the path of the Dreamweaver, to learn the ancient and noble art that hath been passed down through countless generations. In Reverie shalt thou find the means to give form to the formless, to bring forth the wonders of the mind's eye into the waking world."

Arin's heart quickened within his breast, a tempest of excitement and trepidation. With reverence, he bowed his head and replied, "I am most humbled, Lady Lysandra. By my honor, I shall strive to prove worthy of this great trust placed upon me."

A smile graced Lysandra's countenance, as warm and comforting as the first rays of dawn breaking over the eastern hills. "Come then, let us embark upon thy tutelage. The way of the Deamweaver is fraught with trials, yet through steadfast resolve and unwavering dedication, thou shalt unlock the true potential that lies dormant within thee."

They traversed the fair city, passing by Dreamweavers plying their craft with grace and skill. Their hands moved as if weaving invisible threads, bringing forth visions of surpassing beauty and wonder. Arin gazed upon their works with awe, marveling at the mastery with which they wrought their ethereal tapestries.

In a secluded glade, beneath the boughs of a tree whose leaves shimmered with a light akin to captured starlight, Lysandra began to impart her wisdom. She showed Arin how to draw forth the very essence of dreams, to shape and mold the gossamer strands that formed the very heart of Reverie.

"Hearken unto me, Arin," said Lysandra, her voice rich with the lore of ages. "Dreamweaving is an art most sublime, requiring not only the flights of fancy but also the tempering hand of discipline. Thou must learn to balance the light and the shadow, to give form to both the wondrous and the terrible, for such is the nature of dreams."

In the realm of Reverie, where the mists of slumber swirl and dance upon ethereal winds, young Arin labored in his craft. His hands, once unsteady as newborn fawns, now moved with growing surety as he wove the delicate threads of dreams. Under the careful gaze of Lysandra the Wise, he refined his skills, crafting visions of beauty and wonder that seemed to breathe with a life of their own.

With each passing day, his skill in weaving the threads of reverie grew. He crafted visions of such surpassing beauty and wonder that they seemed to draw breath and life of their own accord. Mountains of crystal rose beneath his fingers, their peaks crowned with snow that glimmered like crushed diamonds. Forests of silver and gold sprang forth, their leaves whispering secrets of ages long past. And in the skies of his creation, stars danced in patterns that told stories of love and loss, of triumph and despair.

Yet Lysandra, in her great wisdom, perceived that Arin's journey was but beginning. She knew that to truly master the art of Dreamweaving, he must learn from those whose skills complemented his own. Thus did she call upon Thalia the Swift, a young Dreamweaver, whose nimble spirit could traverse the realms of sleep as easily as a fish glides through water.

Thalia came at Lysandra's summons, her arrival heralded by a shimmer in the air. It felt as though Reverie itself rejoiced at her presence. The young woman's eyes sparkled with mirth and mystery, and her steps were light as thistledown upon the wind.

"Greeting, Lysandra the Wise," spoke Thalia, her voice melodious as a mountain stream. "I have answered thy call, and stand ready to lend my aid in this noble quest."

Lysandra smiled, a warm and gentle expression that belied the power that lay beneath. "Thy coming gladdens my heart, Thalia. For young Arin's path is fraught with peril, and he shall need all the wisdom and skill we can impart."

And so it came to pass that Thalia joined Arin in his studies, her agility in traversing the dreamscape a perfect complement to his gift for weaving visions. Together, they would face the challenges that lay ahead, their combined talents a glimmer of hope in the ever-shifting realms of dream and nightmare.

***

As the great wheel of time turned, Arin's mastery blossomed like the first flowers of spring. He conjured dreams of towering peaks crowned with snow, of forests ancient and deep where the very trees whispered secrets of old. Cascading falls of silver water sang in his creations, and the heavens above sparkled with stars undimmed by mortal sight. Each vision bore testament to the artistry that now flowed from his fingertips, and Lysandra's heart swelled with pride to see her apprentice flourish so.

Yet in the vastness of the dreamscape, not all was fair and wondrous. On a day when the sun rode high and golden in the skies of the waking world, Arin's wanderings led him to a place of shadow and dread. There, writhing like a thing alive, he beheld a nightmare most foul. It pulsed with malevolence, a darkness given form that seemed to drink the very light from the air around it.

With trepidation did Arin reach forth, his fingers brushing against the nightmare's surface. In that moment, a great darkness surged through him, and his mind was filled with visions of despair and terror beyond mortal ken. He drew back with a cry, his breath coming in ragged gasps as the nightmare continued its fell dance before him.

"Lysandra!" he called, his voice quavering like a leaf in autumn's chill wind. "Some evil is at work here. This dream - it bears the taint of corruption."

In the blink of an eye, Lysandra stood beside him, her countenance grave as stone. She extended her hand, and at her approach, the nightmare shrank away, as if burned by the light of her presence. "This is no common night terror," she spoke, her words heavy with foreboding. "It bears the mark of Malakar, a fell power that seeks to twist and destroy all that we hold dear in the realm of dreams."

As if summoned by the very mention of this dark force, another figure materialized beside them. It was Thalia, her eyes surveying the writhing nightmare with concern. "I felt the disturbance within the fabric of dreams," she said, her voice as melodious as a mountain stream. "Arin, your perception grows keen indeed to have sensed this evil."

Thalia stood shoulder to shoulder with Arin and Lysandra. Her presence brought a sense of calm to the turbulent dreamscape, like the eye of a storm. "Together," she declared, her voice ringing with determination, "we shall unravel this dark tapestry and mend the tears in our realm."

At Thalia's words, a newfound courage surged within Arin. His eyes widened, resolve finding itself upon his youthful features. "Who is this Malakar of whom you speak?"

"Malakar is a shadow that lurks in the deepest hollows of the dreamscape," Lysandra intoned, resonating with the echoes of ancient lore. "Once, he too was an apprentice, like yourself, a weaver of dreams, under my tutelage. But his heart was consumed by darkness and greed. Now he seeks to corrupt all dreams into nightmares most foul, feeding upon the fear and despair they engender in the minds of mortals."

Lo, Lysandra spoke unto Arin with a voice that echoed the wisdom of ages past: "Hearken, Arin, for thy fate and that of Thalia are intertwined of great purpose. As the stars in the firmament shine brighter when joined, so too shall your combined strength and wisdom be forged to overcome the foul corruption of Malakar. Difficult shall be this task, fraught with trials that would test the mettle of the mightiest of heroes. Yet I say unto thee, take heart! For in the union of thy spirits lies a power that can pierce even the deepest shadow, through darkness unimaginable. Have faith, young ones, for in your hands rests the hope of all the free peoples of the dreamscape."

"Together shall we face the dread Malakar," spoke Arin, her eyes alight with the fire of resolve. "We shall cleanse the realm of dreams from his foul taint and restore its former splendor."

As the days of Arin's tutelage waxed and waned, so too did his bond with Thalia strengthen, forged in the crucible of shared trials and triumphs. Side by side they traversed the dreamscape, their skills entwining like the roots of ancient trees, each complementing the other as they braved the perils that lay before them.

Yet ever did the shadow of Malakar loom, a dark pall cast over their noble endeavors. Arin knew in his heart that a confrontation with this malevolent force was as certain as the rising of the sun, and he girded his spirit for the battle to come.

Upon a night when the stars shone bright and cold, as Arin lay betwixt waking and slumber, he found himself thrust into a dream unlike any he had known. He stood in a vast emptiness, the darkness pressing upon him like the burden of countless mountains. A voice echoed through the void, a whisper most foul that chilled the very marrow of his bones.

"Arin," the voice hissed carried on a wind of malice. "Thou cannot escape my grasp. The dreamscape shall be mine, and all within it shall bend to my will."

Arin's hands clenched, his courage rising like a tide. "Never shall I allow such a fate to befall this realm, Malakar. I shall fight to the last breath to protect the dreamscape, whatever the cost may be."

A laugh most sinister rang out, echoing through the endless dark. "We shall see, young apprentice. We shall see."

The dream faded like mist before the morning sun, yet the memory of Malakar's voice lingered in Arin's mind like a shadow. He awoke with a start, knowing in his heart that the hour of battle drew nigh, and he swore to be ready when it came.

In the days that followed, Arin and Thalia trained with a fervor that would have put the mightiest warriors of old to shame. Under Lysandra's guiding gaze, they refined their skills to a razor's edge, preparing for the inevitable clash with the dark force that threatened the very heart of Reverie.

As the sun dipped low one evening, Arin stood at the edge of Reverie, his gaze drawn to the distant horizon. The fair city shimmered in the waning light, its beauty a bittersweet reminder of all they fought to safeguard.

"We shall prevail," he whispered to the wind, his resolve unyielding as the ancient stones. "For Reverie, for Lysandra, and for all who dream."

With Thalia at his side and Lysandra's wisdom to guide him, Arin felt a spark of hope kindle in his breast. Though the path ahead was fraught with peril, he was ready to face whatever darkness lay in wait, to confront the shadow of darkness.

And so, the young artist-turned-apprentice set forth upon a quest that would try the very depths of his spirit, challenge the roots of his convictions, and verily shape the course of his fate. That which lay beyond Reverie, the dreamscape, awaited - vast and wondrous. Arin stood poised to weave anew the threads of destiny, to craft a vision filled with hope and wonder, unsullied by Malakar's foul corruption.

***

Lysandra came to them, her countenance grave yet serene. She spoke in tones that seemed to resonate through the realm that was the dreamscape. "Hearken unto me, Arin, for the hour of our greatest trial is nigh. The fell power of Malakar grows stronger with each passing moment, and we must venture forth into the very heart of the dreamscape to confront this darkness."

Arin nodded, his voice steady despite the fear that gnawed at his heart. "I am ready, Lady Lysandra. Though the way be perilous, I shall not falter in my duty."

Thalia, her eyes alight with the fire of determination, stepped forward. "And I shall stand with thee, Arin. Together, we shall face whatever terrors Malakar may unleash upon us."

With a gesture both graceful and powerful, Lysandra wove dreams around them. The world shimmered and shifted, colors blending and reforming like paint upon a vast canvas. When the transformation was complete, they found themselves standing upon a path of starlight that stretched out before them, winding its way through a landscape of ever-changing wonder and terror.

"Behold," said Lysandra, her voice filled with reverence and caution. "We stand now upon the Dreamer's Path, a road that shall lead us through the many places of the dreamscape. Be wary, for, in this place, the line between dream and nightmare is as thin as gossamer."

As they journeyed forth, the world around them shifted and changed with dizzying speed. One moment, they walked through fields of flowers that sang with voices of pure joy, their petals glistening with colors no mortal eye had ever beheld. The next, they found themselves in a forest of shadows, where trees of smoke and ash reached out with grasping branches.

Arin marveled at the wonders and horrors that surrounded them, his artist's eye drinking in every detail. "'Tis a realm of boundless imagination," his voice filled with awe.

Thalia's keen eyes swept the dreamscape, ever vigilant for signs of peril. "Verily," she spoke, her voice as clear as a mountain stream, "herein lies both the splendor and the danger of this realm. For in a world where thought begets reality, even the darkest imaginings of the mind may take form most fell."

No sooner had her words faded than a great chasm yawned before them as if rent asunder by some unseen force. Its depths roiled with shadows as black as the void between stars, and from its maw came cries of such anguish as to chill the very soul. Arin stepped back, his heart quailing at the sight. But Lysandra, wise in the ways of dreams, strode forth without fear. Her hands moved in patterns ancient and arcane, weaving strands of golden light that coalesced into a bridge spanning the dread abyss.

"Cross swiftly," she commanded. "For the nightmares that dwell in those depths hunger for the essence of dreamers."

They hurried across the shimmering bridge, the wails of the creatures below growing louder with each step. Just as they reached the other side, a curl of darkness lashed out, grasping at Arin's ankle. With a cry of alarm, he stumbled, nearly falling back into the chasm.

"Arin!" Thalia cried, reaching out to grasp his hand. With strength born of desperation, she pulled him to safety as Lysandra's power caused the bridge to dissolve, cutting off the pursuing shadows.

Arin, his breath coming in great gasps, turned his gaze upon his companions, his heart full of thankfulness. "I owe you a great debt," he said, his voice trembling like a leaf in autumn. "For I was nigh unto being ensnared by the fell dreams that lurk in shadow."

The eyes of Lysandra shone with the light of understanding and kindness as she laid her hand upon his shoulder, as one might comfort a child after a storm. "Be of good cheer, young master," she spoke softly. "The way of the Dreamweaver is beset with many dangers, yet it is through these trials that our spirits are tempered and made strong."

As they pressed onward in their quest, the dreamscape about them grew ever more wondrous and terrible to behold. Great mountains hung suspended in the firmament, their lofty peaks crowned with flames that flowed like water. Rivers of purest starlight defied the very laws of creation, flowing upwards towards the heavens. And ever at the corners of their sight, dark shapes moved with furtive malice, a grim reminder of the corruption that Malakar, in his folly and pride, had unleashed upon this once-fair realm.

As they ascended the crest of a hill, its crystal surface gleaming in the pale light, they came upon their first true trial. There stood before them a figure shrouded in darkness, his visage concealed beneath a hood of midnight hue. When he turned to face them, Lysandra's heart faltered, and her breath was stilled.

"Eldrin," she uttered, her voice a mingling of grief and wrath.

The figure cast back his hood, unveiling a countenance that might once have been fair to look upon, but now bore the marks of rancor and loathing. "Good day, my former master," he said with a sneer, his words laden with scorn. "I perceive you have found yourself a new apprentice to lead into folly."

Arin stepped forward, his hand instinctively reaching for the threads of dream stuff that surrounded them. "Who art thou, that speaks with such venom to the Lady Lysandra?"

Eldrin's laugh was cold and mirthless. "I am what your precious mentor made me, boy. A dreamer who saw through the lies and realized the true potential of our power."

Lysandra's voice was filled with regret as she spoke. "Eldrin was once my student, as thou art now, Arin. But he was seduced by the promise of power that Malakar offered, turning his back on all that we hold dear."

Eldrin's eyes blazed with a fell light as he turned his gaze upon Arin. "And what of you, young Dreamweaver? Do you not tire of Lysandra's restrictions, her endless prattling about balance and responsibility? Join me, and I shall show you power beyond your wildest imaginings."

For a moment, Arin felt the pull of temptation. The thought of wielding such power, of shaping reality to his every whim, was intoxicating. But then he remembered the beauty of the dreams he had woven, the joy he had brought to others through his art.

"Nay," he said, his voice firm with conviction. "I shall not forsake the path of light for the empty promises of darkness."

Eldrin's visage twisted with a fell wrath. "Then thou shalt meet thy doom alongside thy master!" he growled, raising his hands as wisps of foul dream-stuff began to gather about him.

Yet ere he could unleash his malice, Thalia sprang forth, her grace honed by countless hours of toil. With a movement swift as an elven arrow, she wove a gossamer web of celestial light, ensnaring Eldrin and scattering his burgeoning sorcery to the winds.

"Quickly," she cried. "We must press on while he is contained!"

As they hurried past the struggling Eldrin, Arin couldn't help but look back. In that moment, he saw not a monster, but a lost soul, consumed by bitterness and regret. And in that instant of clarity, he realized a truth that shook him to his core.

"Lady Lysandra," he said, his voice filled with sudden understanding. "Eldrin is not merely our enemy. He is the key to unraveling Malakar's true intentions."

The eyes of Lysandra grew wide, for she comprehended the implications of Arin's utterance. "Pray, continue, young one. What hast thou discerned in thy contemplations?"

Arin's mind rang like a great bell as he wove together the threads of thought. "Eldrin was once thy pupil, as was Malakar in days of yore. Both strayed from the path of righteousness, yet each for reasons most disparate. Can we discover the means to vanquish Malakar's corruption at its very wellspring within Eldrin?"

Lysandra's eyes darkened with the weight of ancient knowledge, and she shook her head slowly, her voice like a distant wind weaving through the high branches of forgotten trees. "Nay, Arin," she said, sorrow touching her words. " What thou speakest is folly. There is no means by which to redeem those who have fallen such. Eldrin is not the key, nor could he ever be. His path, though intertwined with Malakar's, is one of pride and bitterness, not of redemption. To seek in him the means to understand and therefore vanquish Malakar is to chase a shadow in a land of false light. Both fell from grace, aye, but where Malakar's heart is consumed by the hunger for dominion, Eldrin's soul festers with the poison of jealousy, his will bent not toward the unmaking of his master, but toward his own twisted ambitions. To trust in him is to invite ruin. The wellspring of Malakar's power lies not in Eldrin, but deep within the very heart of the dreamscape, where darkness clings like mist to forgotten places. There, and only there, may his corruption be undone."

Arin bowed his head, his brow furrowed in thought, and when he spoke, his voice was quiet, touched with both understanding and regret. "Thy words ring true, Lady Lysandra, and it grieves me to the core that such a path is beyond us. For if Eldrin, who once walked by thy side and learned the ways of light, cannot be turned from his bitter course, then it is a grievous thing indeed. Unfortunate it is, that in him I saw the hope of unmaking the evil we now face. Yet, if the wellspring of Malakar's corruption lies not in the hearts of men but in the depths of this dreamscape, then we must tread cautiously, for our foe is all the more terrible and cunning. Still, I shall not falter. I will follow thee wherever the darkness leads until it is no more."

As they journeyed forth, the gravity of their newfound knowledge bore down upon their shoulders like a mantle of great responsibility. The road that stretched before them was beset with perils untold, yet they strode with hearts aflame, kindled by a fresh resolve. For even in the deepest shadows of their quest, they now carried a glimmer of hope – not merely to vanquish the fell Malakar, but to mend the very essence of the dreamscape, restoring it to its former glory.

Thus, with courage swelling in their breasts and spirits lifted high, Arin, Lysandra, and Thalia ventured onward into the mysterious depths of the dreamscape. They stood ready to face whatever trials might arise, their noble quest to safeguard the realm of dreams from Malakar's corrupting influence driving them ever forward, like the great heroes of old embarking upon a tale that would be sung for ages to come.

***

In the depths of the slumbering realm, where the very essence of the unseen world swirled and wafted like mist upon the breeze, young Arin stood steadfast with his companions, Lysandra the Wise and Thalia the Swift. Before them rose the gnarled dominion of Malakar, a seething mass of umbra and half-formed terrors that seemed to consume the very radiance that dared approach.

Arin's heart faltered at the sight, yet he held his ground, his hands unwavering as he wove the strands of reverie into a gleaming aegis of celestial light. At his side, Lysandra's eyes glowed with the lore of countless years, her argent tresses flowing like a cascade of lunar brilliance. Thalia crouched, nimble and poised, her form seeming to flit betwixt waking and dreaming as she readied herself for the impending clash.

"Hearken unto me, Arin," spoke Lysandra, her voice carrying the weight of prophecy. "The hour of our greatest trial is upon us. Malakar's corruption hath spread far and wide, but 'tis within thee that the power to vanquish this darkness lies."

Arin inclined his head, his voice unwavering despite the dread that clutched at his very being. "I stand prepared, Lady Lysandra. Though the path ahead be fraught with danger, I shall not waver in my sworn obligation."

As if conjured by their utterance, the very fabric of the air before them rent asunder. From the breach emerged Malakar, his form a ceaseless melding of horrors both primeval and newfound. His gaze, fathomless wells of anguish, settled upon the three with malicious delight.

"Lo, Lysandra," his voice a fell discord that made Arin's very bones quake. "How gracious of thee to bring thy new pupil to behold thy ruin. And Thalia, ever the loyal companion. How ye shall all meet thy doom as one."

Lysandra strode forth, her presence waxing mighty as she confronted her age-old adversary. "Thy reign of dread shall cease this day, Malakar. Overlong hast thou tainted the fount of slumber with thy malice."

Malakar's laughter rang out across the dreamscape, a cacophony of shattered crystal and howling gales. "Witless crone! Canst thou not perceive? I am the true lord of this domain. Both fair visions and fell phantasms bow to my command!"

With a gesture, Malakar unleashed a torrent of living shadows, each one taking the form of the dreamer's deepest fears. Arin gasped as he saw his own nightmares given form – the loss of his talent, the disappointment of his mentors, the failure of his imagination.

But even as the shadows surged forward, Arin felt a wellspring of courage rise within him. He remembered

Lysandra's teachings, the power of imagination to shape reality. With a cry that rang clear as a bell, he began to weave.

His hands moved in intricate patterns, drawing forth visions of beauty and wonder. Mountains of crystal rose beneath his fingers, their peaks crowned with snow that sparkled like crushed diamonds. Forests of silver and gold sprang forth, their leaves whispering secrets of ages long past. And in the skies of his creation, stars danced in patterns that told stories of love and loss, of triumph and despair.

The fell creatures of night recoiled from the radiance of Arin's crafting, their hisses and contortions betraying their retreat into the gloom. Swift as an elven arrow, Thalia wove betwixt the umbral forms, her movements nigh imperceptible to mortal eyes. With touches gentle as newly fallen leaves, she unmade the nightmares, their essence dissipating like mist before the dawn.

Malakar's visage twisted in fury, his form swelling and writhing as he drew upon the terrors that dwell in the hearts of countless dreamers. "Thy paltry magics shall not avail thee, stripling! I am the very embodiment of dread, the darkness that dwells in the deepest recesses of every soul!"

Yet Arin stood firm, his voice resonant with a newfound strength of spirit. "Nay, Malakar. Thou art naught but a shade, a mere semblance of true imagination's power. In the realm of dreams, we find not only fear, but also hope, love, and the might to vanquish all that would threaten us!"

As Arin spoke, his creations grew more vivid and more substantial. The light of a thousand suns blazed forth, driving back the encroaching darkness. Malakar howled in rage and pain, his form beginning to fray at the edges.

As the tide of battle seemed to turn in their favor, the voice of Lysandra rang forth like a clarion call amidst the clamor. "Arin, Thalia, stay thy hands! This final contest must be mine alone to wage."

With a grace that belied the weight of countless ages, Lysandra stepped forth to confront Malakar. There they stood, two ancient powers face to face, as light and shadow, as creation and destruction.

"Come, old friend," spoke Lysandra. "Let us bring this long-wrought dance to its final measure."

Malakar's eyes grew wide with wonder, a flicker of recognition passing over his ever-changing visage. "Lysandra? Can it be so? After all these long years, dost thou still name me - friend?"

Lysandra inclined her head, a smile of sorrow gracing her fair countenance. "Always, Malakar. For what art thou but the shadow I have cast? The fears I could not face, the doubts I could not vanquish?"

As Arin gazed upon the two figures before him, understanding bloomed within his heart. Malakar was not merely an outward foe, but a reflection of the shadow that dwelt in the hearts of all dreamers, even the mightiest among them.

When Lysandra extended her hand to Malakar, their forms began to meld and intermingle. Light and shadow entwined, neither vanquishing the other, but at last finding harmony. The dreamscape trembled and surged as if the very fabric of reality bent and flexed around the uniting entities.

Arin and Thalia beheld with wonder as Lysandra and Malakar became one, a being of perfect equilibrium – neither light nor dark, but the full spectrum of imagination incarnate. The newly formed entity turned to face them, its eyes brimming with the wisdom of ages and the spark of boundless possibility.

"The circle is now complete," it spoke, its voice a melody of Lysandra's gentle tones and Malakar's resonant bass. "Equilibrium is restored to the dreamscape. Yet our task is not finished."

With a gesture from the entity, the world around them began to mend. The warped vistas of nightmare grew smooth and bright, while the overly perfect visions of paradise gained depth and intricacy. Dreams and nightmares alike found their rightful place in the grand tapestry of the unconscious mind.

As the great change drew nigh its end, the being began to wane, its form growing as thin as gossamer. "Arin," it called, its voice but a whisper on the wind. "The burden of Dreamweaver now falls to thee. Guard well the balance we have wrought anew, and forget not the might of fancy to mold the very fabric of the world."

With a final smile, as fair as the first light of dawn, the being that once was Lysandra and Malakar vanished, leaving naught but a sense of tranquility and promise that suffused the very air about them.

Arin stood motionless for a time, his heart full with the weight of all he had beheld. Thalia laid a gentle hand upon his shoulder, her eyes agleam with pride and unshed tears.

"Come," she spoke softly. "We must return to Reverie. There is much to be done in the days ahead."

As they journeyed through the now-peaceful dreamscape, Arin felt a great change within his very being. No longer was he the uncertain apprentice who had set forth on this quest, but a true Dreamweaver, guardian of the delicate balance between light and shadow.

The gates of Reverie rose before them, aglow with renewed vigor. As they passed through, Arin gazed upon the city of his learning with eyes anew. The spires of crystalline light seemed to pierce the very heavens, the gardens of luminous blooms more fair than any mortal flower. Yet he could also perceive the subtle dance of shadow and light, the necessary contrast that lent depth and meaning to the beauty that surrounded him.

***

Arin embraced his new charge with quiet humility and steady determination. He led those who dreamed through the shifting realms of the night, helping them face their most hidden fears and quietly planting the seeds of hope within their souls. He shaped wonders that stretched the limits of mortal imagination, but always remained true to the delicate harmony he had learned, a lesson paid for with Lysandra's selfless sacrifice.

On nights when the world grew still and the boundary betwixt realms thinned to gossamer, Arin would oft espy familiar visages amidst the tapestry of stars above. Friends and foes alike gazed down upon him from that celestial canvas, and in those moments, he knew that though the path of a Dreamweaver might be walked in solitude, he was never truly bereft of companionship.

For in the dominion of dreams, where fancy holds sway and the very fabric of existence yields to the will of the sleeper, naught lies beyond the realm of possibility. And Arin, once but a lowly apprentice, now stood as guardian over that boundless wellspring of potential, ready to shepherd the dreamers yet to come through the vast and wondrous landscapes of the mind.

Yet even as he beheld the grand vistas of slumber unfurling before him, a shadow of doubt crept unbidden into his heart. For Arin knew well the tale of Malakar, and in the hushed moments when the world lay dormant and his thoughts wandered far afield, he found himself beset by a question most grave: might a fragment of his own being, a sliver of darkness buried deep within the recesses of his soul, give rise to another such as Malakar?

The weight of this fear pressed upon him, a burden as vast as the mountains of old. He pondered Lysandra's sacrifice, the balance she had restored at so dear a cost, and wondered if he possessed the fortitude to tread the narrow path betwixt light and shadow.

As these thoughts whirled within his mind like autumn leaves caught in a gale, Arin closed his eyes and drew in a breath, deep and steadying. He sought to quell the tempest of his thoughts, to find solace in the teachings of his mentor and the wisdom he had gleaned on his arduous journey.

And lo! As if in answer to his unspoken plea, a familiar presence seemed to enfold him. In the patterns of starlight that danced behind his closed lids, Arin beheld the visage of Lysandra, her countenance aglow with pride and love. Though no words passed between them, Arin felt a surge of reassurance, a reminder that even in the loneliest watches of the night, he was not truly alone.

But even as this comfort washed over him, a chill wind stirred the air, bearing with it a whisper most foul. A voice, dark and insidious, wormed its way into his mind, its words dripping with malice and temptation:

"Arin," it hissed, a sound like the rustling of dead leaves in a forgotten grove. "Thou art not so different from those who came before. The seed of greatness lies within thee, aye, but so too does the potential for ruin. Embrace the darkness, young Dreamweaver, and know power beyond thy wildest imaginings."

Arin's eyes flew open, his heart thundering like a war drum in his breast. The starlight that had brought such comfort moments before now seemed to flicker and wane as if recoiling from the darkness that had made itself known.

For in the realm of dreams, where fancy holds sway and the very fabric of existence yields to the will of the sleeper, all things are indeed possible - both the sublime and the terrible. And Arin, sentinel over that boundless wellspring of potential, now faced a choice that would shape not only his own fate, but the destiny of all who dwell in the landscapes of the mind.

The Confessional

Jared Morrow stood before the towering spire of the Church of the Cosmic Redeemer, its gleaming surface reflecting the neon-lit skyline of NeoAngeles. The building was a marvel of modern architecture, all sweeping curves and impossible angles that seemed to defy gravity. It was beautiful, in its way, but to Morrow, it looked like nothing so much as a giant finger pointing accusingly at the sky.

He took a deep breath, steeling himself for what was to come. His past transgressions had burdened him for years, a constant pressure on his conscience. With unsteady hands, he pushed open the massive doors and entered.

The interior was a stark contrast to the bustling metropolis outside. Soft, ambient light suffused the space, emanating from no discernible source. The air was cool and still, carrying the faintest hint of incense. Rows of sleek, wooden pews faced a central altar that pulsed with a gentle, blue glow.

Morrow's footsteps echoed in the cavernous space as he made his way to the confessional booths lining the far wall. Each was a self-contained unit, its smooth, white exterior broken only by a simple door. He chose one at random, stood in line, and waited until finally he heard:

"Next."

It was his turn.

The booth was surprisingly spacious, with a comfortably padded kneeler, and a small screen set into the wall. Morrow knelt, his heart pounding in his chest. A moment later, movement came from the other side of the screen.

"Welcome, my child," the priest said, his voice warm and comforting. "How may I assist you in your journey towards spiritual enlightenment?"

Morrow swallowed hard. "I - I've come to confess my sins, Father."

The priest's tone softened. "Very well. Know that this is a safe space, free from judgment. Speak freely, and may your burdens be lifted."

Morrow closed his eyes, took a deep breath, and began to speak. "I've killed people, Father. Many people. I don't even know how many anymore. It started - it started as a job. I was good at it, you see. Efficient. Discreet. But then it became more than that. It became a compulsion, a need. I couldn't stop myself."

The priest remained silent, allowing Morrow to continue.

"I told myself it was justified. That the world was better off without these people. But that was a lie. The truth is, I enjoyed it. The power, the thrill of taking a life. And now - now I can't sleep. I see their faces every time I close my eyes. I hear their screams in every moment of silence. I can't live with it anymore."

The priest's voice was gentle when it spoke. "You carry a great burden, my child. The taking of a life is a grave matter indeed. But tell me, what brings you here now? Why seek absolution after so much time?"

Morrow laughed bitterly. "Absolution? I don't think there's enough forgiveness in the universe to absolve me, Father. I'm here because - because I need to understand. How can a just God allow someone like me to exist? To do the things I've done?"

The priest was quiet for a moment as if considering his response. "The nature of God and the existence of evil is a question that has plagued humanity since the dawn of consciousness. In our modern age, with our understanding of quantum mechanics and the multiverse, some might argue that every possible outcome exists simultaneously. In that view, your actions were inevitable in this particular branch of reality."

Morrow shook his head. "That's cold comfort, Father. It doesn't change what I've done."

"Indeed," the priest agreed. "But consider this: in a universe of infinite possibilities, the fact that you are here now, seeking understanding and feeling remorse, is significant. It speaks to the fundamental capacity for change that exists within all sentient beings."

"Change?" Morrow scoffed. "What good is change now? It won't bring back the people I've killed."

The priest's tone became more forceful. "No, it won't. But it can prevent future harm. It can set you on a path towards making amends, towards using your life to bring more light into the world rather than darkness."

Morrow leaned forward, his voice barely above a whisper. "How? How can someone like me possibly make amends?"

"That is a journey you must undertake yourself," the priest replied. "But it begins with acceptance. Acceptance of your past actions, of your capacity for both great evil and great good. And most importantly, acceptance of the possibility of redemption."

Morrow felt a flicker of hope, quickly extinguished by the weight of his guilt. "Redemption? For a murderer?"

"History is filled with those who have transgressed grievously, only to later become agents of profound positive change," the priest said. "Consider St. Paul, who was once a persecutor of Christians before becoming one of the faith's greatest advocates. Or examine the case of Malcolm X who engaged in criminal activities before becoming a powerful voice for civil rights. This capacity for metamorphosis, for intellectual and moral growth, stands as one of the most remarkable attributes of humanity."

Morrow remained silent, considering the priest's words. When he spoke again, his voice struggled to accurately convey the complexity of his emotions. "But how do I live with what I've done? How do I face each day knowing the pain I've caused?"

The priest's voice was compassionate. "That pain, that guilt, is the price of your awakening. It is not meant to be a burden you carry forever, but a catalyst for change. Use it as fuel for your transformation. Let it drive you to make different choices, to be a force for good in the world."

"And what about justice?" Morrow asked. "Don't I deserve to be punished for my crimes?"

"Justice and punishment are complex concepts," the priest replied. "In many ways, the guilt you feel is a form of punishment. But true justice isn't about retribution; it's about restoration. How can you restore balance to the world? How can you use your life to create more good than the harm you've done?"

Morrow felt tears welling up in his eyes. "I don't know if I'm strong enough for that, Father."

"Strength comes from facing our weaknesses," the priest said. "From acknowledging our faults and striving to overcome them. The very fact that you're here, confronting your past, shows a strength you may not realize you possess."

Morrow wiped his eyes. "So what do I do now? Where do I go from here?"

The priest's voice took on a note of gentle authority. "That is for you to decide. But I would suggest starting with honesty. Confess your crimes to the proper authorities. Face the consequences of your actions in the eyes of society. Use that as a foundation for your new path."

Morrow nodded slowly. "And what about - what about God? Can I ever be forgiven in His eyes?"

"The nature of divine forgiveness is beyond my ability to quantify," the priest said. "But if we accept the premise of an all-knowing, all-loving God, then surely such a being would recognize genuine remorse and the desire for change. The question is not whether God can forgive you, but whether you can forgive yourself."

Morrow took a deep, shuddering breath. "I - I think I'm ready to try. To face what I've done and accept the consequences. To try to make amends, however, I can."

The priest's tone was warm. "That is a courageous decision, my child. It will not be an easy path, but it is a noble one. Are you prepared to receive your penance?"

Morrow straightened. "Yes, Father. I am."

"Very well," the priest said. "Your penance is as follows: confront your past with unflinching honesty and deep self-examination. Let each second of your existence serve as evidence of the individual you aspire to become, an ongoing conversation with the remnants of your previous actions. Employ your abilities to guide those who stumble, as you once did, illuminating their way forward. Recognize that redemption is not a simple task, but a complex, never-ending odyssey through the intricate corridors of your own creation. Traverse this route with humility, allowing each stride to be a reconciliation with your former self."

A sigh escaped Morrow's lips, a whisper of relief that echoed softly in the cavernous interior of the church. He had confessed, unburdened himself of the guilt that had gnawed at him for years. "Thank you, Father. I will do my best to - "

"Oh, one additional matter," came the priest's voice.

"And, what's that, father?" Morrow asked.

But, as he leaned closer to the screen barrier, his nose almost touching the small screen, trying to take a closer look at the familiar silhouette of the priest, he saw something else instead. A chilling blue glow emanated from behind the screen, warping the air itself. He squinted, his heart skipping a beat as he made out the sleek lines of a digital interface, a cold, blue screen taking the place of a human face. A face materialized on the screen, androgynous and serene, its lips seemingly pulsing with each word it spoke.

Then, Morrow's insides ignited. White-hot agony consumed him, reality imploding into a singularity of pain. Then - oblivion.

The serene face on the screen remained placid, unmoved. "May God have mercy on your soul," it droned.

Outside the booth, a wisp of vapor escaped from the seams of the door, quickly dissipating in the cool air of the church. The priest's voice rang out through the large space:

"Next."

Silent Resolve

The soldier crouched in the ruins of what was once a proud edifice, now reduced to a crumbling shell by the relentless bombardment. His uniform, once crisp and pristine, now hung in tatters, stained with the grime of battle and the blood of fallen comrades. He peered through a jagged hole in the wall, his rifle at the ready, scanning the desolate landscape for any sign of movement.

The world outside was a wasteland, a grotesque scene of destruction wrought by the hubris of mankind. Twisted metal and shattered concrete stretched as far as the eye could see, punctuated by the occasional flicker of flames or plume of acrid smoke. The air was thick with the stench of death and the acrid odor of chemicals, a noxious cocktail that burned his lungs and stung his eyes.

His finger twitched on the trigger, a reflex ingrained by years of relentless practice and the unforgiving truths of battle. He was a cog in the great machine of war, a true believer in the Cause that had set the world ablaze. The aliens had to be purged, their taint excised from the face of the Earth. It was a sacred duty, a crusade to preserve the purity of humanity against the encroachment of otherworldly parasites.

A quick movement caught his eye, and the soldier's body tensed. Instinctively, he squeezed the trigger, sending a burst of plasma bolts through the air. The figure collapsed, another nameless casualty in this endless war. The soldier felt nothing - no remorse, no guilt. It was just what had to be done.

As the echoes of gunfire faded, a new sound began to rise, faint at first amid the distant rumble of explosions and the wind sweeping through the ruins. It grew steadily, persistent, until it became unmistakable - a sound that sent a chill through the soldier: the soft, trembling cry of a child.

He whirled, his weapon raised, ready to face this new threat. But what he saw made him hesitate, his finger frozen on the trigger. There, huddled in a corner of the ruined building, was a child. But not just any child.

It was an alien child.

The creature was small, no more than five or six years old by human reckoning. Its skin was a pale greenish, smooth, and slightly luminescent in the dim light. Large, liquid eyes the color of burnished gold stared at the soldier, filled with a mixture of fear and curiosity. A pair of delicate antennae quivered atop its head, and six slender fingers on each hand clutched at a tattered blanket.

The soldier's gaze shifted to the debris-covered floor, where the bodies of adult aliens lay, half-buried beneath heaps of shattered concrete and twisted metal. Their forms were contorted, the evidence of their final moments trapped beneath the collapse. The horror they must have faced was undeniable. For an instant, something stirred within him - pity, perhaps, or a shadow of remorse. He pushed it down, steeling himself. These were the enemy, the cause of the conflict that had ravaged their worlds, and there was no room for compassion now.

The child's voice cut through the tension, musical and innocent, piercing the soldier's resolve. "Please," it said, its English tinged with an accent but clear, pleading. "Don't hurt me."

The soldier's grip tightened around his weapon, knuckles whitening. His duty was clear: The Cause demanded the eradication of these aliens, regardless of age. They were an infection, a malignancy to be excised completely. Yet, despite his training and indoctrination, a hesitant flicker of doubt began to gnaw at the edges of his conviction.

"Why are you here?" he rasped, his voice roughened by the grime of battle and the suffocating stench of polluted air. He could barely catch his breath.

The alien child's golden eyes glistened, holding back the tears that threatened to spill. Its antennae quivered in the dim light, betraying the fragility behind its composure. "This is our home," it said, the words soft yet filled with a kind of certainty. "Our world was dying. We had no choice but to seek refuge."

The soldier scoffed, shaking his head with bitter disdain. "No choice? You could have chosen to perish with some kind of dignity instead of becoming this - infestation on our planet."

The child regarded him with quiet, almost unsettling calm. "Is that truly what you believe?" There was no malice in its question, only a curious innocence. "That we are an infestation?"

"It's the truth," he shot back, but even to him, the words felt hollow. They clanged in the air between them, more brittle than he'd meant them to sound. "You're a threat to everything - our way of life, our survival."

The child tilted its head slightly, antennae moving in confusion. "How? We came in peace, only to seek shelter and offer what we had. Many of us have shared knowledge, skills, things that have helped humanity." Its voice, quiet but clear, carried the heavy questions: What had happened? How had their good intentions led to this?

His stance wavered, the unshakable certainty he had harbored for years beginning to erode. "That - that's not the point," he muttered, struggling to uphold his stance. "You're different. Alien. You don't belong here."

"And for that, we deserve to die?" The child's voice carried a quiet, profound wisdom that seemed out of place in such a small, fragile form. "Even the young? The innocent?"

His mind spun, desperately clutching at the familiar slogans and mantras that had been his lifeline amid the chaos of war. Yet, facing this delicate creature, those reassurances disintegrated like the fragmented structures surrounding them.

"You don't understand," he grumbled, more to himself than to the child. "The Cause - it's about preserving humanity. Protecting our future."

The child extended a small, slender hand toward the wasteland outside. "Is this the future you aimed to protect? A world reduced to ash, poisoned and shattered?"

He sank into silence, his once-solid beliefs unraveling in the presence of this new reality. His grip on the weapon loosened, the sharp edge of his conviction dulling as doubt crept in. For a moment, he stood there, uncertain, the steady ground beneath him shifting, the clarity of his mission now clouded.

"Tell me," the child continued softly, her voice carrying a gentle, probing curiosity. "What do you truly know of us? Beyond the propaganda, beyond the fears that have been stoked?"

His hesitation was intense. "I - I know you're a threat. That you came here to conquer, to replace us."

The child's expression grew sorrowful. "We came as refugees, seeking sanctuary. Many of us were scientists, artists, healers. We sought to offer our knowledge, to work alongside humanity in building a better world for all."

"But the attacks," he interjected. "The bombings, the sabotage- "

"Were the desperate actions of a few," she responded with quiet dignity. "Driven to extremes by fear and persecution. Just as some humans have committed atrocities in the name of your Cause."

He stood still, his thoughts churning with a sudden, overwhelming uncertainty. He had spent years believing in the Cause and had marched into battle with the conviction that his every step was for something greater. But now, with doubt creeping in, he felt as if the ground beneath him was shifting, unsteady. Everything he had been told, everything he had sacrificed, now seemed tainted, the truth unraveling in his mind. He struggled to reconcile the possibility that the mission he had dedicated his life to might not have been what he thought at all.

"You - got a name?" he asked abruptly, surprising himself with the sudden, raw inquiry.

The child blinked, taken aback by the unexpected question. "Zara," she answered, her voice carrying a hint of pride as if she were bestowing a precious gift. "My name is Zara."

"Zara," he repeated, letting the name linger in the air. It felt oddly ordinary yet somehow beautiful on his tongue, a refreshing breath amid the chaos surrounding them. "Female of the species?"

She nodded in affirmation, and a smirk danced across his lips.

"At least you got a name," he said. "I - don't know my own name anymore. They took it from me when I joined the Cause," he confessed, a shadow crossing his face as he recalled the moment his identity was stripped away, leaving behind only a hollow shell. It was an uncomfortable thought, now.

Her golden eyes reflected an understanding that cut through his haze of confusion. "Names hold power," she said, her voice steady and clear. "To strip someone of their name is to erase their identity, their very essence."

A crushing wave of shame washed over him, nearly forcing him to his knees as his legs threatened to give way. The faces of the nameless dead surged into his mind, a ghostly procession of silent reproach. No longer did he see them as faceless adversaries; they emerged as individuals - sons and daughters, fathers and mothers - each carrying their own unfulfilled hopes, dreams, and fears.

How many lives had he extinguished without ever knowing their names? The question throbbed in his mind, an incessant drumbeat of guilt reverberating through the hollow chambers of his conscience. He could still recall the sharp click of his rifle's safety disengaging, the electric rush of adrenaline propelling him to pull the trigger, and the sickening thud of bodies collapsing into the earth. Once, he had reveled in that power, that cruel dominion over life and death. Now, the memory churned in his gut like a bitter poison, a reminder of the price he had paid for that dark control.

He squeezed his eyes shut.

How many lives had he extinguished in the name of a Cause he now saw was nothing more than a masquerade of deceit and fear? The Cause had once gleamed with the illusion of nobility, a grand facade of righteousness. They had fed him lies with his daily rations, and inundated his mind with visions of glory and heroism. But now, amid the smoldering ruins of a ravaged city, the reek of death smothered his senses, and the truth clawed at him. The Cause was a smoldering pit of greed and ambition, the plaything of old men who sacrificed lives like pawns in a game of power.

"I'm sorry," he said, his voice breaking, a ragged whisper lost in the vastness of the silence that enveloped him. The words felt pitifully small, dwarfed by the enormity of his actions. He longed to scream, to howl his contrition to the heavens, yet the shame coiled around his throat, suffocating him and rendering his anguish voiceless.

"I didn't know - I didn't want to know." The confession tasted bitter, like ash on his tongue. He had chosen ignorance, had willfully closed his eyes to the humanity of those he had slain. It had been easier to dehumanize them, to see them as mere targets rather than individuals with stories, families, and dreams. But that deliberate blindness was its own crime, he understood now. His ignorance was no mere shield; it was a damning indictment of his moral cowardice.

As he stood amidst the devastation, his uniform caked with the blood and grime of countless battles, he made a silent vow. No more killing. No more blind obedience. He would dedicate whatever remained of his life to healing, to mending what he had torn apart. It would never be enough to absolve his sins, but it was a beginning - a tentative step on a long, agonizing path to redemption.

She reached out with her six-fingered hand, her touch delicate on his arm. "My parents always said that ignorance born of fear is a wretched thing," she spoke. "But knowledge and understanding can transcend it."

He looked into her eyes, no longer seeing an alien menace but a child - vulnerable, alone, yet filled with compassion. In that brief instant, something within him shifted, a deep reorientation of his entire worldview.

"What do we do now?" he asked, his voice a whisper in the heavy silence. "How do we end this madness?"

Her antennae quivered, her gaze thoughtful. "It starts with individuals," she replied. "With people like you, who are willing to question, to pierce through the lies and propaganda. Change begins with one heart at a time."

He nodded, a renewed sense of purpose igniting within him - a feeling he hadn't known since before the war. "I'll help you," he vowed. "I'll spread the truth. Maybe we can - "

His words were abruptly silenced by a sharp crack that sliced through the ruins. The soldier felt a sudden, intense pain searing in his chest, glancing down to see a crimson stain spreading across his tattered uniform. A sniper's blast, he realized with chilling clarity. One of his own, no doubt, seeing him with the enemy.

As he crumpled to the ground, she rushed to his side, her small hands pressing desperately against the wound. "No," she cried, her musical voice thick with despair. "Please, don't leave us. We need you. The truth needs you."

He coughed, tasting copper on his tongue. He looked up at her, marveling at how beautiful she was – not alien or threatening, but simply a child, full of life and potential. "I'm sorry," he whispered. "For everything. For what we've done to your people. To our world."

She shook her head, tears streaming down her lavender cheeks. "Don't apologize," she said. "Just promise me you'll keep fighting. Not with weapons, but with words. With truth."

He nodded weakly, feeling his life ebbing away. "I promise," he said, his voice fading. "I'll tell them - tell them we were wrong. That there's another way."

As darkness began to close in around the edges of his vision, the soldier felt a sense of peace wash over him. He had been given a gift in his final moments – the gift of understanding, of seeing beyond the lies that had shaped his life. And though he wouldn't live to see it, he hoped that the seed of change had been planted.

With his last breath, the soldier whispered a name – not his own, long forgotten, but one that represented hope for a better future. "Zara," he said, the word a benediction and a promise.

His eyes, once hard with the conviction of the Cause, now softened with understanding and regret. The light faded from them, leaving behind a glassy emptiness that reflected the ruined world around them.

He was gone, leaving Zara alone in the ruins of a world torn apart by hatred and fear. But in his passing, he had kindled a spark – a tiny flame of truth that, with care and courage, might one day grow to illuminate the darkness and bring an end to the madness of war.

She sat there for a long moment, her small hand resting on his still chest. Then, with a determination that belied her years, she stood.

The choking smell of smoke and death hung heavy in the air, a constant reminder of the destruction that had become commonplace. Dust motes danced in the slivers of light that penetrated the crumbling structure, creating an eerily beautiful contrast to the grim scene.

As she took a tentative step towards the jagged opening that once served as a doorway, a shadow fell across the rubble-strewn floor. A figure emerged from the haze of dust and smoke, his outline resolving into that of another soldier. But unlike the one who lay lifeless at her feet, this man's eyes held no trace of compassion or understanding.

The sniper, clad in the uniform of the Cause, moved with the stealth of a predator, his eyes locked onto Zara, a blend of disgust and triumph swirling within him. He held a long-barreled blaster in his hands, its muzzle still radiating a faint red heat from the shot that had taken down his comrade.

"Thought you could turn him, did you?" the sniper sneered, his voice as cold and hard as the barrel of his weapon. "Clever little parasite. But the Cause is stronger than your alien tricks."

She stood her ground, her golden eyes meeting the sniper's with a calm defiance that seemed to unnerve him. "It wasn't a trick," she said softly. "It was the truth. He saw it, in the end. Why can't you?"

The sniper's face contorted with rage. "The only truth is that your kind doesn't belong here. You're a plague, and we're the cure."

With a fluid motion born of countless repetitions, he raised his blaster and took aim. She could hear the weapon charging, its humming a horrific sound. But she didn't flinch, didn't try to run or hide. She simply stood there, a small figure of greenish skin and shimmering antennae, facing down the embodiment of humanity's fear and hatred.

The blaster's crack reverberated through the crumbling remnants of a forgotten world, a sound that was immediately followed by the dull thud of Zara collapsing to the debris-strewn ground. As the lifeblood seeped from her, she heard the sniper's voice cutting through the haze, each word a deliberate puncture of cruelty:

"Your death will barely make a ripple. A mere speck in the grand sweep of our victory. In a century, your kind will be a faded echo, lost to oblivion."

She lay on the cold, unyielding floor, her head tilted sideways, eyes glazed and lost. The dim room transformed into a shifting nightmare of shadows as she struggled to grasp the fragmented reality surrounding her.

Suddenly, a distant explosion shattered the oppressive silence, followed by a heavy thud that resonated through the ruin. Drawing on her dwindling strength, she turned her gaze toward the source of the sound. Her eyes met those of the sniper, now vacant and hollow, reflecting back her own imminent demise in a grotesque mirror of fate.

A faint, twisted smile began to form on her blood-streaked lips, a semblance of triumph seeping through the agony. She tried to speak, but her voice was a strangled whisper, choked by the blood pooling in her mouth and staining her lips with its dark, final hue. The words, though faint and almost devoured by the silence that followed the chaos, carried a grim resonance - a truth that only she could utter in these last moments.

"No one wins," she whispered.

The Man in a Red Suit

The mist hung over the park, heavy and still, turning the familiar into something strange. A boy, not quite a teenager yet, moved through it with wide eyes, part fear, part wonder. Everything he knew seemed to disappear, swallowed up by the shadows. The world had shifted, and now only the quiet and the fog remained, whispering things he couldn't understand.

As he navigated this new reality, a figure emerged from the fog. Seated on a weathered park bench was a man in a red suit, his white beard cascading over his ample belly. The boy froze, his young mind grappling with the impossible sight before him.

The man's eyes twinkled with an otherworldly light as he raised a gloved hand, beckoning the child forward. "Come, boy," he said, his voice a low rumble that seemed to emanate from the mist itself. "Sit with me awhile."

The boy approached cautiously, his feet moving of their own accord. He clambered onto the bench, the wood creaking beneath his slight weight. Up close, the man's scent was a curious mixture of peppermint and something older, mustier – like the pages of a book left too long in a damp attic.

"What is your name, child?" the man asked, his gaze fixed on some distant point beyond the veil of mist.

"Finn," the boy replied, his voice barely above a whisper.

The man smiled as if this information confirmed some long-held suspicion. "And tell me, Finn, what is it you desire most in this world?"

Finn's eyes widened, his mind racing with possibilities. "I- I want a new bicycle," he began, gaining confidence. "And a puppy, and maybe a - "

The man raised a hand, silencing the boy mid-sentence. "I am not who you think I am, child. I am not the bringer of toys and trinkets."

Confusion furrowed Finn's brow. "But you look like - "

"Appearances can be deceiving," the man interrupted, his tone gentle but firm. "I am something other. Something older."

Finn studied the man's face, noting now the subtle differences – the eyes that seemed to hold centuries of wisdom, the lines carved deep by joys and sorrows beyond mortal comprehension. "Who are you, then?" he asked, his voice tinged with awe and a hint of fear.

The old man was silent for a long moment, his gaze distant. When he spoke, his words were carefully chosen. "I am - a giver of gifts, in a way. But not the kind you can hold in your hands or play with on Christmas morning."

Finn leaned closer, intrigued despite his lingering apprehension. "What kind of gifts?"

The man turned to face the boy, his eyes sharp and unwavering. Finn felt the pull to look away, but he didn't. He couldn't. "I can give you a glimpse of what's ahead," the man said. "A look into the course of your life, if you want it."

Finn's breath caught in his throat. "You mean - you can tell me my future?"

The man again smiled. "If that is what you truly desire. But know this – the future is not always kind, and knowledge can be a heavy burden."

Finn paused, turning the man's words over in his mind. He couldn't shake the pull of something deeper, a need he couldn't fully understand. At last, he looked up, his voice calm, though his insides churned. "I want to know," he said, the resolve there, even if he wasn't sure why.

The old man's lips curved into a smile that held no mirth. "Very well," he said, extending his hand. "Take my hand, Finn, and I will show you the path that lies before you."

Finn reached out, his small fingers swallowed up by the man's larger hand. The world around them seemed to change, the mist rolling and forming into solid shapes until the grand architecture of a university auditorium took shape. Finn now stood at the back of a crowded hall, the air tense with expectation. He breathed in the sharp mix of perfume, aftershave, and the worn scent of polished wood, each smell carrying the weight of moments that had come before.

On stage, a familiar figure stood at the podium, resplendent in cap and gown. It took Finn a moment to recognize himself, older now, his boyish features matured into those of a man on the cusp of his prime. The older Finn's eyes sparkled with pride and barely contained excitement as he surveyed the sea of faces before him.

"Look there," the old man in red whispered, pointing to a row near the front. Finn looked over, and his chest tightened.

There were his parents, their faces filled with joy and disbelief. His father, though, seemed smaller, worn down. Gray streaked through his dark hair, and lines from years of worry and laughter marked his face. But his eyes, bright with unshed tears, showed the pride he held, watching his son stand on the stage.

Beside him, Finn's mother sat straight-backed, her hands clasped tightly in her lap. She wore her best dress, the one reserved for weddings and christenings, its fabric a splash of color amidst the sea of dark suits and dresses. Her face, softer now with age, beamed with a radiance that seemed to light up the entire auditorium.

"My parents, older," young Finn whispered, his voice choked with emotion.

The old man looked at her with quiet understanding. "Being a parent isn't easy, child. But times like this make it all worth it."

On stage, Finn started speaking, his voice steady and clear. "Distinguished faculty, honored guests, fellow graduates," he said, each word carrying a confidence that would have surprised his younger self. "Today, we stand at the start of a new chapter in our lives- "

As the speech went on, young Finn's eyes settled on a face in the crowd. A young woman with dark hair falling over her shoulders stood there, watching his older self with steady focus. There was something in her gaze - admiration, maybe more - that made young Finn's heart skip. He couldn't look away.

"Who is she?" he asked the old man.

"Meria," came the reply. "Watch closely, for she plays a significant role in the life you have yet to live."

As if on cue, the older Finn's eyes met Meria's. For a brief moment, the rest of the world seemed to fade away. A smile passed between them, intimate and full of promise, before Finn returned his attention to his speech.

The scene shifted, time accelerating like pages flipping in a book. Finn saw flashes of a life unfolding: stolen glances in library stacks, late-night study sessions that turned into deep conversations, a first kiss beneath the sprawling branches of an old oak tree on campus.

Then, another graduation. This time, it was Meria on stage, accepting her medical degree. Finn sat in the audience, his face beaming with pride. Beside him, his parents watched with the same joy they had shown at his own graduation, having embraced Meria as a daughter of their own.

More images flashed by: a modest wedding in a sunlit garden, Finn's parents dancing with abandon at the reception; the purchase of a first home, a fixer-upper that they poured their hearts into; late nights spent hunched over sales plan and financial reports as Finn's business began to take shape.

Through it all, Meria was a constant presence, her strength and compassion a balm for the stresses and doubts that plagued the older Finn as he climbed the corporate ladder. Her own career flourished, her dedication to her patients earning her a reputation as one of the city's finest physicians.

The old man in red placed a hand on young Finn's shoulder. "So many moments, charting a path forward," he said softly. "The start of a journey that will shape not only your life but the lives of many others."

As the vision began to fade, dissolving back into swirling mist, Finn felt a profound sense of hope. Whatever challenges lay ahead, he knew that he would face them with the support of family and the love of a partner who would stand by his side through it all.

The park bench materialized beneath him once more, the damp air a stark contrast to the warmth of the many visions. Finn blinked, the memory of his possible future self still vivid in his mind. He turned to the old man in red, a thousand questions on the tip of his tongue, but found only silence and the swirling mist as his companion. The damp air of the park was replaced by the crisp, climate-controlled atmosphere of a high-rise office.

"Look," the old man in red said, his voice a whisper that seemed to come from everywhere and nowhere at once.

Finn blinked, his eyes adjusting to the scene before him. He saw himself, but not as he was. This Finn was older still, perhaps in his late forties, dressed in an impeccably tailored suit that spoke of wealth and power. His hair was perfectly coiffed, streaked with distinguished gray at the temples. The boyish roundness of his face had given way to chiseled features, his jaw set with determination.

The older Finn sat behind a massive desk of polished mahogany, its surface adorned with a sleek computer and a few carefully arranged objects – a crystal paperweight, a fountain pen that probably cost more than his entire childhood home, a framed photo of a beautiful woman and two smiling children.

"Is that - me?" young Finn asked, his voice low, almost uncertain.

The old man smiled. "This is one possible future. Watch."

A knock came at the office door. The older Finn looked up, his face moving from focus to a smile that seemed easy, but well-worn. "Come in," he said, his voice steady and sure.

A young man stepped in, tense and gripping a folder close to his chest. "Sir, I've got the quarterly reports you wanted," he said, his words stumbling out.

The older Finn gestured for the young man to approach. "Let's see them, then," he said, his tone not unkind but carrying an undercurrent of impatience.

The young man laid the reports on the desk. The older Finn's eyes moved over the pages, quick and steady. He paused, tapping a finger on one of the sheets. "These numbers for Eastern Europe," he said. "They're off from what we projected."

The young man swallowed hard. "No, sir. There were some unexpected complications with the merger. Currency fluctuations and- "

The older Finn raised a hand, cutting off the explanation. "I don't need excuses. I need solutions. What's your plan to get us back on track?"

The young man shifted, clearly uneasy. "Well, sir, I thought maybe if we restructured the - "

"No," the older Finn interrupted, his voice sharp. "That's not good enough. We need bold action, not timid restructuring." He leaned back in his chair, locking eyes with the young man. "You have until the end of the week to devise a plan that will not only fix this shortfall but also exceed our original projections. Do you understand?"

The young man's face was pale."Yes, sir. I'll have it on your desk by Friday."

"See that you do," the older Finn replied, dismissing the young man with a wave of his hand.

As the young man hurried from the office, young Finn turned to the old man in red. "Is that really me? I seem so - harsh."

The old man's expression was unreadable. "The path to success is often paved with difficult decisions. Watch."

The scene continued to unfold. The older Finn picked up his phone, his fingers dancing across the keypad. "Janet," he spoke into the device, "get me Yashira in Tokyo. We need to discuss accelerating the Asian expansion."

A moment later, his older self was engaged in rapid-fire conversation, his words a mix of business jargon and strategic planning that young Finn could barely follow. He watched in awe as his older self navigated complex negotiations with ease, his voice commanding respect even across thousands of miles.

As the call ended, the older Finn allowed himself a small smile of satisfaction. He reached for the framed photo on his desk, his expression softening as he gazed at the faces of his family.

The intercom buzzed, and Janet's voice filled the room. "Sir, your wife is on line one. She wants to know if you'll be home for dinner tonight."

A brief flash of something – regret? Frustration? – crossed the older Finn's face. He paused before answering. "Tell her I'm sorry, but I have to work late. The Tokyo deal is too important. I'll make it up to her this weekend."

As he placed the photo back on his desk, young Finn saw a sadness in his older self's eyes that hadn't been there before. "He seems lonely," Finn said.

The old man sighed. "Success often comes at a price. The higher you climb, the more you leave behind."

The older Finn turned back to his computer, immersing himself in work once more. The office hummed with quiet efficiency – the soft whir of the air conditioning, the muted tapping of keys, and the occasional ping of an incoming email. It was a world of order and control, every element carefully managed and optimized.

Young Finn watched as the hours ticked by, the sky outside the floor-to-ceiling windows darkening as night fell over the city. Still, his older self worked on, pausing only to order a quick dinner that he ate absently at his desk.

"Is this what it means to be successful?" Finn asked, a note of uncertainty in his voice.

"Success is defined differently by each person," the old man replied. "This version of you has achieved great things in the business world, but at what cost? It's up to you to decide if this is the path you wish to follow."

As the vision began to fade, dissolving back into the mist of the park, Finn felt a conflicting mix of emotions. The power and wealth his older self commanded were alluring, but the loneliness and strain were equally apparent. He realized that the choices he would make in the years to come would shape not just his career, but the very essence of who he would become.

The park bench materialized beneath him once more. Finn blinked, the memory of his possible future self still vivid in his mind. He turned to the old man in red, more questions on the tip of his tongue, but found only silence and the swirling mist as his companion.

But then the scene shifted again. The mist swirled and coalesced, forming a stark, antiseptic hospital room. The change was jarring, like a discordant note in a symphony of life. Finn found himself standing at the foot of a bed, the harsh fluorescent lights casting an unforgiving glow on the scene before him.

In the bed lay a woman, her form so frail and diminished that Finn barely recognized her as his mother. Her skin, once vibrant and warm, now had the pallor of old parchment, stretched taut over the sharp angles of her bones. The machines surrounding her beeped and buzzed, a mechanical chorus that seemed to mock the fragility of human life.

Beside the bed sat an older version of Finn, his face lined with worry and sleepless nights. He held his mother's hand, his warm flesh enveloping her papery skin, a clear reminder of the distance between life and the approach of death.

"Your mother," the old man in red said softly, his voice steady, shaped by countless such scenes witnessed through the years. "Her final days."

Finn watched as his future self leaned close to his mother, his lips moving in quiet words of comfort that the younger Finn couldn't quite hear. The words didn't matter. It was the love and anguish behind them that traveled through time and space.

Tears streamed down both their faces, glistening trails of shared grief that seemed to connect them more profoundly than any umbilical cord ever could. The older Finn's shoulders shook with silent sobs, a man reduced to a child in the face of inevitable loss.

"Why?" Finn asked the old man in red, his voice choked with emotion, barely able to force the word past the lump in his throat. "Why do you show me this?"

The old man's expression was one of infinite compassion, his eyes holding depths of understanding that no mortal could fully comprehend. "Life is not only joy, child. It is also sorrow, loss, and pain. These experiences shape us, mold us into the people we become."

He took young Finn's hand, the touch both comforting and oddly cold. "Your father passed only three months prior," he said, his voice gentle but matter-of-fact. "A sudden heart attack. He was never able to say goodbye to her."

The words hit Finn like a physical blow. He stumbled back, his mind reeling with the implications. His father, gone? The man who had always seemed larger than life, indestructible in his child's eyes, reduced to a memory in the span of a heartbeat?

"No," Finn whispered, shaking his head in denial.

The old man's eyes softened with sympathy. "Your father's journey ended sooner than anyone expected, but his influence lives on in you."

Finn turned back to the scene before him, seeing it with new eyes. He noticed now the absence of his father, the empty space beside the bed where he should have been standing. The older Finn seemed to carry an extra burden, his posture speaking of not just the impending loss of his mother, but the still-fresh wound of his father's passing.

"How?" Finn asked the old man, his voice barely above a whisper. "How does he - I mean - how do I go on?"

The old man gestured to the scene. "Watch," he said simply.

The door to the hospital room opened. Meria walked in, her face tight with worry. She moved to Finn's side and placed her hand gently on his. The older Finn looked up at her, his eyes red and lost. Without saying anything, she wrapped her arms around him, offering silent strength and comfort.

"Love," the old man in red said. "Love carries us through the darkest times. It doesn't erase the pain, but it gives us the strength to bear it."

Young Finn watched as Meria pulled up a chair, sitting close to his older self. She took his mother's other hand, forming a circle of connection and care. The atmosphere in the room shifted subtly, the cold sterility softened by the warmth of human connection.

"Your mother lingers for three more days," the old man continued. "In that time, you and Meria rarely leave her side. You share stories, sing her favorite songs, and remind her of a lifetime of love."

Finn felt tears rolling down his cheeks, mirroring those of his older self. "It seems so unfair," he said. "To lose them both so close together."

The old man smiled. "Life often is unfair. But it is in facing these challenges that we discover our true strength. Your parents' passing becomes a crucible, forging you into a man of deep compassion and resilience."

The scene before them began to shift, time accelerating. Finn saw flashes of a funeral, of quiet nights spent sorting through old photographs, of conversations with Meria that lasted until dawn. He saw his older self throwing himself into work, then pulling back, finding balance with Meria's gentle guidance.

"You honor their memory," the old man said, "not by dwelling in grief, but by living the values they instilled in you. Your father's work ethic, your mother's kindness – these become the cornerstones of the man you grow to be."

As the visions faded back into mist, Finn felt a deep sense of loss, but also a glimmer of hope. "Will it always hurt this much?" he asked.

The old man's smile was gentle. "The pain dulls with time, but it never truly disappears. Nor should it. That ache is the echo of love, a reminder of the bonds that shaped you."

Finn wiped his eyes, feeling older. It was as if future grief had already settled upon him. Yet beneath it all, a new determination took root in his heart, a resolve to live a life that would make his parents proud.

"Thank you," he said to the old man. "For showing me this. For preparing me."

The old man's eyes twinkled with an ageless wisdom. "Knowledge of the future is a double-edged sword, child. But you have shown the strength to wield it well. Remember, even in the darkest moments, there is always light to be found – if you have the courage to look for it."

As the mist swirled around them once more, Finn took a deep breath, ready to face whatever vision the old man would show him next. He knew now that life held both joy and sorrow, triumph and loss. But armed with this knowledge, he felt prepared to embrace it all, to live fully and love deeply, no matter what the future might hold.

The mist swirled slowly, forming shapes that solidified into the warm, intimate confines of a living room. The air was heavy with the scent of cinnamon and wood smoke, a comforting aroma that spoke of home and hearth. Finn found himself standing in a corner, an unseen observer of a scene of familial bliss that both warmed and disquieted him.

An elderly man, his face a roadmap of years lived and hardships endured, sat ensconced in a well-worn armchair. The leather was cracked and faded, bearing the imprints of countless hours spent in quiet contemplation and animated conversation. The old man's hair was a shock of white, like freshly fallen snow, and his face was deeply lined, each wrinkle a testament to joys savored and sorrows weathered.

But it was his eyes that captured Finn's attention. They sparkled with a vitality that belied his advanced years, a light that seemed eerily familiar. With a start, Finn realized he was looking at himself, decades hence, the boy he was transformed by time into the patriarch he would become.

"Your twilight years," the old man in red murmured, his voice barely above a whisper. "A life well-lived, filled with love and family."

Surrounding the elderly Finn was a lively scene filled with life. Children of various ages sprawled on the floor, their faces turned up, intent on his words. Some looked like him, while others had Meria's features mixed in with his. They were his grandchildren, and he felt both awe and a deep unease.

A fire crackled in the hearth, casting shadows on the walls, which were covered with photographs and mementos from a long life. Finn's gaze landed on one image—a younger version of himself and Meria, arms wrapped around each other, standing against snow-capped mountains. They were smiling, joy radiating from their faces, a moment of pure happiness caught in time.

The elderly Finn leaned forward in his chair, his voice carrying the weight of years yet tinged with an undercurrent of mischief. "Now, my little ones," he began, his words immediately silencing the soft murmurs of the children, "let me tell you about the time your grandmother and I found ourselves lost in the wilds of Patagonia- "

As the story unfolded, Finn watched in fascination as his future self wove a tale of adventure and discovery. The children hung on every word, their eyes wide with wonder and excitement. Even the older ones, teenagers on the cusp of adulthood, listened with rapt attention, occasionally exchanging knowing glances that suggested they'd heard this particular story before but enjoyed it no less for the repetition.

The elderly Finn's hands moved as he spoke, punctuating key moments with gestures that seemed both practiced and spontaneous. A flick of the wrist to indicate a treacherous mountain path, fingers splayed to mimic the span of a condor's wings, a gentle tap on his chest to convey the pounding of his heart during a moment of peril.

Laughter erupted at regular intervals, the sound rich and genuine. It filled the room with a warmth that went beyond the physical, creating an atmosphere of love and belonging that made young Finn's heart ache with longing.

As the tale reached its conclusion, a young girl with Meria's eyes and Finn's smile piped up. "But Grandpa, weren't you scared? All alone in the wilderness?"

The elderly Finn's face softened, his gaze distant as if looking back through the years. "Scared? Oh yes, little one. But you see, I wasn't alone. I had your grandmother with me. And when you're with someone you love and trust, even the wildest wilderness becomes a little less frightening."

A collective "aww" rose from the assembled children, accompanied by good-natured eye-rolling from the older ones. But Finn could see the truth of the words reflected in their eyes – the love and admiration they held for this man who had shaped their lives in countless ways.

As the story came to an end, the children began to drift away. Some went to the kitchen, drawn by the smell of freshly baked cookies. Others returned to the books or electronic devices they had set aside. A few, however, stayed close, climbing into the elderly Finn's lap or settling on the arms of his chair. They were eager for more stories or simply happy to be near him.

Young Finn watched his older self with the children. He gave hugs, offered words of encouragement, and playfully ruffled their hair. Each interaction was smooth and natural, a familiarity that showed years of love and guidance.

In a quiet moment, as the elderly Finn sat surrounded by his family, his gaze seemed to drift to the corner where young Finn stood watching. For a heartbeat, it felt as if their eyes met across the gulf of years. A smile played at the corners of the old man's mouth, tinged with a hint of melancholy as if acknowledging the long and sometimes difficult road that lay between the boy and the man he would become.

The scene began to fade, the edges of the room blurring as the mist crept back in. But before it dissolved completely, young

Finn caught a final glimpse of his future self. The elderly Finn had closed his eyes, his face a study in contentment. One gnarled hand rested on the head of a dozing child, while the other clasped a framed photograph – the same image of himself and Meria in their youth that hung on the wall.

As the vision faded, Finn found himself back on the park bench, facing the old man in red. He felt a deep longing mixed with unease. The life he had seen was filled with love and meaning, made up of countless moments of joy, sorrow, triumph, and quiet contentment.

But the burden of years yet unlived pressed upon him, along with the knowledge of all that must unfold to create that future. He faced losses, challenges, and choices that would shape his life and the lives of those who would follow.

Finn turned to the man in red, his voice thick with emotion. "Is this- is this really my future?"

The old man's eyes sparked with an inscrutable light. "It is a possibility, child. One of many paths that stretch before you. The choices you make, the love you give and receive, the courage you show in the face of adversity – these will determine the man you become."

Finn's young mind wrestled with thoughts too big for him. He imagined his old age, surrounded by family, filled with memories from a life well-lived. The thought excited him, but it also frightened him. It was a future filled with possibility, but he knew it would demand sacrifice and hard work to reach.

As the park around them reasserted its reality, the mist retreating to the corners of Finn's vision, he felt a renewed sense of purpose. The path ahead was long and uncertain, but the glimpse of what could be – of the man he might become and the lives he might touch – filled him with a determination that belied his years.

The man in red observed Finn's face as determination took hold. A slight smile tugged at the corners of his mouth. In that instant, the boy's potential felt alive in the air around him, a promise of what was to come and lives yet to be molded by his existence in the world.

"What comes next?" Finn asked, almost scared to have asked.

The old man reached out and gripped his hand tightly. "What comes to all men, child. The final journey."

The mist swirled again, forming shapes that hardened into the stark environment of a hospital room. Finn stood at the foot of the bed, the sharp scent of disinfectant mixing with the low, mechanical hum of machines. The room was dim, lit only by the soft glow of monitors and the muted light filtering through the drawn blinds.

On the bed lay an old man, his features thin and worn by time. Finn saw himself in that frail figure, breathing slow and shallow. The rhythmic beeping of the heart monitor broke the silence, each sound a reminder of life slipping away.

Beside the bed sat his children and Meria, her face marked by worry and sorrow. She held the elderly Finn's hand, her grip firm yet gentle, much as he had held his mother's hand so many years before. Her eyes, red from crying, held a fierce determination to be there for every moment that remained.

"Your beloved," the old man said, his voice soft, blending with the sounds around them. "She stays with you until the end."

Finn watched in silence as his future self took a final, shuddering breath.

"Goodbye," he told Meria.

Then, the heart monitor's steady beeping faded into a single, unchanging tone, a stark contrast to the muffled sobs of the woman. The room felt heavy, the moment pressing down on everything around them.

"No," Finn whispered, tears streaming down his face. "I don't want to die. Why do I have to die?"

The old man knelt before him, his eyes level with Finn's. They were eyes that held centuries of wisdom and sorrow, eyes that had seen countless lives begin and end. "Death is not an ending, child. It is a transition, a doorway to what comes next. It is the price we pay for the gift of life, for all the joys and sorrows that shape our existence."

Finn shook his head, unable to accept this truth. "But it's not fair. Why give us life if it just ends?"

The old man's smile was sad but knowing. "Life is precious because it is finite. If we lived forever, would we truly appreciate the beauty of a sunset, the laughter of a child, and the warmth of a loved one's embrace? It is the knowledge of our mortality that gives meaning to our days, that drives us to create, to love, to leave our mark upon the world."

Finn considered these words, his young mind struggling. "But- but what's the point? If we all die in the end, why does anything matter?"

The old man gave a wonderous smile. "The point, dear child, is the journey itself. The lives we touch, the love we share, the differences we make – however small they may seem. Each act of kindness, each moment of joy, each lesson learned ripples outward, affecting the world in ways we may never fully understand."

He gestured to the hospital room around them, to the grieving daughter and the still form on the bed. "This man – the man you will become – he lived. He loved. He left the world a little better than he found it. And in doing so, he achieved a kind of immortality. For as long as those who loved him remember him, as long as the effects of his actions continue to shape the world, he lives on."

Finn wiped his eyes, his gaze fixed on the scene before him. "Will it hurt? Dying?"

The old man shook his head. "For some, it is as gentle as falling asleep. For others, it may be more difficult. But it is a journey we all must take, and one we need not face alone."

Finn took a deep breath, trying to process everything he had seen and heard. "I think I understand. Or at least, I'm starting to."

"That is all anyone can ask, child," the old man said. "To seek understanding, to embrace the great mysteries of existence – that is what it means to be truly alive."

Finn kept watching as the scene in the hospital room changed. Meria, her face still wet with tears, leaned down to kiss the old Finn's forehead. "Goodbye, my love," she said, her voice cracking. "Thank you for everything."

The room was heavy with love and loss, a reflection of a life lived and connections made. Finn felt a strange blend of sorrow and peace, recognizing the beauty in the cycle of life and death.

The old man in red stood, his presence a comforting anchor in the midst of Finn's emotional turmoil. "You see, child, it is not the length of our days that matters, but the depth of our experiences. Your future self has lived a life rich with meaning, surrounded by love and family. That is a gift beyond measure."

Finn looked at the ground, his heart heavy but his spirit lifted by the understanding he had gained. "I think I understand now. Life is about the moments we create, the people we touch, and what we leave behind."

The old man placed a hand on Finn's back, steady and reassuring. "Yes, child. And remember, even in the face of death, there is always hope. The love you give and receive, the kindness you show - these are the things that endure."

As the vision began to fade, the hospital room dissolving into the swirling mist once more, Finn felt a profound sense of gratitude. He had been given a glimpse of his future, a chance to see the impact of his life on those he loved. It was a gift that would shape his choices, guiding him toward a life of purpose and connection.

The park bench materialized beneath him once more, the damp air returning. As he sat there, contemplating all he had seen and learned, Finn felt a newfound sense of resolve. He would live his life with intention, cherishing each moment and striving to make a positive impact on the world around him. And when the time came for his final journey, he would face it with the knowledge that he had lived fully and loved deeply.

The old man's words echoed in his mind, a gentle reminder of the wisdom he had been given. "Life is precious because it is finite. Embrace each day and let the love you share be your legacy."

With a deep breath, Finn stood, ready to face the future with courage and hope. The mist began to clear, revealing the familiar shapes of the park, and Finn walked forward, his heart light and his spirit strong.

"Remember what you have seen, Finn," the old man's voice faded like the last notes of a distant song. "Live each day fully, love deeply, and fear not the night that comes to all. For in the end, it is not the years in your life that matter, but the life in your years. I hope you liked my gifts."

Finn blinked. The world around him shifted like a kaleidoscope coming into focus. The bench beside him was empty, a void where moments before sat the old man who had shown him visions of futures not yet lived. Only a trace of peppermint hung in the air, making Finn question if the man had been real or just a creation of his fevered mind.

As the mist faded into the dark corners of the park, Finn stood still, his legs trembling like young trees in a storm. The visions pressed on him, neither a burden nor a gift, but something strange and heavy. Tears had fallen from his eyes, revealing a world so clear and vivid it almost hurt to see. Each moment lay before him, full of possibility and marked by the knowledge of its fleeting nature.

The park around him was alive in a way he had never seen before. Blades of grass stood tall and green, vibrant and bright. The trees whispered secrets in a language he could not understand, their leaves woven together in intricate patterns. Finn turned his head, his eyes scanning for a flash of crimson, a sign of the mysterious figure who had stripped away his innocence. But the bench was empty, a void where moments before sat the man who had opened his eyes. The old man had disappeared, lost in the fog of time and memory.

As the full weight of his experience settled upon him, Finn felt words rising unbidden to his lips, a truth that both terrified and exhilarated him: "Ho – ho - ho," he whispered to the indifferent park.

Messages from Beyond

From: Grayson Demeter-7291
To: Yarla Demeter-7291
Date: 15 Solas, 2784
Subject: Missing you already

My dearest Sevika,

It's only been a few hours since the Stellaris left orbit, yet the absence of your presence and the children's laughter is already deeply felt. The emptiness of space seems all the more profound without the sound of our family's joy to fill it. How are Orion and Nova managing with this sudden change? I hope they're finding comfort in each other and not causing too much trouble.

The ship is alive with excitement as we set out on this unprecedented voyage to the edge of known space. Captain Myrokos has been tirelessly briefing us on our mission objectives, and while the prospect of what lies ahead is exhilarating, it is also filled with a certain gravity. The unknown stretches out before us, vast and mysterious.

Our velocity is astonishing - so fast that the familiar starfield has become a blur, a smear of light that we barely register. The automated systems onboard manage the navigation and shield us from any errant space debris, a small comfort in this boundless expanse.

Please give the children a warm hug from me and remind them that no matter how far I travel, they and you are always with me, carried in my heart across the stars.

All my love,
Grayson

From: Sevika Demeter-7291
To: Grayson Demeter-7291
Date: 16 Solas, 2784
Subject: Re: Missing you already

Dearest Grayson,

We miss you more than words could ever capture. The house feels like a cavern without you, the rooms echoing with the quiet that has become our constant companion. We're filling the days with small tasks and cherished routines. Orion has been gazing up at the night sky with a kind of wonder that only children possess, asking with a seriousness that belies his years about the stars you'll be seeing. Nova, too, keeps pointing up, her little voice calling out "Dada." She is so precious.

I am proud of you, of the courage and curiosity that push you forward on this mission. It's an honor to share in your journey, even from a distance. The universe may hold unimaginable wonders, but I believe the greatest adventure is the one we share here, together, as a family.

Please, stay safe, my love. We'll be here, holding our breath and waiting for the day you return.

With all my heart,
Sevika

From: Grayson Demeter-7291
To: Sevika Demeter-7291
Date: 30 Solas, 2784
Subject: First discoveries

Sevika, my star,

We've made our first significant discovery! We've encountered a previously unknown nebula that seems to defy our understanding of astrophysics. The colors are unlike anything I've ever seen – imagine if a rainbow had a thousand more hues. I wish you could see it.

How are things back home? Has Orion started his new learning module? And has Nova taken her first steps yet? I hate missing these milestones, but knowing that you're there, capturing every moment, gives me comfort.

The work here is challenging but rewarding. Sometimes, when I'm elbow-deep in the ship's engines, I close my eyes and pretend I'm back in our garage, tinkering with that old hover-car while you bring me iced tea.

I love you all so much.

Forever yours,
Grayson

From: Sevika Demeter-7291
To: Grayson Demeter-7291
Date: 2 Equos, 2784
Subject: Re: First discoveries

My darling Grayson,

Your description of the nebula brought tears to my eyes. I showed your message to Orion, and he immediately started drawing what he imagined it looked like. Our son has quite the imagination – I've attached a holo-image of his artwork for you.

You haven't missed Nova's first steps yet, but she's getting close. She can stand on her own now and has been cruising along the furniture, holding herself up. It is so cute. I have a feeling it won't be long before she's running circles around me.

Orion has indeed started his new learning module. He's particularly fascinated by the history of space exploration. I think he wants to follow in your footsteps someday.

We miss you terribly, but hearing about your discoveries makes the separation a little easier to bear. Keep reaching for the stars, my love.

Yours always,
Sevika

From: Grayson Demeter-7291
To: Sevika Demeter-7291
Date: 18 Equos, 2784
Subject: Strange phenomena

My beloved Sevika,

Things are getting interesting out here. We've been encountering more and more phenomena that challenge our understanding of the universe. Just yesterday, we passed through a region of space where time seemed to flow differently. It was as if we lived a week in the span of a few hours.

I find myself thinking about you and the kids constantly. In quiet moments, I replay memories of our life together – our first date at the antigravity gardens, the day Orion was born, Nova's naming ceremony. These memories are my anchor in this vast, strange cosmos.

How are you holding up? I know it can't be easy managing everything on your own. You're the strongest person I know, Sevika. I couldn't do this without your support.

All my love,
Grayson

From: Sevika Demeter-7291
To: Grayson Demeter-7291
Date: 20 Equos, 2784
Subject: Re: Strange phenomena

Grayson, my heart,

Your latest message has left me in awe. A place where time flows differently? It sounds like something out of Orion's bedtime stories. Speaking of which, he's been asking more questions about your mission. I do my best to explain, but I think he senses there's more to it than I'm letting on.

Nova took her first steps yesterday! I wish you could have been here to see it. She toddled right over to the holo-projector where your last message was playing and tried to grab your image. It was the sweetest thing.

Don't worry about us, love. We're managing. Your mother has been a great help, coming over a few times a week to assist with the children. And yes, it's challenging, but knowing that you're out there, pushing the boundaries of human knowledge, makes it all worthwhile.

Stay safe, and keep those memories close. They're what bind us across the vastness of space.

Loving you always,
Sevika

From: Grayson Demeter-7291
To: Sevika Demeter-7291
Date: 5 Nix, 2785
Subject: Uncharted territories

My dearest Sevika,

We've crossed into the uncharted reaches of the cosmos. As we delve deeper into this mysterious expanse, we're methodically setting up communication relays, each one linking seamlessly to the next, ensuring that our voices can still cut through the immense silence of the void. Rest assured, our connection with home remains intact.

The stars here present a riddle, their patterns shifting in ways that defy any familiar constellation. It's a sight both captivating and unsettling, as we behold this celestial canvas, crafted from beams of light previously unknown to human sight. The majesty of it all leaves me feeling both minuscule and profoundly moved, as though we're trespassing upon a cosmic enigma.

I can't help but ache for the moments I've missed, especially Nova's first tentative steps. The holo-projection of her tiny feet stretching out was a wrenching reminder of the life I'm absent from. Please, keep capturing every detail. I need to experience those precious moments, even if it's only through your recordings.

Lately, the ship has been showing some odd quirks. Nothing severe, but enough to keep me vigilant. During the quiet hours, when the crew is lost in sleep, I can almost swear I hear faint whispers coming from the engine room. Perhaps it's just the isolation of deep space playing tricks on my mind.

Give Orion and Nova extra hugs for me. Let them know that despite the endless expanse of stars that separate us, Daddy's love for them spans far beyond all the constellations combined.

Missing you terribly,
Grayson

From: Sevika Demeter-7291
To: Grayson Demeter-7291
Date: 18 Tellus, 2785
Subject: Re: Uncharted territories

My brave Grayson,

I am utterly enchanted by the way you describe the vast, uncharted stretches of space. Orion has taken your celestial adventures to heart and transformed his bedroom ceiling into his own starry canvas. Each constellation he dreams up has a name as playful as his imagination, and he even insists on mapping out nebulas and distant galaxies, as if he's crafting an entire universe in the quiet sanctuary of his room. It's a charming spectacle, with glowing stars and swirls of color that make his room feel like a miniature cosmos.

I must confess, though, I am a little worried about the equipment problems you mentioned. Is everything working properly over there? I know how committed you are to this mission, but don't push yourself too hard. It's easy to get lost in the excitement of making new discoveries, but your health matters just as much as whatever you're trying to uncover.

As for the whispers you've been hearing, they might be the universe's way of revealing its secrets to you, or perhaps they are simply echoes of our love reaching out to you across the distance. I like to think of them as messages from home, reminding you that you're not alone in the vast expanse.

Back home, life moves with its gentle cadence. Nova's vocabulary is expanding. She's taken a particular shine to the word "stars," and her fascination is boundless. Orion has even started a space exploration club at school, proudly telling everyone that his dad is out there charting new worlds. His enthusiasm is contagious, and he often regales his friends with stories of your missions and the incredible things you're discovering.

We miss you so much and keep you in our thoughts each and every day.

Yours eternally,
Sevika

From: Grayson Demeter-7291
To: Sevika Demeter-7291
Date: 22 Tellus, 2785
Subject: Edge of reality

Sevika, my anchor,

Things are growing increasingly bizarre out here. The laws of physics, once solid and sure, are coming apart. Light bends and twists in ways I can't explain. Time feels loose like it's stretching one moment and shrinking the next. The whispers I've been hearing aren't just in my head anymore. Some of the crew are hearing them too, and the same confusion I feel is written on their faces. Something is wrong, but no one can say what it is.

Captain Myrokos keeps pushing us onward, always certain of the breakthrough he believes is just within reach. He doesn't waver, not even when the rest of us begin to question if we should keep going. But with every day that passes, a creeping dread settles deeper in my gut. It feels like we're moving toward a place where the world we know starts to unravel, where the rules that have always guided us no longer hold, and something strange waits, watching from the other side.

In these moments of disorientation, my thoughts drift more frequently to home. I imagine our life together, our house with its garden brimming with both Terran and Nacentaurian flowers. The image of our little sanctuary, so full of normalcy and love, is a beacon amid this encroaching chaos. It grounds me, even if just for a moment.

And you - how are you managing? Are you finding time to relax amidst the daily grind? I think about the small moments we used to share: those quiet evenings when we'd cook dinner together, the way you'd hum a tune while you worked in the garden, or the conversations we'd have over our morning tea. Your presence, your warmth, was a constant source of comfort for me.

I yearn for the routine of our life, the rhythm of ordinary days.

Please, tell me more about the children, about you, and the day-to-day of our life together. Anything that can pull me closer to the world I left behind. It's this connection to the ordinary, that I cling to now more than ever.

Love you always,
Grayson

From: Sevika Demeter-7291
To: Grayson Demeter-7291
Date: 24 Tellus, 2785
Subject: Re: Edge of reality

My dearest Grayson,

Your message worries me. I wish I could be there, to give you comfort and tell you that things will turn out fine. Though we are far apart, know that our love for you never falters. It's always there, like a steady light to lead you home.

In our little world, life marches on with its own rhythm. Orion lost his first tooth yesterday. His excitement was contagious. He dashed around the house, eager to show everyone his new smile. Nova has started saying "I love you." Every night before bed, she says it to your picture with such sweetness that it breaks my heart and heals it all at once. As for me, I've been spending more time in the garden. Do you remember how we used to dream about expanding the garden? Well, I've begun working on it. It gives me a purpose, a way to feel closer to you and to hold onto the dreams we shared.

I can only imagine the challenges you face out there, ones beyond our understanding. But take solace in knowing that you have a family here who loves you unconditionally. Let our love be your anchor amidst the chaos.

Think of our mornings together, the laughter we share, and the quiet moments we cherish. Reflect on our daily routines, our conversations, and the comfort we find in each other's presence. Our love is a steady thread that connects you to a world of warmth and familiarity, even from afar. You are always with us, regardless of the distance or the strangeness of your surroundings. Let this thought be a source of comfort and a grounding force that keeps you tethered to the love and stability waiting for you at home.

Stay strong, my love. We are here, waiting for you with open arms.

All my heart,
Sevika

From: Grayson Demeter-7291
To: Sevika Demeter-7291
Date: 10 Celeste, 2785
Subject: Shadows at the edge

Sevika,

I don't know if this message will reach you. We're continuing to drop relays, but we're getting closer to the point where our communications will be slower. But I'm sending it anyway, hoping against hope that it finds its way to you relatively soon.

We've reached something. I don't know how to describe it. It's like a wall of darkness at the edge of everything. The whispers have become a constant chorus now, speaking in languages no human tongue has ever uttered.

Some of the crew are changing, and there's no easy way to explain it. Their faces are shifting, their bodies too, like the darkness around us is creeping in, reshaping them into something different, something wrong. Even the toughest among us find it very disconcerting. The Med Unit is overwhelmed. It feels like we aren't just watching this happen but are part of it, pulled into something darker than we ever expected.

I can't quite articulate the fear that's taking root inside me, Sevika. It's a fear that extends beyond my own safety and grips me with worry for you and the children.

What if, by venturing into this unknown, we've triggered something far more sinister? What if whatever is festering here, whatever dark force we've unwittingly encountered, finds a way to follow us back? The thought of bringing such a threat into our home, into the lives of those I cherish most, is almost too much to bear. The possibility of this darkness reaching out from its lair and touching our world is a chilling notion, one that keeps me awake at night, tormented by the implications.

If this is my last message, know that I love you. You, Orion, and Nova are the best things that ever happened to me. Whatever happens, whatever I become, that will always be true.

I see shadows moving in the darkness. They're calling to us. I have to go now.

Forever yours,
Grayson

From: Sevika Demeter-7291
To: Grayson Demeter-7291
Date: 12 Celeste, 2785
Subject: Re: Shadows at the edge

Grayson, my love,

Your message reached me, but it left me with an icy knot of dread in my chest. Please, take care of yourself. Don't let the strangeness out there push you into hasty actions. Hold tight to your training and remember who you are, the person we love and depend on.

We need you here with us. Orion and Nova miss their father dearly, and I'm clinging to the hope that you'll come home safe. Whatever dangers you face, they aren't worth losing you over. The thought of you being lost to the void is unbearable.

I'm reaching out to the Space Exploration Bureau to see if they're sending a rescue mission. We need to find a way to bring you back to us. Just hold on a little longer, my love. Find a path through this uncertainty and return to us.

I love you more than words can capture. We all do. Stay strong, and remember that we're waiting for you, yearning for your safe return.

Your Love,
Sevika

From: Sevika Demeter-7291
To: Grayson Demeter-7291
Date: 20 Celeste, 2785
Subject: Please respond

My dearest Grayson,

It's been days since we last heard from you, and the silence grows heavier with each passing hour. The worry is relentless, a shadow that clings to me day and night, wrapping itself around every thought. I find myself staring at the empty spaces where you should be, haunted by the absence of your voice, your presence. If you can, please reach out. Just let us know that you're safe, or even that you're still out there. The children ask for you every day, their small faces pressed against the window panes, their voices a fragile blend of hope and confusion that pierces through the quiet of our home. I'm at a loss for what to tell them. I try to offer comfort, but inside, the uncertainty weighs on me like a leaden shroud, pulling me into a darkness I can barely escape.

The Bureau says they're doing everything they can, but their reassurances feel hollow against our fear. They've lost all contact with the Stellaris, and while they're preparing a rescue mission, it'll be weeks before they reach your last known position. Time drags on, each moment stretching longer than the last, filled with questions no one will answer and the quiet dread we don't dare speak aloud.

We cling to hope with every ounce of strength we can muster. Please, do whatever it takes to find your way back to us. Your absence permeates every corner of our lives, leaving a horrible emptiness. Your return is the light we are holding onto, and the thought of losing that hope is unbearable.

Please, come back to us.

All my love,
Sevika

From: Sevika Demeter-7291
To: Grayson Demeter-7291
Date: 8 Nix, 2786
Subject: Still waiting

My dearest Grayson,

It's been months now, and the silence is an unbearable weight. The rescue mission returned empty-handed, their reports filled with the stark finality of failure. They found no trace of the Stellaris or its crew, leaving us with nothing but the cold, unyielding void of uncertainty. But I refuse to let go of the hope that you might still be out there.

Orion and Nova ask about you with a regularity that breaks my heart. I've told them that you're engaged in a crucial mission, one that's taking longer than anticipated. I've crafted stories of your bravery and the importance of your work, hoping that they offer some comfort. I fear that in my desperation, I might be deceiving them more than protecting them.

Wherever you are, whatever has transpired, please know that our love for you remains unshaken and steadfast. We hold onto the hope that one day, against all odds, you'll come back to us. We wait for you with open hearts, knowing that you'll return to us once more.

Always yours,
Sevika

From: Sevika Demeter-7291
To: Grayson Demeter-7291
Date: 26 Tellus, 2786
Subject: Hope

Grayson, my true love,

The Bureau has officially declared the Stellaris and its crew lost. There was a memorial service today, a somber gathering where they honored what they presumed was the end. I didn't attend. The thought of standing among the mourners, listening to eulogies that cast you in the past tense, was too much to bear.

I refuse to accept that you're truly gone. Deep down, I can sense that you're still out there, somewhere beyond the grasp of our current reach. I can't stop sending these messages, hoping against hope that somehow, they will bridge the void and bring you back to us. Each transmission is an act of faith, a silent plea that you will hear me and find your way home.

Orion and Nova are growing fast, faster than I expected. Nova looks more like you every day, her face and the way she moves remind me of you in quiet moments. Orion, always full of energy, never stops talking about becoming an explorer like his father. He's been pouring over star charts with a focus that's hard to break, convinced that he'll be the one to bring you home.

We are here, waiting with a patience that's settled into us over time. The house isn't the same without you, and the days go on longer than they should. We love you, and no words can say how much we miss you. We keep hope close, believing that one day, you'll return to us.

Always with my love,
Sevika

From: Sevika Demeter-7291
To: Grayson Demeter-7291
Date: 26 Tellus, 2786
Subject: Hope

Oh, Grayson,

I am writing to you before I go to bed. My heart reaches for yours across the expanse of this endless night. In the quiet of these hours, when the world is hushed, I stretch my hand into the darkness, searching for yours. I yearn for the warmth of your touch, a fleeting moment of connection in this vast solitude.

If you are out there, find my spirit and take my hand. Kiss it for me.

Your only love,
Sevika

From: Sevika Demeter-7291
To: Grayson Demeter-7291
Date: 12 Celeste, 2787
Subject: Always

My Grayson,

It's been two years since your last message, two long years of clinging to hope, waiting, dreaming of the day when you'll return. The world outside has continued its relentless march forward, but here, we've remained suspended in time, unable to move on. We haven't, and we can't.

Orion and Nova are growing up, their laughter and energy a reminder of the family we once were. Still, there's always a sadness in their eyes, a quiet ache for the father they miss. I feel it too, the absence of you, every day. I miss you - my husband, my partner, my best friend. The days are full of the memory of your voice and the places you once filled.

But I want you to know this: wherever you are, whatever you've become, don't fear the darkness that surrounds you. Embrace the changes, even if they are beyond our current comprehension. You once described a nebula with colors that defied imagination. Perhaps your new reality is something akin to that, a place of beauty and wonder, even if it lies beyond our understanding.

And if you cannot find your way back to us, remember this: someday, somehow, we will find our way to you. In this life or the next, in this universe or another, our paths will cross again. The bond we share is not confined by time or space.

Until that day arrives, my love, know that you are deeply cherished. You are missed more than words can express. You are remembered in every moment of our lives.

We will meet again, my darling. Whether it be in starlight or shadow, across any expanse of existence, we will find each other once more.

All my love, for all time,
Sevika

Messages from Within

The nursing facility was a marvel of futuristic design, all sleek lines and soft, ambient lighting. It was a place meant to provide comfort and care, but to Sevika Demeter, it felt more like a gilded cage. The years had not been kind to her; her once vibrant hair had turned silver, and her eyes, still keen, carried the burden of a lifetime's joys and sorrows. She spent her days in quiet contemplation, her thoughts often drifting to Grayson, her husband who had vanished into the void of space so many years ago.

Sevika's room was filled with mementos of her life: photographs of Orion and Nova, now grown with families of their own, and a small garden of Terran and Nacentaurian flowers that she tended with care. But it was the old holo-projector, a relic from a bygone era, that held her attention most. She would sit for hours, replaying the last message she had received from Grayson, his words a haunting song of the love they had shared.

The world outside the facility had changed dramatically. A race of aliens, known as the Xylar, had begun their invasion of the homeworld. The news was filled with reports of cities falling, governments collapsing, and people fleeing in terror. The caregivers at the nursing facility were no exception; one by one, they left, seeking safety for themselves and their families.

It was on a particularly stormy night that Sevika found herself alone in the common room, the rain lashing against the windows like a thousand tiny fists. The other elderly residents were scattered throughout the facility, some uneasy while others were oblivious to reality. Sevika, in her cherished armchair by the window, clutched her faded photographs, their edges frayed from years of tender handling. One was of Grayson in his Space Exploration Bureau uniform.

"Grayson," she whispered, her voice a hush over the storm. "Where are you? I need you now more than ever."

The common room, usually filled with the soft hum of conversation and the gentle clinking of teacups, was eerily silent. The storm outside seemed to mirror the turmoil within the facility, the wind howling like a wounded animal. Sevika's eyes, though clouded with age, still held a spark of determination as she gazed at another photograph in her hands. It was an image of her and Grayson on their wedding day, their faces radiant with the unrestrained joy of youth and the boundless promise of a shared future.

She glanced around the room, once a sanctuary of comfort and warmth for those in their twilight years. Now, it felt transformed into a prison, the walls pressing in as the world outside descended into chaos. The quiet murmurs of the other residents reached her, their voices tinged with anxiety. They turned to her for strength, seeking reassurance that all would be well. Yet, how could she offer them comfort when her own heart was heavy with uncertainty?

As the rain continued to batter the windows, Sevika's thoughts drifted back to the early days of her marriage. Grayson had been a mechanic on a star vessel, exploring the outer reaches of the universe. His messages had been her lifeline. She remembered the joy she felt reading his descriptions of distant nebulae and uncharted territories, the pride she felt knowing he was part of something so grand. But those messages had also been tinged with fear, as Grayson recounted the strange phenomena and eerie whispers that haunted the edges of known space.

"Grayson," she whispered again, her voice trembling. "Where are you?"

The room fell into blackness as the power failed. Cries of alarm rose from some of the residents. Sevika's pulse quickened, her imagination conjuring a multitude of dreadful scenarios. She rose slowly, her aging body protesting, and shuffled to the window. Outside, the tempest raged, but it was the alien vessels emerging from the clouds that sent ice through her veins.

"Sevika?" a voice called from the doorway. It was Elda, one of the residents. "What's happening?"

Sevika turned to face her, her expression grim. "The aliens are here, Elda. They're taking over the city."

Elda's eyes widened in fear. "What are we going to do?"

Before Sevika could respond, the door to the common room burst open, and a group of alien soldiers, the Xylar, stormed in. Their silhouettes strode purposefully, towering figures cloaked in the oppressive anonymity of their suits. They weren't the sleek, tailored kind, but suits built for function, not fashion. The exoskeleton frame beneath the matte black armor hinted at hidden power, its every line tracing the outline of powerful servos and reinforced polymers.

Mirrored visors, like featureless black eyes, scanned the environment, their edges occasionally flickering with internal diagnostics. A faint mechanical whirring whispered with each step, the only sound betraying the suit's wearer. Utility pouches hung on their hips, their contents unknown but no doubt essential for whatever task lay ahead.

Sevika observed the soldiers, their metallic suits gleaming under the harsh lights. Yet, beneath the imposing exterior, she discerned a hint of the human form, a gentle contour that spoke of flesh and bone. One of the figures moved, and in that moment, Sevika glimpsed a gloved hand, its digits curling with an unexpected elegance that seemed at odds with the suit's imposing frame. The realization dawned on her: these were not the soulless machines of her nightmares, but individuals - enhanced by science, certainly, but still very much alive and breathing beneath their technological armor.

Sevika's mind wandered to the people concealed behind those luminous shields. What stories did they carry? What aspirations had they nurtured before embracing this armored existence? As a figure drew near, Sevika experienced an odd blend of trepidation and inquisitiveness. These were undoubtedly soldiers, prepared to confront the perils hiding in the urban darkness. Yet beneath it all, they shared a common humanity with her. This realization brought both solace and dread.

One of the alien Xylar soldiers spoke. "Sevika Demeter-7291," it said, its voice a mechanical monotone. "You will come with us."

Sevika's heart pounded in her chest. "Why? What do you want with me?"

The soldier did not answer. Instead, he gestured to the other soldiers, who moved to either side of Sevika, their grip firm but not unkind. As they slowly and carefully led her out of the common room, she caught a glimpse of Elda, her face a mask of terror.

"Don't worry, Elda," Sevika called over her shoulder. "I'll be back."

The Xylar soldiers guided Sevika through the dimly lit hallways of the facility with an unexpected gentleness, their movements careful and measured as they supported her frail frame. Outside, a series of canopies had been erected, leading the way to an alien ship that loomed ominously against the stormy sky. The rain drummed incessantly on the fabric above, creating a rhythmic, almost soothing backdrop to the tension in the air.

They halted before a large, reinforced door that slid open with a quiet hiss, revealing a room bathed in a cold, sterile light. The space was filled with advanced technology, sleek and otherworldly, glowing softly in hues of blue and green. Strange devices lined the walls, their purposes a mystery to Sevika's aging eyes.

At the center of the room, illuminated by the harsh overhead lights, stood a figure that made her heart stop. Encased in a suit of gleaming metal, it was both awe-inspiring and terrifying. The armor, seamless and polished, reflected the sterile light, giving the figure an almost spectral appearance. Its presence commanded the room, an embodiment of both power and enigma.

The soldiers released their gentle hold on Sevika, allowing her to take a tentative step forward. She took in the sight before her. The figure before her seemed to vibrate with an unseen energy, its presence amplified by the soft whirring of machinery all around. As understanding dawned, Sevika drew in a sharp breath, grasping the magnitude of what she witnessed.

It was Grayson, she could feel him. But it wasn't the Grayson she remembered. His body was encased in the same sleek, metallic exoskeleton, face partially obscured by a visor, as the others. He looked like something out of a nightmare, a fusion of man and machine.

"Grayson?" her voice trembling. "Is it really you?"

The figure turned, revealing its face as it raised the visor.

"It is you," she breathed.

Though still youthful, his visage bore marks of hardship - scars and deep gashes marring the once-familiar features. But his eyes, those eyes she knew intimately, held a complex blend of grief and awareness. Here was the man she had cherished for so long, now trapped within this fearsome armor. Her heart ached as she understood that despite the altered exterior, Grayson's essence endured somewhere inside.

"Sevika," his voice was a robotic approximation of its former self. "I have returned."

Tears filled her eyes as she took a step forward. "What happened to you? Where have you been all these years?"

Grayson's gaze softened, and with a tenderness that belied the cold metal of his mechanical hand, he reached out to touch her cheek. The contrast between the unyielding steel and the warmth of her skin was striking, yet there was a surprising gentleness in his touch. "I was lost, Sevika," he began, his words laden with unspoken tales. "Lost in the darkness at the edge of the universe. The Xylar found me, saved me, and transformed me."

As his hand lingered on her cheek, she could feel the faint hum of his internal mechanisms. "I am one of their leaders now," he continued, his eyes searching hers for understanding.

The revelation lingered between them, carrying unspoken meaning, yet all Sevika could focus on was the curious ease his touch brought her.

The moment seemed to bridge the vast chasm of time and space that had separated them. Sevika's heart ached at the sight and feel of him, so familiar yet so changed. "But why? Why did you come back?"

Grayson's expression grew serious. "The Xylar are here to take control of the homeworld, to bring order to the chaos. But I came back for you, Sevika. I could never forget you."

Sevika wept, her face awash with the release of years of buried feelings. Her heart raced, a tempest of conflicting emotions threatening to overwhelm her. With quivering fingers, she reached for Grayson's metallic hand, still cool against her skin. "Grayson," she whispered, her voice breaking. "Your changes don't matter to me. I don't care what you've become."

The words tumbled out, raw and earnest, each one carrying a piece of her soul. "I love you," she continued, her gaze locking onto his, trying to bridge the years and the transformations that had come between them. "And I always will."

Grayson's metallic hand, surprisingly warm against her skin, gently wiped away her tears with an unexpected delicacy. "And I love you, Sevika," he said, his voice a soft murmur that seemed to drift from a distant memory. His gaze, intense yet tender, searched hers as if trying to convey the depth of his feelings through the layers of transformation he had undergone.

"But I need your help," his tone shifted to one of urgency and determination. "The Xylar will not harm you or the other residents, but we need your cooperation." The plea in his voice was clear, filled with an unspoken promise of safety amidst the chaos. His mechanical fingers lingered on her cheek for a moment longer, a bridge between the human warmth of their shared history and the cold, unyielding reality of his current existence.

"Alright," she replied, her determination growing as she looked at Grayson, this fusion of the known and the unfamiliar. Their shared memories and the uncertain days ahead tugged at her. "I'll do whatever it takes to keep everyone safe," she said, her voice steady despite the tremor in her hands.

Grayson's eyes mellowed, and he drew close, his metallic lips brushing her brow with tender care. The gesture, so human in its affection, seemed at odds with the gleaming circuitry and polished steel that now composed his form. "Thank you, my darling," he murmured, his voice a blend of warmth and synthetic tones. "With you by my side, we'll reshape this world into something beautiful."

"But I am old," Sevika whispered, her eyes searching his, seeking reassurance. "I don't have many days left."

"Your days are more precious than ever," he said, a slight smile on his face. "We will honor every moment. Your wisdom and strength are what we need now. And I will be with you, every step of the way." His words were a promise, a vow that transcended the boundaries of time and transformation, binding them together in a shared mission, a shared hope.

As the Xylar soldiers gently led Sevika back to the common room, she couldn't help but feel a sense of hope. Grayson had returned, and though he was changed, their love remained. She would do whatever it took to protect her family and the other residents, even if it meant working with the very beings who had invaded their world.

***

In the aftermath, everything moved quickly. The Xylar seized the city with remarkable precision, their advanced technology and strategic maneuvers allowing no space for rebellion. While Grayson met with the Xylar leaders, outlining plans for the future and exploring how to blend Xylar systems with human governance, Sevika, and the other nursing facility residents were treated with care. The Xylar soldiers, now a constant presence in the corridors, ensured their needs were met. Servo-droids attended to the frail, delivering meals, maintaining cleanliness, and administering medication with methodical efficiency.

Sevika devoted her days to a different kind of labor - one marked by quiet resolve and tender care. Instead of the conference rooms and strategy sessions with Grayson and the Xylar leaders, she found herself amidst the residents, working side by side with the Xylar soldiers and servo-droids who had been assigned to help manage the facility. Their interactions, once fraught with tension, had evolved into a rhythm of cooperation and mutual respect.

Each day, Sevika walked the halls of the facility, quietly tending to the needs of the residents. She assisted with medications, supported their daily routines, and listened intently to their concerns. The servo-droids, despite their mechanical nature and distant demeanor, performed their duties with an unexpected gentleness, a calmness that grew under her steady direction. Their presence brought a kind of quiet reassurance, and Sevika's calm guidance gave the residents a sense of steadiness that helped them navigate their uncertain days.

Despite the difficulty of merging Xylar technology with the facility's existing systems, Sevika's attention stayed rooted in the well-being of the people she cherished. Every small success - a resident's smile, a shared laugh, a fleeting moment of ease - deepened her determination. The challenge of reconciling two worlds, of finding a balance between her past and the current demands, became less important than her personal mission to protect those around her. In these quiet, everyday moments of compassion, Sevika discovered a renewed sense of direction and a hope that quietly lingered for what lay ahead.

"Do you remember our garden back home?" Sevika asked, her voice soft with nostalgia.

Grayson nodded, his gaze distant. "I do. It was our sanctuary, a place where we could escape from the world and just be together."

She smiled, her heart aching with the memory. "I miss those days. But I'm grateful that we're together now, even if things are different."

Grayson's metallic hand gently squeezed hers. "I am too, Sevika. I never thought I would see you again, but fate has brought us back together. And now, we have a chance to build something new, something better."

One night as they sat together, watching the stars appear in the night sky, Sevika felt a sense of peace. The future was uncertain, and the challenges ahead were great, but she knew that as long as she had Grayson by her side, she could face anything.

However, their newfound harmony was soon shattered. While Sevika was tending to her small garden, Grayson approached, his mechanical form casting a long shadow across the flowers. She looked up, smiling, but the expression faded as she saw the tension in his posture.

"Sevika," he began, his voice strained, "there's something I need to tell you."

She stood slowly, brushing the dirt from her hands. "What is it, my love? What's wrong?"

He hesitated, and in that moment, she felt a cold dread slink through her. "The Xylar command has made a decision. About the elderly residents here."

Sevika's heart began to race. "What kind of decision?"

His eyes, still so human despite his transformation, were filled with pain. "They've determined that the elderly are - disposable. They want to remove them from the facility."

The words hit Sevika like a physical blow. She stumbled back, her hand reaching out to steady herself against the wall. "Disposable? What do you mean, disposable? These are people, Grayson. My friends."

"I know, my dearest. I tried to argue against it, but the Xylar believe it's for the betterment of the homeworld. They say the resources used to care for the elderly could be better allocated elsewhere."

Sevika's shock quickly gave way to anger. "How dare they? After everything we've been through, after all the promises of a better world. This is barbaric, Grayson. You can't let this happen."

His metallic hands clenched at his sides. "I don't have a choice, Sevika. The Xylar are in control now. Their command is final."

"And what about your word?" she demanded, her voice rising. "You said we would be safe!"

Grayson remained still. "I am sorry. "

Her gaze burned with scorn. "And your humanity? Did they strip that from you when they locked you in that suit?"

Her words settled between them, sharp and painful. Grayson winced, as though the blow had landed. "Sevika, please. Try to understand. This isn't easy for me either."

But she was beyond listening. She pushed past him, her feet carrying her swiftly through the facility. She had to warn the others, had to do something to stop this madness.

The next few hours were chaos. Sevika moved from room to room, telling the residents what was happening, urging them to resist. But most were too frail, too confused to understand. Some, like Elda, rallied to her side, determined to fight.

With the sun sinking lower on the horizon, the Xylar approached, their massive metal cargo transports rumbling steadily. Sevika's heart tightened watching her friends being corralled into the cold, steel vessels, their faces marked by a grim acceptance and silent fear. She remained at the entrance of the facility, arms extended wide, creating a fragile barrier between herself and the advancing force, a final act of resistance against what seemed impossible to prevent.

"You can't do this," she shouted at the Xylar soldiers. "These are people, not things to be discarded!"

But her words fell on deaf ears. The soldiers moved around her, their movements efficient and impersonal. Grayson stood to the side, his face a mask of anguish as he watched the scene unfold.

As the final residents were carefully loaded into the cargo transports, Sevika's weariness settled heavily upon her. The frenetic pace of the day had taken its toll, leaving her with a sense of weary resignation. In a moment of quiet amidst the turmoil, she turned to her friend Elda, taking her hand with a tenderness that spoke volumes.

Leaning in, Sevika whispered softly into Elda's ear, her words a gentle reassurance in the midst of uncertainty. Elda's response was a solemn nod, her eyes glistening with the beginning of tears. They shared a brief, poignant look, a silent understanding passing between them.

Together, hands clasped, they quietly moved toward one of the cargo vehicles. They slipped inside, seeking a brief refuge amongst the other residents. Sevika and Elda settled into a rare moment of calm, their breaths meeting in the quiet, anticipating the unknown course ahead.

Elda's voice, a fragile whisper, broke the silence. "We are ready." Sevika squeezed Elda's hand and smiled.

Meanwhile, in the facility, Grayson was in a frenzy. He combed through every room, calling out for Sevika, his mechanical voice carrying through the vacant corridors. It wasn't until a Xylar soldier approached him that the truth finally came to light.

"Sir," the soldier said, "We believe she may have stowed away in one of the cargo vehicles."

Grayson's world shifted in an instant. "Sevika," he whispered, the name heavy with both longing and regret. Without pausing to think, he raced toward the nearest skycraft, his mechanical body propelling him forward with an almost unnatural swiftness.

The disposal center towered on the horizon, an immense structure of steel and cables that appeared like a dark sentinel against the sky. Its brutalist architecture exuded an unspoken menace, the hard edges and unforgiving surface absorbing the somber light of the day. Grayson pushed the hover vehicle to its limits, the engine's hum sharp and discordant amid the confusion of thoughts racing through his mind. Each possibility, each scenario that flitted through his consciousness, grew increasingly bleak and daunting, intensifying his sense of urgency.

As the vehicle drew closer, Grayson could make out the slow, methodical dance of the cargo vehicles unloading their grim contents. The sight was almost hypnotic in its monotony, the whir of machinery and the clatter of metal creating a harshness of relentless efficiency. Grayson's eyes darted through the crowd with mounting desperation, searching for any sign of Sevika amidst the sea of unfamiliar faces. But as the seconds ticked by, his heart sank deeper - there was no sign of her. The crowd was a shifting sea of shadows and movement, and Sevika remained elusive, swallowed up by the cruel, indifferent expanse of the disposal center.

The reinforced doors sighed open with a hiss as Grayson forced his way in. His metal frame dwarfed the startled Xylar guards, their bioluminescent markings flashing in alarm. He swept through the sterile corridors, a relentless determination driving every thrust of his hydraulic joints. Each empty holding cell he passed filled Grayson's chest with an unsettling void. At last, he arrived at a vast chamber, where the metallic clang of the conveyor belt resonated like a solitary heartbeat. A harsh light cast elongated shadows across the churning furnace, turning it into a gaping maw poised to consume something invaluable. Time, which had once flowed leisurely, now felt like a relentless drumbeat in Grayson's ears. He had to arrive before it was too late.

And then, he saw her.

Sevika lay on the conveyor, a small figure against the unforgiving steel, almost childlike in her stillness. Her hands, usually a whirlwind of activity, rested quietly across her chest, a serene image in the face of the impossible. Anesthesia had cast a mask of tranquility over her typically expressive features, yet beneath that calm, the slow rise and fall of her chest revealed a turbulent sea of emotions. Each rhythmic click of the conveyor felt like a hammer blow, pushing her closer to the furnace, a hungry, orange giant waiting at the end of the line.

"Sevika!" Grayson shouted, his voice resonating in the vastness of the room. He raced toward her, his augmented legs allowing him to move with an extraordinary swiftness that surpassed any ordinary human.

Sevika's eyes fluttered open at the sound of his voice. She turned her head, a sad smile spreading across her face as she took in his presence. "Grayson," she said gently, her voice a whisper, nearly lost in the soft hum of the machinery surrounding them.

Grayson reached the conveyor belt, his hands stretching out to grab her. But at that moment, the belt surged forward, carrying Sevika towards the furnace at an alarming speed.

"No!" his scream was primal, filled with a pain that transcended his mechanical form. He lunged forward, his fingers just brushing her outstretched hand before she disappeared into the flames.

The world seemed to stop. He stood there, his arm still extended, as if by sheer will he could bring her back. But there was nothing but the roar of the furnace and the acrid smell of smoke.

He sank to his knees, his mechanical body making a harsh sound as it hit the floor. He stayed there, unmoving, as Xylar soldiers surrounded him, their weapons raised.

Grayson's eyes, now pools of anguish, fixed on the furnace, holding the smoldering remnants of what had once been Sevika. He felt an unbearable heaviness in his chest, the weight of a thousand unspoken goodbyes pressing down on him. The mechanical augmentations that had once defined him - his lifeline to strength and endurance - now felt like chains binding him to a fate he could no longer accept.

With an intense ferocity, Grayson started to rip away the augmentations attached to his body. The metal plates and synthetic limbs came off in jagged pieces, each removal accompanied by a cry of agony that filled the vast, sterile room. His hands, trembling from the effort, were smeared with the dark grease of the Xylar machinery, leaving them bloodied and raw. As he tore away the last remnants of the once-proud armor, the floor around him became littered with broken fragments of metal and tangled wires. Each discarded fragment told a story of its own, traces of strength now reduced to mere debris.

With each piece he removed, the visage of the man beneath became increasingly apparent - a figure far older and more fragile than the powerful machine he had embodied. Once concealed by sleek steel, his body was now exposed as a withered shell of its former self. Wrinkled skin, pallid and sagging, hung loosely from his bones. Veins, once hidden tributaries, now bulged like blue rivers across the pale expanse of his flesh. Time had taken its ruthless toll, picking apart his once-strong physique that was now marked by bloodied, jagged wounds crisscrossing his skin, where wires and tubes had once tunneled into him.

As the last of the augmentations clattered to the ground, he swayed unsteadily, his movements now labored and slow. The machinery that had granted him power lay discarded, and he stood exposed and vulnerable. Yet, his eyes still held a fierce glint, a resolute spark that defied his physical frailty.

He turned towards the conveyor and took a step forward, then another, each movement deliberate and measured. Every step, every breath stung with the agony. As he approached the conveyor, his heart pounding in his chest.

With great effort, he climbed onto the belt, carefully positioning himself. He placed his hands gently over his chest, trying to steady his trembling form. The belt moved forward with a relentless pace, pulling him closer to the furnace's blistering heat, which pressed against his face with an almost overwhelming intensity. The furnace roared like a beast, its flames writhing and reaching toward him with an insatiable hunger. As the belt carried him inch by agonizing inch, the pain became a searing force.

Grayson closed his eyes, the oppressive heat piercing through his despair. He released a desperate shout, his voice breaking under the strain. "Sevika! Remember us! Let this be our end!" His cry resonated through the fiery chamber, a final plea that was swallowed by the searing heat.

Guardians of the Golden Tree

In the hazy realm of Misty Glen, where ancient trees whispered their secrets to the passing winds and shadows danced like phantoms beneath their towering boughs, there dwelt a young orphan boy named Thorne. His days were passed under the care of the kindly folk who kept the orphanage at the village's edge - a weathered, timeworn building that, though showing the wear of many seasons, still offered warmth and refuge to those without hearth or home.

Thorne was a quiet lad, his eyes reflecting the very spirit of the mist that hung over the land. He possessed a gentle manner, one that drew the creatures of the forest close to him, and beneath that gentleness was a strength beyond his years. Oftentimes, he would wander to the very border of the great forest that surrounded Misty Glen, standing as if peering into its deep shadows, searching for some elusive truth he could not yet name.

It was on one such day, as the sun struggled in vain to break through the ever-present mist, clinging like a ghostly veil to the world, that Thorne's path was irrevocably altered. His destiny arrived in the form of Eldrin the Enlightened One, an aged wizard of ancient renown. Eldrin had journeyed far from forgotten realms, and the years were etched deeply upon his face, once regal and proud, now marked by the passage of many long roads. Where once he had strode tall, his frame now bore the wear of innumerable trials, and the burdens of many years seemed to pull him nearer to the earth.

He leaned heavily upon a staff of twisted oak, its surface etched with ancient runes, pulsing with a faint, inner light. It seemed as though the very heart of the forest's magic had been bound within the wood, casting eerie shadows upon the ground as the runes glimmered in the misty air. Atop the staff sat a great sapphire, set within silvered mounts of intricate design, its deep blue hue gleaming faintly beneath the day's dim light. His robes, though woven from fine cloth embroidered in rich greens and silver threads, were frayed and worn at the hems, and the clasp at his throat - a relic from a forgotten age - was shaped like a crescent moon, adorned with a single radiant star that sparkled even in the gloom.

His eyes, though clouded with age, still gleamed with the fire of wisdom and ancient knowledge, borne through many ages and countless trials. As he approached, his steps were measured, each one deliberate, heavy with the weight of fate itself. The very air around him seemed to hum with a faint, unseen power, as though the world itself acknowledged his presence and held its breath in anticipation.

As Eldrin neared the village, a shift stirred in the air, subtle yet undeniable. There was magic nearby, a presence that beckoned him like a star in the darkness. His weary eyes brightened, and with what strength his limbs could still muster, he quickened his pace, his heart lifting with long-sought purpose. "At last," he murmured, the words barely audible above the breeze. "The one I seek is near."

The wizard wandered the winding ways of Misty Glen, offering gentle nods to the villagers whose curious eyes followed him. Though strangers seldom came to this remote hamlet, and rarer still were those who carried the unmistakable presence of magic, Eldrin moved with an air of calm familiarity. The power that surrounded him, though veiled in humility, was felt by all who crossed his path.

As Eldrin drew closer to the heart of the village, he felt a shift in the breeze, something subtle yet profound. The very air seemed to hum with the presence of ancient enchantments, and the wizard's tired gaze brightened with recognition. His steps quickened, though the wisdom of his years tempered his pace. "At last," he whispered to the wind, "the one I seek is near."

Eldrin continued his journey through the glen, each step deliberate, his expression kind and open as he greeted the villagers. "Good day to you," he called out, his voice smooth as a summer breeze, carrying the rich tone of a storyteller. The villagers watched him with a blend of awe and wonder. An old woman, her arms laden with herbs, bowed as he passed. "Wizard Eldrin," she greeted, her tone reverent. "A rare visitor, indeed. What brings a man of your gifts to such humble lands?"

Eldrin paused, his dark robes stirring gently with the wind as he inclined his head. "I seek one whose path is set by powers unseen," he said softly, his voice deep as distant thunder. "A flame kindled by the fates themselves, one that must not be extinguished."

The old woman's eyes narrowed, and her voice, though tempered by respect, held the weight of caution. "Sorcery has its own ways, wizard. We are a simple folk, and magic is but a story whispered by the fireside, one that brings more trouble than ease."

A knowing smile tugged at the corner of Eldrin's lips. "Perhaps," he replied, his voice laced with mystery. "But I am drawn here for reasons beyond mere tales." With a nod, he turned away, his presence fading like mist as dusk settled over the village.

His path led him through the quiet lanes, and he paused for a moment where the sun warmed a gathering of cats stretched lazily upon the stones. One, sleek and black, with eyes bright as emeralds, caught his attention. Kneeling beside it, Eldrin extended a hand, his voice soft. "And what wisdom do you carry, guardian of these lands?"

The cat purred, leaning into his touch, and Eldrin chuckled quietly. His journey continued, taking him through the woods where the scent of damp earth rose to greet him, and before long, a cottage nestled in the verdant hollow appeared its thatched roof and weathered timbers whispering tales of seasons past. Children, like wildflowers scattered across a meadow, frolicked in the sunlit yard, but one stood apart from the rest - a boy, silent and watchful, gazing into the woods as though he could see beyond the veil of the present.

The wizard stopped and regarded the boy. There was something more to him than mere youth - a quiet spark that resonated with the timeless forces Eldrin knew all too well. "Greetings, young one," the wizard called, his voice deep and ancient as the trees themselves. "Do you know of the stories the wind carries?"

The boy turned, startled by the presence of the stranger. His eyes grew wide, taking in the figure before him. Eldrin, with his silvered beard and midnight robes speckled with stars, seemed to carry the weight of a thousand untold tales. "Who - who are you?" the boy asked in a whisper.

Eldrin's lips curved into a gentle smile, and though shadows lined his face, there was warmth behind his gaze. "I am Eldrin, keeper of the Golden Tree, whose roots have stretched into the heart of this land long before your time." He paused, his eyes narrowing slightly as if searching for something within the boy. "And you, child? What name do you bear?"

The boy hesitated before answering. "Thorne," he said at last, his voice soft, as if the name itself was unfamiliar on his tongue.

Eldrin frowned thoughtfully, his brow furrowing like the roots of an ancient oak straining against the earth. "Thorne, is it? Names are like seeds, young one - they grow into the roots of all that is yet to come. And yours, I think, carries the mark of something greater."

The boy lowered his head. "I am but an orphan," he muttered. "Thorne they call me, and nothing more."

A slow smile crept across the wizard's face. "Orphaned, you say? Then you are like a stone, unburdened by the weight of history, yet capable of becoming something far greater. The roots of your strength lie not in the blood that flows through your veins, young Thorne, but in the spirit that burns within your heart." His gaze softened, filled with a profound understanding. "Remember this: the wind may howl and the rain may fall, but the oak that stands alone is often the mightiest of them all." Gently, he brushed the boy's wayward hair. "Yet know this, young one: you have been sought by fate, a destiny woven long before your birth."

Thorne's expression clouded with uncertainty. "Me? But I am nothing - just a boy from Misty Glen, with no name or legacy."

The wizard chuckled softly, a sound like the rustling of autumn leaves in a forgotten wood. "Ah, young Thorne, therein lies your error. You are not as ordinary as you believe. Within you burns a flame, faint but steadfast, a spark of ancient magic that has called to me across wood and water, hill and hollow."

The wizard chuckled softly, a sound like the rustling of autumn leaves in a forgotten wood. "Ah, young Thorne, therein lies your error. You are not as ordinary as you believe. Within you burns a flame, faint but steadfast, a spark of ancient magic that has called to me across wood and water, hill and hollow."

A mist, pale and ethereal, began to drift between them. It coiled and shifted, like the breath of the forest itself, weaving forms that flickered and dissolved as swiftly as they appeared. Thorne's eyes widened as the mist deepened into something more - a curtain drawn from the memories of the earth. Shadows stirred within its depths, shapes of forgotten beings, whispering of ages long past. A tremor ran through him, not of fear, but a reverence that stirred his very soul.

"Come, young one," Eldrin's voice rolled low and steady, like the rumble of distant thunder. "The path before us is as old as the world itself, and the tales I carry stretch back to the dawn of time. Your journey awaits, and it is not one you can turn from."

Thorne's voice was a fragile murmur, barely audible amid the gathering twilight. "But what of those who care for me? Will they not search for me? Will they not grieve?"

Eldrin cast his gaze toward the far horizon, where the mist seemed to part ever so slightly, revealing faint outlines of realms beyond. "The world is vast, young Thorne, and time flows differently in lands untouched by mortal concerns. Those who love you will be comforted, knowing that you walk a path of purpose. Worry not for their sorrow, but trust in the unfolding of fate."

With hesitation lingering in his steps, Thorne moved to follow the wizard deeper into the forest. The trees around them grew mightier with every stride, their trunks gnarled and ancient, their branches stretching skyward like arms raised in eternal supplication. Golden light filtered through the leafy canopy, casting a soft, otherworldly glow upon the forest floor. The air grew thick with the rich scent of damp earth, of moss-covered stones, and the deep hum of nature's quiet pulse. Now and again, the silence was broken by the distant call of unseen creatures.

As they walked, Eldrin spoke again, his voice like the cadence of an ancient song, drawing Thorne's attention deeper into the mysteries of the world. "In the days when the stars were young, and the rivers of magic flowed free through all living things, there stood a tree unlike any other - a tree of untold beauty and power. Its trunk gleamed with the sheen of gold, its leaves shimmered like polished silver, and its roots sank deep into the heart of the world itself."

Thorne listened, entranced, as Eldrin wove the tale of the Golden Tree. It was more than mere legend - Thorne could feel it in the air around them, as though the very essence of the tree lingered in every shadowed glen and sunlit grove. Yet, as the wizard spoke, a weariness settled into his words, the strength of his voice waning, like the final light of a setting sun. Eldrin leaned heavily upon his staff, his steps slower, more labored, as if the weight of his years pressed harder with each passing moment.

"Alas," the wizard sighed, pausing to catch his breath, "my time as the tree's guardian is drawing to a close. As the seasons pass, so too must I, and this may be the last for both of us."

Thorne's heart quickened. "But if the tree withers, what will become of the magic?"

Eldrin's smile was fraught with sorrow. "The tree shall not perish in the way you fear. In its final season, it will bear golden seeds, each a promise of renewal. Yet, there are those who would seek to claim these seeds for their own, or worse, to ensure they never take root."

At that very moment, as though summoned by the wizard's warning, a cold wind stirred through the trees, bringing with it the scent of rot and the distant echo of cruel laughter. Thorne felt a chill creep over him, drawing him closer to Eldrin's side.

"Who would commit such evil?" Thorne asked, his voice trembling.

Eldrin's gaze darkened, his eyes sharp as flint. "There is one, a sorcerer of great malice and ambition - Goroth the Shadowmancer. He has long coveted the power of the Golden Tree, and his greed knows no bounds. He will stop at nothing to seize its magic, or destroy it utterly if he cannot."

Turning to Thorne, Eldrin's eyes gleamed with a fierce resolve. "That is why I have come to you. The task of safeguarding the tree and its legacy cannot rest upon my shoulders much longer. It must pass to one with the strength of spirit and purity of heart - to one such as yourself."

Thorne recoiled, doubt gripping him. "But I am no more than a child. How can I face one so powerful?"

Eldrin reached out, placing a gnarled hand upon Thorne's shoulder. His touch filled with ancient knowledge and unspoken strength. "Listen well, young Thorne," he said, his voice deepening with an almost mythical resonance. "You are far more than you know. In your blood runs the legacy of kings - rulers who once held sway over this land when the world was new and the stars themselves whispered songs of creation. Within you lies power untapped, a magic forgotten by the passing ages."

The wizard's words struck deep, and in that moment, Thorne felt a strange warmth rising within him, as though the very earth itself was stirring in answer to Eldrin's call. He looked down at his hands and saw a faint glow, like sunlight refracted through amber, begin to shimmer upon his skin.

"But how can this be?" Thorne whispered. "I have no lineage, no claim to such things."

Eldrin smiled, his expression softening. "Your true lineage has been kept hidden from you, shielded from those who would seek to exploit it. But now, in this time of need, it calls to you. Hear the song of your ancestors, young Thorne, those you have never known, and feel the magic that stirs within your heart. It is your destiny."

The forest grew still, as though the very trees themselves listened, awaiting Thorne's response. All around him, the air shimmered with a strange, expectant energy, and he felt the weight of the moment press upon him.

"Will you take up this mantle?" Eldrin asked, his voice solemn and filled with purpose. "Will you become the guardian of the Golden Tree?"

For a long moment, Thorne stood in silence, torn between the life he had known and the great unknown stretching out before him. But then, as if carried on the wind itself, the whisper of destiny stirred his soul. Slowly, he nodded. "Yes," he said, his voice gaining strength with each word. "I will protect the tree and its seeds."

Eldrin's face broke into a smile, and a light seemed to return to his weary features. "Then let us begin, young one. There is much to teach, and little time before the forces of darkness descend."

As Eldrin spoke, the wind stirred again, this time carrying with it the scent of flowers and the soft murmur of distant music. From the shadow of the trees emerged a figure, graceful and luminous, her form shifting with the light like water flowing over smooth stone.

"Greetings, Eldrin the Enlightened One," she said, her voice as clear as a mountain stream. "And to you, Thorne, chosen guardian of the Golden Tree."

Eldrin bowed deeply. "Mira, spirit of the forest, your presence honors us."

Thorne could only stare in awe at the forest spirit, her ethereal beauty like something from a dream, her eyes aglow with ancient wisdom. She smiled, and Thorne felt a warmth spread through him once more, filling him with confidence for the journey ahead.

"The forest has long awaited your coming, young Thorne," Mira said, her voice gentle yet filled with power. "We shall aid you in your task, for the fate of the Golden Tree is tied to the fate of all living things."

As Mira spoke, the forest around them seemed to come alive. Flowers bloomed where there had been none before, and the very air sparkled with motes of golden light. Thorne felt a surge of confidence, knowing that he would not face the coming trials alone. Then, in a blink of an eye the forest muse was gone.

***

The mists wove themselves about the ancient trees like delicate veils, their tendrils stretching forth with ethereal fingers as Eldrin the Enlightened One led young Thorne deeper into the forest's secret heart. The old wizard's staff struck a rhythmic beat against the moss-covered stones, and with each soft thud, a faint shimmer of light pulsed through the fog, as if the very air acknowledged his passage.

"Mark my words, Thorne," Eldrin intoned, his voice resonant and rich, like the deep roots of the earth itself. "The path that lies ahead of you is not one to tread without care. It is a charge passed down since the First Age, a sacred duty borne by those of unwavering heart and steadfast mind. The Golden Tree, the very lifeblood of this land, must be guarded by one worthy, for on its protection depends the fate of all free peoples."

Thorne listened with reverence, his gaze wide with awe as the splendor of the forest unfolded around him. Never before had he ventured beyond the familiar bounds of Misty Glen, and each step brought him closer to wonders that seemed to outshine even the ancient tales. Flowers of unimaginable color glowed in the shaded groves, their petals illuminated by a soft light from within. Strange creatures, perhaps born in the world before the rising of the Sun and Moon, darted through the branches overhead, their songs strange and haunting, like whispers of forgotten times.

"Will you teach me how to be its guardian?" Thorne asked, his voice quiet in the vastness of the wood, though beneath it lay a flicker of strength not yet fully kindled.

Eldrin turned toward him, the faintest spark of mirth dancing in his ancient eyes, eyes that seemed to hold within them the endless memory of the world. "I will show you the path, as it was shown to me long ago. Yet remember, Thorne, it is not the circumstance of one's birth that shapes destiny, but the choices made in the face of great trials. Even the smallest among us may alter the course of the future, should they possess the courage to stand firm."

As they walked along paths that had not felt the tread of mortal feet for an age, Thorne's attention was drawn to a shimmering pool that lay off the path, its waters clear, its surface as smooth as polished glass, reflecting the canopy above with perfect clarity, as if it were a window into another world. But as he approached, drawn by an unseen force, the water began to ripple, and from its depths rose a being of such ethereal beauty that Thorne's breath caught in his throat.

The creature was nimble and graceful, with skin that shimmered like moonlight on water and hair that flowed like liquid mithril. Its eyes, deep and fathomless as the pool itself, fixed upon Thorne with an intensity that made him shiver, as if his very soul were laid bare before this ancient being.

"Greetings, young guardian," the being spoke, its voice like the gentle lapping of waves. "I am Naiada, spirit of these waters and kin to Aolma, Lord of Waters. Long have I awaited your coming."

Eldrin bowed low, a gesture of respect that Thorne hastily mimicked, feeling the weight of history and legend pressing upon him. "Lady Naiada," the wizard intoned, his voice reverent, "we are honored by your presence. What wisdom do you offer to my apprentice, who stands at the threshold of a great and perilous journey?"

Naiada's gaze never left Thorne as she replied, her words carrying the weight of prophecy. "The path of the guardian is not always clear, young one, for it winds through shadow and light, through joy and sorrow. There will be times when the mists of doubt cloud your vision and the currents of fear threaten to sweep you away. But remember this: just as water finds its way through the tiniest cracks in stone, so too can courage and determination overcome even the greatest of obstacles. Trust in the strength that lies within you, for it is greater than you know."

With these words, Naiada sank back into the pool, leaving only ripples to mark her passing, like the fading memory of a dream. Thorne stood in awe, his mind reeling from the encounter, feeling as if he had glimpsed a fragment of the great tapestry of creation.

As they continued their journey through the ancient wood, Eldrin began to teach Thorne the ancient lore of the forest, passed down from his master who had walked these lands in ages past.

He spoke of the delicate balance that existed between all living things, of the magic that flowed through every root and branch, a remnant of the power that had shaped the world in its beginning. Thorne listened with rapt attention, his young mind expanding to encompass concepts that would have bewildered most grown men, feeling as if he were unlocking secrets hidden since the dawn of time.

It was as they approached a gnarled old oak, its trunk twisted into fantastic shapes by the passage of centuries, that they encountered their next magical being. From a hollow in the tree emerged a creature no taller than Thorne's knee, with skin like weathered bark and eyes that glowed with an inner fire reminiscent of a blacksmith's forge.

"Ho there, wizard!" the creature called out, its voice surprisingly deep for its small stature, resonating with the strength of the earth itself. "What brings you to old Rootbeard's domain? And who's this spindly sapling you've got with you? He looks no more substantial than a birch in winter!"

Eldrin chuckled, a sound like distant thunder rolling over the forest. "Well met, Rootbeard, old friend. This 'spindly sapling' is Thorne, soon to be guardian of the Golden Tree. We seek your counsel, if you would be so kind as to share it, for your wisdom is as deep as your roots are long."

Rootbeard hopped down from his perch, circling Thorne with a scrutinizing gaze that seemed to see through flesh and bone. "A guardian, is it? A bit thin, if you ask me. Yet, even the mightiest oaks spring from the smallest acorns, and the great tree itself was once naught but a seed." He fixed Thorne with a penetrating stare that delved into the depths of his spirit. "Listen closely, lad, for the words of Rootbeard are not given lightly. The forest is alive, woven with wonders beyond your imagining, a vast web of life crafted by the hand of the divine. Learn to heed its whispers and feel its rhythms in your very marrow, as your master does. In doing so, you shall never truly be alone, for you will carry the strength of every tree and every blade of grass within your heart."

As the day unfolded and the lessons progressed, Thorne felt a swell of confidence blossom within him. The forest, once foreign and foreboding, began to feel like a second home as if he were rediscovering a piece of himself long obscured.

When the sun dipped low, painting the mist in golden and pink hues, they at last reached their destination. In a clearing that emanated its own soft glow stood the Golden Tree, its leaves shimmering like beaten gold in the fading light, a living testament to the glory of the divine.

There, waiting at the base of the tree, was Mira. The spirit of the forest captivated Thorne, her form shifting gracefully like sunlight dancing upon leaves, as though she were neither entirely of this world nor entirely of the next.

"Welcome, Thorne," Mira greeted, her voice a gentle murmur like the wind rustling through the boughs, carrying echoes of ancient songs sung at the dawn of creation. "I have been observing your journey with great interest, for upon you rests the hope of many."

As Thorne stepped closer, he sensed a bond forming between himself and Mira, a connection resonating with the essence of the forest itself. It felt as if he could perceive the flow of life surrounding him, from the smallest insect to the grandest tree, a harmonious symphony of existence that had played since the world first awoke.

"Mira," Thorne spoke, his voice rich with wonder, "I feel - transformed. As though I am part of something grander, a vast web of life stretching beyond time and space."

Mira's smile lit up the clearing, causing Thorne's heart to flutter. "Indeed, young guardian. The forest has embraced you, welcoming you as it did the firstborn children of this realm. You now stand at the threshold of a great destiny."

In that moment, Mira's form shimmered and shifted, growing taller and more radiant until she became a being of pure golden light. Thorne and Eldrin fell to their knees, awe-struck, as if witnessing the unfolding of a profound mystery.

"Hark, Thorne!" Mira's voice resonated with a power that seemed to tremble the very fabric of the world. "I am the heart and soul of this Golden Tree. My life intertwines with that of the forest, and now, with yours. The path before you shall be fraught with peril, for darkness encroaches upon the verdant realms. Yet, take heart, for you do not walk alone. Within you dwells the strength and wisdom of those who came before you."

As the golden light receded and Mira returned to her familiar form, Thorne felt a torrent of emotions wash over him - fear of the monumental task ahead, excitement for the adventures that awaited, and a deep sense of purpose resonating with the essence of creation itself. Whatever trials lay before him, he was prepared to confront them, armed with Eldrin's wisdom, the forest's strength, and Mira's unwavering support. In that moment, Thorne grasped that he was woven into a narrative far greater than himself, a tale that had unfolded since time began and would endure long after he became legend.

***

In the heart of the great forest stood the Golden Tree, its presence grand and resplendent. Leaves of a luminous gold shimmered in the soft glow of twilight, casting a warm light that filtered through the dense canopy above. At its base, Eldrin, the venerable guardian and wise wizard, rested his staff firmly against the earth. Beside him, Thorne, a young boy from the orphanage on the outskirts of Misty Glen, gazed up in awe, his heart filled with wonder.

"Eldrin, it is truly magnificent," Thorne breathed, the beauty of the tree overwhelming him.

"Indeed, young one," Eldrin replied, his eyes glimmering with a blend of pride and solemnity. "Yet, beauty bears a heavy burden. The time approaches for the tree to shed its seeds, and we must shield them from those who would seek to wield their power for darkness."

As if acknowledging Eldrin's words, the Golden Tree shivered, a soft hum resonating in the air, growing in strength and vibrancy. Leaves rustled, and branches swayed, as if caught in an unseen wind. Thorne watched in rapture as golden seeds, each pulsating with an inner light, began to detach from the tree, hovering delicately above.

"They're so small," Thorne said, reaching out, curiosity dancing in his eyes.

"Small, yet imbued with great power," Eldrin replied. "These seeds contain the essence of life and magic. They must be safeguarded, for they are precious."

Suddenly, a chill swept through the clearing, and a dark shadow loomed, casting a pall over the sacred space. Thorne shivered, a deep sense of foreboding gripping him. He turned to see a figure emerging from the gloom, clad in tattered leather and dark metal. His eyes, cold and predatory, seemed to drain the very light from the world around him.

"Goroth the Shadowmancer," Eldrin hissed, gripping his staff with renewed resolve.

Beside Goroth, a smaller figure slinked forward, its eyes glinting with malice. Hornbark, the goblin, cackled with delight as he surveyed the hovering seeds.

"Look, Master! The treasures of the Golden Tree, ripe for the taking!" Hornbark jeered.

Goroth's lips curled into a menacing grin. "With these seeds, we shall wield the power to reshape reality itself."

Thorne stepped forward, his heart racing. "You will not take them! We will protect the seeds!"

Goroth's gaze turned to Thorne, a sneer crossing his face. "And who is this child to defy the Shadowmancer?"

Before Thorne could respond, Eldrin raised his staff, its crystal tip glowing with radiant light. "Begone, Goroth! The seeds shall not fall into your grasp!"

Goroth laughed, a sound that chilled Thorne to the bone. "You are frail, Eldrin. Your time has passed."

With a flick of his wrist, Goroth unleashed a bolt of dark energy, hurtling it towards Eldrin. The wizard raised his staff in defense, but the force sent him staggering back. Thorne gasped, rushing to Eldrin's side as he crumpled to the ground, his staff clattering beside him.

"No!" Thorne cried, fear gripping his heart.

Eldrin's eyes, though filled with pain, shone with a flicker of hope. "Thorne, you must guard the seeds. Within you lies a power yet untapped."

"I have no power," Thorne protested, tears brimming in his eyes. "I am just a boy."

Eldrin placed a trembling hand upon Thorne's shoulder. "You are more than you realize. Believe in yourself."

As Goroth and Hornbark approached, Thorne felt an unfamiliar energy coursing through him, as though a dam had burst, releasing a tide of power. Standing tall, his eyes alight with determination, he shouted, "Stay back!"

To his astonishment, a radiant barrier sprang forth between him and the encroaching darkness. Goroth's eyes widened, and Hornbark yelped in fear.

"Impossible!" Goroth hissed. "The boy possesses magic!"

Thorne felt the energy swell within him, growing stronger with each heartbeat. Focusing on the seeds, he willed them to safety, and the barrier expanded, encasing the seeds and forcing Goroth and Hornbark back.

Mira, the spirit of the forest, appeared beside Thorne, her form shimmering with ethereal light. "Well done, Thorne," she said, her voice gentle as the breeze rustling through leaves. "Yet the battle is not yet won."

Goroth's face contorted with rage. "You may have found your power, but you cannot prevail against me!"

With a roar, Goroth unleashed a torrent of darkness, aiming to shatter the barrier. Thorne gritted his teeth, pouring all his strength into maintaining the shield. Mira joined him, her magic entwining with his to fortify their defense.

Seeing an opportunity, Hornbark darted around the barrier, desperate to seize the seeds. Mira's eyes flared with fury, and she summoned a snarl of vines to ensnare the goblin. Hornbark fought and struggled, his sharp teeth gnashing at the thick tendrils, but Mira's magic held fast.

Goroth's assaults grew more frenzied, each blow a test of Thorne's resolve. He could feel his strength waning. "I cannot hold it much longer," he gasped.

Mira placed a calming hand on his shoulder. "You are not alone, Thorne. Together, we shall protect the seeds."

With renewed vigor, Thorne and Mira merged their powers, creating a brilliant display of light and magic. The barrier blazed brighter, pushing Goroth back with every strike.

Just as it seemed victory was within reach, Goroth let out a triumphant howl. "Do you believe mere light can defeat me? I am the master of shadows!"

With a desperate effort, Goroth summoned a vast wave of darkness, crashing it against the barrier. Thorne and Mira fought to withstand the onslaught, but the force was overwhelming. The barrier shattered, throwing them both to the ground.

Goroth advanced, eyes glinting with malice. "The seeds belong to me!"

Yet, as he reached for the radiant seeds, a blinding light erupted from within them. Goroth recoiled, his hand seared by the intense heat. Thorne, struggling to rise, realized that the seeds were safeguarding themselves.

"Impossible!" Goroth howled. "What sorcery is this?"

Mira smiled, hope shining in her eyes. "The seeds are pure magic, Goroth. Your darkness cannot corrupt them."

Fury and frustration twisted Goroth's features. "This is not the end, boy. I will return, and I will claim those seeds!"

With one last furious glare, Goroth and Hornbark melted back into the shadows, leaving Thorne and Mira standing amidst the glowing seeds.

Thorne sank to his knees, exhaustion washing over him, yet relief filled his heart. Eldrin, still weak but alive, managed to sit up, pride illuminating his face. "You have done it, Thorne. You have safeguarded the seeds."

Thorne stared at his hands, still tingling with residual magic. "I never knew I had this power."

Eldrin nodded sagely. "Magic lies dormant until called upon. You have proven yourself worthy, Thorne. The Golden Tree and its seeds are secure because of you."

Mira knelt beside Thorne, her touch gentle. "A great destiny awaits you, Thorne. The forest and its magic shall ever be with you."

Thorne looked at the glowing seeds, a newfound sense of purpose igniting within him. "I will protect them, Eldrin. I vow it."

Eldrin placed a reassuring hand on Thorne's shoulder, wisdom and kindness reflecting in his gaze. "You are the guardian now, Thorne. The future of the Golden Tree rests in your hands. Yet, I fear they may return, stronger than before."

As the first light of dawn filtered through the trees, casting a golden hue over the clearing, Thorne felt a profound sense of peace. Though the battle had been won, the journey was just beginning. With Eldrin and Mira at his side, he felt prepared to face whatever trials lay ahead.

***

In the heart of the ancient forest, where the mists of Misty Glen clung to the gnarled branches and whispered secrets of old, a great battle loomed on the horizon. The Golden Tree, resplendent in its autumnal glory, stood sentinel, its leaves shimmering with an otherworldly light. At its base, Thorne, a young orphan, stood resolutely alongside Eldrin, the Enlightened One, and Mira, the ethereal spirit of the woods.

Across the clearing, emerging from the shadows like a nightmare brought to life, came Goroth, the Shadowmancer. His eyes glimmered with malevolent intent, and at his side loomed Hornbark, the goblin henchman, leading a horde of his kin. Tension hung heavy in the air, the very forest pausing in anticipation of the impending clash.

Eldrin stepped forward, his staff raised high, the crystal tip radiating a fierce light. "Goroth!" he called, his voice resonating with the authority of ages. "Turn back now, lest you bring doom upon yourself and your misguided followers!"

Goroth's laughter was harsh, akin to the sound of stone scraping against bone. "Doom, old man? The only doom here is for those who stand in my way. The power of the Golden Tree shall be mine, and with it, I shall reshape this world in my image!"

Thorne felt a chill run down his spine but steeled himself, drawing strength from Eldrin's unwavering presence and Mira's gentle touch upon his shoulder. He had journeyed far from the timid orphan he once was, and now, with the fate of the forest - and perhaps the world - hanging in the balance, he knew he could not falter.

"Remember your training, young Thorne," Eldrin murmured, his gaze fixed upon Goroth. "Trust in the magic that flows through you and in the strength of your heart."

Mira's voice flowed like the rustling of leaves in a summer breeze. "We stand with you, Thorne. The forest itself is at your side."

With a guttural roar, Hornbark signaled the attack. The horde of goblins surged forward, crude weapons glinting dully in the golden light. Eldrin raised his staff, and a barrier of shimmering energy sprang into existence, momentarily halting the goblin's advance.

"Now, Thorne!" the old wizard cried. "Show them the power you possess!"

Thorne closed his eyes, reaching deep within for the wellspring of magic Eldrin had taught him to harness. He felt it surge through him, warm and vital, and with a gesture, he unleashed a cascade of golden light toward the goblin ranks. Where it touched, the creatures shrieked and fell back, their weapons crumbling to dust in their grasp.

Mira danced among the trees, her form shifting and blurring. Wherever she passed, roots erupted from the earth, entangling the goblins and pulling them into the hungry soil. The forest itself joined the fray, ancient trees creaking and groaning as they moved to defend their domain.

Goroth snarled in frustration, dark tendrils of shadow coiling around him like living smoke. With a sweeping gesture, he sent them lashing out, cutting through Eldrin's barrier and scattering the defenders. Thorne stumbled back, momentarily overwhelmed by the sheer malevolence of Goroth's power.

"Stand firm, lad!" Eldrin called, his own magic flaring to life. Bolts of pure energy crackled from his staff, pushing back the encroaching darkness. Yet Thorne could see the strain upon the old wizard's face, the trembling of his hands as he wielded power beyond mortal comprehension.

The battle raged on, a tumult of light and shadow, primal magic clashing with corrupted power. Thorne found himself fighting back-to-back with Mira, her lithe form a blur of motion as she fended off goblin after goblin. He marveled at how his own magic responded, almost instinctively, to counter each new threat.

But despite their valor, the defenders were slowly being pushed back. Goroth's power seemed to swell with each passing moment, fed by the fear and pain of the conflict. Eldrin's spells, once mighty, began to falter, and the old wizard's breathing grew labored.

"We cannot hold them much longer!" Mira cried, desperation tinging her voice.

Thorne looked to Eldrin, seeking guidance, hoping for a secret weapon that could turn the tide. But dread filled him as he saw the old wizard's face pale, his eyes dimming as the life force that had sustained him for so long began to wane.

"Eldrin!" Thorne called, fighting his way to his mentor's side. "Hold on! We need you!"

The wizard managed a weak smile. "My time is ending, young Thorne. Yet yours - yours is just beginning. Remember all that I have taught you, and trust in the power that lies within your heart."

With trembling hands, Eldrin pressed his staff into Thorne's grasp. The moment their hands touched, Thorne felt a surge of energy, unlike anything he had ever known. It was as if all of Eldrin's knowledge, all of his power, flowed into him in a torrent of pure magic.

"No!" Goroth's voice sliced through the chaos. "The power is mine! Mine alone!"

The Shadowmancer lunged forward, dark tendrils reaching for Eldrin and Thorne. But before they could touch them, Mira interposed herself, her form shimmering with inner light. She threw herself into the path of Goroth's attack, crying out in pain as the darkness enveloped her.

"Mira!" Thorne screamed, his heart aching at the sight of his friend's sacrifice.

In that instant, something inside Thorne tore loose. The power that had been building within him, nurtured by Eldrin's teachings and strengthened by the forest's magic, erupted outward in a blinding nova of golden light. It swept over the battlefield like a tidal wave, driving back the shadows and sending the goblins fleeing in terror. Yet, amid the retreat, one creature remained, stubbornly clawing at the earth beneath the great tree, its gnarled hands tearing at the soil in a desperate grasp.

Goroth howled in rage and pain, his form wavering and distorting as the pure magic tore at his very essence. "This isn't over, boy!" he snarled.

With a final, defiant gesture, Goroth vanished in a swirl of darkness, taking the cowering Hornbark with him. The remaining goblins scattered, disappearing into the depths of the forest.

***

As the golden light waned, Thorne found himself alone in the clearing, Eldrin's staff gripped firmly in his hands. The venerable wizard lay before him, breathing shallowly, his gaze clouded and unfocused.

"Eldrin," Thorne murmured, kneeling beside his beloved mentor. "Pray, do not depart. I am not prepared for such loss."

Eldrin's hand, though feeble, sought out Thorne's, squeezing it with what little strength remained. "You are prepared, my boy. Always have you been. The power you displayed today is but a mere fraction of your true potential. Trust in yourself, as I have always trusted in you."

With a final, shuddering breath, Eldrin, the Enlightened One, closed his eyes and grew still. A profound emptiness engulfed Thorne, a void that no magic could mend. Tears cascaded down his cheeks as he held the old wizard's form, the sounds of the forest fading until only the rhythm of his own heart remained.

"Thorne." A gentle voice broke through the shroud of grief - Mira, her presence shimmering like the softest light. He lifted his gaze to her, noting her ethereal form, insubstantial and delicate. The darkness wrought by Goroth's attack had taken its toll on her as well.

"Mira," he choked, a wave of sorrow washing over him. "Forgive me. I could save neither of you."

Mira smiled, a warm and understanding light in her expression. "You saved us all, Thorne. The forest, the Golden Tree, the very balance of nature itself. Eldrin and I knew the price we would pay. Our choices were made freely, out of love for this world and unwavering faith in you."

Rising to his feet, Thorne grasped Eldrin's staff - now his own. "What must I do now? How can I be the Guardian when I have lost so much?"

Mira's form shimmered as she began to merge with the mists swirling about them. "The Golden Tree will wither, Thorne. It is the way of all things - the cycle of life and death that governs all. Yet from its seeds, new life shall emerge. You must nurture these seedlings with your magic and your love. One will rise to take its place, and thus the cycle shall begin anew."

She gestured toward the Golden Tree, which Thorne saw indeed was beginning to fade, its luminous leaves dimming. Yet, even as he gazed, a cascade of seeds drifted down, each glowing with potential.

"But how shall I know which to choose?" Thorne asked, feeling smaller than ever.

Mira's voice began to blend with the soft whispers of the wind through the leaves. "Trust in your heart, Thorne. The magic within you shall guide your way. Eldrin and I shall watch over you. Though we may no longer tread this earth, our spirits shall remain, forever entwined with the forest you now guard."

As Mira's form dissolved entirely, Thorne felt a warmth envelop him, as if the very essence of the forest embraced him. He closed his eyes, inhaling the rich, earthy scents that surrounded him. When he opened them once more, he saw the world anew, perceiving the intricate web of life and magic binding all things together.

With a heavy heart yet a spirit resolute, Thorne began to gather the fallen seeds of the Golden Tree. Each seed pulsed with vitality, a tiny heartbeat of magic resonating with his own. He understood that the journey ahead would be long and fraught with challenges he could scarcely imagine, yet he knew he was not truly alone.

As the sun dipped beneath the horizon, casting the sky in hues of gold and crimson, Thorne gazed up at the branches of the Golden Tree. For a fleeting moment, he believed he saw two figures standing among the leaves - Eldrin, his eyes sparkling with pride, and Mira, her smile as radiant as ever. They nodded once, then faded away, leaving behind a sense of peace and purpose.

Thorne squared his shoulders, feeling the mantle of responsibility settle upon him. He was no longer the orphan from Misty Glen, nor merely Eldrin's apprentice. He was now the Guardian of the Golden Tree, protector of the forest, and keeper of its ancient magics.

With Eldrin's staff in one hand and a pouch of golden seeds in the other, Thorne ventured into the heart of the forest. The path ahead was uncertain, yet he walked with newfound confidence, knowing each step drew him closer to fulfilling his destiny.

As night enveloped the world and the first stars began to twinkle, Thorne discovered a small clearing that seemed to call to him. Here, he realized, he would plant the first of the Golden Tree's seeds. Kneeling to prepare the soil, he heard Mira's voice one final time, carried gently on the evening breeze:

"Remember, Thorne, that true strength lies not merely in power, but in the wisdom to wield it wisely. The forest has chosen you, and in doing so, it has chosen hope. Nurture that hope, allowing it to grow within you as these seeds will flourish into mighty trees. For in the darkest hours, it is hope that will illuminate the way forward."

A smile broke through Thorne's sorrow, a sense of peace settling over him. He may have lost his mentor and his friend, yet their legacy lived on within him and the magic coursing through his veins. As he planted the first seed, murmuring words of encouragement and protection, he recognized that this marked the beginning of a new chapter - not just for himself, but for the entire forest and all its inhabitants.

Thus, beneath the watchful eyes of the stars and the spirits of those who had come before, Thorne commenced his vigil as the new Guardian of the Golden Tree. The forest around him seemed to sigh in contentment, assured that it rested in capable hands. The cycle of life, death, and rebirth would continue, and with it, the promise of a brighter future for all.

***

Deep within the shadowy recesses of the caverns, concealed in the very heart of the mountains, a malevolent darkness writhed and churned. Hornback, his visage contorted with a cruel glee, dragged the trembling goblin before Goroth, the Shadowmancer. The dark master's eyes, aglow with a sinister light, pierced through the wretched creature, promising untold horrors to come.

"Reveal it," Hornback growled, shoving the goblin forward with a harsh push.

With trembling, gnarled fingers, the goblin slowly unfurled its hand, exposing a single, radiant seed from the Golden Tree. The light it emitted was a strange beacon amidst the oppressive gloom.

A chilling laughter erupted from Goroth, echoing through the cavern and freezing the very marrow of those who dared to listen. He snatched the seed with a skeletal hand, and as his fingers brushed its golden surface, the light was snuffed out, consumed by an inky blackness that seemed to devour all life's essence.

"At last!" Goroth's voice, rich with malevolent triumph, resounded throughout the chamber. "I shall plant this seed, and from it shall arise a tree of darkness that will overshadow all others. Its roots shall weave through the earth, spreading corruption; its branches will eclipse the sun, shrouding the world in eternal night; and its fruit will be a poison, tainting the land and all who dwell upon it. All that is cherished shall fall before me! The age of shadow begins now! "

As Goroth's proclamation filled the air, the shadows thickened, and a crushing weight settled upon the land, heralding the dawn of an era steeped in darkness and despair.

The Human Touch

Edgar and Mildred sat quietly on their balcony, watching the city stretch out before them. The glass towers caught the late afternoon light, their reflections casting long lines across the streets below. Hovercars passed in steady streams, trails of light tracing their paths through the busy airways. Robotic assistants moved seamlessly among the crowds, their movements smooth and calculated. The city, gleaming and orderly, stood as a vision of progress, its achievements hailed in the brochures they had read so many times before. Yet, as they looked out, the distance between that promise and the life they felt seemed to grow.

Edgar let out a sigh, a sarcastic smile creeping onto his worn face. "Well, Millie, here we are in our crystal prison," he said, gesturing toward the endless stretch of city beyond them. His voice carried a resigned amusement, as though the gleaming structures surrounding them were some grand, ironic joke.

Mildred chuckled, her laughter a soft, comforting sound. "You always know how to put things, Ed. But you have to admit, it's a beautiful prison."

"Beautiful, yes. But it lacks a certain - humanity." Edgar leaned back in his chair, the synthetic cushions adjusting to support his frail frame. "Remember when cities had character? When you could walk down the street and actually talk to people instead of these damn robots?"

Mildred's gaze drifted, distant and unfocused. "I remember. There was noise, chaos, life everywhere. Now, it all feels so - sterile."

"Sterile is right," Edgar grunted. "I mean, look at that!" He pointed to a nearby building, its surface a perfect mirror. "It's like the whole city's trying to pretend it's something it's not. Just like those emotion-simulating pills everyone's popping. Artificial happiness in a bottle."

Mildred sighed. "It's a different world now, Ed. Sometimes I miss the unpredictability of it all. You never knew what was going to happen next."

"Like the time we met," Edgar said, a rare smile breaking through. "Remember that? 2267, wasn't it? A protest turned into a block party. You threw a shoe at a police drone."

Mildred laughed, her eyes lighting up. "I thought it was spying on us! Turns out it was just monitoring traffic."

"Those were the days," Edgar said, shaking his head. "Everything was simpler, more chaotic. People actually interacted with each other."

Mildred's smile faded slightly. "Do you think we did the right thing, Ed? Embracing all this technology?"

Edgar looked thoughtful. "I don't know, Millie. We live longer, we have more conveniences, but at what cost? Our children are scattered across the sectors, too busy with their tech-driven lives to visit us. We rely on robots for companionship. Hell, our butler's the closest thing we've got to a friend these days."

Jeeves, the robotic butler glided onto the balcony, its polished surface catching the sunlight. "Would you like some refreshments, Mr. Edgar, Mrs. Mildred?" it inquired, its voice smooth and composed.

"Scotch, neat," Edgar grumbled.

"Cosmic crush, please," Mildred said with a polite nod.

The robot whirred away, leaving the couple in silence.

"Cosmic crush? Living dangerously tonight, my love?" Edgar remarked.

Mildred winked at him. "Always. "

Edgar smiled, then looked out over the city again, his expression softening. "You know, sometimes I wonder if this progress is worth it. We've got everything we ever wanted, and yet- "

"- and yet we still feel empty," Mildred finished for him.

"Yeah. But at least we've got each other." Edgar reached for her hand, holding it gently. "You're ice cold, my dear. We can have Jeeves bring you a sweater."

"No. I'm fine. I have you to keep me warm."

They sat quietly, the sun slipping below the horizon, painting the city in shades of orange and pink. The lights of the towers blinked on, and the hum of the city moved forward without pause.

"Do you remember the blackout of '78?" Mildred asked suddenly. "The whole city plunged into darkness, and people came out of their apartments, talking, sharing whatever they had. It was like the old days, for a moment."

Edgar laughed. "Yeah, I remember. I think that was the last time I felt like we were part of a community. After the power came back, everyone just went back to their screens and robots."

Mildred looked away. "I miss those times, Ed. I miss the human touch."

"Me too, Millie. Me too." Edgar looked down at their joined hands, then back out at the city. "You know, I read somewhere that they're refining robots that can simulate human emotions perfectly. Imagine that, robots pretending to be human so we don't feel so lonely."

Mildred shook her head. "It sounds so - sad. We've come so far, and yet we're still trying to fill the same void."

The robotic butler returned with their drinks, placing them carefully on the table. "Your refreshments, Mr. Edgar, Mrs. Mildred."

"Thank you, Jeeves," Edgar said, raising his glass to Mildred. "To progress."

"To progress," Mildred repeated, gently clinking her glass against his.

They sipped their drinks in silence, the city lights reflecting in their eyes. Despite the advancements, the conveniences, and the marvels of modern technology, there was something timeless about their bond, something that no amount of progress could replicate or replace.

"You know, Millie," Edgar said after a long pause, "I've been thinking. Maybe we should take a trip. Get out of the city for a while. See some real nature, feel the earth under our feet."

Mildred's eyes sparkled with excitement. "Do you think we can? At our age?"

"Why not? We've got the time, and I'm sure Jeeves can handle things here."

The robot, ever attentive, responded, "I would be delighted to manage your affairs in your absence, Mr. Edgar."

Edgar laughed softly, the corners of his eyes crinkling with amusement. "See? Even Jeeves thinks it's a good idea."

Mildred smiled, a sense of adventure kindling in her heart. "All right, Ed. Let's do it. Let's go on an adventure, just like the old days."

Edgar raised his glass again. "To adventures, then."

"To adventures," Mildred agreed, her voice filled with renewed hope. "To adventures- to adventures- to adventures- "

Edgar's frustration with countless malfunctions seeped through his words. "Goddammit. Jeeves! She's skipping again."

"To adventures- to adventures- to adventures- "

As Mildred's voice looped, Jeeves glided across the room. With a precise tap to her cranial casing, he reset her vocal subroutines.

Mildred's eyes whirled, recalibrating. "Ah, that's better," she said, her smile reconfiguring. "Where were we?"

"Adventures," Edgar reminded her, his voice tinged with a blend of affection and resignation.

"Oh, yes. Adventures."

They sat together, an aging man and his companion, planning their escape from the technological marvel that was their city. The future suddenly seemed a little brighter, a little more human. And in that moment, Edgar felt truly alive, ready to embrace whatever came next, his hand resting on Mildred's cool synthetic one.

As night deepened, the city hummed with its artificial life. But on that balcony, a human heart beat alongside a mechanical one, finding an unlikely harmony. Two hearts beating with a timeless rhythm, finding comfort and strength in each other, proving that no matter how advanced the world became, some things would always remain beautifully, irreducibly human.

A Harvest of Dreams

Somnium was a city that never truly slept, even as its inhabitants dreamed. It rose from the ground like a metallic forest, its skyscrapers piercing the perpetually smog-raked sky, their windows glowing with an eerie blue light that pulsed in rhythm with the city's heartbeat. The streets below were a maze of neon and shadow, where hover-cars zipped between towering structures and holographic advertisements flickered in and out of existence, hawking the latest in dream-enhancing technology.

At the center of it all stood the Dream Spire, a colossal structure that dwarfed all others, its tip lost in the clouds above. It was here that the dreams of Somnium's citizens were harvested, processed, and transformed into the lifeblood of the city – pure, unadulterated energy.

Luna Rivera stood at her bedroom window, her dark eyes reflecting the pulsing lights of the city beyond. At sixteen, she was old enough to understand the importance of dreams in Somnium, but young enough to still question the world around her. She pressed her palm against the cool glass, feeling the faint vibration of the city's energy coursing through it.

"Luna!" her father's voice called from downstairs. "It's almost time for bed. Don't forget your dream cap!"

Luna sighed, turning away from the window. The dream cap sat on her nightstand, its sleek design belying its true purpose. She picked it up, running her fingers over the smooth surface. It was cool to the touch, almost uncomfortably so.

As she settled into bed, Luna placed the cap on her head, feeling the familiar tingling sensation as it connected with her neural pathways. The soft hum of the device filled her ears, drowning out the distant sounds of the city.

"Sweet dreams, honey," her father said, poking his head into her room. Marcus Rivera's kind reflected a weariness that seemed to afflict all adults in Somnium these days. "Remember, dream big. It's good for the city."

Luna nodded, forcing a smile. "Night, Dad."

As the lights dimmed automatically, Luna closed her eyes, willing herself to sleep. But sleep, as always, was elusive. Her mind wandered, thinking about the dream harvesting process she'd learned about in school.

Every citizen of Somnium wore a dream cap to bed. As they slept, the cap would monitor their brain activity, capturing the electrical impulses generated during REM sleep. These impulses were then transmitted to the Dream Spire, where they were collected, amplified, and converted into energy. This energy powered everything in Somnium, from the simplest household appliances to the massive factories that churned out more dream tech.

It was a perfect system, or so they were told. Dreams, endlessly renewed with every night's sleep, provided an inexhaustible supply. Somnium, by harnessing this energy, had overcome its scarcity issues, emerging as a leader in technological innovation in a world grappling with depletion.

But lately, there had been whispers. Rumors of people waking up feeling drained, their memories fuzzy, their emotions muted. Some spoke of a rising tide of mental instability sweeping through the city, hidden behind closed doors and masked smiles.

Luna had noticed it in her own father. Marcus, once full of laughter and stories, had grown quieter over the years. His eyes, once bright with imagination, now seemed dulled, as if the very essence of his being was slowly being leeched away.

As these thoughts swirled in her mind, Luna felt herself drifting off, the dream cap's hum fading into the background as sleep finally claimed her.

And then, something strange happened.

Luna found herself standing in a vast, empty space. It was neither dark nor light, neither warm nor cold. It simply - was. She looked down at her hands, surprised to find that she could see them clearly, despite the absence of any visible light source.

"Hello?" she called out, her voice ringing through the void.

Suddenly, the space around her began to shift and change. Colors swirled into existence, forming shapes and patterns that into a familiar scene. Luna gasped as she recognized her own bedroom, but not as it was. This was her room from years ago when she was a little girl.

A younger version of herself sat on the bed, clutching a stuffed rabbit. Little Luna was crying, her face buried in the rabbit's soft fur.

"It's okay," Luna found herself saying, approaching her younger self. "What's wrong?"

To her surprise, Little Luna looked up, her tear-stained face registering shock at seeing her older self. "You - you can see me?" the child asked, her voice trembling.

Luna knelt beside the bed. "Of course I can. This is a dream, isn't it?"

Little Luna shook her head vigorously. "No, no, it's not a dream. It's a memory. My memory. But it's fading, and I can't hold onto it anymore."

As if to emphasize her point, the edges of the room began to blur, colors running together like wet paint. Luna felt a surge of panic. "What do you mean, fading?"

Little Luna held out the stuffed rabbit. "Take Mr. Flopsy. If you have him, maybe the memory won't disappear completely."

Without thinking, Luna reached out and took it. As soon as her fingers closed around it, the room dissolved into a whirlwind of color and light. Luna felt herself being pulled away, the stuffed rabbit clutched tightly to her chest.

She woke with a start, sitting bolt upright in bed. The dream cap fell off her head, clattering to the floor. Luna's heart was racing, her breath coming in short gasps. It had felt so real, so vivid. She could still feel the soft fur of the stuffed rabbit in her hands.

Luna glanced down, anticipating the familiar presence of Mr. Flopsy in her grasp. Instead, a small, delicate clump of soft, white fur lay nestled in her palm.

Rising, she moved toward the closet. On a shelf, untouched for what felt like ages, sat Mr. Flopsy - the once-beloved doll. She carefully lifted it, turning it over in her hands, her eyes catching on the patch where its fur had been ripped away. A chill coursed through her at the sight.

"Impossible," she whispered, staring at the fur in disbelief.

The sound of hurried footsteps in the hallway snapped Luna out of her shock. Her bedroom door burst open, and Marcus rushed in, his face pale with worry.

"Luna! Are you alright? The house systems alerted me to a spike in your heart rate and- " He stopped short, noticing the dream cap on the floor and the wild look in his daughter's eyes. "What happened?"

Luna opened her mouth to explain, but the words caught in her throat. How could she describe what she'd experienced? It was more than a dream, more than a simple flight of fancy. It felt like she had touched something fundamental, something that shouldn't be possible.

"I had a strange dream," she murmured at last, choosing to hold back the specifics for now. "It felt so real."

Her father's expression shifted, marked by a quiet worry. He settled beside her on the bed, his hand resting gently on her shoulder. "It's alright, sweetheart. Vivid dreams come to everyone from time to time. It's all part of the journey."

Luna nodded, not trusting herself to speak further. She discreetly slipped the tuft of fur under her pillow, out of sight.

He picked up the fallen dream cap, turning it over in his hands. "The cap seems to be functioning normally. Must've just slipped off when you woke up." He placed it back on the nightstand. "Try to get some more sleep, okay? You have school tomorrow."

As he stood to leave, Luna caught his arm. "Dad? Do you - do you ever feel different after dreaming? Like something's missing?"

A shadow passed over her father's face, there and gone so quickly Luna almost thought she'd imagined it. "Of course not, honey. Dreams are natural. The harvesting process is completely safe. You know that. Now get some sleep. I have to go in to work for a bit."

But there was something in his voice, a slight tremor that betrayed his words. Luna realized that this was the first time she'd ever heard her father lie to her.

After he left, closing the door softly behind him, Luna retrieved the tuft of fur from under her pillow. She examined it closely in the dim light filtering through her window. It was real, tangible proof that something extraordinary had happened.

Luna's mind raced with questions. How had she brought something back from a dream? Was it really a dream, or something else entirely? And if she could do this, could she do more?

The rest of the night passed in a blur of fitful sleep and half-formed dreams. Luna kept the dream cap off, too afraid of what might happen if she put it back on. When morning finally came, she felt groggy and disoriented, but also filled with a strange sense of excitement.

As she got ready for school, Luna couldn't shake the feeling that everything had changed. The city outside her window looked the same as always, but now she saw it with new eyes. The pulsing lights of the buildings, once a comforting rhythm, now seemed ominous. The Dream Spire, towering in the distance, was no longer a symbol of progress, but a question mark on the skyline.

At breakfast, her father seemed distracted, his movements mechanical as he prepared their meal. Luna watched him closely, noticing the dark circles under his eyes, the slight tremor in his hands as he poured his coffee.

"Dad," she said carefully, "are you feeling okay?"

Marcus looked up, startled, as if he'd forgotten she was there. "What? Oh, yes, I'm fine. Just a bit tired. Busy night at the facility."

Luna nodded, not pressing further. She knew her father worked at one of the dream processing plants, but he rarely talked about his job. Now, she wondered what exactly went on in those facilities. What happened to the dreams after they were harvested?

As Luna headed off to school, a quiet resolve settled within her. She needed answers about dream harvesting, about the strange events affecting the people of Somnium. Her search for the truth would begin with unraveling the mystery of what had happened to her the previous night.

The streets of Somnium were busy as always, a sea of people moving with purpose, their eyes glazed and distant. Luna weaved through the crowd, her mind whirling with possibilities. She was so lost in thought that she almost didn't notice when someone fell into step beside her.

"Rough night?" a gruff voice asked.

Luna looked up, startled to see Inspector Tobias Black walking next to her. The inspector was a familiar sight around their neighborhood, his imposing figure and perpetual scowl a constant reminder of the city's ever-watchful eye.

"Oh, um, good morning, Inspector Black," Luna stammered. "I'm fine, thank you."

Black's eyes narrowed, studying her face. "You look tired. Not sleeping well?"

There was something in his tone, a hint of suspicion that made Luna's heart race. "Just stayed up too late studying," she lied, forcing a smile.

Black grunted, seemingly satisfied with her answer. "Make sure you get enough rest. Can't have the youth of Somnium burning out, can we? Dreams are a precious resource, after all."

With that, he peeled off, disappearing into the crowd. Luna let out a breath she didn't realize she'd been holding. Something about the encounter left her feeling uneasy.

As she continued her walk to school, Luna's gaze was drawn once again to the Dream Spire. From this angle, she could see the constant flow of energy pulsing up its length, a river of stolen dreams powering the city.

A chill came over her as a thought occurred to her. If dreams were so vital to Somnium's survival, what would happen if people stopped dreaming? Or worse, what if someone could somehow interfere with the harvesting process?

Luna quickened her step, her thoughts racing with the revelations from the previous night. She had brushed against something more than a dream - something real, something remembered - and carried a fragment of it into the daylight. What else might be within her grasp?

Nearing the massive structure of glass and steel that was her school, she quietly resolved to gain control over this strange ability, whatever it might be. Only then would she begin to uncover the mystery of the dream harvesters, determined to pursue the truth, no matter the consequences.

The city of Somnium pulsed around her, oblivious to the small revolution brewing in the heart of one of its youngest citizens. But as Luna stepped through the school's doors, she couldn't shake the feeling that everything was about to change.

In the distance, the Dream Spire continued its relentless harvest, drawing in the hopes, fears, and fantasies of millions. But for the first time in its history, suddenly there was a dreamer it couldn't touch, a mind beyond its reach.

Luna Rivera, the girl who could walk in dreams, had awakened. And Somnium would never be the same again.

***

Luna watched her father from the corner of her eye as he shuffled about the kitchen, his movements slow and deliberate as if each action required immense concentration. He reached for a mug, his hand shaking ever so slightly, and poured coffee with painstaking care.

"Dad?" Luna's voice was soft, hesitant. "Are you feeling okay?"

Marcus Rivera turned to his daughter, a wan smile stretching across his tired face. "I'm fine, honey. Just a little tired, that's all."

But Luna knew better. She'd seen the signs growing more pronounced over the past few weeks – the forgetfulness, the mood swings, the vacant stares into nothingness. It was as if pieces of her father were slowly being chipped away, leaving behind a hollow shell of the man she knew.

"Maybe you should take a day off," she suggested, trying to keep the worry from her voice. "Rest a bit. You work too hard."

Marcus shook his head, his eyes regaining some of their usual warmth. "No, no. Can't do that. The city needs its power, and we all have to do our part." He ruffled Luna's hair affectionately. "Don't worry about your old man. I'll be right as rain in no time."

As he turned away, Luna caught a flicker of something in his eyes – fear, perhaps? Or was it resignation? Before she could ponder it further, Marcus was heading for the door, his lunch pail in hand.

"I'll see you tonight, Luna. Be good, okay?"

The door closed behind him with a soft click, leaving Luna alone in the suddenly too-quiet apartment. She stood there for a moment, listening to the fading sound of her father's footsteps in the hallway. Then, with a determined set to her jaw, she grabbed her jacket and followed.

The streets of Somnium were a whirlwind of sights and sounds, starkly different from the quiet calm of their apartment. Luna kept to the shadows, her dark hair and slight frame allowing her to merge seamlessly with the crowd as she followed her father through the winding streets.

The city itself seemed to pulse with an otherworldly energy, neon signs flickering like fevered dreams against the perpetually twilight sky. Luna had always found it beautiful in a haunting sort of way, but now she couldn't shake the feeling that something sinister lurked beneath the glittering surface.

As they neared the industrial sector, the crowds thinned, replaced by towering structures of glass and steel. Luna's heart raced as she caught sight of it – a Dream Harvesting Facility, a behemoth of a building that seemed to swallow the light around it.

She watched as her father approached a side entrance, swiping his ID badge and disappearing inside. Luna hesitated, her courage faltering for a moment. What she was about to do was illegal, dangerous even. But the memory of her father's trembling hands steeled her resolve.

With a deep breath, she crept towards the building, searching for a way in. It was then that she noticed a service entrance, propped open by a worker taking a smoke break. Luna waited, her heart pounding in her ears, until the worker stubbed out his cigarette and headed back inside. Before the door could swing shut, she darted forward, holding onto the door and then quickly slipping into the facility unnoticed.

The interior of the building was a maze of sterile white corridors and humming machinery. Luna moved cautiously, every sense heightened as she navigated the unfamiliar terrain, making sure to remain unnoticed. The air seemed to thrum with a hidden energy, causing the hairs on the back of her neck to stand on end.

As she rounded a corner, she froze. Through a large observation window, she saw a sight that would be forever etched into her memory.

The chamber stretched on, a cathedral of slumber. Rows of reclining figures filled the room, each enveloped by a strange, softly glowing blue sphere. From these orbs, tubes and wires wound their way toward a central tower, a towering structure humming with a quiet, pervasive energy. The sleepers lay entwined in this intricate network, a silent assembly bound by forces beyond their control.

Luna's chest tightened at the sight before her. This was the place where dreams were extracted, where these individuals were locked in perpetual slumber, their essence drawn away to fuel the city's life.

She asked herself – why the dream caps?

Pressing closer to the glass, her eyes wide with a mixture of fascination and horror. It was then that she spotted her father, moving between the rows of sleepers, checking readouts and adjusting dials.

As Luna watched, her father approached one of the sleeping figures – a young woman with fiery red hair. He hesitated for a moment, his hand hovering over the control panel. Then, with a resigned sigh, he pressed a series of buttons.

The dome above the woman shone with an intense light, her body rising from the chair, her face twisting as if seized by some deep sensation. Luna, startled, pressed her hand to her mouth to keep from crying out.

Her father noticed anyway. His head snapped upward, his gaze meeting hers through the glass. In that instant, everything around them fell away - father and daughter, caught in the sudden grip of realization.

Then, everything happened at once.

Her father rushed to the door, his face twisted with panic. "Luna! What are you doing here? You can't be here!"

She stumbled backward, her mind spinning from what she'd seen. But as she moved, something strange happened. The world around her seemed to shimmer, reality bending like a reflection in a funhouse mirror.

And suddenly, she wasn't in the facility anymore. She was - somewhere else.

Luna found herself standing in a sun-drenched meadow, wildflowers swaying gently in a warm breeze. The sky above was an impossible shade of blue, dotted with clouds that seemed to form and reform into fantastic shapes.

"What - where am I?" she whispered, her voice sounding oddly distant to her own ears.

"You're in my dream," a soft voice answered.

Luna turned to see the red-haired woman from the facility standing behind her. The woman appeared far more vibrant and full of life than she had in the chamber.

"Your dream?" Luna asked, a look of bewilderment crossing her face.

The woman nodded, a sad smile playing at her lips. "Yes. Though it won't be mine for much longer. They're taking it, you see. Bit by bit, dream by dream, until there's nothing left but an empty shell."

Luna was trying to make sense of what was happening. "But how am I here? How are we talking?"

The woman's smile widened, a spark of curiosity lighting her eyes. "Now that is interesting. You're not supposed to be here, are you? You're not one of them."

Before Luna could respond, the dream world around them flickered, like a television with bad reception. The woman's face writhed in pain.

"They're taking more from me," she gasped. "Please, if you can hear me in the waking world, tell them to stop. Tell them we can't take much more of this."

Luna reached out, wanting to help, to comfort, but her hand passed right through the woman's arm. "I - I don't know how to stop it," she admitted, feeling helpless.

The woman's form began to fade, her voice growing fainter. "Wake us up. Wake us all up before it's too late."

With a jolt, Luna was thrust back into the facility, stumbling against the observation window. Below, the sleepers were stirring, coming to life, and ripping away the wires and tubes that had bound them. Just then, her father's hand clamped around her arm, his face a turbulent blend of fear and anger.

"Luna, what have you done?" he hissed, pulling her away from the window.

But Luna's attention was fixed on the red-haired woman in the chair. To her horror, she saw that the woman's eyes were open, darting around in panic.

"Dad, stop it!" Luna cried, wrenching her arm free. "You're hurting her!"

He looked torn, his gaze darting between his daughter and the now-awake dreamer. "I - I can't, Luna. This is my job. This is how we keep the city running."

"But at what cost?" Luna demanded, her voice rising. "Look at what it's doing to people. Look at what it's doing to you!"

As if to punctuate her words, alarms began to blare throughout the facility. Red lights flashed, and the hum of machinery rose to a fevered pitch.

"Warning: Dream sequence interrupted. Harvesting process compromised," an automated voice announced over the loudspeakers.

Chaos erupted in the harvesting room as more and more dreamers began to stir, their cries of confusion and fear audible even through the thick glass.

Her father's face paled. "Oh god, what have you done?"

Luna grabbed her father's hand, tugging him towards the exit. "We need to get out of here, Dad. Now."

As they ran through the corridors, dodging panicked workers and malfunctioning equipment, Luna's mind raced. She had done this. Somehow, she had entered that woman's dream and woken her up. And in doing so, she had caused a chain reaction that threatened to bring the entire system crashing down.

They burst out into the street, the cool air a shock after the stifling atmosphere of the facility. Behind them, the Dream Harvesting Facility loomed, its windows now dark, the usual hum of power noticeably absent.

Luna turned to her father, seeing the fear and uncertainty in his eyes. "Dad, I'm sorry. I didn't mean to - I just wanted to understand."

Her father pulled her close, his arms encircling her with a tremor that seemed to come from deep within. "Oh, sweetheart," he said, his voice a mix of regret and revelation. "I'm the one who should be apologizing. I've been walking around with my eyes shut tight, not seeing what's been right in front of me. Not seeing what I've been a part of all this time."

Luna leaned back, just enough to look up at him. "Those people," she said. "Are they – "

Her father's eyes, usually so certain, now held a sadness she'd never seen before. "Dreamers," he said. "People of our city who lost a kind of terrible lottery. They give their lives - their dreams - to keep everything running during the day."

"That - " Luna started, but the word 'horrible' felt inadequate, far too simple to encompass the enormity of what she had witnessed.

As they stood there, holding each other in the shadow of the silent facility, Luna knew that everything had changed. The city around them flickered and dimmed, the constant flow of dream-energy now disrupted.

But amidst the darkness, Luna felt a glimmer of hope. She had woken one dreamer. Perhaps, with time and understanding of her newfound abilities, she could wake them all.

"What do we do now?" she asked.

Her father took a deep breath, squaring his shoulders. "We hide away. They'll be coming for us."

She knew why.

As they turned to face the city, now cloaked in an eerie twilight, Luna sensed the burden of responsibility settling onto her shoulders. She had initiated this, albeit unwittingly, and now it was up to her to follow it to its conclusion.

The woman dreamer had awakened something in her – an ability she didn't yet understand.

Luna took her father's hand, squeezing it tightly. "But where will we go?"

"I have an idea," he told her, and together they stepped into the encroaching darkness of the city.

***

The city of Somnium stretched above them like a great inverted mountain, its towers disappearing into the hazy darkness overhead. Luna and her father moved through the lower levels, their footsteps echoing in the cavernous spaces between buildings. The air grew thicker as they descended, heavy with the scent of damp stone and something else - something electric and alive.

Luna's hand found her father's in the dimness. "Dad," she whispered, "where are we going?"

He squeezed her fingers gently. "Somewhere safe," his voice low and reassuring. "Somewhere we can figure this out."

They passed through a series of narrow alleys, each one darker and more constricted than the last. Luna felt the walls pressing in on either side, heard the distant hum of machinery growing fainter with each step. She thought of the dream harvesting facility they'd left behind, its banks of gleaming pods now silent and dark. The memory of what she'd seen there - of what she'd done - made her shiver.

"Are you cold?" her father asked, glancing back at her.

Luna shook her head. "No, I'm just - thinking."

Her father's face softened with understanding. "I know, sweetheart. It's a lot to take in."

They emerged into a wide tunnel, its ceiling lost in shadow. Luna could hear the faint drip of water somewhere in the distance. "How much further?" she asked.

"Not far now," he replied. He paused, studying the featureless walls around them. "It should be - ah, here we are."

He led her to what looked like a blank section of wall, running his hand along its surface until he found what he was looking for. There was a soft click, and a portion of the wall swung inward, revealing a dark passageway beyond.

Luna hesitated. "Dad, how do you know about this place?"

He sighed, his shoulders sagging slightly. "Someone told me. Someone I trust. He's been helping people - people like us. "People running from the dream harvesters."

"People with an ability like mine?" she asked.

"Yes," he said. "A similar gift that your mother had."

"Mommy," Luna breathed.

"She lost the lottery," he explained, his voice low and weary. "They wanted to take her away, put her to sleep forever, to steal her dreams. Like those you saw. She didn't want that, so she ran away. She found Henk, a friend who helped her hide."

Luna's heart tightened with an ache she struggled to comprehend. "But Mommy missed me," she whispered. "She came back to see me, didn't she? But they caught her."

His voice cracked with exhaustion. "I tried to find her, Luna, working at the Dream Harvesting Facilities. Going from one to the next, hoping to catch a glimpse. But I never did."

"But the dream caps we wear at night?" she asked.

"Those are just fleeting dreams," he replied. "They don't generate enough energy to truly sustain the city. You and your mother - along with a select few - possess something unique. Your dreams are more vivid, and the energy they hold is far greater."

Luna's tears fell softly as she grasped her father's hand, his warmth providing a momentary escape from the harshness that enveloped them. She had always sensed her difference, but today brought a realization that cut deeper than she had anticipated.

"Come now. We've no time to waste," he urged her.

They moved through the hidden passage, the air growing cooler and damper. Luna could hear faint voices ahead, a low murmur of conversation that grew louder as they approached. Finally, they came to a heavy metal door. Her father raised his hand to knock, then hesitated.

"Luna," he said softly, turning to face her. "Whatever happens, know that I love you. I will always protect you."

She nodded, her throat tight with emotion. Her father knocked three times, paused, then knocked twice more.

There was a long moment of silence, then the scrape of metal on metal. The door swung open, revealing a tall, slender man with graying hair and kind eyes.

"Marcus," the man said, his voice warm with relief. "I was beginning to worry."

"Henk," Marcus replied, clasping the other man's hand. "Thank you for this."

Henk's gaze shifted to Luna, and his eyes widened slightly. "Is this- ?"

Marcus nodded. "My daughter, Luna."

Henk stepped back, gesturing for them to enter. "Quickly, come inside. We have much to discuss."

The room beyond was larger than Luna had expected, its walls lined with mismatched furniture and shelves overflowing with books and strange devices. A dozen or so people milled about, their conversations falling silent as Luna and her father entered.

Henk closed the door behind them, engaging a series of heavy locks. "Now then," he said, turning to face them. "Tell me everything."

Marcus took a deep breath. "It's happened, Henk. Just like we always feared it might. One of the facilities went dark."

Henk's expression grew grave. "Which one?"

"Mine," Marcus replied, "where I work,"

"Where I was," Luna finished quietly.

Henk's gaze snapped to her, his eyes narrowing. "You were there?"

Luna nodded. "I snuck in. I - I did something. To a dreamer."

A murmur ran through the room. Henk held up a hand for silence. "Start from the beginning," he said. "Leave nothing out."

Over the next hour, Luna and her father recounted the events of the past day – why she followed her father to work, how concerned she had become over his tiredness and mood swings, how she made her way into the facility, saw what was happening, and finally, the moment when she'd somehow reached out and touched the dreams of those in the harvesting pods, setting off a chain reaction that had shut down the entire facility.

As they spoke, Henk's expression cycled through disbelief, wonder, and finally, a grim determination. When they finished, he paced the room for several long moments before speaking.

"This changes everything," he said at last. "Luna, what you can do - it's extraordinary. It's what we've been waiting for."

Luna shifted uncomfortably. "What do you mean?"

Henk exchanged a look with her father. "There have always been whispers," he explained. "Rumors of someone who could manipulate dreams, who could free the dreamers and bring down the whole system. We never truly believed it was possible, but now- "

"Now we have hope," her father finished.

Luna felt the weight of their expectations settling on her shoulders. "But I don't even know how I did it," she protested. "It just - happened."

Henk nodded. "Of course. You'll need training, guidance. But first, we need to get you somewhere safe. Both of you."

He led them deeper into the underground complex, through a maze of tunnels and chambers. As they walked, Luna caught glimpses of other rooms - makeshift dormitories, kitchens, even what looked like a small medical bay. And everywhere, there were people. Dozens, maybe hundreds of them, all ages and backgrounds, but with the same haunted look in their eyes.

"Are these all- " Luna began.

"- Dreamkeepers," Henk confirmed. "People who fled before their time in the dream harvesters. Some have been here for years."

They came to a small, private room with two cots and a table. "You can rest here for now," Henk said. "We'll bring you some food and clean clothes."

As Luna sank onto one of the cots, exhaustion finally catching up with her, Henk pulled Marcus aside. Their voices were low, but in the quiet of the underground, Luna could still make out their words.

"There's something else you should know," Henk was saying. "An investigator has been sniffing around. Getting too close."

Marcus tensed. "Who?"

"Tobias Black," Henk replied. "He's tenacious, Marcus. And if he's figured out what happened at the facility - "

"He'll be looking for Luna," Marcus finished, his voice tight with worry.

Henk nodded. "We need to move quickly. Get her somewhere even he can't find her."

"But where?"

"There's a place," Henk said hesitantly. "Deep in the old city. It's dangerous, but it might be our only option."

Marcus was quiet for a long moment. "Whatever it takes," he said at last. "To keep her safe."

As their conversation continued in hushed tones, Luna closed her eyes, trying to process the whirlwind of events. She thought of the dreamers she'd seen in the harvesting pods, of the strange power that had awakened within her, a gift both terrifying and exhilarating. And somewhere above them all, in the towering city of Somnium, she imagined Inspector Tobias Black, a relentless predator, beginning his pursuit. A memory flickered in her mind, a fleeting image of her mother, a woman she barely remembered, a woman who had possessed a similar ability, a woman who had been a dreamer too.

Sleep, when it finally came, was fitful and filled with strange visions. Luna dreamed of vast, shimmering webs of light, flowers of glass that sung, of voices calling out in the darkness. And through it all, a sense of urgency, of time running out.

She woke with a start, her heart pounding. For a moment, she didn't know where she was. Then the events of the past day came rushing back, and she sat up, blinking in the dim light of the underground room.

Her father was asleep on the other cot, his face lined with worry even in slumber. Luna watched him for a moment, feeling a surge of love and protectiveness. Whatever happened next, she knew they would face it together.

A soft knock at the door made her jump. "Come in," she called quietly.

The door opened, revealing Henk. He looked tired, but there was a sparkle of excitement in his eyes. "I'm sorry to wake you," he said, "but there's something you need to see."

Luna glanced at her father, still sleeping. Henk shook his head. "Let him rest. This is for you."

Curious and a little apprehensive, Luna followed Henk through the winding tunnels of the underground. They passed more rooms filled with escapees, some sleeping, others talking in hushed voices or tending to various tasks. Luna marveled at the scale of the operation, hidden away beneath the city.

Finally, they came to a small, circular chamber. Its walls were covered in intricate designs - swirling patterns that seemed to move in the flickering light of the single lamp that illuminated the space.

"What is this place?" Luna asked.

Henk smiled. "This," he said, "is where we've been waiting for you."

He gestured to the center of the room, where a simple wooden chair sat. "Please, have a seat."

Luna hesitated, then slowly lowered herself into the chair. As soon as she made contact, the designs on the walls began to glow faintly, pulsing with a soft, blue light.

"Oh!" Luna gasped, her eyes wide.

Henk nodded, looking pleased. "It's responding to you. Just as we hoped it would."

"But what is it?" Luna asked, her gaze darting around the room. "What does it do?"

Henk's expression grew serious. "It's a dreamcatcher, a gateway," he explained. "A way to access the deepest levels of the dreamscape. Your mother helped us with it. We've always believed that someone with your abilities would be able to use it to its full potential."

Luna felt a mix of excitement and fear. "And what is its full potential?"

"To free all the dreamers," Henk said simply. "To bring down the entire system of dream harvesting, once and for all."

Luna felt her breath hitch. "But how?"

Henk shook his head. "That, we don't know. It's something only you can discover." He paused, his eyes searching her face. "Luna, we believe your abilities are extraordinarily powerful. You have the potential to channel the dreams of all the sleepers and expand them. You can liberate them. Are you willing to take that chance?"

Luna thought of the people she'd seen in the underground, of the countless others still trapped in the dream harvesting facilities. She thought of her father, risking everything to protect her. And she thought of the strange ability she'd felt, the connection to something vast and unknowable.

Slowly, she nodded. "Yes," she said. "I'll try."

Henk smiled, relief evident in his features. "Good. We'll begin tomorrow. For now, get some rest. You'll need your strength."

As they made their way back to the small room where her father slept, Luna's mind raced with possibilities and fears. She didn't know what the future held, but she knew that everything had changed. The city of Somnium, with its soaring towers and colossal Dream Spire, and hidden depths, would never be the same.

And somewhere above them, in the waking world, Inspector Tobias Black was drawing ever closer, driven by a relentless need to uncover the truth. The clock was ticking, and Luna knew that soon, very soon, she would have to face the full extent of her newfound powers - and the dangers that came with them.

***

The office of Inspector Tobias Black was a sanctuary of stillness, a world apart from the busy precinct beyond its walls. The room, illuminated by the harsh, unyielding light of fluorescent bulbs, felt suspended in time as Black sat motionless behind his desk, his gloved hands resting neatly before him. The silence was so complete that the soft hum of the air conditioning unit sounded like a thunderous roar.

When the communication device on his desk chirped to life, it was as if a spell had been broken. Black's eyes, previously unfocused and distant, snapped to attention. He reached for the device with a deliberate slowness that belied the sudden tension in his shoulders.

"Black here," he growled, his voice rough from disuse.

As he listened, his expression remained impassive, but a keen observer might have noticed the slight tightening around his eyes, the almost imperceptible quickening of his breath.

"I see," he murmured after a long pause. "And you're certain? This isn't another false lead?"

Another pause, shorter this time.

"No, no, I understand the gravity of the situation. If what you're saying is true, if there really is someone down there with the ability- " He trailed off, his free hand clenching into a fist on the desk.

"Yes, I'll handle it personally. Send me the coordinates. And keep this quiet, understood? The last thing we need is a panic."

As the communication ended, a smile spread across Black's face. It was not a pleasant expression. It was the smile of a predator that had finally caught the scent of its prey.

Rising from his chair with an ease that defied his years, Black walked to the door. He paused briefly, his hand resting on the handle, inhaling deeply. As he opened the door and entered the precinct, his face was marked by a determined resolve.

"I need a squad of guards," he barked to no one in particular. "Now."

As the precinct erupted into frantic activity, Black allowed himself a moment of satisfaction. After years of searching, of false starts and dead ends, he was finally closing in on his quarry. The Dreamkeepers had eluded him for too long, but now - now he had them.

The underground awaited.

***

In the depths of the city, far below the gleaming towers and bustling streets, the underground hummed with its own peculiar rhythm. It was a world unto itself, a haven for those who had fled the dream harvesters, a place where hope still flickered like a candle in the wind.

Luna sat at a makeshift table with her father, their breakfast a meager affair of synthesized protein and recycled water. Despite the humble fare, there was warmth in their shared glances, a sense of gratitude for another day together, safe from the terrors that lurked above.

"You're quiet this morning," her father observed, his voice gentle. "Bad dreams?"

Luna shook her head, pushing a strand of long black hair behind her ear. "No, not bad. Just - strange. I was in a field of flowers, but they were all made of glass. When I touched them, they sang."

Her father chuckled, reaching across the table to squeeze his daughter's hand. "That doesn't sound so bad. Better than nightmares, at least."

"I suppose," Luna agreed, though her expression revealed unspoken worries. "Dad, do you ever wonder if - "

Her words were cut short by a sound that didn't belong in their underground sanctuary. It was a crash, followed by screams that echoed through the tunnels with terrifying clarity.

Her father was on his feet in an instant, his chair clattering to the floor behind him. "Luna, we need to go. Now."

They ran, merging with the frantic crowd that surged through the corridors. Voices erupted around them - shouts and cries - each face a portrait of fear. Luna caught fleeting glimpses of robotic guards, their cold metal bodies jarring against the chaotic humanity that enveloped them. Leading the way, a figure emerged who sent a chill through her: Inspector Tobias Black.

"This way," her father urged, pulling Luna down a side passage. They could hear the sounds of violence behind them, the harsh reports of weapons fire, the sickening thuds of bodies hitting the ground.

Luna could feel her heart pounding, her breath coming in ragged gasps. She wanted to stop, to help those who had fallen, but her father's grip on her arm was unyielding. They ran until the sounds of battle faded until the only noise was their own labored breathing and the distant drip of water.

"In here," her father whispered, ushering Luna into what appeared to be an electrical closet. The space was cramped and dark, filled with the hum of machinery and the smell of ozone.

They huddled together in the darkness, Luna burying her face in her father's chest as he held her close. Time seemed to lose all meaning as they waited, straining to hear any sign of pursuit.

The screams had faded to a terrible silence, broken only by the rhythmic thud of approaching footsteps. Luna felt her father tense, his arms tightening around her protectively.

The footsteps grew louder, closer. Luna held her breath, her eyes squeezed shut as if that could somehow make them invisible.

The door to their hiding place creaked open.

A hand reached in.

Luna bit back a scream, certain that their time had run out, that they were about to join the countless others who had fallen victim to Black's relentless hunt.

But the voice that spoke was not the harsh bark of Inspector Black or the emotionless tones of a robotic guard. It was a voice they knew, one that carried with it a glimmer of hope.

"Luna? Marcus? It's me, Henk. You need to come with me. Now."

Luna's eyes flew open, meeting her father's gaze in the dim light. For a moment, they hesitated, their caution warring with the desperate need for salvation.

"Please," Henk urged, his voice tight with urgency. "There isn't much time."

Marcus nodded, his decision made. "Alright," he said. "Lead the way."

As they emerged from their hiding place, Luna blinked in the harsh light of the corridor. Henk stood before them, his slender frame taut with tension, his eyes darting nervously from side to side.

"Quickly," he gestured for them to follow. "I know a way out, but we have to hurry."

They set off at a brisk pace, Henk leading them through a maze of tunnels and passageways that Luna had never seen before. The sounds of pursuit seemed to fade, but the tension in the air remained palpable.

"What happened?" Marcus asked as they ran. "How did they find us?"

Henk's expression darkened. "I don't know. Someone must have talked, or- " He trailed off, shaking his head. "It doesn't matter now. What matters is getting you two to safety."

Luna's mind raced as they moved through the underground. She thought of the others she had met in their little time below. How many had survived? And what of those who had been captured? The thought of being at the mercy of the dream harvesters sent a shudder through her body.

They came to a junction, and Henk held up a hand, signaling for them to stop. He peered cautiously around the corner, then quickly pulled back.

"Guards," he whispered. "Two of them."

Marcus tensed, his hand instinctively tightening on Luna's shoulder. "Can we go another way?"

Henk shook his head. "This is the only route I know that leads to the surface. We'll have to find a way past them."

Luna took a deep breath, steeling herself. "I might be able to help," she said softly.

Both men turned to look at her, surprise evident on their faces.

"Luna, no," her father began, but she cut him off.

"Dad, please. You know what I can do. Let me try."

Henk's eyes widened in understanding. "The dreams," he murmured. "You can enter them, can't you?"

Luna nodded, her expression a mixture of determination and fear. "Even robotic guards have a kind of consciousness. If I can access it, maybe I can - I don't know, confuse them or something."

Her father looked torn, his protective instincts warring with the knowledge that his daughter's unique ability might be their only chance. Finally, he nodded. "Be careful," he said.

Luna closed her eyes, reaching out with her mind. It was different from entering human dreams, more like navigating a complex network of data and algorithms. But at its core, there was something akin to consciousness, a spark of awareness that she could latch onto.

She felt herself slipping into the guards' shared network, their perceptions becoming hers. For a moment, she was overwhelmed by the flood of information, the constant stream of data that made up their reality.

But then she found what she was looking for. With a mental push, she introduced a new variable into their programming, a false sensor reading that indicated a disturbance in the opposite direction.

Luna opened her eyes, swaying slightly as she readjusted to her own body. "It's done," she whispered. "They should be moving away from us now."

Sure enough, they heard the metallic footsteps of the guards retreating, heading off to investigate the phantom disturbance Luna had created.

Henk let out a low sigh. "Impressive," he said, a note of awe in his voice. "Come on, let's move while we have the chance."

They pressed on, the tension easing slightly now that they had overcome this obstacle. But Luna couldn't shake the feeling that their troubles were far from over.

As they rounded another corner, they found themselves face to face with Inspector Tobias Black himself.

For a moment, everything seemed to come crashing down upon them. Black's eyes widened in surprise, then narrowed with a predatory gleam. "Well, well," his voice a low rumble. "What have we here?"

Marcus stepped in front of Luna, shielding her with his body. "Leave her alone," he growled. "She's just a child."

Black's laugh was cold and humorless. "A child? No, I don't think so. She's much more than that, isn't she? She's the one we've been looking for."

Luna suddenly felt cold. How could he know she was here?

Henk moved to stand beside Marcus, presenting a united front against the inspector. "You have no jurisdiction here, Black," he said, his voice steady despite the fear Luna could see in his eyes. "This is our home."

"Home?" Black sneered. "This cesspool? No, this is a den of thieves, of Dreamkeepers, people who think they can hide from the law. But the law always finds a way."

He took a step forward, and Luna could see the robotic guards moving into position behind him, their weapons aimed at her father and Henk.

"Come quietly," Black said, his gaze fixed on Luna. "There's no need for anyone else to get hurt."

Luna felt a surge of anger, of defiance. She stepped out from behind her father, ignoring his attempt to pull her back.

"No," her voice rang out clear and strong. "I won't let you hurt anyone else. I won't let you take me."

Black's eyebrows rose in amusement. "And how do you plan to stop me, little dreamer?"

Luna took a deep breath, centering herself. She could feel the power within her, the ability that had both blessed and cursed her. With a mental push, she reached out, not to the robotic guards this time, but to Black himself.

She felt resistance, a mind trained to withstand psychic assault. But Luna was not trying to control him, not trying to bend his will to hers. Instead, she showed him a dream.

In an instant, the underground faded away. Black found himself standing in a vast field of glass flowers, each one singing a haunting melody. The beauty of it was overwhelming, bringing tears to his eyes.

And then the flowers began to shatter, one by one, their crystalline shards cutting deep. Black cried out, falling to his knees as the dreamscape crumbled around him.

In the real world, barely a second had passed. Black staggered, his eyes unfocused, a trickle of blood running from his nose.

"Run!" Luna shouted, grabbing her father's hand.

They fled, leaving the disoriented inspector and his confused guards behind. Henk led them through a series of twisting passages.

Henk's hand closed around Luna's wrist, his grip firm but not unkind. "This way," he urged, his voice barely above a whisper. "Quickly now."

They ducked down another passage, the sounds of pursuit fading behind them. Luna's heart hammered in her chest, each breath a struggle as they raced through the pre-dawn gloom. Her father brought up the rear, his eyes constantly scanning for any sign of danger.

"Where are we going?" Luna managed between gasps.

Henk's response was cryptic. "Somewhere safe. Somewhere they can't follow."

They wound their way through a maze of hallways until finally, Henk slowed his pace, coming to a stop before a nondescript door set into a weathered brick wall. He turned the knob and Luna heard a faint click.

"Inside," Henk said, ushering them through the now-open door. "Quickly."

The interior was dark and musty, the air thick with the scent of old books and dust. Henk closed the door behind them, plunging them into total darkness for a moment before a soft, blue-tinged light flickered to life.

"What is this place?" Marcus asked, his voice hushed with awe.

Henk's expression was solemn. "A sanctuary. And perhaps our last hope."

"Luna," Henk said, turning to face her. "This is where we were last night. Are you ready?"

Luna glanced at her father, who looked perplexed. "I'm ready," she said, her voice steadier than she felt.

They stepped into the small, circular chamber. Its walls were covered in intricate designs - swirling patterns that seemed to move in the dim light of the single lamp that illuminated the space. In the center of the room stood the chair.

"The dreamcatcher," Luna breathed, unable to take her eyes off the chair.

Henk's voice was soft, reverent. "Yes. It's how you can free the sleepers."

Her father stepped forward, his brow creased with concern. "Henk, what are you talking about?"

Henk turned to face them both, his expression grave. "All those trapped in the dream harvesting machines. The ones whose minds are being used to power the city above. Luna, her ability - it's the key to setting them free."

Again, she felt cold. "I understand."

"The chair will amplify your natural abilities," Henk explained. "It will allow you to enter the shared dreamscape of all the sleepers at once. From there, you can guide them back to consciousness."

Her father shook his head, stepping between Luna and the chair. "No. Absolutely not. It's too dangerous."

"Dad," Luna said softly, placing a hand on his arm. "We have to try. All those people - we can't just leave them. For mom."

Henk nodded. "She's right, Marcus. Luna may be our only chance to end this nightmare."

For a long moment, Marcus said nothing, his eyes locked with Luna's. She could see the fear there, the desperate need to protect her. But there was something else too - pride, and a grudging acceptance.

Finally, he stepped aside. "Alright," he said, his voice rough with emotion. "But I'll be right here. If anything goes wrong- "

"Nothing will go wrong," Henk assured him. "Luna, are you ready?"

Luna took a deep breath, steeling herself. She approached the chair, feeling a faint hum of energy emanating from it. As she sat down, the material seemed to mold itself to her body, cradling her in its strange embrace.

"Close your eyes," Henk instructed. "Focus on your breathing. Let your mind open up, just like when you enter a dream."

Luna did as she was told, her eyelids fluttering closed. She could feel the energy of the chair flowing through her, amplifying her own abilities. It was exhilarating and terrifying all at once.

"Remember," Henk's voice came from somewhere far away. "You're not just entering one dream now. You're entering thousands. Stay focused. Find the thread that connects them all."

Luna took another deep breath, letting her consciousness expand. She could feel the minds of the sleepers now, a vast landscape of dreams and nightmares stretching out before her.

"I'm ready," she whispered, and then she was falling, plunging into the shared dreamscape of a thousand captive minds.

The last thing she heard before the real world faded away entirely was her father's voice, filled with a mixture of fear and hope:

"Be careful, my little dreamer. Come back to us."

And then Luna was gone, lost in the sea of dreams.

***

In the dreamworld, Luna found herself standing in a vast, ethereal landscape. The ground beneath her feet was soft and shifting, like sand, and the sky above was a swirling mass of colors. She could see the sleepers, their forms flickering in and out of existence like ghosts.

"Hello?" she called out, her voice echoing in the dreamscape. "Can you hear me?"

One by one, the sleepers turned to face her, their eyes wide with confusion and fear. Luna felt a pang of sympathy for them; they were trapped in a nightmare, unable to wake.

"Don't be afraid," she said, her voice soothing. "I'm here to help you."

As she reached out to them, she felt a sudden, chilling cold wash over her. It was a familiar sensation, one she had felt before, but never this intense. The cold seemed to seep into her very bones, freezing her in place.

"No," she whispered, her breath visible in the frigid air. "Not now."

The cold continued to spread, and Luna felt her connection to the dreamscape weaken. She tried to focus, to push the cold away, but it was no use. It was as if the dreamworld itself was rejecting her.

In the real world, Marcus watched in horror as Luna's body tensed, her face contorting in pain. "Luna!" he shouted, rushing to her side. "What's happening?"

Henk placed a hand on Marcus's shoulder, his expression grim. "She's fighting something. We need to give her time."

But time was running out. The door to the circular room burst open, and Inspector Tobias Black strode in, flanked by robotic guards. His eyes locked onto Marcus, and a cruel smile spread across his face.

The robotic guards moved forward, their weapons trained on Marcus. He didn't flinch, his gaze never leaving Black's.

"Take him," Black ordered.

The guards grabbed Marcus, pulling him away from Luna. He struggled, but it was no use. They were too strong.

As Marcus was dragged towards the door, Black turned to Henk. "And you," he said, his eyes narrowing, "you'll be rewarded for your assistance."

"I expect the hefty deposit to be in my account within the hour," smirked Henk.

Black clapped Henk on the back. "Consider this your receipt."

Before Henk could react, a laser blast shot through him, fired by one of the robotic guards. He crumpled to the ground, his eyes wide with shock.

Black gazed down at Henk's still form, the smile on his face unyielding. "Payment in full," he remarked, before turning his back and walking away.

Luna, on the other hand, felt the cold envelop her. She attempted to connect with the sleepers, but her ability had vanished. Instead, she was engulfed by something far more sinister. It was as if the dreams of the entire city surged within her, overwhelming her senses.

"No," she breathed, her voice a fragile murmur. "I can't- "

It was too late. The dreams wrapped around Luna, transforming her into a vessel for the countless visions swirling through the city. The energy surged within her, a force both exhilarating and overwhelming. She became acutely aware of the myriad emotions - the aspirations, the anxieties, the haunting fears of so many souls. And then, amidst the tumult, she spotted a woman seated in a chair much like her own.

"Luna, my sweet," the woman murmured. "We're together at last."

"Mommy," Luna cried.

In the real world, Luna's body convulsed, her eyes rolling back in her head. Marcus, still struggling against the guards, saw what was happening and screamed her name.

"Luna!"

But she couldn't hear him. She was lost in the dreamworld, a prisoner of her own power.

Black watched with a satisfied expression, his eyes gleaming with triumph. "We've done it," he said, turning to his guards. "A harvest of dreams."

As Marcus was pulled away, he caught one last, fleeting glimpse of his daughter, her body motionless in the chair. A profound wave of despair washed over him, heavy and suffocating.

Black's laughter erupted, sharp and malevolent. He pressed a button on the wall, and the circular room released a hiss as its walls slid apart, revealing another chair. In it sat an older woman, her form unmoving, trapped in a state that suggested she had long since drifted away from the world around her.

***

Marcus found himself in a small prison cell, the walls stark and white. The bright lights overhead were blinding, casting harsh shadows on the floor. He sat on the narrow cot, his head in his hands, trying to make sense of what had happened.

The sound of footsteps echoed in the corridor, and Marcus looked up as a guard approached. The guard slipped a tray of food through the door slit, his expression unreadable.

"Don't know what they've done," the guard said, his voice flat. "But we sure have all the power we need now."

Cartwheels 'Cross the Floor

Eddie Raines stumbled through the alleys bathed in neon light, his thoughts tangled in a haze of scattered memories and incomplete theories. Above him, the towering skyline bore down, a symbol of the corporate giants that had seized control, replacing what was once a free society. He held onto a worn datapad, its dim screen showing remnants of stories he knew he would never write again.

"Jasper," Eddie muttered, his voice hoarse from disuse, "run another scan on that thing we found. There's gotta be something we missed."

The AI materialized beside him, a holographic projection of calm in Eddie's chaotic world. "Certainly, Eddie. Though I must remind you, this is the seventeenth scan I've performed in the last hour."

Eddie's eyes darted nervously, scanning for unseen threats. "Yeah, well, make it eighteen. You know they're always watching, always one step ahead."

Jasper's expression remained neutral, but there was a hint of concern in his synthesized voice. "Eddie, perhaps we should discuss your current state of mind. Your cortisol levels are- "

"Shut it, Jasper!" Eddie snapped, then immediately regretted his outburst. "Sorry, I just - I can't shake this feeling. Not after what happened at the Pulse."

Jasper gave a knowing glance. Eddie's fall from grace at the New Angeles Pulse had been spectacular and public. He'd been their star investigative reporter, always one scoop ahead of the competition. But his relentless pursuit of the truth behind the government's "Nexus Program" had cost him everything - his job, his reputation, and very nearly his sanity.

Eddie pulled the odd gadget from his pocket, his fingers moving over the unfamiliar markings carved into its surface. It was no larger than a standard comm box, yet it vibrated with a charge that made his jaw tighten. "This is it, Jasper. This is the key to blowing the whole thing wide open. I can feel it."

Jasper's holographic form flickered as he processed the latest scan. "Eddie, I've detected an anomaly in the device's quantum signature. It appears to be - fluctuating in a way that defies our current understanding of physics."

Eddie's eyes widened, a manic grin spreading across his face. "I knew it! We need to get this to Sarah. She'll know what to make of it."

Jasper interjected, his tone cautious, "Are you certain Sarah will want to see you? The last time you two spoke, it didn't end well."

Eddie's grin faltered for a moment, replaced by a flash of doubt. "She'll understand, Jasper. This is bigger than our past. It's about the truth."

"Sarah is a logical and analytical individual," Jasper continued, "but she also values her privacy and has distanced herself from past associations for a reason. She might not be receptive to your arrival, especially unannounced."

Eddie's paranoia flared up, but he was determined. "I know, I know." He took a deep breath. "But she can't ignore this. She has to see the potential here. This device could change everything."

Jasper's holographic eyes seemed to soften, a programmed empathy shining through. "I understand your urgency, Eddie. But it might be wise to consider her perspective. She has her own reasons for staying hidden."

Eddie sighed, running a hand through his unkempt hair. "But I don't have a choice. If this device is what I think it is, we need her expertise. She's the only one who can help us."

Jasper's image wavered for a moment. "Very well. But I suggest approaching her with caution and respect. She may need time to process your reappearance and the implications of this discovery."

Eddie took a deep breath, bracing himself for what was to come. "Alright. Alright. Let's go find Sarah. And let's hope she's willing to listen."

As they made their way through the crowded streets, Eddie couldn't shake the feeling of being watched. Every face in the crowd seemed to hide secrets, every shadow concealed potential threats. He clutched the device closer, his paranoia a constant companion, but Jasper's calm presence beside him offered some reassurance.

"Remember, Eddie," Jasper said softly, "this is about more than just the device. It's about rebuilding trust and forging alliances. Tread carefully."

The door to Sarah Kim's small street-level lab burst open, startling her from her work. Clean lines, sterile surfaces, and the soft hum of advanced machinery created an atmosphere of controlled precision. Eddie stumbled in, his eyes wild and unfocused, clutching the strange device. Sarah's cybernetic enhancements whirred to life, scanning for potential threats.

"Eddie?" Sarah was surprised and irritated. "What the hell are you doing here?"

Eddie's eyes moved rapidly around the lab, tension clear in his every movement. He thrust the unfamiliar device toward her. "Sarah, I need your help. This thing - it's the key to everything."

Sarah's enhanced eyes narrowed, her posture stiffening. "You shouldn't be here, Eddie. Not after what happened last time. Or have you conveniently forgotten how you nearly got us both killed?"

Eddie winced at the memory but pressed on. "I know, I know. But this thing is different. This thing is bigger than us, bigger than anything we've ever encountered."

Sarah's cybernetic hand clenched into a fist. "Bigger than the Nexus Program? Bigger than your obsession that cost me my career and nearly my life? I told you I was done with your conspiracy theories, Eddie."

"Please, Sarah," he pleaded, placing the device on her workstation. "Just take a look. You're the only one who can help me make sense of this."

Sarah studied the object, her scientific mind grappling with frustration and suspicion. "What am I supposed to make of this?"

Jasper's hologram appeared abruptly, causing Sarah to jump. "I apologize for the interruption, Dr. Kim. The device seems to be generating quantum fluctuations that challenge our grasp of time's mechanics "

Sarah's composure cracked for a moment, genuine interest seeping through. "Impossible. The energy required for such fluctuations would be - "

"Astronomical, I know," Eddie interrupted, his excitement building. "But it's real, Sarah. I can feel it. This thing - it's not from here. Not from our time."

Sarah's fingers hovered over her console, torn between initiating a scan and throwing Eddie out. "Even if what you're saying is true, Eddie, why should I help you? Last time I got involved in one of your 'big stories,' I lost everything. My job, my reputation, my- "

She trailed off, her cybernetic hand unconsciously touching the implants at her temple. Eddie's face fell, guilt washing over him.

"I know I hurt you, Sarah. I never meant for any of that to happen. But this - this could change everything. We could make it right."

Sarah's eyes sparked with a blend of anger and frustration. "Make it right? Eddie, you can't just stroll in with some strange gadget and think I'll forget everything that's gone on between us."

As their voices rose in debate, neither of them caught the device's soft, eerie glow, now shifting to a vivid blue. Strange symbols moved rapidly along its surface, weaving patterns that made it almost painful to observe.

Eddie, alarmed, placed the device on a nearby table, stepping away. "What is this?"

Reacting swiftly, Sarah's enhanced instincts took over, recognizing the threat. "It's powering up! Jasper, start the containment protocols now!"

But it was too late. A wave of energy exploded outward, enveloping the three of them in a cocoon of shimmering light. For a moment, reality itself seemed to bend and warp around them.

When the light faded, they found themselves still in the lab, but something was - off. Objects seemed to flicker in and out of existence, and through the windows, they could see the cityscape shifting and changing like a fevered dream.

"What - what did you do?" Sarah's voice broke, breathless.

Eddie, eyes wide, stared at the device that he now held. His hands trembled slightly as if he were unsure whether to let go or clutch it tighter. "I think - we might have just changed time."

Jasper's hologram wavered again, cutting in and out, its voice distorted. "Warning: Temporal anomalies detected. Reality - unstable. Immediate action is - "

But his were cut off as another pulse of energy erupted from the device. This time, when the light faded, they found themselves in a completely different location - a dimly lit warehouse filled with outdated technology.

"Where are we?" Sarah's cybernetic enhancements scanning their surroundings.

Eddie's paranoia kicked into overdrive. "When are we? This tech - it looks like stuff from at least a decade ago."

Jasper materialized, his form still unstable. "Based on available data, we appear to have shifted approximately 12 years into the past. However, the temporal field is highly unstable. We may experience further shifts at any moment."

Sarah grabbed Eddie by the arm. "Do you realize what you've done? We're trapped in a temporal loop, bouncing through time like – like - "

"Like a glitch in the system," Eddie finished, his reporter's instincts kicking in despite the insanity of the situation. "But don't you see, Sarah? This is our chance! We can go back, and stop the Nexus Program before it ever starts!"

Sarah shook her head, her enhanced mind racing through calculations. "It's not that simple, Eddie. Any changes we make could have catastrophic consequences. We could erase ourselves from existence, or worse."

Eddie's eyes blazed with a manic intensity. "Or we could save millions of lives! We could stop the corporations from taking over, prevent the government from becoming the puppet it is now!"

As their voices clashed, neither noticed the figures slipping into view at the far corners of the warehouse. Figures dressed in sleek black armor emerged, their weapons aimed steadily at the three.

"Quite the surprise," a voice cut through the air, cold and sharp. "It seems our temporal experiment has produced some rather interesting outcomes."

Eddie, Sarah, and Jasper turned to face a new threat, the device pulsing ominously in Eddie's hands.

"Who are you?" Eddie demanded, his paranoia now fully justified.

The leader of the black-clad group stepped forward, peeling away his helmet to reveal a face that sent a chill through Eddie, its familiarity unsettling.

With a malevolent grin, the man spoke. "I'm you, Eddie. More precisely, I'm what you become in about five years. And I'm here to ensure you don't alter a thing."

Eddie's thoughts raced, grappling with the weight of this revelation. Sarah, her heightened senses keenly attuned, surveyed the surroundings for any possible escape routes. Meanwhile, Jasper's hologram wavered between them, its programming struggling to adapt to the impossibility of the moment.

The future Eddie raised his hand, revealing a device identical to the one they'd found in the junkyard. "You see, we've been playing this little game for quite some time now. Jumping back and forth, trying to 'fix' things. But the truth is, there's no fixing it. There's only the loop, and our part in maintaining it."

Sarah's eyes narrowed, her analytical mind piecing together the puzzle. "You," she accused. "you are the architect of this loop. You've been manipulating events, ensuring that the future unfolds exactly as you remember it. And you - you're the reason for the Nexus Program."

The future Eddie clapped slowly, a mocking grin spreading across his face. "Bravo, Dr. Kim. Always the quick one, aren't you? Yes, we are the designers of our own dystopia. And we do it all in the name of preserving the timeline."

Eddie felt this revelation wash over him like a sudden storm. All his paranoid theories, all his investigations - they had brought him face-to-face with himself. He realized he was the villain he had been pursuing all along.

"No," Eddie whispered, tightening his grip on the device. "I won't become you. I won't let this happen!"

The warehouse began to shimmer and distort as the device in Eddie's hands pulsed with increasing intensity. Reality itself seemed to be tearing at the seams.

"Eddie, don't!" Sarah shouted, reaching for him. "You'll destroy everything!"

Jasper's hologram stabilized for a moment, his voice cutting through the chaos. "Warning: Temporal paradox imminent. Recommend immediate action to stabilize the timeline."

The future Eddie and his team raised their weapons, preparing to fire. "You can't change it, Eddie. You can't escape the loop. It's who we are!"

As the energy from the device reached a crescendo, Eddie made a split-second decision. He looked at Sarah, tears in his eyes. "I'm sorry. I have to try."

With another thought, he activated the device, enveloping them all in a blinding flash of temporal energy. The warehouse, the future Eddie, and the very fabric of reality seemed to dissolve around them.

When the light faded, Eddie found himself back in the junkyard where he'd first discovered the device. But something was different. The city skyline had changed, the oppressive megacorporate towers replaced by a more diverse, hopeful landscape.

Sarah appeared at his side, her cybernetic enhancements replaced by her natural limbs, radiating an unexpected warmth. Jasper's hologram materialized, more stable and vibrant than he had ever been before.

"What - what did you do?" Sarah asked, her voice filled with wonder and confusion.

Eddie stared at the device in his hands, which was now nothing more than an inert piece of metal. "I think - I think I broke the loop. I chose a different path."

Jasper's voice was calm, almost serene. "Timeline stabilized. New reality established. Congratulations, Eddie. You've created a new future."

As they stood there, taking in this new world they'd inadvertently created, Eddie couldn't help but wonder about the consequences of his actions. Had he truly broken free of the cycle, or merely started a new one?

The device in his hands disintegrated into dust, its mission complete. Eddie understood that regardless of what the future held, he would meet it with clarity, liberated from the anxiety that had colored his life for far too long.

A genuine smile lit up Sarah's face. "Well, Mr. Raines, it seems you've got quite a story to share. Shall we go discover what kind of world we've created?"

Eddie smiled back, a sense of true hope blossoming within him for the first time in years. "Yeah, let's go see what lies ahead. Together."

As they moved toward the new skyline, Jasper's hologram shimmered briefly before disappearing, leaving Eddie and Sarah to navigate this courageous new world on their own.

***

Eddie and Sarah stepped out of the junkyard and into a world that was both familiar and alien. The city skyline, once a monolithic monument to corporate dominance, now pulsed with a chaotic energy that defied easy categorization. Holographic advertisements blinked and danced across the faces of buildings, their messages shifting and mutating like fevered dreams.

"What have we done, Eddie?" Sarah whispered, her eyes wide as she took in the transformed landscape.

Eddie's paranoia, momentarily subdued by their apparent victory, began to creep back in. "I think we may have broken the loop, Sarah. We changed everything."

Jasper's hologram materialized beside them, his form more stable than ever before. "Caution advised. While the timeline has been altered, the full extent of the changes remains unknown. Recommend proceeding with extreme care."

As they made their way down the rain-slicked streets, the neon glow reflecting off puddles like psychedelic oil slicks, Eddie couldn't shake the feeling that they were being watched. Every shadow seemed to harbor potential threats, every passing face a possible enemy.

"Something's not right," Eddie muttered, glancing anxiously at the dimly lit alleyways. "It's too quiet. Where are all the people?"

Sarah, her analytical mind working overtime to process their new reality, nodded in agreement. "The population density doesn't match the infrastructure. It's as if - "

Her words were cut short by the sudden appearance of a hulking figure at the end of the street. It was a man, standing there, a muscular frame silhouetted against the pulsing neon backdrop. His eyes, cold and unyielding, locked onto Eddie and Sarah with predatory intensity.

"Well, well," his voice carried through the empty street, a hint of amusement coloring his words. "The prodigal children return. Did you really think you could change the game so easily?"

Eddie's hand instinctively went to the pocket where he'd kept the device, only to remember it had crumbled away. "Who are you? What do you want?"

His laugh held no trace of warmth. "They call me Zelle. I am the constant, Mr. Raines. The one variable you can never truly eliminate from the equation." With a deliberate motion, he raised a hand, displaying a device identical to the one Eddie had used to manipulate reality. "You see, some of us remember the old world. And we're here to set things right."

At that moment, a squad of robotic enforcers emerged from the shadows, their metallic bodies gleaming in the neon light. Sarah grabbed Eddie's arm, her voice urgent. "We need to run. Now!"

They dashed down a narrow side street, the clatter of mechanical footsteps trailing close behind. Jasper's hologram materialized beside them, his voice steady amidst the chaos. "Accessing local surveillance networks. Calculating optimal escape route."

Eddie's lungs burned as they sprinted through the tangled alleyways, each turn revealing new and bizarre aspects of this altered reality. Holographic street vendors hawked impossible wares, their faces shifting between human and animal features. Gravity seemed to fluctuate sporadically, causing trash and debris to float momentarily before crashing back to the ground.

"This way!" Sarah shouted, pulling Eddie into a dimly lit doorway. They found themselves in a cramped elevator, its walls covered in throbbing, organic-looking circuitry. "Down," Sarah commanded, and the elevator plunged into the depths of the city.

As they descended, Eddie turned to Sarah, his breath coming in ragged gasps. "How did you know about this place?"

A flicker of vulnerability crossed Sarah's features, her earlier detachment softening. "I was part of its creation, Eddie. A long time ago, in a reality that's vanished."

"What?" Eddie stared at her, disbelief etched on his features.

The elevator doors opened, revealing a vast underground chamber filled with banks of humming computers and holographic displays. Figures hunched over workstations, their bodies a mix of flesh and cybernetic enhancements.

"Welcome to the Nexus Program," Sarah spoke softly, her tone laden with significance.

Eddie's thoughts spiraled, grappling with the enormity of her words. "You - you were involved in this? From the beginning?"

Before Sarah could respond, a familiar voice cut through the air. "Well, look who decided to pay us a visit." A man stepped forward, his face a mirror image of Eddie's, but marked by the passage of time. "Welcome home, Sarah. We've been expecting you."

Eddie stumbled back, his paranoia reaching a fever pitch. "What the hell is going on? Who are you people?"

The older Eddie smiled, but it didn't reach his eyes. "We're you, Eddie. All of us. Every version of you that's ever existed, across every timeline and reality. And we're here to fix the mess you've made."

Sarah stepped between the two Eddies, her voice firm. "That's enough. We don't have time for this. Zelle and his enforcers will be here any minute."

Suddenly, the chamber shook with the sound of an explosion from above. Alarms blared, and the assembled hackers and resistance fighters sprang into action.

"Jasper," Eddie called out, his mind racing to keep up with the rapidly unfolding events. "What's our status?"

The AI slowly formed, his expression grave. "Multiple hostiles detected. Zelle appears to be leading a full-scale assault on the facility. Recommend immediate evacuation."

The older Eddie barked out orders, his voice carrying over the chaos. "Initiate Protocol Alpha! We need to scatter and regroup at the secondary site!"

As the resistance members began to disappear through hidden exits and shimmering portals, Sarah grabbed Eddie's arm. "Eddie, listen to me. What I'm about to tell you will sound insane, but it's the truth. I was part of the team that created the device. We thought we were building a tool to fix the world's problems, to create a perfect future. But we were wrong."

Eddie's eyes widened, his reporter's instincts kicking in despite the madness surrounding them. "What happened?"

A wave of regret colored Sarah's voice. "We succeeded beyond our wildest dreams. The device didn't just alter reality; it created new ones. Infinite timelines, infinite possibilities. But with that power came a terrible price. The fabric of reality itself began to unravel."

Another explosion rocked the chamber, closer this time. The older Eddie shouted over the din, "We need to move!"

Sarah continued, her words tumbling out in a rush. "I fled when I realized what we'd done. I tried to hide, to forget. But the truth is, Eddie, there's no escaping it. We're all caught in the loop, every version of us, trying to fix what we broke."

Eddie's mind struggled to process the implications. "So, what do we do now?"

Before Sarah could answer, a section of the ceiling collapsed, revealing Zelle and his enforcers. Zelle's eyes locked onto the device in the older Eddie's hand. "Hand it over, and this all ends peacefully."

The older Eddie laughed, a note of insanity threading through it. "Peace? There's no such thing, not anymore. Not since we shattered the mirror of reality."

With that, he activated the device, enveloping the chamber in a blinding light. Eddie felt reality shift and warp around him, his consciousness stretching across infinite possibilities.

When the light faded, Eddie found himself back on the rain-soaked streets, Sarah and Jasper by his side. But something was different. The city seemed to shimmer and shift, as if layers of different realities were overlapping.

"What happened?" Eddie exclaimed, his head spinning. "Where are we?"

Sarah's eyes were wide with a mix of wonder and terror. "Everywhere and nowhere, Eddie. We're in the space between realities, the nexus point of all possible timelines."

Jasper's hologram wavered erratically, his voice strained. "Warning: Reality instability reaching critical levels. Recommend immediate action to stabilize the temporal field."

As they stood there, caught between worlds, Eddie realized the true nature of their predicament. They weren't just fighting to save one reality; they were fighting to save all of them.

Zelle's voice echoed from everywhere and nowhere, a constant across all possible timelines. "You can't run forever. The loop will always find you."

Eddie gripped Sarah's hand, his resolve hardening. "Then we'll keep running. We'll keep fighting. Until we find a way to break the loop once and for all."

As they set off into the shifting, fragmented landscape of broken realities, Eddie couldn't help but wonder: In a world where every choice creates a new timeline, where every decision spawns infinite possibilities, what does it truly mean to be free?

Blurred streets stretched out before them, a labyrinth of potential futures and forgotten pasts. And somewhere amid this intricate web of options, the key to unraveling the greatest conspiracy of all awaited discovery.

Eddie, Sarah, and the shifting presence of Jasper ventured forth, each step taking them deeper into the heart of a mystery that spanned not just worlds, but entire universes. The hunt for truth had never been more perilous, nor more essential.

***

Eddie stood at the edge of reality, his thoughts swirling with the vivid possibilities that stretched out before him. Sarah Kim, her cybernetic enhancements now remnants of a timeline wiped clean, clutched his arm firmly. Jasper's hologram sputtered between worlds, a digital ferryman of souls guiding them through this impossible river of time.

"Which one, Eddie?" Sarah's voice faltered, her analytical mind grappling with the unfathomable. "How can we possibly choose?"

Eddie's gaze flitted from one shimmering portal to the next, each revealing glimpses of worlds that were both awe-inspiring and daunting. In one, gleaming spires of impossible design reached toward otherworldly skies. In another, a desolate wasteland unfolded as far as he could see.

"I - I don't know," Eddie stammered, his instincts as a reporter slipping away amid the vastness of the unknown.

Jasper's voice pierced the confusion, a clear thread of reason. "According to quantum probability calculations, the timeline most likely to resolve the temporal loop seems to be - that one."

His holographic hand gestured toward a portal ahead that appeared somehow more substantial than the rest. Eddie spotted what looked to be the imposing facade of a massive government building, its architecture a fusion of concrete and streamlined, modern lines.

"That's it," Eddie whispered, a surge of certainty cutting through his uncertainty. "That's where we need to go."

Without waiting for agreement from the others, Eddie stepped through the portal, pulling Sarah along with him. Jasper's hologram followed, flickering and reforming as it passed through the barrier between realities.

They materialized on a pristine sidewalk, the air around them humming with the barely perceptible buzz of advanced technology. The government building towered above them, its windows reflecting the setting sun in hues of crimson and gold.

"Temporal shift complete," Jasper announced, his form stabilizing. "Current date: August 15, 2384. Location: Central Government Complex, Nova City."

Sarah's eyes widened in amazement as she surveyed their surroundings. "2384? We're so far into the future!"

Eddie's usual paranoia, temporarily dulled by the awe of their arrival, surged back. "We need to move. If this is where the loop ends, you can bet they're ready for us."

As if responding to his words, a patrol of sleek, robotic drones buzzed overhead, their sensors scanning the area. Eddie, Sarah, and Jasper pressed tightly against the wall of the building, narrowly avoiding detection.

"How are we supposed to get in there?" Sarah whispered, her gaze fixed on the heavily fortified entrance.

Eddie's mind raced, piecing together fragments of half-remembered conspiracies and hushed revelations. "There's always a back door. We just need to find it."

Jasper's hologram dimmed a bit, his eyes glowing as he interfaced with the building's security systems. "I've detected a vulnerability in their quantum encryption. If we can access a terminal, I may be able to create a temporary breach in their defenses."

They made their way around the building, ducking into shadows and narrowly avoiding patrols of both human and robotic guards. Finally, they found an unattended maintenance hatch, its control panel glowing softly in the gathering dusk.

"Jasper, do your thing," Eddie whispered, his gaze fixed on the AI as its holographic fingers moved gracefully over the keypad.

With a soft hiss, the hatch opened, revealing a dimly lit service tunnel. They slipped inside, the door sealing behind them with a sense of finality that sent a shiver through Eddie.

As they made their way through the facility's winding corridors, Eddie felt an unsettling sense of being directed, as if an invisible force was pushing them toward a specific goal. Every security camera they eluded, every locked door that opened effortlessly, seemed almost too convenient.

"I don't like this," Sarah voicing Eddie's unspoken concerns. "It's like they're expecting us."

Eddie nodded grimly. "Maybe they are. Maybe this is all part of the loop."

They emerged into a vast, circular chamber, its walls lined with screens displaying a dizzying array of data streams and probability matrices. At the center stood a figure, a man, shrouded in shadow, his features obscured by a hood of shimmering, light-absorbing material.

"Welcome, Mr. Raines," the figure spoke, its voice a discordant blend of tones and timbres. "We've been expecting you."

Eddie stepped forward, his hand instinctively reaching for the device that no longer existed. "Who are you? What is this place?"

The figure chuckled, a sound that pricked at Eddie's skin. "I am the Director, Mr. Raines. And this - this is where all realities connect."

With a wave of his hand, the screens around them erupted into life, each displaying a different version of Eddie, Sarah, and Jasper. In one, they were triumphant heroes. In another, broken and defeated. In yet another, they had never existed at all.

"You see, Mr. Raines," the Director continued, "the device you so rashly destroyed was never intended to merely manipulate time. It served as a key, a means to unlock the very essence of reality itself."

Sarah stepped forward, her scientific curiosity overriding her fear. "But why? What could possibly be worth risking the stability of the entire universe?"

The Director faced her, their features shrouded in shadow, yet Eddie sensed the intensity of their scrutiny. "Control, Dr. Kim. Absolute and total control. Not just over time and space, but over thought itself. Imagine a world where every decision, every fleeting impulse, could be predicted and manipulated. A world where free will is nothing more than an illusion, a comforting lie we tell ourselves to stave off the existential dread of our own insignificance."

Eddie's thoughts whirled, struggling to process the implications. "You're out of your mind. You can't possibly think you can control every possible reality!"

"Can't I?" the Director's voice dripped with smug confidence. "We've been doing it for eons, Mr. Raines. Like cartwheels 'cross the floor. Every loop, every iteration, has been meticulously planned to lead us here. You, Sarah, Jasper - you're merely players in a game far beyond your understanding."

As the Director spoke, the room began to shift and warp around them. Reality itself seemed to be fraying at the seams, fragments of other timelines bleeding through.

"What's happening?" Sarah cried out, her voice distorted by the temporal flux.

Jasper's hologram pulsed erratically, his words a jumbled mess. "Warning: Temporal integrity critical. Reality collapse imminent."

The Director raised his arms, his form seeming to grow and expand until it filled the entire chamber. "You see, Mr. Raines? This is the power we wield. The power to reshape reality itself!"

Eddie experienced a sudden clarity that pierced through his fear and confusion. Although the device was no longer in his possession, he still possessed his intellect and his resolve. He was determined not to be manipulated by anyone.

"Absolutely not," he growled, advancing a step. "I refuse to allow this. I won't let you dominate us!"

With a fierce yell, Eddie lunged forward, colliding with the Director. In that moment of impact, a blinding surge of energy erupted, overwhelming Eddie's senses. He felt as though he were being pulled apart, his essence splintering into countless fragments, each scattering into a myriad of realities.

For what felt like an eternity condensed into a single heartbeat, Eddie Raines was no longer a singular being. He existed in every place and none, living every conceivable version of himself at once. He glimpsed worlds where he had never come into being, realms where he had triumphed over galaxies, and landscapes where he had met his end in countless ways.

And then, just as suddenly as it had begun, it ended.

Eddie inhaled sharply, his eyes snapping open as he shot upright in bed. His heart pounded, and his mind grappled with the remnants of a dream that felt astonishingly real.

The room around him was ordinary. Sunlight filtered through half-closed blinds, illuminating a messy apartment that unmistakably belonged to him. There was no advanced technology, no hints of a sprawling dystopia. Just the familiarity of home.

"Jasper?" Eddie croaked, his voice rough. "Jasper, are you there?"

Silence was his only answer. Of course, there was no AI assistant. There had never been an AI assistant. Had there?

Eddie stumbled out of bed, his legs shaky as he made his way to the bathroom. The face that stared back at him from the mirror was his own, but somehow different. Older? Younger? He couldn't quite put his finger on it.

As he splashed water on his face, fragments of memories began to resurface. Sarah Kim. The device. Zelle. The Director. Yet, it felt like a dream, didn't it? It had to be.

Still, a persistent doubt lingered at the periphery of his thoughts. Eddie fumbled for his phone, scrolling through his contacts with unsteady fingers. No Sarah Kim. No trace of anyone by that name.

He opened a search engine and typed "Nexus Program," an uneasy sensation creeping in. No results appeared. No whispers of government conspiracies, no mention of time-altering devices. Just silence.

"What have I done?" Eddie whispered, staring at the blank screen.

As he stood there, lost in a whirlpool of confusion and doubt, a notification popped up on his phone. It was a news alert from his old employer, the New Angeles Pulse. The headline made his blood run cold:

"BREAKING: Mysterious Temporal Anomalies Reported Worldwide"

Eddie's heart pounded in his chest as he read the article. Reports of people experiencing déjà vu on a massive scale. Instances of objects appearing and disappearing without explanation. Eyewitness accounts of buildings shifting and changing before people's eyes.

At the bottom of the article was a blurry photograph, clearly taken in haste. It showed a hooded figure standing in the middle of a crowded street, their features obscured by a shimmering, light-absorbing material.

Eddie's phone slipped from his numb fingers, clattering to the floor. As he bent to retrieve it, he caught a glimpse of his reflection in the black screen. For just a moment, he could have sworn he saw another face superimposed over his own. A face with a cruel smile and eyes that held the weight of centuries.

"The loop," Eddie whispered, his voice barely audible. "It's starting again."

Outside his window, the sky began to ripple and shift, reality itself bending under the weight of infinite possibilities. It was as though a cosmic painter had begun to smear and smudge the very fabric of existence. Through the distorted glass, Eddie watched the world buckle and warp, a grotesque, mesmerizing ballet of impossible angles. In the cracks of this cosmic chaos, a sound, a whisper carried on the wind – laughter, it seemed, but a laughter both alien and familiar, a mirth born of a madness he couldn't comprehend.

The game, it seemed, was far from over.

Rise of the Dragonlord

In the deep recesses of the world, where light had never ventured and shadows held dominion, lay an ancient cavern. The air was thick with the scent of damp stone and the faint whisper of forgotten magic. Here, in this subterranean world, two figures moved with purpose, their footsteps echoing softly against the cavern walls.

Elara, a young mage apprentice, walked with a mixture of awe and determination. Her petite frame was dwarfed by the immense stalagmites and stalactites that surrounded her, but her bright green eyes shone with curiosity. Her long auburn hair, tied back in a loose braid, swayed gently with each step. She clutched a staff, its tip glowing faintly with a soft, ethereal light that illuminated their path.

Beside her strode Master Thorne, an elderly archmage of great renown. Tall and thin, he moved with a grace that belied his age. His long white beard flowed down to his chest, and his piercing blue eyes seemed to see beyond the physical realm, into the very essence of the world around them. He held his own staff with a practiced hand, its light a steady beacon in the darkness.

"Master Thorne," Elara began, her voice breezing slightly in the vastness of the cavern, "what do you hope to find down here? We've been exploring for hours, and the air grows colder with each step."

"Patience, Elara," Master Thorne replied, his voice calm and measured. "The secrets of the world are not revealed to those who rush. We must move with care and respect for the ancient magic that dwells here."

Elara simply nodded, though her curiosity burned brighter than ever. She had been under Master Thorne's tutelage for several years, and though she had learned much, there was still so much she did not understand. The mysteries of magic, the hidden knowledge of the ancients – these were the things that drove her, that filled her dreams with wonder and possibility.

As they ventured deeper into the cavern, the air grew colder, and the light from their staffs seemed to struggle against the encroaching darkness. The walls of the cavern began to change, adorned with intricate carvings and ancient runes that glowed faintly with their own inner light.

"Master Thorne, look at these carvings," Elara said, her voice filled with awe. "They seem to depict some kind of ritual or ceremony."

Master Thorne paused, his eyes scanning the carvings with a practiced eye. "Indeed, Elara. These runes are ancient, even by my reckoning. They speak of a time long before our own, when the world was young and magic flowed freely through the land."

Elara's fingers danced across the stone, tracing the intricate carvings with a reverence that belied her youth. The magic hummed beneath her touch, a faint vibration that spoke of ancient power and forgotten secrets. She glanced up at Master

Thorne, her eyes wide with curiosity and barely contained excitement.

"What tales do these runes whisper, Master?" she asked, her voice hushed in the stillness of the chamber.

Master Thorne leaned closer, his weathered face creasing with concentration as he deciphered the cryptic symbols. When he spoke, his voice carried the weight of ages. "They speak of a magnificent dragon and its mistress, a woman of extraordinary grace and might. Together, they stood as guardians of our world, entrusted with a sacred duty – the protection of an egg of unimaginable power, a gift bestowed by the gods themselves."

These mythical creatures, with their wisdom and strength, had always captivated her imagination. "The Dragonlord," she murmured, tasting the word on her tongue like a prayer. "Could she truly exist?"

A shadow passed over Master Thorne's face. "No, child. The Dragon Hunters extinguished their light long ago, leaving only whispers and stone to remember them by."

Undeterred, Elara's mind whirled with possibilities. The discovery of a dragon's egg, especially one of such legendary significance, would shake the very foundations of their world. She leaned closer to Master Thorne. "Master, do you think - could the egg still be hidden here, waiting to be found?"

"It is possible," Master Thorne replied, his eyes gleaming with a rare excitement. "But we must be cautious. Such a relic would be protected by powerful magic, and we do not know what dangers may lie ahead."

With renewed purpose, they continued their exploration, following the path of the carvings deeper into the heart of the cavern. The air grew colder still, and the light from their staffs sputtered as if in response to some unseen presence.

At last, they came upon a vast chamber, its ceiling lost in the shadows above. In the center of the chamber, bathed in a soft, otherworldly glow, lay an enormous dragon's egg. Its surface was smooth and iridescent, shifting colors like the surface of a tranquil lake. The egg pulsed with a gentle, rhythmic light as if it were alive and breathing.

"By the gods," Elara breathed, her eyes wide with wonder. "It's beautiful."

Master Thorne approached the egg with reverence, his eyes never leaving its surface. "This is indeed a rare and precious find, Elara. The magic that surrounds it is ancient and powerful. We must be careful in our examination."

As they drew closer, the egg began to pulse more rapidly, its light intensifying. Elara sensed an unusual warmth radiating from it, stirring a blend of wonder and unease deep within her.

"Master, do you feel that?" she asked, her voice trembling slightly.

"I do, Elara," Master Thorne responded, calm though tinged with unease. "The egg is stirring, reacting to us. It begins to wake." He allowed a small smile to soften his expression. "There's an old legend, a quiet promise of peace, foretelling a dragon that will heal the divide between our people. Perhaps- "

His words were cut short by a sound as sharp as a dagger, the egg rending itself open. Fine cracks, like spiderwebs spun by a malevolent weaver, spread across its shell. The light within, once a gentle glow, intensified, casting the chamber in an ethereal radiance.

Elara stepped back, her heart pounding in her chest. "Master, what should we do?"

"Stay calm, Elara," Master Thorne said, his eyes fixed on the egg. "We must see this through. The hatching of a dragon is a rare and wondrous event. We must be prepared for whatever comes next."

The cracks in the egg widened, and with a final, resounding snap, the shell broke apart, revealing a small, shimmering dragon. Its scales were a brilliant shade of blue, and its eyes, though still clouded with the haze of birth, held a spark of intelligence and curiosity.

The dragon unfurled its wings, shaking off the remnants of the eggshell, and let out a small, tentative roar. Elara felt a surge of emotion - joy, and a deep, instinctual connection to the creature before her.

"Master Thorne, it's magnificent," her voice full of wonder.

"Indeed, Elara," Master Thorne replied, his gaze alight with pride. "This is a momentous occasion. The birth of a dragon heralds great change, both for us and for the world."

The dragon looked up at them, its eyes now clear and focused. It took a tentative step forward, its movements graceful and fluid. Elara reached out a hand, and the dragon nuzzled against her palm, its scales warm and smooth.

"Hello, little one," she said softly, her heart swelling with affection. "You are a wonder."

Master Thorne watched the interaction with a thoughtful expression. "Elara, this dragon has chosen you. It is a bond that cannot be broken. You must care for it, protect it, and learn from it."

Elara remained focused on the dragon. "I will, Master. I promise."

The dragon let out another small roar, and Elara couldn't help but laugh. "I think he's hungry."

Master Thorne smiled, a rare sight that filled the chamber with warmth. "Then we must find food for our new friend. Come, Elara. Our journey is far from over."

As they made their way back through the cavern, the dragon following closely at Elara's side, she couldn't help but feel a sense of excitement and anticipation. The discovery of the dragon's egg had been unexpected, but it had awakened something within her – a sense of purpose, a connection to the ancient magic that flowed through the world.

She glanced at Master Thorne, who walked with a renewed vigor, his eyes alight with the possibilities that lay ahead. Together, they had uncovered a secret that had been hidden for centuries, and with it, the promise of a new beginning.

As they emerged from the cavern into the light of day, Elara took a deep breath, feeling the warmth of the sun on her face. The dragon, now perched on her shoulder, let out a contented sigh, its eyes half-closed in contentment.

"Welcome to the world, good friend," she murmured, a voice filled with hope and determination. "Your name shall be Zephyr"

***

In the heart of the bustling city of Eldoria, the Mage's Tower rose with quiet strength, holding centuries of wisdom within its stone walls. Its towering spires stretched skyward, while ancient symbols traced into the stonework glowed softly in the early evening. This was a place of deep learning, where those skilled in magic gathered from far and wide, seeking to refine their abilities and unlock mysteries long forgotten.

Elara returned from her journey to the cavern and settled into her modest chamber. The room held shelves lined with old books and brittle scrolls, a narrow bed tucked in one corner, and a window that opened to the movement of the streets below. Zephyr rested on her shoulder, his scales catching the light in a soft shimmer, as the day's last light filtered through the room.

Though small and innocent, Zephyr had already formed a strong bond with Elara. His playful nature brought a sense of joy and wonder to her life, but she knew that his presence had to be kept a secret. Dragons were creatures of legend, and their existence would surely attract unwanted attention.

As Elara sat at her desk, poring over a well-worn book on dragon lore, Zephyr nuzzled against her cheek, his warm breath tickling her skin. She smiled and scratched behind his tiny horns, eliciting a contented purr from the little dragon.

"You must stay hidden, Zephyr," she whispered affectionately. "But we must be careful. The world is not ready for you yet."

Zephyr cocked his head, his lively eyes brimming with curiosity and comprehension. Though her words held weight, his mischievous spirit always seemed eager to break through.

A sharp knock rang out against the chamber door, and Elara's heart stuttered. She quickly gathered Zephyr into her arms, his scales warm, gently shifting under her touch. Tucking him beneath her cloak, she felt the quiet flutter of his wings brush against her. She paused, drawing in a breath to steady herself, and pulled open the door. Councilor Vex stood there, his smile easy but sharp, the glint in his dark eyes reflecting both curiosity and a watchful edge.

"Good evening, Elara." Vex's voice slipped through the dim corridor, smooth and deliberate. His gaze lingered on her, sharp and inquisitive. "May I come in?"

Elara paused, unsure of her next move. The councilor's visits carried a weight she could never quite shake, his intentions tangled with schemes she was wary to confront. She stepped aside, offering him passage. "Certainly, Councilor Vex. What brings you to the Mage's Tower at this hour?"

Vex strode into the room with the confidence of one who is seldom refused. His gaze swept over the chamber, taking in the modest furnishings, the shelves strewn with ancient books, and the faint glow of magical wards that shimmered in the corners. The wards, intricate spells of protection and concealment, hummed softly, their light casting long shadows on the stone walls. "I was passing by and thought I might pay a visit. It has been some time since we last spoke, and I have heard whispers of powerful magic emanating from this tower."

Elara's heart raced, each beat a drum of warning. She knew Councilor Vex's nature well - ambitious, power-hungry, ever the manipulator. His visits were seldom casual, always laden with ulterior motives. She had to tread carefully. "The Mage's Tower is always a place of powerful magic, Councilor. We are constantly studying and experimenting with new spells and enchantments." She forced a smile, hoping to veil the tension coiling within her.

Vex turned to face her, his eyes narrowing slightly as he considered her words. "Indeed, Elara. But there is a difference between the routine hum of academic magic and the resonant echoes of something far more ancient and potent. I have always had a keen ear for such distinctions, as you know."

Elara felt Zephyr stir beneath her cloak, his tiny claws digging into her side as if sensing the unease she fought to conceal. She moved to the small table in the center of the room, gesturing to the chair opposite her. "Please, have a seat, Councilor. Perhaps you can share more about these whispers that have reached your ears."

Vex took the offered seat, his gaze never leaving her. "There are always whispers in a place like this, Elara. Whispers of power, of ancient relics and untapped potential. It is said that you have been particularly - active, as of late."

Elara forced herself to remain calm, her mind seeking just the right words. "Master Thorne and I recently returned from an expedition to an ancient cavern. We discovered some old relics and runes that we are currently studying. Perhaps that is what you are sensing."

Vex smiled. "I see. And where is Master Thorne now? I would very much like to speak with him about your findings."

Elara's heart sank. She had not seen Master Thorne since their return, and his sudden disappearance had left her feeling vulnerable and alone. "I'm afraid Master Thorne is not here at the moment. He often goes on solitary journeys to meditate and seek guidance from the arcane forces."

Vex's smile faltered for just a moment, a slight hint of something darker passing through his eyes. "How unfortunate. I do hope he returns soon. In the meantime, I trust you will continue your studies and keep me informed of any significant discoveries."

Elara nodded, her grip tightening on the cloak that concealed Zephyr. "Of course, Councilor. I will do my best."

Vex turned to leave, but paused at the door, his gaze lingering on Elara. "Take care, Elara. The world is full of dangers, and one must always be vigilant."

As he left Elara felt Zephyr shift beneath her cloak once more, his presence a comforting warmth against the chill of the councilor's visit. She watched Vex's silhouette fade into the shadows of the corridor, the door closing with a soft thud behind him.

With a breath of relief, Elara revealed Zephyr, the dragon's golden eyes locking onto hers with a blend of curiosity and trust. She gently caressed his head, her mind racing with the ramifications of Vex's visit.

"It's alright, Zephyr," she said, holding him close. "We just have to be cautious. We can't let anyone discover you."

Zephyr nuzzled against her, his warmth and presence a soothing balm to her frayed nerves. She knew that keeping him a secret would be a challenge, but she was determined to protect him at all costs.

Days passed and Elara continued her studies, delving deeper into the ancient texts and scrolls that filled the Mage's Tower. She learned about the history of dragons, their powers, and the bond they shared with their chosen companions. Zephyr grew stronger and more playful, his wings still too small for flight but his spirit undaunted.

One evening, as Elara sat by the window, watching the sun set over the city, she felt a strange sensation in the air. It was as if the world had shifted, a ripple of magic that made her shiver.

Elara's gaze swept across the distant skyline, her voice barely above a murmur. "Zephyr, something's not right."

The diminutive dragon, attuned to her disquiet, scampered up to perch on her shoulder. It issued a gentle, inquisitive trill. Elara rose, her pulse quickening as she approached the threshold, anxiety rising within her chest.

"You stay here," she told the Zephyr, putting him down on the floor.

Closing the door behind her, Elara stepped into the hallway, where mages and apprentices bustled about, their expressions clouded with worry. Rumors of Master Thorne's disappearance had permeated the tower, thickening the atmosphere with tension.

Determined, Elara made her way to the central chamber, the usual meeting place for the archmages' council. She sought answers, hoping for direction amid the chaos. As she entered, her eyes fell on Councilor Vex, who stood at the center, addressing the assembly of mages.

"Master Thorne has not been seen for some time now," Vex declared, his tone commanding. "We must assume that he has been taken or is in grave danger. We cannot afford to be complacent. We must strengthen our defenses and prepare for whatever may come."

Elara's anger bubbled beneath the surface, fueled by her frustration. It was clear to her that Vex was exploiting Master Thorne's absence to advance his own ambitions, to tighten his grip on the tower. She stepped forward, her voice cutting through the tension with an unexpected clarity that took even her by surprise.

"Councilor Vex, with all due respect, we should be focusing on finding Master Thorne, not just fortifying our defenses. He is a wise and powerful mage, and we cannot abandon him."

Vex turned to Elara, his gaze sharp and intent. "What do you suggest? Do you know where he could be? Perhaps you have a hint about who might have taken him?"

Elara paused, sensing the council's scrutiny enveloping her. She lacked definitive answers, only a deep instinct that something was profoundly amiss. "I—I'm not certain. Yet, I feel we should be searching for him, utilizing every resource available to us."

Vex offered a smile that failed to warm his expression. "A commendable thought, Elara. However, we must remain pragmatic. Our immediate concern is the safety of the tower and everyone within its walls. Once we secure that, we can focus on locating Master Thorne."

Elara clenched her fists, frustration boiling within her. She knew that Vex was manipulating the situation, using fear to consolidate his power. But she also knew that she had to be careful, that any rash actions could put Zephyr in danger.

As the council meeting continued, Elara slipped away, her mind wheeling with thoughts and plans. She needed to find Master Thorne, to uncover the truth behind his disappearance. And she needed to protect Zephyr, to keep him safe from those who would seek to exploit his power.

In the quiet of her chamber, she settled beside the window, Zephyr nestled in her lap. The small dragon gazed up at her, his eyes full of trust.

"We will find him, Zephyr," she said, determination threading through her words. "We will locate Master Thorne and bring him home. And we will keep you safe, no matter what happens."

Zephyr let out a soft, reassuring chirp, and Elara felt a sense of calm wash over her. She knew that the road ahead would be difficult, filled with challenges and dangers. But she also knew that she was not alone. She had Zephyr by her side, and together, they would face whatever came their way.

Days turned into weeks, and Elara continued her studies, honing her skills and learning more about the ancient magic that surrounded Zephyr. She practiced spells and enchantments, her bond with the little dragon growing stronger with each passing day.

One night, as she sat by the window, absorbed in her thoughts, a gentle knock rapped at the chamber door. Elara's heart quickened, and she swiftly concealed Zephyr beneath her cloak before she opened the door.

To her surprise, it was one of the tower's apprentices, a young boy named Arin. He gazed up at her, his eyes wide with concern. "Elara, I need to talk to you. It is important."

She stepped aside, inviting him in. "What is it, Arin? What is troubling you?"

Arin glanced around nervously before speaking in a hushed tone. "I have been hearing things, whispers among the mages. They say that Councilor Vex is planning something,

something big. I do not know what it is, but I think it has to do with Master Thorne's disappearance."

Elara's heart raced. "What do you mean? What have you learned?"

Arin hesitated, his expression clouded with worry. "I overheard some senior mages discussing Vex's recent meetings. They mentioned he has been conferring with unfamiliar faces, individuals who shouldn't be in the tower. They also spoke of a powerful artifact - something that could alter everything we know."

Elara's thoughts spun with a whirlwind of scenarios. Was it possible that Vex had a hand in Master Thorne's vanishing? Did he possess knowledge of Zephyr? Was he attempting to seize the power of the Zephyr for his own gain?

"Thank you, Arin," she replied, her tone unwavering even amid the chaos inside her. "You made the right choice in confiding this to me. However, you must remain vigilant. Trust no one, and stay alert. We need to uncover Vex's intentions."

Arin's expression was resolute. "I will, Elara. I will do whatever I can to help."

As he walked away, a fresh urgency surged within Elara. Time was of the essence; she needed to unveil Vex's intentions and locate Master Thorne before it slipped from her grasp. Her gaze fell on Zephyr, who peered out from the shadows of her cloak, curiosity dancing in his eyes.

"We will find him, Zephyr," she declared, her voice steady with determination. "We will track down Master Thorne and put an end to Vex's schemes."

***

The royal palace stood proudly at the city's heart, a symbol of the realm's enduring power and elegance. Its towering spires stretched toward the sky, adorned with banners that danced in the soft breeze. The walls, hewn from the finest marble, sparkled under the sun, their surfaces embellished with intricate designs narrating the land's rich history.

Elara moved through the grand halls with a sense of unease, her footsteps resounding on the polished floors. Beside her, Zephyr, now nearly full-grown, glided silently, his iridescent scales catching the light with each graceful motion. Though he had matured, his eyes retained the same innocence and wonder that had enchanted Elara since the day he hatched. Gasps filled the chamber at the sight of Zephyr, and Elara's heart sank as she grasped the weight of the moment.

As they neared the throne room, Elara felt a surge of anticipation. Being summoned by Queen Isolde was an extraordinary privilege for a mage apprentice. Yet, a disquieting sensation twisted in her stomach, firm and persistent. She understood, without a doubt, the reason for her summons.

Glancing at Zephyr, she offered him a reassuring smile.

"Don't worry," she told him. "All will be well."

The massive doors of the throne room creaked open, unveiling a space of stunning elegance. The walls were lined with woven depictions of legendary exploits, their hues lively and fresh. Sunlight poured through the stained glass windows, casting an array of colors across the marble floor.

At the far end of the hall, upon a dais of polished stone, sat Queen Isolde. Her crown of silver leaves glinted in the light, a symbol of her authority and wisdom. Her face, though lined with the cares of rulership, retained a regal beauty that commanded respect and admiration.

To the Queen's right, Councilor Vex stood, his eyes shining with a triumphant glimmer that sent a chill through Elara. She stepped closer to the throne, bowing deeply before her sovereign.

"Rise, Elara of the Mage's Tower," Queen Isolde's voice resonated, authoritative and unwavering. "You have been summoned to respond to serious accusations."

Elara straightened, her brow furrowed in confusion. "Accusations, Your Majesty? I do not understand."

Councilor Vex stepped forward, his voice dripping with false concern. "Your Majesty, as I have informed you, and as you can plainly see, this apprentice has been harboring a dangerous creature within the walls of our fair city. A dragon, no less."

Elara cast a quick glance at Zephyr, who looked up at her with unyielding trust, blissfully unaware of the peril that loomed over them.

Queen Isolde's eyes narrowed as they landed on Zephyr, a blend of awe and trepidation crossing her features. "Elara, enlighten me about this dragon now revealed before me."

Taking a deep breath, Elara steeled herself for the inevitable. "Your Majesty, I raised Zephyr from an egg that Master Thorne and I discovered. I promise you, he poses no danger to the kingdom. He is gentle and intelligent, and he has forged a bond with me that- "

"Silence!" Councilor Vex's voice cut through her words like a knife. "Your Majesty, surely you can see the danger this creature poses. Dragons are creatures of legend, known for their destructive power and insatiable greed. We cannot allow such a beast to roam freely within our borders."

Queen Isolde considered Vex's words with a seriousness that drew Elara's attention. The conflict in her eyes revealed a battle between fear and reason, a silent struggle that weighed heavily in the room. "Councilor Vex offers wise counsel," the Queen finally declared. "The welfare of our people must take precedence. I regret it, Elara, but I cannot overlook the potential danger that dragon poses."

As the Queen spoke, Elara felt the ground shift beneath her, the reality she had long feared now manifesting. Though she had anticipated this moment, she had clung to the hope of keeping Zephyr safe. "Your Majesty, I implore you," she urged, her voice thick with emotion. "Zephyr is no threat. He is gentle and steadfast. If you would only allow him the chance- "

"Enough!" Councilor Vex's voice boomed through the chamber. "Your Majesty, we must act swiftly. I propose that the dragon be taken into custody immediately, and swiftly disposed of - for the protection of the realm, of course."

Queen Isolde's expression hardened, firm and composed. "I agree. Guards, seize the dragon."

As the royal guards advanced, their armor clanking with each step, causing Zephyr to draw closer to Elara, instinctively aware of the impending threat. Elara's mind searched for a way out of this nightmare.

"Wait!" she implored, her voice cutting through the tension. "Your Majesty, I beseech you to reconsider. Zephyr is more than just a dragon; he is a sentient being, capable of thought and feeling. To act on Councilor Vex's proposal would be an egregious injustice."

Queen Isolde paused, her hand raised to signal the guards to halt. For a moment, Elara dared to hope. Yet, Councilor Vex leaned closer, murmuring something urgent into the Queen's ear. Elara observed as the Queen's demeanor shifted, her features tightening once again.

"I am sorry, Elara," Queen Isolde replied, her voice heavy with sorrow. "But the safety of the kingdom must come first. The dragon will be taken into custody."

As the guards approached, Zephyr's mournful cry pierced Elara's heart. She clutched him tightly, feeling the warmth of his fur beneath her trembling fingers. "It's alright, Zephyr," she whispered, her voice quivering as tears cascaded down her cheeks. "I won't let them hurt you. I promise."

Yet, deep down, she sensed the emptiness in her own assurances. The guards closed in, their spears menacingly pointed toward them. Elara felt a rough hand grasp her shoulder, yanking her away from Zephyr. Panic surged within her as she fought against the grip, her voice rising in desperation.

"No! You can't do this! Zephyr has done nothing wrong!"

As Zephyr was escorted away, his gaze remained fixed on Elara, a tether that seemed unbreakable. Suddenly, a disturbance erupted at the far end of the throne room. The grand doors swung open, and a figure entered, his robes swirling around him like dark clouds on the horizon.

"Cease this nonsense at once!" The voice boomed, powerful and commanding.

Elara's pulse quickened as recognition washed over her. "Master Thorne!"

The venerable archmage advanced purposefully down the center of the throne room, his striking blue eyes locked onto Queen Isolde. The guards stepped aside, transfixed by his presence.

"Your Majesty," Master Thorne intoned, bowing deeply. "I beg you to reconsider this course of action. The dragon you see before you is not a threat, but a miracle. A creature of ancient magic, reborn in our time."

Queen Isolde leaned forward, her interest piqued. "Master Thorne, we had feared you lost. Where have you been?"

"I have been on a journey of great importance, Your Majesty," Master Thorne replied. "A journey that has revealed to me the true nature of a threat we face. And it is not from this young dragon."

Councilor Vex stepped forward, his face a mask of barely contained rage. "This is preposterous! The dragon must be disposed of for the safety of the realm. Master Thorne, your judgment has clearly been clouded by your long absence."

Master Thorne turned to face Vex, his gaze sharp and narrow. "It is not my judgment that is obscured, Councilor. It is your true intentions that have remained concealed for far too long."

A hush enveloped the hall, as if time itself had paused. The only sound was the gentle rustling of fabric as Master Thorne withdrew a scroll from within his robes. It emerged, bearing a seal unfamiliar to those gathered. "Your Majesty," he began, his tone imbued with a gravity that filled the room, "I come bearing news of betrayal. Councilor Vex, a serpent hidden among us, is not who he claims to be. He belongs to the once-exiled secret society, now reformed, known as the Kulkodar Hunaveruk."

A gasp, sharp as a dagger, sliced through the hushed assembly. Whispers, like venomous snakes, slithered amongst the crowd, carrying the chilling name, "Dragon Hunters."

Master Thorne continued, his voice a relentless hammer upon the anvil of truth. "His design was sinister, a web of deceit spun with diabolical cunning. To ensnare the dragon, a captive in our care, and cast its power forth for his own devices. To seek and destroy all dragons, and even the Dragonlord herself."

Queen Isolde, her complexion as pale as winter's frost, accepted the scroll with trembling hands. "Where did you acquire this?" she inquired of Master Thorne.

"From the Grand Librarian himself of the Emerald Arbor. In Everwood," Master Thorne replied.

"Ah, the elves," the Queen murmured. She turned sharply to Vex. "Explain yourself, Councilor Vex," she commanded, her voice rising like a storm on the horizon.

Vex's face twisted with rage. "Lies! All lies! What do elves know! This old fool seeks to undermine the safety of our kingdom with his wild tales!"

As the Queen unfurled the parchment, her previously calm expression now marked by disbelief. "These symbols," she breathed, her voice as fragile as spun glass, "they bear your hand, Councilor. They are of the Kulkodar Hunaveruk and speak of a vile scheme to enslave dragons, to bend their ancient power to your will. Is this truth?"

Vex's eyes darted like frightened quail, seeking sanctuary in the shadows. "Your Majesty," he stammered, his voice a thin reed in the storm of her accusation, "these creatures, they hold power beyond measure. Power that is difficult to control. We sought not to enslave, but to understand. To use for the kingdom's benefit. But to do this, the Dragonlord needs to be found and eliminated."

"For the kingdom's benefit, Councilor?" Master Thorne's voice, a thunderclap in the chamber, slashed through Vex's deceit. "To bind the noble dragons and tarnish such ancient magic? Do you take us for simpletons? Your thirst for power knows no limits!"

"For the kingdom's benefit, Councilor?" Master Thorne's voice crashed like thunder in the chamber, cutting through Vex's web of deceit. "To bind the noble dragons and tarnish such ancient magic? Do you take us for simpletons? Your thirst for power knows no limits!"

Queen Isolde, a tempest in her regal bearing, rose from her throne. "Seize him," she ordered, her voice a storm wind. "Bind this traitor. We will reveal the full extent of his treachery."

As the guards advanced to capture Vex, the Councilor's mask of composure shattered. "Fools!" he spat, his voice laced with venom. "You are blind to the power you waste! The Dragon Hunters will not be denied their prize!"

Vex moved quickly, drawing a small vial from his robes and shattering it against the ground. A dense, acrid smoke erupted, quickly saturating the throne room. Amidst the ensuing turmoil, Elara caught the fading sound of footsteps racing away, accompanied by Vex's derisive laughter, gradually disappearing into the distance.

As the smoke cleared, Elara rushed to Zephyr's side, embracing the young dragon. "Everything is fine now," she whispered, her voice choked with relief. "You're safe."

Queen Isolde descended from her throne, her gaze directed toward Elara and Zephyr, a blend of wonder and remorse painted across her features. "Elara, I owe you an apology. I allowed fear and misguided counsel to cloud my judgment. Will you find it within yourself to forgive me?"

Elara, cradling Zephyr close, offered a reassuring smile. "Of course, Your Majesty. You acted out of a desire to protect your people."

The Queen knelt before Zephyr, her eyes shining with admiration. "And you, noble dragon. I hope you can forgive us for how we treated you. You are welcome in our kingdom, now and for all time."

With a slight tilt of his head, Zephyr regarded the Queen with understanding. To everyone's astonishment, he leaned in and gently nudged her hand, a gesture that conveyed forgiveness and acceptance.

Master Thorne stepped forward, his face grave. "Your Majesty, while this crisis has been averted, I fear our troubles are far from over. The Dragon Hunters are a powerful and far-reaching organization. They will not give up their pursuit easily."

Queen Isolde nodded, her face set with determination. "Then we must be prepared. Elara, your bond with Zephyr may be the key to understanding and protecting dragons. I would ask that you continue your studies, but now with the full support of the crown."

Elara felt a rush of pride and purpose surge within her. "It would be my honor, Your Majesty."

As the sun dipped low in the sky, casting elongated shadows through the vibrant stained glass of the throne room, Elara remained resolute, with Zephyr at her side, a silent sentinel. Master Thorne, framed by the waning light, loomed behind her - a figure of wisdom and counsel. Queen Isolde, her silhouette embodying regal grace against the deepening colors, regarded them with a blend of hope and apprehension.

"The path before us stretches long and perilous," Master Thorne declared, his voice resonating with the authority of ages past. "We must confront the Dragon Hunters, those who defile the sacred bond between man and beast." He turned his gaze upon Elara and Zephyr, their youthful faces illuminated by the fading light. "Your courage will be tested, your hearts tried. Yet, in this darkness, hope shall be your guiding star."

As the first stars began to pierce the twilight sky, they charted a path forward, their spirits buoyed by the Queen's unwavering support. Indeed, the journey loomed with uncertainty, yet they found comfort in their shared mission, a deep-rooted belief in the sanctity of the dragons and the fragile equilibrium of their world. And so, they set forth, their hearts filled with both trepidation and a resolute determination to protect all that they held dear.

Leaving the castle behind, Elara, Zephyr, and Master Thorne carried the significance of their mission like a mantle across their shoulders. The night air was crisp and invigorating, infused with the promise of adventure and the remnants of ancient magic. Stepping into the unfamiliar, the castle lights faded into the distance, leaving them bathed in the ethereal glow of the moon, their path illuminated only by the hope that flickered within their hearts.

***

Time flowed as a swift river, bearing the company of Elara, Zephyr, and the aged Master Thorne upon its tide. Seasons ebbed and flowed, their passage marked only by the subtle shift in the angle of the sun and the changing hues of the world beyond their journey. At length, their odyssey culminated in the heart of the ancient mountains, where shadows clung to the land like clinging mist.

There, shrouded in a constant twilight, was the sanctuary of the dragons. A vast expanse stretched out before them, its ceiling fading into the impenetrable blackness above. The air hung thick with the scent of earth and history, a potent blend of life and decay. The walls were adorned with carvings, ancient and significant, depicting beings of myth and legend, their forms rendered with an artistry that spoke of ages long gone. Crystals, akin to the mountain's heart, pulsed with a soft light, casting an otherworldly glow on the moss-covered stone. In this place, it felt as though the very walls carried the weight of dragons, their presence lingering in the shadows. It was to this hallowed place that they had come, seekers of the elusive Dragon Hunters.

Elara stood at the entrance, her eyes scanning the shadows that danced along the cavern walls. Zephyr, now almost fully grown and majestic, stood beside her, his scales glimmering like polished sapphires. His eyes, molten gold, reflected the flickering light of the crystals. Master Thorne, his robes flowing like water, stood with a staff in hand, his expression one of grim determination.

"We must be cautious," Master Thorne warned in a low rumble. "The Kulkodar Hunaveruk are cunning and ruthless. They will not hesitate to strike."

Elara placed her hand on Zephyr's flank, feeling the warmth radiate from the creature. "We will be ready," she replied, a knot of fear twisting in her chest.

As they ventured deeper into the sanctuary, the air grew colder, and the light dimmer. The silence was oppressive, broken only by the occasional drip of water from the cavern ceiling. Suddenly, a figure emerged from the shadows, his eyes gleaming with malice.

"Councilor Vex," Elara spat, her voice filled with contempt.

Vex stepped forward, a sinister smile playing on his lips. "Ah, Elara. How fitting that you should be here to witness your own demise."

Before Elara could speak, a thunderous roar erupted, shattering the tranquility of the cavern. From the depths, a titan emerged, a creature cloaked in darkness and fire. Illska, the dragon claimed by Vex, filled the space with its enormous presence. Its scales glistened like polished obsidian under the soft glow of the moon, exuding an otherworldly brilliance. Eyes that blazed with a fierce, malevolent red pierced the gloom, instilling an icy fear. A being born from nightmares had risen from the depths of despair.

"Back!" Master Thorne commanded, forcefully urging Elara away. But she quickly stepped forward.

"Zephyr, to me!" Elara shouted, leaping onto the dragon's back with practiced precision. Zephyr roared fiercely, his wings unfurling as he braced himself for the impending fight.

Vex climbed onto Illska's back, his eyes never leaving Elara. "You cannot win, girl. The Kulkodar Hunaveruk will prevail."

The battle erupted with such intensity that it rattled the sanctuary's walls. Zephyr and Illska collided in the sky, their roars echoing throughout the cavern. Elara held tightly to Zephyr, her pulse racing as she guided him with sharp commands. Below, Master Thorne unleashed his formidable magic, his staff radiating a bright light. Streams of energy surged toward Illska, but the dragon easily deflected each one.

Vex laughed at Thorne, his voice a cruel mockery. "Your magic is useless against Illska the Dark, old man. Give up now, and I may spare your life."

Master Thorne's eyes narrowed, his grip tightening on his staff. "I will never surrender to the likes of you, Vex."

As the battle raged on, Elara felt a surge of power within Zephyr. His scales began to glow, and a strange energy enveloped them both. She realized with a start that this was the moment the prophecy had foretold. Zephyr was the prophesied dragon, destined to restore balance between humans and dragons.

"Zephyr, now!" Elara shouted, her voice filled with newfound confidence.

Zephyr let out a mighty roar, and a wave of energy burst forth from his body. The force of it knocked Illska back, sending

Vex tumbling from his perch. The dark dragon roared in pain, its eyes filled with rage.

The cavern trembled, not with the approach of a living beast, but with the whisper of a memory so powerful it seemed to bend reality. From the depths of history, a presence unfurled - a dragon, but not of flesh and blood. This was a creature of legend made manifest, its form shimmering like starlight on water, scales the color of forgotten seas. It moved with a grace that defied its enormous size, each ripple of spectral muscle a testament to the power it once wielded in life.

Astride this magnificent apparition sat a figure that seemed to exist between worlds. Dragonlord Azura, no longer of mortal form, but a presence that commanded awe even in death. Her beauty was that of a fading dream, ethereal and haunting. As they entered the cavern, both dragon and rider began to materialize, their ghostly forms solidifying into tangible beings. Scales shimmered into existence, iridescent and alive with an inner fire. Azura's flesh took on a pale, luminous quality, her hair flowing like liquid starlight. Around her neck, an amulet, red as blood, rested.

When she spoke, her voice carried the weight of centuries, a sound like wind through ancient ruins, filled with wisdom and sorrow in equal measure. The cavern air trembled with each word as if reality itself recognized the power of her presence.

The pair - dragon and rider – now fully formed, filled the cavern not just with their physical presence, but with the weight of their legend. They were a reminder of a time when magic ran wild and the boundaries between the mundane and the extraordinary were as thin as gossamer. In their newly corporeal forms, they embodied both the glory and the tragedy of a world long past, their very existence a bittersweet lament for what once was and could never be again. The dragon's breath misted in the cool air, and Azura's fingers, now solid enough to touch, traced patterns on its scales - a gesture both familiar and impossibly ancient.

"Cease!" Azura's voice echoed through the cavern, a sound of thunder and authority. "This battle ends now."

Illska, sensing the power of the phantom dragon, hesitated. Vex, scrambling to his feet, looked up in horror. "No, this cannot be!"

Azura's eyes fixed on Vex, her gaze piercing. "You have betrayed your kind and sought to enslave the noble dragons. For that, you will pay the ultimate price."

With a swift motion, Azura unleashed a torrent of fire, engulfing Illska and Vex in its searing heat. The dark dragon let out a final, agonized roar, a mournful lament, before succumbing to the inferno. Vex's screams, a desperate plea for mercy, were silenced by the flames, a cruel epitaph to his life.

The cavern fell silent, the only sound the crackle of dying flames. Elara dismounted Zephyr, her legs trembling with exhaustion. She looked up at Azura, her eyes filled with gratitude and awe.

"Thank you, Dragonlord Azura," she said, her voice barely above a whisper.

Azura nodded, her expression softening. "You have shown great courage, Elara. And you, Zephyr, have proven yourself to be the dragon of prophecy. You shall be Dragonlord, Elara, and herald a new era of harmony between our kinds."

Azura's words hung in the air, heavy with the weight of destiny. Elara felt a sudden dizziness, as if the world had tilted on its axis. She reached out to steady herself against Zephyr's warm scales, feeling the dragon's heartbeat thrumming beneath her palm.

"But - I am just an apprentice," Elara whispered, her voice small in the vastness of the cavern. "I can't possibly be - "

Azura's laughter, rich and melodious, echoed off the stone walls. "My dear, destiny rarely announces itself with fanfare. It slips in through the cracks of ordinary days, disguised as coincidence or chance."

Zephyr lowered his great head, nuzzling Elara's shoulder with surprising gentleness. She felt a surge of warmth, of belonging, that defied explanation. It was as if a piece of herself she hadn't known was missing had suddenly slotted into place.

"The bond between you is already forming," Azura observed, her eyes twinkling. "It's a rare and precious thing, this connection between dragon and rider. It will grow stronger with time, until your thoughts and hearts beat as one."

Elara tried to grasp the enormity of what was happening. She thought of her small room in the Mage's Tower, of the rows of scrolls and the comforting smell of ink and parchment. How could she leave all that behind?

And yet - there was an exhilaration building in her chest, a wild joy that threatened to burst free. She looked at Zephyr, saw the same excitement mirrored in his eyes, and knew that her life would never be the same.

"What happens now?" she asked, her voice steadier than she felt.

Azura's smile was both kind and enigmatic. She reached up and unclasped the red amulet that hung around her own neck. With graceful movements, she placed it over Elara's head, letting it rest against her chest. "Now, my dear, your real training begins. The world is changing, and it will need both of you to face the challenges ahead." Her voice took on a formal tone as she continued, "I pronounce you Dragonlord, Elara. May you wield this power with wisdom and courage." She paused, her gaze intense. "Are you ready?"

Elara took a deep breath, feeling the weight of the amulet and the echoes of history and expectation enveloping her. She straightened her spine, lifted her chin, and met Azura's gaze with newfound resolve. "Yes," she affirmed, surprised by the strength that surged through her voice. "We're ready."

Master Thorne moved closer, his features reflecting both relief and pride. "It is as I had hoped. The prophecy has come to pass."

Elara turned to him, her gaze brimming with unshed tears and dawning comprehension. "You knew, didn't you? All this time. Your journey wasn't truly to Everwood. You sought out Azura."

A gentle smile played across Master Thorne's lips, his expression radiating the warmth of a long-held secret finally revealed. "Not entirely, my dear. Everwood did indeed welcome me, old friends awaiting my arrival. Yet I understood that only with her aid could we hope to overcome the Dragon Hunters."

With the battle behind them and the truth finally laid bare, Elara, Zephyr, and Master Thorne journeyed back to the kingdom. Though the road stretched long before them, their hearts were light. They recognized that they had accomplished something remarkable, a feat destined to reshape the very fabric of history.

When they arrived at the royal palace, they were met with a hero's welcome. Queen Isolde, her eyes filled with wonder and respect, greeted them personally. The people of the kingdom, once fearful of dragons, now looked upon them with admiration and hope.

In a ceremony that seemed to stretch across time itself, Zephyr and Elara stood before a sea of faces. The air thrummed with anticipation, a living thing that wound its way through the crowd. As they were proclaimed the new bridge between their two worlds, Elara felt a deep shift within herself, as if the very essence of her being had realigned.

Master Thorne, his eyes bright with unshed tears, received his accolades with quiet dignity. Elara, now bearing the mantle of Dragonlord, felt the expectations settle upon her shoulders like a cloak of responsibility.

As twilight painted the sky in hues of lavender and gold, Elara and Zephyr found themselves atop a hill overlooking their kingdom. The vastness of what lay before them was both exhilarating and daunting. Challenges lurked on the horizon, nebulous but undeniable. Yet Elara felt a curious calm, a readiness that seemed to hum in her very bones.

"Zephyr," she said softly, her voice carrying the quiet strength of a mountain stream, "are you ready?"

The dragon's response was a low, melodious rumble that vibrated through the earth beneath their feet. His eyes, reflecting the last golden rays of sunlight, held a wisdom and determination that matched her own. In that moment, Elara knew with absolute certainty that together, they would forge a new path. They would write a future where the bonds between humans and dragons grew stronger with each passing day.

And so began the tale of the Dragonlord and Zephyr, a story that would be whispered around firesides and sung in great halls for generations to come. It was a legend born of courage, nurtured by friendship, and sustained by the indomitable power of hope.

Tick. Tock. Tick. Tock.

Tick. Tock. Tick. Tock.

I wake to the sound of a clock. Darkness surrounds me, and my breath catches within the hard casing that covers my face. The cold, unyielding mask of metal presses against my skin, a constant reminder of my imprisonment. My limbs feel heavy, and as I attempt to move, I hear the clinking of chains. I am bound to a wall, my freedom stripped away by unseen captors.

Where am I? I just had gone to bed for the night. What manner of fiends had wrought this upon me?

Tick. Tock. Tick. Tock.

The room around me is shrouded in an impenetrable gloom, my eyes straining to discern any shape or form in the inky blackness. Yet, despite the visual void, my other senses heighten, attuning themselves to the slightest stimuli. The air is stale and musty, carrying the faint scent of decay and abandonment.

Tick. Tock. Tick. Tock.

The rhythmic sound of a clock pierces the silence, each second measured with deliberate precision. Its sound carries an eerie sense of inevitability, a constant reminder that time presses on, indifferent to the madness building inside me. I focus on my breathing, trying to calm the rising panic that threatens to overwhelm me.

Inhale. Exhale.

The faint sound of air rushing through the mask's narrow openings joins with the clock's incessant ticking.

How long have I been here? Hours? Days?

The absence of light and the monotonous ticking have robbed me of any sense of time. My mind desperately tries to recall the events that led to my current predicament, but my memories are as shrouded as the room itself.

Tick. Tock. Tick. Tock.

The clock continues its merciless march, each tick seeming to grow louder, more insistent. I struggle against my bonds, the metal biting into my flesh. Sweat, a traitorous accomplice, begins to bead upon my brow. My breath quickens, the sound of my own desperate gasps filling my ears.

What cruel fate has befallen me? What transgression have I committed to deserve such torment?

The questions swirl in my mind, each one giving birth to a hundred more, a maelstrom of uncertainty and fear.

Tick. Tock. Tick. Tock.

The clock's rhythm seems to mock me now, a constant reminder of my powerlessness. I try to focus on something, anything else, but in this sensory deprivation, the ticking becomes my entire world. It sings in my skull, reverberating through my very being.

I close my eyes, though it makes little difference in the oppressive darkness. I attempt to steady my breathing, to find some semblance of calm in this nightmare. But with each inhale, the musty air reminds me of my confinement, and with each exhale, I hear the whisper of my own despair.

Tick. Tock. Tick. Tock.

How easy it would be to surrender to madness, to let my mind unravel in the face of this unending torment. Yet something within me rebels against this fate. A spark of defiance ignites in my soul, urging me to resist, to endure.

I begin to count my breaths, trying to establish a rhythm separate from the clock's tyrannical ticking.

One. Two. Three. Four.

With each number, I feel a small measure of control returning. It is a pitiful rebellion against my circumstances, but it is mine.

As I count, I become aware of subtle changes in my environment. The air seems to shift, carrying new scents – damp stone, rusted metal, and something else, something organic and unsettling. My skin prickles with gooseflesh, a primal response to an unseen threat.

Tick. Tock. Tick. Tock.

The clock's rhythm remains unchanged, but now it seems to pulse with an ominous energy. Each tick feels like a hammer blow, each tock a death knell. I strain my ears, desperate to hear anything beyond my own breathing and the clock's relentless march.

For a moment, I think I hear something – a whisper, a sigh, the rustle of fabric. But is it real, or merely the product of my increasingly fragile mind? The uncertainty gnaws at me, adding another layer to my torment.

I try to move again, testing the limits of my bonds. The chains rattle, their metallic song a haunting melody in the darkness. As I shift, I feel something brush against my leg – something soft and yielding. I recoil instinctively, my heart pounding in my chest. What horrors lurk in this lightless chamber?

Tick. Tock. Tick. Tock.

The clock continues its merciless count, each second stretching into an eternity. I find myself wondering about the nature of time itself in this unchanging darkness.

Does time truly pass here? Or am I trapped in a single, endless moment, doomed to experience this torment for all eternity?

My thoughts turn to the mask that encases my face.

Why am I forced to wear it? Is it merely another form of restraint, or does it serve some more sinister purpose?

I try to recall my own face, but the memory seems to slip away like water through cupped hands.

The steel is cold against my skin, its weight a constant presence. I can feel the edges where it meets my flesh, a boundary between my self and the void that surrounds me.

If I removed it, would I still exist? Or would I dissolve into the darkness, becoming one with the nothingness?

Tick. Tock. Tick. Tock.

The clock's rhythm seems to quicken, though I know it must be my imagination. My pulse races to match it, sweat beading on my skin beneath the unforgiving mask. I feel as though I am balancing on the edge of a precipice, one misstep away from plunging into the abyss of insanity.

I try to ground myself in physical sensation – the cold of the chains, the pressure of the mask, the hardness of the wall at my back. These discomforts become anchors, tethering me to reality as my mind threatens to drift away on currents of fear and confusion.

As I focus on these sensations, I become aware of a new sound – a faint scratching, barely audible beneath the clock's ticking and my labored breathing. It seems to come from all around me, a soft, insidious noise that sets my nerves on edge.

Tick. Tock. Scratch. Tick. Tock. Scratch.

The new rhythm terrifies me more than the unending darkness. It speaks of life, of movement, of something sharing this hellish space with me. My imagination runs wild, conjuring images of unspeakable creatures lurking just beyond my perception.

I strain against my bonds with renewed vigor, desperate to escape whatever horror approaches. The chains bite into my flesh, but I barely notice the pain. It is nothing compared to the fear that now consumes me.

Tick. Tock. Scratch. Tick. Tock. Scratch.

The scratching grows louder, more insistent. I can hear it moving, circling me in the darkness. My breath comes in ragged gasps, the sound amplified by the mask. I want to scream, to cry out for help, but my voice seems trapped in my throat.

Suddenly, I feel something brush against my hand. It is soft, almost gentle, but the touch sends a jolt of terror through my body. I jerk away, the chains rattling violently. The scratching stops for a moment, then resumes, closer than before.

Tick. Tock. Scratch. Tick. Tock. Scratch.

The twin rhythms of the clock and creature merge into a maddening dissonance. I feel as though I am being crushed between them, my sanity crumbling under the relentless assault. I close my eyes tightly, though it makes no difference in the pitch blackness.

In this moment of utter despair, a strange calm descends upon me. It is not peace, but rather the stillness that comes when one has reached the limits of fear. I realize that whatever fate awaits me, I am powerless to prevent it. This understanding brings with it a kind of freedom.

I open my eyes, facing the darkness. The scratching continues, drawing ever nearer, but I no longer shrink from it. Instead, I listen intently, trying to discern its nature, to understand the thing that shares my prison.

Tick. Tock. Scratch. Tick. Tock. Scratch.

As I listen, the scratching reveals itself not as chaos, but as intention. Each scrape and drag carries purpose, a rhythm that speaks of consciousness. My ears strain, decoding the sound, and suddenly I understand - this is language, a message being carved into the very stone itself. The realization gives me a chill.

Is some unseen hand inscribing my fate upon the walls of this chamber?

Tick. Tock. Scratch. Tick. Tock. Scratch.

I strain to decipher the message, to glean some meaning from the rhythmic scratching. But the darkness is absolute, and the sound alone is not enough to convey its content. I am left with only questions and the maddening uncertainty of my situation.

The scratching stops abruptly, leaving only the ticking of the clock and the sound of my breathing. The sudden absence is more terrifying than its presence had been. I hold my breath, waiting for something, anything to break the silence.

Tick. Tock. Tick. Tock.

The clock resumes its solitary vigil, marking the passage of time in this timeless place. I exhale slowly, the air hissing through the mask's openings. The moment stretches, taut with anticipation.

Then, without warning, I feel a touch on my face – not on the mask, but on my skin beneath it. It is impossible, yet I feel it clearly – a cold, dry finger tracing the contours of my cheek. I try to recoil, but there is nowhere to go. The touch continues, exploring my features as if trying to memorize them.

A scream builds in my throat, finally breaking free. It reverberates inside the mask, filling my ears and mind with its raw, animal intensity. The touch withdraws, but I continue to scream, unable to stop. My voice grows hoarse, but still, I cry out, railing against the darkness, the clock, and the unseen presence that torments me.

Tick. Tock. Tick. Tock.

The clock continues its relentless count, indifferent to my anguish. As my screams subside, replaced by ragged sobs, I become aware of a change in the air. A faint light begins to seep into the room, so gradually, that at first, I believe it to be a hallucination.

But it grows stronger, revealing the contours of my prison. The walls are covered in strange symbols, carved into the stone. The floor is littered with bones. And there, in the center of the room, stands the clock – a towering monstrosity of gears and pendulums.

Tick. Tock. Tick. Tock.

As the light reaches its full strength, harsh and unforgiving, a flicker of motion comes at the edge of my vision. I turn, every muscle tensed, every nerve screaming. There, in a mirror I had not noticed before, is my reflection.

But it is not me. Not really. Where my face should be, there's a mask. I had thought it was metal, cold, and unyielding. Now I see the truth. It is bone. Yellowed, ancient bone, grown into my skull like some nightmarish parasite.

I cannot look away. I want to, God how I want to, but my eyes are locked on this grotesque visage.

And then, as if this horror were not enough, the mask begins to move. Its jaw drops open, wider and wider, in a silent scream that seems to swallow all sound, all hope.

I want to run. I want to claw at my face until this abomination comes off. But I can't move. I can only watch as the scream goes on and on, a soundless howl of despair that threatens to consume me entirely.

The clock chimes.

Tick. Tock. Tick. Tock.

Hunger, Hunger, Everywhere

The city loomed like a decaying colossus, its once-gleaming towers now tarnished monoliths stretching towards a perpetually smog-choked sky. Streams of acid rain trickled down the pockmarked facades, etching new scars into the already ravaged urban landscape. The streets below were a labyrinth of shadows and despair, where the unfortunate masses scurried like vermin, their eyes hollow and their spirits broken.

Amidst this dystopian display, a solitary figure moved with deliberate purpose. His worn coat, patched and frayed, billowed behind him like tattered wings as he navigated the detritus-strewn alleys. To the casual observer, he was just another lost soul, indistinguishable from the countless others who haunted these forsaken streets. But beneath his unremarkable exterior lurked a terrible secret, a darkness that set him apart from the common herd.

As he walked, the voice whispered to him, a constant companion that both tormented and guided him. It had been with him for as long as he could remember, a spectral presence that lived in the recesses of his mind. Sometimes it spoke in soothing tones, other times it shrieked with manic intensity. But always, always, it demanded blood.

"Why me?" his words were lost in the sounds of the dying city. "Why am I cursed with this burden?" He had asked himself these questions a thousand times, but answers remained elusive. Did others hear voices too? Were there more like him, walking among the masses, their inner demons hidden behind masks of normalcy?

The man's gaze darted from face to face as he moved through the throng, searching for - something. A sign, perhaps, or a kindred spirit. But all he saw were the same vacant expressions, the same defeated slouch of shoulders. These people were already dead inside; what difference would it make if he hastened their journey to oblivion?

A woman bumped into him, muttering an apology as she hurried past. For a moment, their eyes met, and he saw a flicker of - what? Fear? Recognition?

The voice surged within him, urging, *Follow her.*

His fingers twitched, longing to wrap themselves around her throat, to feel the life drain from her body.

No, not here. Not yet.

The voice could be impatient, but he had learned to bide his time. The hunt was as much a part of the ritual as the kill itself. So he continued his aimless wandering, allowing the city's oppressive atmosphere to seep into his bones.

As night fell – or what passed for night in this place of eternal twilight – the man found himself in a part of the city he didn't recognize. The buildings here seemed older, their architecture a departure from the utilitarian structures that dominated most of the urban landscape. Ornate gargoyles leered down from crumbling cornices, their stone faces twisted in silent screams.

The streets were quieter here, the usual bustle of the city muted to a distant hum.

Perfect. The voice became more demanding, its whispers rising to a fever pitch. *Soon*, it promised. *Soon the craving will be fulfilled.*

A figure emerged from the shadows, a young man barely out of his teens. His eyes were glazed, his movements jerky – clearly in the throes of some chemical escape from reality.

Easy prey, but perhaps too easy. The voice demanded more of a challenge.

The man approached nonetheless, his posture carefully crafted to appear non-threatening. "Excuse me," he spoke, the roughness of his voice surprising even him. How long had it been since he'd spoken aloud? "I seem to be lost. Could you point me towards the central district?" he asked the other man.

The young man's unfocused gaze struggled to settle on the man's face. "Central - yeah, man. It's - that way." He waved vaguely in no particular direction.

"Thank you," the man said, his voice a low, predatory growl masked as casual conversation. He took a step closer, closing the distance between them like a closing noose. "Do you hear them? The voices, the whispers in the dark? The ones that no one else can hear?"

Confusion, a thick fog, rolled across the young man's face. "Voices? Man, everyone's got noise in their head, right? The stuff that makes you want to scream."

Wrong answer! The voice, a monstrous thing within him, shrieked in frustration.

This was a waste of time, a pointless detour on the road to his destiny. But patience, a mask he'd learned to wear well, held him back. He forced a smile, a rictus grin that felt like a betrayal of his true self. "Yeah, ain't that the truth. Thanks for your help." He backed away, a slow, deliberate retreat as if facing a rabid animal.

As he continued his journey through the nightmarish urban sprawl, the man's thoughts turned inward. Was he truly alone in his affliction? Or were there others out there, hiding their own inner demons behind carefully constructed facades?

The hours blurred together as he walked, each step taking him deeper into the heart of the city's rot. Cascading around him, the buildings were little more than skeletal remains, their windows gaping wounds that stared sightlessly into the gloom. The few people he encountered scurried away at his approach, their animal instincts warning them of the predator in their midst.

And still, the voice whispered, growing more insistent with each passing moment. *I am hungry!*

The hunger was becoming unbearable, a physical ache that threatened to consume him from within. Soon, he promised himself. Soon.

He walked down an alley, a shadowy passage that seemed to stretch into darkness, an opening that hinted at nothingness. Ahead, in the muted light, a figure began to take shape from the despair - a man, or perhaps something claiming to be one. His clothes were a tattered banner of defeat, his gait a drunken lurch.

He muttered to himself, a broken record of nonsense, oblivious to the world around him.

The voice, a persistent parasite, urged him forward. *This time, no hesitation.*

He moved closer, a predator stalking its prey.

"Pardon me," he began, his tone a silken lie. "I have a question."

The drunkard blinked, his eyes twin pools of confusion. "Huh? Whaddya want?"

"Do you hear them?" he pressed, closing the distance. "Voices in the night, whispers on the wind?"

The drunk's face, a roadmap of misery, twisted in incomprehension. "Voices? All the time. Don't know if it's the booze talkin'. But yeah. I hear 'em."

A smile, cold as winter, touched his lips. "Right answer," he purred.

In one fluid motion, he closed the distance between them, his hands finding the drunk's throat with the practiced precision of a virtuoso pianist striking a perfect chord.

The voice in his mind burst into a raucous symphony of delight, each neuron firing in orgasmic glee as he felt the life force ebb from his victim. *Finally, we can feast! Yes, yes, this is what we've been waiting for. Feel the pulse beneath your fingers, the desperate struggle for air. Isn't it exquisite? Remember how we used to resist this urge? How foolish we were, denying ourselves this sublime pleasure.*

His grip tightened, fingers digging into soft flesh. The drunk's eyes bulged, a silent plea for mercy that only fueled the voice's excitement.

Look at those eyes, so full of fear. Drink it in. This is what it means to be alive, to hold power over life and death. We are gods in this moment, you and I.

The hunger, that insatiable void that had gnawed at his insides like a rabid beast, finally subsided. It was a moment of transcendent bliss, a fleeting second of nirvana in this cesspool of a city. The man savored it, knowing all too well how quickly the respite would fade.

As the body slumped to the ground, a discarded marionette with its strings cut, the man straightened up. He adjusted his coat with meticulous care, smoothing out the wrinkles as if preparing for a society gala rather than standing over a fresh corpse in a piss-stained alley. The act was automatic, a ritual as ingrained as the killing itself.

The encounter with the drunk lingered in his mind, a splinter of doubt lodged in the calloused surface of his psyche. For a moment - brief as a hummingbird's heartbeat - he had felt a connection, a shared madness. But ultimately, it changed nothing. The relentless voice in his head, that ever-present puppeteer of his actions, had reasserted its dominance with brutal efficiency.

He was what he was: a predator among prey, a shark gliding through schools of unsuspecting fish. The city served as his hunting ground, its inhabitants little more than nourishment for his unquenchable desire.

Perfect, utterly perfect. We did well with this one. But there will be more. Many more. The voice offered its approval, a sinister lullaby that promised more hunts, more kills, more fleeting moments of relief.

He melted back into the shadows, leaving the corpse as a grim offering to the decaying city. Tomorrow would bring a new hunt, a new victim, and always, always, the voice would be there to guide him. The cycle would continue, unbroken and unrelenting, until either the voice fell silent or the city ran out of prey. And in this sprawling metropolis of lost souls and broken dreams, the latter seemed as unlikely as the former.

The city swallowed him up, its endless maze of streets and alleys offering ample hunting grounds for those who listened to the whispers in the dark. And as he walked, the man continued to ponder the eternal question: Why me? Why am I cursed with this burden?

But deep down, he knew there would never be an answer. There was only the voice, the hunt, and the fleeting moments of release when the hunger was finally sated. It was, he realized, a perfect microcosm of the city itself – a place of endless appetite and momentary satisfactions, where the lines between sanity and madness blurred into meaninglessness.

Then, as if in answer to his unspoken need, a figure appeared at the end of the street. A woman, her posture erect and purposeful, so unlike the shuffling gait of the city's usual denizens. She moved with confidence, her head held high as she navigated the treacherous terrain.

The voice surged within him once again, a tidal wave of anticipation and desire. *Yes*, it hissed. *This one. This one is worthy.*

He followed her, keeping to the shadows, his footsteps silent on the debris-strewn pavement. She led him on a winding path through the decaying cityscape, seemingly oblivious to his presence. But as they entered a narrow alley, she suddenly stopped and turned to face him.

"I know you're there," she called out, her voice steady and unafraid. "Show yourself."

For a moment, he hesitated. This was not how the hunt usually unfolded.

Do it! Do it! What are you waiting for? The voice urged him forward, eager for the kill.

He stepped into the dim light, his face a mask of calm neutrality.

"Good evening," he said, his tone conversational. "I apologize if I startled you. I was merely heading in the same direction."

The woman's eyes narrowed, assessing him with a keen intelligence that both thrilled and unnerved him. "You've been following me for the past twenty minutes," she stated flatly. "What do you want?"

Not yet! First, the question! Always the question! The voice screamed.

"Tell me," he said, taking a step closer, "do you ever hear voices? Voices that no one else can hear?"

Something flashed in the woman's eyes – recognition? Understanding? For a breathless moment, he dared to hope that he had finally found another like himself.

Then she laughed, a harsh, bitter sound that echoed off the alley walls. "Voices? No, I don't hear voices. But I see things. Things that aren't there. Things that can't possibly be real."

What the fuck! Get her! Do it now!

But the man froze, his mind reeling. This was - unexpected. The voice fell silent, as if unsure how to proceed.

"What kind of things?" he asked, genuinely curious despite the hunger for flesh and blood that still gnawed at him.

No! Get her now! Do it!

The woman's gaze became distant, unfocused. "Monsters," she whispered. "Creatures from nightmares, lurking in every shadow. Sometimes I think they're more real than the world around us."

For a moment, the man forgot his murderous intent, silencing the voice. Here, at last, was someone who understood the burden of living with an altered perception of reality. Not voices, perhaps, but something equally isolating and terrifying.

"How do you cope?" he asked, his voice barely audible.

"I do my best," she smiled with a twitch.

Her smile, a fleeting, almost predatory gesture, widened into a grin of otherworldly hunger. Then her body lengthened, contorting with sickening cracks and pops like a time-lapse of evolution gone mad. The skin on her face stretched taut, cracking like sun-baked earth in a forgotten desert, revealing a grotesque, alien visage beneath - all angles and jagged protrusions. Her eyes, once deceptively human, now blazed with an unnatural, predatory light that seemed to suck the very warmth from the air.

He stumbled backward, his reality shifting as if the universe had decided to play a cruel trick.

The voice, that insistent whisper that had been his constant companion in this hellscape, returned, screaming at him. *Get her! Get her now!*

But his body, that traitorous sack of meat and bone, refused to obey. He was frozen, a deer caught in the headlights of an oncoming truck.

Her smile grew ever wider, stretching into something unnerving, as her body uncoiled like a spring made of razors and broken glass. The darkness of the alley seemed to bend around her, reality itself recoiling from the wrongness of her existence. With a roar that shattered the silence and a few laws of physics, she lunged forward, pinning him to the grimy pavement. Her claws, long and razor-sharp, extended from her inhuman hands like switchblades made of nightmares and broken promises.

"Do you see things?" she asked him, saliva dripping from fangs that gleamed with the sickly iridescence of an oil slick on a polluted river. Her voice was a discordant noise of whispers and screams, the sound of a thousand lost souls crying out in the void.

Don't answer! Don't answer!

He shook his head in fear, his eyes wide with the dawning realization that he was staring into the abyss, and the abyss was not only staring back but preparing to swallow him whole. "I hear only voices," he managed to croak, his own voice a pathetic whimper in the presence of unimaginable dread. "In my head. Tormenting whispers and anguished cries."

"Right answer," she cackled.

The world erupted into a frenzy of pain as she tore into him - her teeth transformed beyond any human form - sinking deep into his flesh with the eagerness of a junkie finding their next fix. Each bite unleashed a universe of pain, an explosion of suffering that birthed new realms of torment with every fleeting moment.

The voice, once an ever-present echo in this urban wasteland of broken dreams and shattered realities, was silenced, drowned out by the brutal melody of his own terror and death. Its absence left a void more terrifying than its presence had ever been, a silence so profound it screamed.

With that horrific act of violence, she turned and continued down the alley, her form already shifting back to its human disguise. She disappeared into the shadows as suddenly as she had appeared, melting into the city's dark underbelly like a nightmare fading at dawn.

Just another monster among monsters, in a world where such distinctions had long since ceased to matter, where the line between predator and prey was as distorted as the smeared reflections in rain-slicked streets.

The city swallowed her whole, digesting her presence like it had countless others, leaving behind only the cooling corpse of her latest victim and the lingering stench of fear and violated reality.

Across the Veilwater

In the fair lands that lay upon the banks of the Veilwater, two realms stood sundered by its meandering course. Upon the eastern shore, the elven settlement of Allundel gleamed with a beauty beyond the craft of mortal hands, its silver-leafed dwellings of crystal catching the light of sun and stars alike. Westward, the village of Riverton, home to the race of Men, nestled amidst gentle hills and fields of golden wheat that swayed in the breeze. Here, thatched roofs and stout stone walls spoke of the brief yet industrious lives of those who dwelt within, a testament to the resilience of those whose days were numbered by the swift passage of time.

It was upon these shores that young Aelindra first beheld Callum, though neither yet knew the other's name. The elven child, with hair like unto spun moonbeams and eyes of deepest violet, had stolen away from her lessons, drawn by the siren song of adventure that whispered upon the wind. Her bare feet, light as falling leaves, danced across sun-warmed stones as she approached the water's edge, her laughter a melody that seemed to make the very air shimmer with delight.

Across the expanse of the Veilwater, Callum paused in his task of gathering kindling for his father's hearth. The boy's green eyes, as vibrant as new leaves in the first flush of spring, widened with wonder at the sight of the elven child. He had heard tales of the Fair Folk, of course, whispered around the village fires on long winter nights when the wind howled fiercely beyond the walls, but never had he dreamed that his own eyes might behold one of that ancient and noble race.

In that moment, as the two children gazed upon one another across the flowing waters of the Veilwater, a great silence fell upon the land. It was as if the entirety of the land held its breath, witnessing the meeting of two worlds long sundered. The young ones stood thus, hearts aflutter with a mixture of wonder and trepidation, each marveling at the other's strangeness and beauty.

It was Aelindra, daughter of the elven, who first found the courage to break the spell of silence. Her voice, clear and melodious, carried across the water like the gentle chiming of bells in great halls.

"Hail and well met!" she called, raising a slender arm in greeting. "I am Aelindra, of the house of Elowen. Pray tell, who might you be?"

Young Callum, son of Men, hesitated for but a moment, casting a furtive glance over his shoulder as if fearing the reproach of the Wise. Yet the allure of this encounter, like the call of the sea, proved too strong to resist. With halting steps, he drew nigh to the water's edge.

"Callum am I," he answered, his voice tinged with awe, "son of Gareth of Riverton. Tell me true, fair one - are you indeed of the Elves of whom our legends speak?"

At this, Aelindra's laughter rang out, a sound of such pure joy that it seemed to set the leaves of nearby trees dancing upon their boughs. "Indeed I am, young Callum! And you, I perceive, are of the race of Men. Never before have I had converse with one of your kind."

"Nor I with one of yours," Callum admitted, a shy smile playing upon his lips. "My father oft warns that we ought not trouble your folk, for you dwell apart from the world of Men."

"As does my mother caution me," Aelindra confided, her eyes alight with the mischief that has ever been the birthright of the young, be they elf or man. "Yet long have I wondered of the lands beyond our forests. I pray you, Callum of Riverton, tell me of your home and people."

And so began a conversation that would span hours, the two children sharing tales of their respective homes and lives. Callum spoke of the changing seasons, of planting and harvest, of the warmth of a hearth on a cold winter's night. Aelindra, in turn, painted pictures with her words of moonlit glades where elves danced beneath the stars, of ancient trees that whispered secrets to those who knew how to listen.

As the sun, the fire-golden, began its descent towards the lands, casting the Veilwater in hues of silver and flame, both children were struck with the sudden realization of time's swift passage.

"Alas, I must take my leave," said Aelindra, her voice tinged with the sorrow of parting. "My mother shall surely be seeking me ere long."

"And my father likewise," Callum concurred, his words heavy with reluctance. "Yet - might we not meet again on the morrow? When the day is young and full of promise?"

At this, Aelindra's countenance brightened, her smile rivaling the radiance of the sun itself. "Indeed! Oh, indeed we shall! I shall come when the sun reaches its zenith. Will you await me here?"

"Nay, not all the wild steeds of the plains could stay me from this place," Callum vowed, his joy mirroring that which shone in Aelindra's eyes.

As they went their separate ways, each returning to the lands of their kin, neither could have divined the intricate weave of destiny that had begun to enfold them, intertwining their fates in a manner that would alter the very fabric of both their realms.

Aelindra and Callum found themselves drawn again and again to the shores of Veilwater, where their companionship grew, delicate and vibrant, spanning the divide between their worlds. They exchanged stories, dreams, and the pure insights of youth, discovering in one another a spirit that transcended the long-standing rifts between their peoples. In those moments, the histories that had separated them felt distant, replaced by the bond that quietly deepened with every shared word.

Aelindra, with a voice as sweet as a nightingale's song, endeavored to teach Callum the flowing phrases of the elven tongue. Her laughter, like the tinkling of silver bells, filled the air as he stumbled over the lilting syllables, his human tongue struggling to capture their grace. In return, Callum imparted to her the simple delight of skipping stones across the river's surface, a pastime that brought boundless joy to the elven child.

"Look, Callum!" Aelindra exclaimed one sunlit afternoon, her face radiant with triumph as her stone danced five times upon the Veilwater before sinking into its depths. "I have mastered it!"

"Well done!" Callum called from the opposite bank, his green eyes gleaming with pride for his companion. "You are a natural, Aelindra. Soon you shall outdo me!"

As the seasons wove their tapestry of change, their meetings grew beyond the bounds of mere play. They began to share the burdens of their youthful hearts, the dreams and fears that shaped their awakening minds.

"Do you ever ponder what lies beyond the horizon, Callum?" Aelindra inquired one day, her violet gaze fixed upon the distant mountains that rose like sentinels to the east. "At times, it seems to me that the world is vast beyond measure, and we glimpse but a fragment of its wonders."

Callum nodded, his expression contemplative. "Indeed, I do. In the village hall, there are maps that speak of lands far beyond our own—realms of desert and ice, of mighty cities and boundless forests. At times, I dream of beholding them all."

"As do I," Aelindra admitted, a wistful smile gracing her lips. "Yet my mother insists that an elf's place is within the forest, tending to the trees and singing beneath the stars. She believes the world of Men to be too - transient for our kind."

At her words, a shadow flitted across Callum's face, a reminder of the chasm that lay between their peoples. "And my father claims that elves are too ethereal, that we ought not to mingle with those who dwell eternally while we fade and perish."

For a long moment, silence lay heavy between them, disturbed only by the gentle whisper of the Veilwater. Then Aelindra spoke, her voice soft yet imbued with a determination that belied her years.

"But they are mistaken, are they not, Callum? We are friends, you and I. What does it matter that you are human and I am an elf?"

Callum's smile was like the sun breaking through a veil of clouds. "Indeed, Aelindra. Friends we are, and friends we shall remain, regardless of what others may say."

Yet even as they forged this bond, the winds of change began to stir. Whispers of their friendship spread through both Allundel and Riverton, attracting the attention of those who viewed such a connection with suspicion and fear.

It was on a crisp autumn morning that Elowen, Aelindra's mother, confronted her daughter. The elven matriarch's face was a mask of stern disapproval as she gazed down upon the young girl.

"Aelindra," she began, her voice as cold and unyielding as mountain stone, "I have heard tales of your - associations with a human child across the Veilwater. Is there truth to these rumors?"

Aelindra lifted her chin, meeting her mother's gaze with a courage born of conviction. "It is true, Mother. His name is Callum, and he is my friend."

Elowen's eyes narrowed, a flicker of something akin to pain passing through them before being swiftly concealed. "Oh, my naive child. Do you not grasp the folly of such a friendship? Humans are as fleeting as mayflies, here and gone in the blink of an eye. To bond with them is to invite only sorrow."

"But Mother," Aelindra protested, her young voice trembling with emotion, "Callum is kind and brave and wise beyond his years. Surely not all contact with humans must end in grief?"

"Enough!" Elowen's voice cracked like a whip, causing Aelindra to flinch. "I forbid you from seeing this human boy again. Our ways are not their ways, Aelindra. It is time you embraced your heritage and left childish fancies behind."

In the humble dwelling of Gareth the husbandman, a scene of no less import was unfolding. The weathered tiller of the soil, his countenance furrowed with the cares of many harvests, stood before his only son, Callum.

"My child," spake Gareth, his hand, roughened by years of honest toil, resting upon Callum's shoulder with the weight of paternal concern, "Word has reached mine ears that thou hast been in communion with a child of the Elves by the river's edge. Speak true, is this so?"

Callum, though his heart did quicken within his breast, met his sire's gaze with unwavering mien. "It is as you say, Father. Her name is Aelindra, and in her I have found a companion most dear."

A sigh, heavy with the burden of ages past, escaped Gareth's lips. "Hearken unto me, Callum. The Elves, fair though they may be, dwell not in our realm of fleeting days. They abide unchanging, while we, the children of Men, wither and pass into shadow. No good can come of the mingling of our kindreds."

"But Father," Callum's voice rang with the fervor of youth, "Aelindra has unveiled to me marvels beyond my imagining. Through her eyes, I have beheld the world anew. How can such enlightenment be deemed amiss?"

"For it shall bring naught but sorrow!" Gareth's tone rose, imbued with a father's fear for his child. "When the winters have silvered thy hair and bent thy back, she shall remain as the spring, ever-blooming. 'Tis not the way of things, Callum. I bid thee, see her no more. Dost thou comprehend?"

Though Callum's shoulders bowed as if beneath a great burden, a spark of defiance yet smoldered in the depths of his verdant gaze. "Yea, Father. I comprehend."

As the sun sank beyond the western hills, casting the lands sundered by the Veilwater into shadow, two young hearts were rent with the anguish of enforced parting. Yet neither Aelindra nor Callum could have divined that this tribulation was but the first of many trials that would test the strength of their bond, a bond destined to shake the very foundations of their sundered realms.

In the days that unfolded, both children found themselves under the vigilant eyes of their respective kin. Aelindra's instruction in the ancient lore and arcane arts of her people was intensified, her mother resolute in her desire to steep her daughter in the traditions of the Elves. Callum, meanwhile, found his days filled with an abundance of tasks and duties, his father hoping that the rigors of labor would banish thoughts of elven companionship from the boy's mind.

Yet no measure of distraction could efface the memories of their shared moments, nor quench the yearning for the companionship they had discovered in one another. In stolen instances, each would gaze across the Veilwater, longing for a glimpse of the other, a silent vow that their friendship had not been a mere illusion.

It was on a night bathed in moonlight, when both hamlets lay in the embrace of slumber, that Aelindra resolved upon her course. With the grace inherent to her elven nature, she slipped from her bed and made her way to the river's edge. There, in the argent glow that danced upon the water's surface, she began to sing.

Her voice, pure and crystalline, carried across the Veilwater, a melody of friendship and longing that seemed to draw the very stars nearer to listen. It was a song of two realms sundered by fear and misunderstanding, yet bound by the indissoluble threads of love and hope.

In his modest chamber in Riverton, Callum stirred from his rest, drawn by the haunting melody that whispered through his window. Without hesitation, he rose and crept from his dwelling, his bare feet swiftly carrying him to the riverbank.

There, illuminated by the moon's gentle radiance, stood Aelindra, her silver hair gleaming like a beacon. As Callum approached the water's edge, their eyes met across the divide, and in that moment, both knew that no force in the world could truly keep them apart.

"Aelindra," Callum murmured, his voice carrying effortlessly across the still water. "I feared I might never behold you again."

"As did I," Aelindra replied, her violet eyes glistening with unshed tears. "But I could not endure the thought of losing your friendship, Callum. Regardless of what our parents may say, I know in my heart that our bond is right and true."

Callum nodded, a fierce resolve settling upon his young features. "We shall find a way, Aelindra. No matter how long it takes, no matter what obstacles we encounter. Our friendship will endure."

As they stood there, separated by the Veilwater yet united in spirit, neither child could have foreseen the trials and triumphs that lay ahead. For at that moment, on the banks of a river that divided two worlds, a seed had been planted - a seed of understanding and love that would, in time, grow to bridge the chasm between elf and human, altering the course of both their lives and the very fabric of their world.

***

In the turning of many seasons, Aelindra and Callum grew from the tender shoots of youth into the full bloom of adulthood. Their clandestine meetings, once filled with childish wonder, now bore the weight of deeper understanding and shared dreams. They found sanctuary in a hidden glade deep within the woods that bordered their realms, a place where the very air seemed to shimmer with ancient magic, and the veil between their worlds grew thin as gossamer.

It was in this hallowed place, on an eve when summer's warmth still lingered in the air, that Callum awaited with heart aquiver. The setting sun cast its dying rays through the boughs of ancient trees, painting the sky in hues that would make the most skilled of elven artisans weep with envy. His breath caught as he heard the soft whisper of approaching footsteps, and then Aelindra emerged from the shadows, her silver tresses catching the fading light like silver spun by the hands of the angels themselves.

"Callum," she breathed, her eyes, violet as the twilight sky, alight with joy. "I feared the watchful gaze of my mother would prevent my coming. Her vigilance has been as keen as that of the great hawks these past fortnights."

Callum rose to greet her, taking her hands in his own. He marveled, as he had countless times before, at how they seemed to fit together as perfectly as if crafted by the same maker, despite the differences wrought by their separate kindreds.

"My heart sings to see you, Aelindra," he said, his voice soft as a summer breeze. "These fleeting moments we share are as precious as the rarest gems, yet never enough to sate the longing in my soul."

A shadow, like a cloud passing before the sun, flickered across Aelindra's fair countenance. "Indeed, each day grows heavier with the weight of pretense. To return to Allundel, to feign contentment when my very being yearns for the world beyond the Veilwater - it is a burden that grows ever more difficult to bear."

Callum's grip tightened upon her hands, his eyes, green as the deepest forest, burning with intensity as he gazed upon her. "Then let us cast aside these chains of duty and expectation. Come with me, Aelindra. Surely there exists a place in this vast world where elf and man may dwell in harmony, side by side."

Aelindra's breath caught in her throat, hope and trepidation warring within her breast. "Callum, do you speak in earnest? Would you truly forsake all you have known, for my sake?"

"Nay, not for your sake alone, but for ours," Callum gently corrected. "So many seasons we have spent in secret communion, sharing the very essence of our beings - they have shown me that what we possess is a treasure beyond price. My love for you,

Aelindra, is not in spite of our differences, but because of them. You have unveiled to me wonders I had never dreamed existed, and I yearn to spend my days exploring them at your side."

Tears, like liquid starlight, welled in Aelindra's eyes as she hearkened to Callum's impassioned words. With trembling fingers, she reached up to caress his face, marveling at the strength and vulnerability she beheld there.

"Oh, Callum," she whispered, her voice thick with emotion. "My love for you surpasses all I once believed possible. Yet the world beyond our sheltered realms can be cruel to those who dare to be different. Are you certain this is the path you wish to tread?"

Callum's response was to draw her close, pressing his lips to hers in a kiss that spoke more eloquently than any words could hope to convey. It was at once tender and fervent, a vow of devotion that transcended the boundaries of kindred and custom. When at last they parted, both were breathless, their eyes shining with the light of newfound resolve.

"Never in all my days have I been more certain of anything," Callum declared, his voice ringing with conviction. "Whatever trials may lie ahead, we shall face them as one."

As they stood thus entwined, the very air of the glade seemed to pulse with an otherworldly energy. The ancient trees whispered their approval in voices as old as the world itself, and the very air sparkled with the promise of destiny unfolding.

Yet their moment of blissful communion was not to last. A sharp crack, as of a branch sundered beneath a careless foot, shattered the tranquility of their sanctuary. Aelindra and Callum turned as one to face the source of the disturbance, their hearts filled with sudden dread.

From the shadows emerged Elowen, Aelindra's mother, her face a mask of fury and disappointment that would have cowed the bravest of warriors. Behind her stood Gareth, Callum's father, his countenance a storm of conflicting emotions.

"So," Elowen's voice cut through the air like the keenest of elven blades, "this is how you repay the trust of your people, Aelindra? By consorting with a mortal, betraying your heritage and the very essence of who you are?"

Aelindra straightened, her hand finding Callum's and gripping it with a strength born of desperation and love. "Mother, I beseech you to see reason. This is no betrayal, but a union that could bridge the chasm between our peoples. Can you not see that our bond strengthens both our kindreds, rather than diminishing them?"

Gareth stepped forward, his weathered face creased with worry that spoke of long years of toil beneath the sun. "Son, I implore you to consider well the path you tread. The life of an elf is not for one of mortal blood. You will wither and grow old while she remains ever young. Is that truly the future you desire?"

Callum met his father's gaze unflinchingly, his voice steady and sure. "Father, the future I desire, is one spent at Aelindra's side. Be it fifty years or five hundred, I would count each moment a blessing beyond measure."

Elowen's eyes narrowed to slits, her voice dropping to a dangerous whisper that seemed to chill the very air around them. "You speak of matters beyond your ken, child of Men. The weight of immortality is not a burden to be borne lightly. Aelindra, come. We depart this place, and you shall not lay eyes upon this boy again."

"No!" Aelindra's cry echoed through the glade, startling birds from their roosts and sending small creatures scurrying for cover. "I shall not go, Mother. My heart belongs to Callum, and I choose to stand with him, come what may."

For a long moment, silence reigned in the clearing, as if the very forest stilled in anticipation. Then, with a swiftness that belied her graceful appearance, Elowen lunged forward, grasping Aelindra's arm and attempting to pull her away from Callum's side.

"Enough of this folly," she hissed, her voice filled with a mother's fear and anger. "You return home with me, this very instant."

But Callum, though mortal, was not slow to act. With a swift movement born of love and protective instinct, he pulled Aelindra behind him, shielding her with his own body. "You shall not take her against her will," he declared, his voice ringing with the conviction of one who has found his true purpose in life.

Gareth moved to intervene, his face a tempest of conflicting emotions. "Do not play the fool, boy. This path can lead only to heartache and sorrow."

As the tension in the glade reached its zenith, it was Aelindra who broke the impasse. With a gesture of her free hand, she summoned forth a blinding flash of elven light, a magic as old as the stars themselves. The radiance momentarily stunned both Elowen and Gareth, leaving them blinking and disoriented.

"Run!" she cried, her hand finding Callum's once more. Without hesitation, they plunged into the depths of the forest, leaving their stunned parents behind.

They ran as if pursued by all the dark creatures of legend, their feet barely seeming to touch the ground. The forest blurred around them, ancient trees and shadowed glades melding into a tapestry of green and shadow. When at last they could run no more, their lungs burning and legs trembling with exertion, they found themselves in a part of the woods neither had ever laid eyes upon before.

"What now?" Callum gasped, his gaze never leaving Aelindra's face, as if she were his lodestone in this sea of uncertainty.

Aelindra's expression was a mixture of wild exhilaration and tremulous fear, like one who stands upon the brink of a great adventure. "We press on," she declared, her voice filled with a determination that could move mountains. "There lies a world beyond the Veilwater, beyond our forests and fields. Together, we shall find our place within it."

Callum nodded, a slow smile spreading across his face like the dawn breaking over the eastern hills. "Together," he echoed, drawing her close once more.

As they stood thus embraced, poised upon the threshold of a new life, neither could have foreseen the trials and tribulations that awaited them. At that time, beneath the watchful gaze of the ancient forest, Aelindra and Callum exchanged a quiet promise. They would confront whatever awaited, side by side, their bond a steady light in a world so often veiled in uncertainty.

Days passed in a whirlwind of excitement and unease, each moment filled with both wonder and wariness. They journeyed under the cover of darkness and sought rest in the light of day, ever alert for signs of pursuit. Aelindra's innate knowledge of the forest, passed down through countless generations of her people, kept them fed and on a true course. Callum's practical skills, shaped by years of mortal toil, ensured they had shelter from the elements and warmth in the chill of night.

As they traversed the wild lands, their bond deepened and strengthened, tempered by the challenges they faced together. They shared tales of their childhoods, of the dreams they had nurtured in secret, and of the future they hoped to forge together.

One evening, as they sat beside a small campfire whose flames danced like spirits in the gathering gloom, Callum turned to Aelindra, his expression grave. "I have been pondering," he began, his voice low and thoughtful, "the words my father spoke. Of how I shall age and wither while you remain ever young."

Aelindra's heart clenched within her breast, fear gripping her like a cold hand. "Callum, I - "

He raised a hand, gently silencing her. "Pray, let me finish, my love. I would have you know that I have considered this matter deeply. And I stand firm in my conviction. Whether fate grants us fifty years or five hundred, I wish to spend them at your side. Your immortality does not fill me with dread, Aelindra. It is as much a part of you as the color of your eyes or the timbre of your voice, and I love all that you are."

Tears, like liquid starlight, welled in Aelindra's eyes as she hearkened to his words. "Oh, Callum," she whispered, reaching out to caress his face with fingers that trembled with emotion. "I swear to you, I shall cherish every moment we are granted together, be it the span of a mortal lifetime or the endless march of eternity."

As their lips met in a kiss as tender as it was passionate, the forest around them seemed to hum with approval. The ancient trees whispered their blessing in voices as old as the world itself, and the stars above twinkled with the promise of adventures yet to come.

Yet even as they reveled in the depths of their love and the exhilaration of their newfound freedom, both Aelindra and Callum were keenly aware that their journey was far from its end. The world that lay beyond the borders of their homes was vast and often unforgiving, particularly to those who dared to challenge the established order of things.

Yet as they held each other close that night, watching the embers of their fire slowly fade to ash, both felt a sense of peace and rightness settle over them like a warm mantle. Whatever trials might lie ahead on the winding road of their shared destiny, they would face them together, their love a beacon of hope in a world that too often forgot the power of unity between peoples long sundered.

And so, hand in hand, Aelindra and Callum stepped forth into the unknown, their hearts full of love and their spirits buoyed by the promise of a future forged together. The forest glade where their love had first blossomed faded into memory, yet the magic of that place lived on within their hearts, a constant reminder of the power of love to transcend all boundaries, be they of race, custom, or the very fabric of the world itself.

**

In the embrace of the sea and the shelter of ancient forests lay the coastal village of Tidewhisper, a refuge for those weary of the divisions that marked the wider world. Here, after many moons of journey and trial, Aelindra and Callum found their sanctuary.

The village was a vibrant tapestry woven from the threads of many cultures, where elves and humans lived alongside dwarves and the occasional halfling. Thatched cottages stood in harmony with the elegant dwellings of the elves, and the air was alive with the mingling of languages and the scent of exotic spices.

As Aelindra and Callum walked hand in hand through the bustling marketplace, they marveled at the harmony that surrounded them. An elven herbalist haggled good-naturedly with a human fisherman, while dwarven craftsmen displayed their wares beside the delicate artistry of the elves.

"It is everything we dreamed of," Aelindra breathed, her violet eyes wide with wonder. "A place where our love is not seen as something to fear or shun."

Callum squeezed her hand, his heart brimming with joy and hope. "Aye, love. It seems we have found our home at last."

The villagers welcomed the young couple with open arms and curious minds. Many were intrigued by their tale of love that crossed the boundaries of race and custom. Elindril, an ancient elf whose eyes held the wisdom of ages, took a particular interest in them.

"You have chosen a path both blessed and fraught with peril," Elindril told them one evening, as they sat in his home overlooking the sea. "The union of elf and man is rare and not without its challenges. But in your love, I see the potential for great beauty and understanding between our peoples."

"Our parents were against such a bond," Aelindra spoke. "But you, you are different in your thoughts. Why?"

Elindril smiled, his ageless face softening. "I am old, even by the reckoning of my kind. I have seen the turning of many seasons and the rise and fall of kingdoms. In all that time, I have learned that the heart's wisdom often surpasses the mind's caution. "

He rose and walked to the window, gazing out at the twilight sea. "The world is changing, as it ever does. The old ways fade, and new paths must be forged. Your union, though it may seem strange to some, is a harbinger of hope - a bridge between two kindreds long sundered."

Turning back to the couple, Elindril's eyes gleamed with a light both ancient and new. "Do not fear the whispers of those who cling to the past. Your love is a gift, a rare flower blooming in the midst of winter. Nurture it well, and from it may grow a forest of understanding that will shelter generations to come."

Aelindra and Callum exchanged a glance, their hands intertwining almost unconsciously. "We are prepared to face whatever comes," Callum said firmly.

Elindril's gaze softened as he regarded them. "Then let Tidewhisper be your haven, young ones. Build your life here, and may your love be an example to all."

And so they did. Callum's skills as a farmer found new purpose in tending the village's coastal gardens, coaxing life from the salt-touched soil. Aelindra's knowledge of elven lore and magic made her a valued healer and teacher, bridging the gap between elvish wisdom and human practicality.

They made a home in a small cottage on the outskirts of the village, where the forest met the sea. Aelindra filled it with the ethereal beauty of her people, while Callum added touches of human comfort and warmth. It became a symbol of their union, a perfect blend of both their worlds.

Years passed in what seemed like the blink of an eye to Aelindra, but which marked the steady march of time for Callum. Their love deepened with each passing season, weathering storms both literal and metaphorical.

There were challenges, of course. Some of the more traditional elves in the village viewed their union with quiet disapproval, while a few, those of Men, muttered about the unnaturalness of Aelindra's ageless beauty. But for every voice of dissent, there were many more raised in support and admiration.

In the fullness of time, as the seasons waxed and waned, Callum and Aelindra's love blossomed like the fair flowers of Lórien. Yet, in their wisdom, they chose not to bring forth children into a world shadowed by uncertainty.

For Aelindra, being of the elven kind, the weight of immortality lay heavy upon her heart. She knew that any offspring born of their union would be granted the gift of choice, to embrace either the fate of Men or the longevity of Elves. This burden of decision, she deemed too great to bestow upon an innocent soul.

Callum, though mortal, shared in his beloved's foresight. He understood that the joining of their bloodlines would create beings unlike any other, caught between two worlds, never fully belonging to either. The path of such children would be fraught with sorrow and isolation, for they would find no true kinship among either race.

Thus, in their love and wisdom, Callum and Aelindra chose to remain childless. Their union became a bridge spanning the divide of mortal and immortal. In this way, they nurtured not children of flesh and blood, but the seeds of harmony between their kindreds, which would bear fruit long after they had passed into memory and song.

It was on the eve of their twentieth year in Tidewhisper that Aelindra first noticed the subtle changes in Callum. A few strands of silver had appeared at his temples, and fine lines had begun to etch themselves at the corners of his eyes. To Aelindra, he was as handsome as ever, but the sight stirred a deep, primal fear in her heart.

That night, as they lay in their bed listening to the distant crash of waves, Aelindra voiced her fears. "Callum," she whispered, her fingers tracing the contours of his face, "I saw gray in your hair today."

Callum chuckled softly, catching her hand and pressing a kiss to her palm. "Aye, love. It seems time is leaving its mark on me at last."

"But I remain unchanged," Aelindra said, her voice quivering slightly. "While you age, I stay as I am. The truth of what that means - it terrifies me, Callum."

Callum propped himself up on one elbow, gazing down at her with eyes full of love and understanding. "Aelindra, my heart, we knew this day would come. I do not fear growing old, not when each year brings new joys with you by my side."

Tears glistened in Aelindra's eyes as she looked up at him. "But I do fear it, Callum. The thought of losing you, of continuing on alone - it is more than I can bear."

Callum gathered her in his arms, holding her close as she wept. "Hush, my love," he murmured into her hair. "We have many years yet before us. Let us not borrow sorrow from a future that is yet to come."

But Aelindra could not shake the fear that had taken root in her heart. In the days that followed, she threw herself into research, poring over ancient tomes and seeking out every scrap of elven lore she could find. She spoke with Elindril and other elders of the village, searching for any hint of a way to extend Callum's life or to shed her own immortality.

Callum watched her quest with a mixture of love and concern. One evening, as Aelindra sat surrounded by scrolls and books, he approached her gently.

"Aelindra," he said softly, kneeling beside her chair. "My love, you are wearing yourself to the bone with this search. Please, come walk with me by the sea. Let us watch the sunset together."

Aelindra looked up, her eyes red-rimmed from strain and lack of sleep. "But Callum, I am so close. There are references to ancient rituals, to magic that could-"

Callum placed a finger gently on her lips, silencing her. "And they will still be here tomorrow. Come, love. Let us not waste the precious time we have in fear of its ending."

Reluctantly, Aelindra allowed herself to be led from their cottage. As they walked hand in hand along the shore, the setting sun painting the sky in breathtaking hues of gold and crimson, she felt some of the tension leave her body.

"It is beautiful," she murmured, leaning into Callum's embrace.

"Aye," he agreed, his eyes on her rather than the sunset. "And made all the more so by sharing it with you."

Aelindra turned to face him, her heart swelling with love. "Oh, Callum. How did I become so fortunate as to find you?"

Callum smiled, the lines around his eyes crinkling in a way that Aelindra found utterly endearing. "I ask myself the same thing every day, my love. Every moment with you is a gift, Aelindra. I would not trade our time together for all the immortality in the world."

As they stood there, silhouetted against the dying light of day, Aelindra felt a shift within herself. The fear did not vanish entirely, but it receded, overtaken by a fierce determination to cherish every moment she had with Callum.

"You are right," she said softly. "I have been so focused on the future that I have been neglecting our present. Forgive me, my love."

Callum's response was to draw her close, kissing her with a passion that spoke louder than words. When they parted, both breathless, he rested his forehead against hers.

"There is nothing to forgive," he whispered. "We will face whatever comes together, Aelindra. That is all that matters."

As they made their way back to their cottage, the first stars of evening twinkling overhead, Aelindra felt a renewed sense of purpose. She would continue her research, yes, but not at the cost of the precious time she had with Callum. Their love had already overcome so much; surely it could conquer even the relentless march of time.

And so life in Tidewhisper continued, each day bringing new joys and challenges. Aelindra and Callum's home became a gathering place for those seeking understanding between the races, a living testament to the power of love to bridge even the widest of divides.

As the years continued to pass, Callum's hair turned from dark to silver, and lines of laughter etched themselves deeper into his face. But his eyes, when they looked upon Aelindra, held the same love and wonder they had that day by the Veilwater so long ago.

And Aelindra, though her outward appearance remained unchanged, felt herself growing in wisdom and compassion with each passing year. She cherished every moment with Callum, storing up memories like precious gems to be treasured for all the long years of her immortal life.

Their love, born on the banks of a river that divided two worlds, had become a beacon of hope in Tidewhisper and beyond. It was a love that defied convention, that challenged the very notions of what was possible between elf and human. And though the shadow of mortality loomed ever present, Aelindra and Callum faced it as they had faced every other challenge - together, hand in hand, their hearts beating as one.

***

As the great wheel of ages turned, its spokes marking the passage of countless moons, Aelindra and Callum dwelt in their home upon the cliffs, where the vast waters of the sea stretched forth to the uttermost horizon. Their dwelling, a humble cottage wrought of stone and timber, stood as a bulwark against the tempests of the world, both those of wind and wave, and those of the heart.

Long did Aelindra, fairest of the Elves, seek to unravel the mysteries of immortality, that she might bestow upon Callum the gift of endless days. In her quest, she delved into tomes of lore long forgotten, sought counsel from the wisest of her kindred in lands far-flung, and ventured into the depths of forests primeval, where the very trees whispered secrets of ages past. Yet for all her labors, the prize she sought remained ever beyond her grasp.

Callum, whose locks had turned to silver and whose countenance bore the marks of years well-spent, observed her ceaseless toil with a heart full of love and gentle concern. As the sun dipped below the western sea on an eve of golden splendor, he took her hand in his, weathered by time and toil.

"Aelindra, light of my life," he spoke, his voice soft as the evening breeze, yet his eyes shone with the same devotion that had burned therein for nigh on half a century, "I fear that thy search hath become as a consuming fire. Can we not, instead, cherish the moments granted to us by the grace of the maker?"

Aelindra turned to him, her face as fair and ageless as the day they first met, a stark contrast to his mortal visage. "But Callum, how can I accept the fleeting nature of our time together, when the span of my days stretches forth beyond the count of years? The very thought of thy passing-"

Her words faltered, choked by the wellspring of emotion that rose within her breast. Callum drew her close, his embrace as strong and comforting as it had ever been, despite the changes wrought by the inexorable march of time.

"My beloved," he murmured into her tresses of silver, "thou shalt never truly lose me. Our love hath been a gift beyond measure, one that shall endure long after I have passed beyond the circles of this world. Let not the fear of its ending rob us of the joy we may yet share in the present."

Aelindra clung to him, her tears falling silent as starlight upon the waters. "Thy wisdom surpasses thy years, my love. I shall endeavor to heed thy counsel."

And so they did, treasuring each moment as though it were the last gift of the maker. They walked upon the shore, hand in hand, gathering shells and memories alike. They tended their garden in harmony, Callum's knowledge of growing things blending seamlessly with Aelindra's elven touch. They opened their home to all, sharing their tale with the younger generations, a witness to love that transcended the boundaries of kindred and custom.

Yet time, that most implacable of foes, marched ever onward, heedless of the joys and sorrows it wrought. Callum's once-vigorous steps grew slower, his breath more labored with each passing day. Aelindra, steadfast and unwavering, tended to him with the devotion of one who has pledged her heart for all eternity. Her healing arts, learned from the ancient lore of her people, eased his pain, yet they were powerless against the inexorable doom that awaited all Men.

On a crisp morn in autumn, when the world was cloaked in the golden raiment of falling leaves, Callum's appointed hour drew near. The sea-breeze carried with it the scent of salt and the promise of distant lands, as if whispering of journeys yet to come. He lay upon their bed, his hand clasped in Aelindra's, his gaze fixed upon her face as though to memorize every line and curve, every shadow and light. In her eyes, he saw the reflection of the countless moments they had shared, a tapestry woven from the threads of joy and sorrow, laughter and tears.

"Grieve not overmuch, my Aelindra," he whispered, his voice weak yet filled with love undimmed. "Our time together hath been more precious than all the jewels in the depths of the earth. I go now to a place where I shall await thee, for all the ages of the world if need be."

Aelindra's tears fell like rain. "Oh, Callum. How shall I bear the weight of eternity without thee by my side?"

Callum's lips curved in a gentle smile. "Thou art strong, my love. Stronger than thou knowest. Live, Aelindra. Live and remember our love, and in so doing, I shall never truly be gone."

With those words, Callum drew his last breath, his hand growing slack in Aelindra's grasp. A great keening cry rose from Aelindra's throat, a sound of such raw anguish that it seemed to shake the very foundations of the land.

For days uncounted, Aelindra sat motionless by Callum's grave, heedless of the concerned murmurs of the villagers. The very sky wept with her, rain mingling with her tears. It was Elindril, wisest of their kindred in Tidewhisper, who finally approached her, his ancient eyes filled with compassion born of countless years.

"Aelindra," he said gently, "Callum would not wish for thee to fade away in grief. Come, child of the Elves. Return to the world of the living."

Slowly, like one waking from a dream of deepest night, Aelindra rose. She allowed Elindril to lead her back to the cottage, though every step felt as a betrayal of Callum's memory.

As the wheel of seasons turned and the leaves of countless autumns fell, Aelindra moved through the twilight of her days as one caught between waking and dreaming. Her grief, born of mortal loss, hung about her like a cloak of mist, dimming the light of stars and sun alike. Through the rooms of their humble cottage she drifted, a wraith of sorrow, her slender fingers caressing the remnants of a life shared and now sundered.

It was upon an eve when the moon hung low and full, bathing the world in silver light, that Aelindra found herself in the study where Callum had spent many an hour bent over ancient texts. The scent of parchment and ink still lingered, a ghostly reminder of his presence. With hands that trembled like leaves in a gentle breeze, she reached for a tome bound in leather so old it had cracked and faded to the color of autumn wheat. As she opened its weathered pages, her eyes, keen even in the dim light, fell upon markings that stirred something deep within her fëa, her immortal spirit.

In that moment, as the candlelight flickered and danced upon the walls, casting long shadows that seemed to whisper of ages past, Aelindra felt the first stirrings of a change. It was as though a veil had been lifted, revealing a path hitherto hidden from her sight. The discovery within those yellowed pages would set her upon a journey that would lead her beyond the circles of the world, to a fate that neither Elf nor Man had foreseen.

There, hidden in the margins of a text long forgotten, was a reference to an ancient ritual of the Elves. A rite that would allow her to relinquish her immortality and join her beloved in the halls beyond the circles of the world.

Aelindra's heart raced as she read the faded script. Here, at last, was a way to be with Callum again. But the price was steep – not only would she have to give up her immortal life, but all memories of her existence would be erased from the world of the living.

For days uncounted, Aelindra wrestled with the decision. She thought of the life she and Callum had built, of the example their love had set for others. Would it all be for naught if none remembered?

But in the end, the thought of an eternity without Callum proved too great a burden to bear. With trembling hands, Aelindra began to gather the components needed for the ritual.

On the night when the moon was full and bright, Aelindra stood upon the cliff overlooking the sea, the same spot where she and Callum had shared so many sunsets. The components of the ritual were arrayed before her – herbs of great rarity, crystals that pulsed with the magic of a time lost and forgotten, and a lock of Callum's silver hair.

As she began to chant the words of the spell, her voice carrying upon the wind, a strange peace settled over her fëa. Images of her life with Callum flashed before her eyes – their first meeting by the Veilwater, their flight from their families, the joy of building a life together in Tidewhisper.

The air around Aelindra began to shimmer, her form becoming as translucent as the mists of dawn as the magic took hold. She felt no fear, only a profound sense of rightness. As the last words of the spell left her lips, Aelindra closed her eyes, a smile of pure joy illuminating her face.

"I come to thee, Callum," she whispered.

In that moment, Aelindra's physical form dissolved into motes of light, scattering upon the sea breeze. The components of the ritual crumbled to dust, leaving no trace of what had transpired.

As dawn broke over Tidewhisper, a curious thing occurred. The villagers awoke with a vague sense of something missing, though none could quite discern what it might be. The cottage upon the cliff stood empty, its contents fading like half-remembered dreams.

Yet in the hearts of those who had known them, a warmth remained – a legacy of love that transcended memory. And in the whispered tales told around hearth fires, a legend began to take shape. A story of an elven maiden who loved a mortal man so deeply that she followed him beyond the veil of death itself.

In a realm beyond mortal understanding, two souls reunited. Aelindra and Callum, no longer bound by the constraints of race or mortality, embraced. Their love, which had defied custom and time itself, now blazed eternal, a beacon of hope in the vast tapestry of existence.

And so their tale, though forgotten by the world of the living, became etched in the very fabric of creation. It was a tale to the power of love to overcome all boundaries, even those between life and death.

As the seasons passed, in Tidewhisper, life continued its endless cycle. The sea danced its eternal dance with the shore, and new loves blossomed in the shadow of ancient trees. And on quiet nights, when the moon was full and the wind whispered secrets from ages past, some swore they could hear the faint sound of laughter and see, just for a moment, the shimmering forms of two figures walking hand in hand along the moonlit beach – an elven woman and a man, their story a song that would be sung in the halls of eternity.

Last Call

Benno polished the glass with an old rag, the kind that probably should've been retired centuries ago but somehow kept doing its job. It was a quiet night in The Dead Star, the little bar floating on the edge of nowhere. A few regulars sat scattered around the room, each wrapped up in their own tragic stories of regret, failure, or just plain bad luck. They were the usual crowd - a couple of space miners on a long break, a synthetic philosopher contemplating the meaning of an asteroid, and some bounty hunter waiting on a target that had probably died of boredom.

Benno didn't mind the quiet. He'd been behind that bar for - well, longer than he cared to think about. The stars outside hadn't changed in eons. The station orbited a dying red giant, a bloated corpse of a sun that had no fight left in it, just like most of the bar's patrons.

The bell above the door chimed, and Benno didn't bother looking up. He never did. He knew who'd walk in before they even turned the handle. You tend bar at the edge of the universe long enough, you start to notice patterns. Most of the beings who drifted in were looking for the same thing - a place to rest, to forget, to escape from the infinite blackness they'd spent their lives staring into.

But this one was different. He knew it the second they stepped in.

"Whiskey," said the newcomer, sliding onto a stool.

Benno glanced up. Human - or at least mostly human, though with features that didn't quite match up. The eyes were too bright, the skin too smooth, like someone had sketched out the idea of a human but hadn't quite nailed the details.

Benno grabbed the bottle and poured a shot. "You got it."

The stranger picked up the glass and took a sip, eyes drifting over the room. "Quiet night."

Benno shrugged. "Always is."

The stranger smiled, a thin, tired expression that spoke of centuries rather than years. "I've been looking for a place like this. Somewhere - final."

Benno raised an eyebrow. It wasn't the first time he'd heard that line, and it wouldn't be the last. Every traveler through the bar seemed to think they were special, that their story was the one that mattered. They were wrong, of course. In the end, none of the stories mattered.

"Don't know if you're in the right place, then," Benno said, wiping down the counter. "We're not exactly the end of the line. More like the station you stop at before you realize there is no line."

The stranger chuckled, but it was a humorless sound. "I've been traveling a long time. From one corner of the universe to the other. Seen it all - stars being born, worlds crumbling into dust, civilizations rising up only to tear themselves apart. And now here I am, at The Dead Star, talking to a bartender who looks like he's been here since the Big Bang."

Benno smirked. "Something like that."

"What's your name?"

"Benno."

"Benno." The stranger rolled the name around in his mouth like he was tasting it. "I'm Cass."

Benno nodded, filing the name away like he did with all the others. In his line of work, you meet so many Casses and Zorvans and Maaliks that they all start to blur together after a while. But something about this one stuck, like a splinter he couldn't quite shake.

"So, Cass," Benno said, pouring himself a drink, "what brings you to this corner of the cosmos?"

Cass took another sip of whiskey, staring into the amber liquid as if it held the answers to the universe. "You ever get the feeling that none of it matters? That all this - " he gestured vaguely to the stars outside the bar's windows, " - is just noise? Like no matter what you do, you're just - waiting?"

"Waiting for what?"

"That's the question, isn't it?" Cass leaned forward. "I've been running for so long, Benno. I don't even know what I'm running from anymore. But when I heard about this place - this little bar floating in the shadow of a dead star - I figured maybe, just maybe, I'd find what I'm looking for."

Benno poured him another drink. "And what's that?"

"I don't know." Cass chuckled, but the sound was hollow. "Maybe you do."

Benno said nothing, just watched Cass with the same quiet patience he'd cultivated over the millennia. There was always a pattern to these conversations, a rhythm. It always led to the same place.

"I've heard stories," Cass continued, his voice low now, like a confession. "Stories about this place. About you."

"Oh yeah?" Benno leaned back, arms folded. "What kind of stories?"

"The kind that says you're not just a bartender. That this isn't just some outpost at the edge of nowhere."

Benno grinned, but it didn't reach his eyes. "Sounds like someone's been drinking too much."

Cass's expression didn't change. "I'm not some drifter with a sob story. I've seen things, Benno. Things most beings can't even imagine. And I've been looking for you for a long, long time."

Benno's smile faded. "You sure about that?"

"I am." Cass set the glass down gently, his eyes locking onto Benno's. "You're not just a bartender. You're entropy. The end of all things."

For the first time in what felt like an eternity, Benno was quiet. Not that it mattered - he knew where this was going, knew it had always been heading here.

"What gave me away?" Benno asked, his voice casual like he was asking about the weather.

"I don't know. Something about the way you talk. The way you seem - detached. Like you've already seen everything that's ever going to happen."

Benno sighed, pulling out another glass and filling it for himself. "Can't say you're wrong. But it's not exactly something I advertise."

Cass leaned back, a weary smile on his face. "I knew it. I knew you were more than just some old bartender." He paused, watching Benno closely. "So what now?"

"What now?" Benno shrugged. "You tell me. You're the one who came looking."

"I came here to stop running. To find peace. Maybe to end it all."

"That's the thing, though." Benno downed his drink and poured another. "There's no peace. Not really. Everything ends, sure. But not the way you think. Not in some big, cosmic blaze of glory. It's slow. It's quiet. And most of the time, no one even notices."

Cass frowned. "What do you mean?"

"I mean, when it's over, it's over. One day, you just stop. The universe doesn't care. Time moves on. Stars fade. People forget. You stop running not because you find peace, but because you get tired."

Cass stared at him, the weight of the words sinking in. "So that's it? I've been looking for answers, and you're telling me there aren't any?"

"There's one answer," Benno said, leaning in close. "It doesn't matter. Not you, not me, not the universe. We're all just - waiting."

Cass's face darkened. He stood up, pushing the stool back. "I refuse to believe that. There has to be more."

Benno watched him for a moment, then sighed. "Suit yourself." He poured another drink, this time for Cass. "But if you ask me, you came here because you already knew the truth. You just didn't want to admit it."

Cass stared at the glass, then back at Benno. "And what if I don't accept it?"

Benno shrugged. "That's up to you. But sooner or later, you'll stop running."

For a long time, Cass stood there, the silence of the bar wrapping around him like a blanket. Finally, he sat back down, picking up the glass. "And then what?"

"Then you finish your drink," Benno said, his voice soft, "and you go."

Cass's hand trembled as he raised the glass to his lips. He drank slowly, savoring each drop, as if it were his last. Maybe it was.

When he finished, he set the glass down gently, stood up, and nodded to Benno. No words were exchanged; there was no need. Cass knew the answer now. He had always known.

As Cass walked out the door, the bell chimed one last time. The stars outside the window flickered, dimmed, and blinked out one by one. Benno watched in silence, polishing the same glass he'd been polishing for eons, waiting for the next soul to wander in.

Because they always did. Eventually.

The Beast

The crystalline spires of Galadorn glittered in the ethereal light of the aurora, their facets refracting the dancing colors across the landscape. Seraphina and Kaelan huddled close to their grandfather on the observation deck, their eyes wide with wonder as they watched the celestial light show. The wind whistled through the towering structures, carrying with it the scent of ozone and stardust.

Seraphina, a precocious girl with bright green eyes and unruly auburn hair, tugged gently on her grandfather's sleeve. "Grandpa," she said, her voice filled with excitement, "tell us about your adventures on the TradeStar!"

The old man chuckled, his worn face crinkling with fondness. His once-dark hair had long since turned silver, but his eyes still sparkled with the light of countless stars he'd navigated. "Ah, you two never tire of those tales, do you?" He settled back in his chair, a comfortable old thing that had seen better days but fit him perfectly. His gaze grew distant as he recalled his days as a navigator. "Very well. Let me tell you about a planet called Aegis Terra."

Kaelan, Seraphina's younger brother, leaned in, his voice hushed with excitement. His mop of blond hair fell into his eyes as he asked, "Was it beautiful like Galadorn?"

"Oh, it was beautiful indeed," their grandfather nodded, a shadow passing over his face. "But beauty can hide terrible secrets. Now, listen closely- "

***

Aegis Terra hung like a jewel in the vast expanse of space, its surface a tapestry of lush forests and crystalline seas. As the TradeStar entered orbit, I marveled at the planet's pristine beauty. The ship's viewports were filled with swirling greens and blues, punctuated by wispy white clouds. Little did I know the dark truth that lay beneath its gleaming exterior.

We made planetfall in a clearing near one of the larger settlements. The descent was smooth, the TradeStar's engines barely disturbing the lush vegetation that surrounded us. As the landing ramp lowered, we were hit by a wave of sweet-scented air, rich with the fragrance of alien flora.

The Floreans, the planet's inhabitants. There was excitement on their faces, but also anxiety. They were delicate-looking people, catching the light in soft ripples, almost as if they carried the glow of their vibrant surroundings. Their eyes, wide and luminous, seemed to hold every hue of their world, mirroring both its beauty and its mysteries.

"Welcome, travelers," their leader, a tall, willowy being named Creaniul, said. His voice was melodious, almost musical, but there was an undercurrent of tension that I couldn't quite place. "We hope your stay on Aegis Terra will be - peaceful."

There was something in Creaniul's tone that set me on edge. I glanced at Captain Ralius, a grizzled veteran of a thousand voyages, who gave a subtle nod. We'd both picked up on it.

As we toured the settlement, I couldn't help but notice the nervous energy that seemed to be everywhere. The Floreans moved with a constant sense of urgency, their eyes darting to the horizon every few moments. Their homes were beautiful structures that seemed to grow from the planet itself, but there was something - temporary about them. As if they were ready to be abandoned at a moment's notice.

As we sat down to our evening meal, a spread of unfamiliar yet surprisingly tasty fruits and what I guessed were local specialties, the rumble came. A low, resonant noise, seemed to emerge from all around us. The Floreans went still, their expressions seized with fear. The lively conversation that had buzzed only moments earlier fell away, leaving behind an eerie quiet.

"What was that?" Captain Ralius demanded, his hand instinctively moving to his sidearm.

Creaniul's voice was barely above a whisper, his earlier melodious tones replaced by raw fear. "The Beast. It hungers."

And so we learned of the terrible bargain that ruled life on Aegis Terra. The Beast, a creature of unimaginable size and appetite, demanded tribute from the Floreans. In exchange for not devouring them outright, it allowed them to live and cultivate the land – only to feed it later.

"How long has this been going on?" I asked, horrified by the implications.

"As long as our histories record," Creaniul replied, his eyes filled with a sorrow that seemed to stretch back eons. "The Beast was once no larger than a hill. But with each feeding, it grows. Now- " He gestured to the horizon, where a massive shape loomed, blotting out the stars.

Over the next few days, we witnessed the grim ritual. They gathered their meager harvests, their livestock, and even the very stones of their homes, and brought them to the base of the colossal creature. The Beast, a monstrous entity, consumed it all with terrifying efficiency, its massive maw swallowing entire fields in single gulps, its eyes cold and dark. The ground trembled beneath its weight, the air thick with the stench of decay. It was a horrifying spectacle.

"But surely you'll run out of resources eventually," Captain Ralius argued, his voice filled with frustration and disbelief. "This can't be sustainable."

Creaniul's eyes were filled with a resigned sadness. "We know. But what choice do we have? To refuse is to die immediately. To comply - gives us time."

As our stay lengthened, we saw the toll this arrangement took on the planet. Forests that once stretched to the horizon, their canopies a vibrant tapestry of emerald and jade, now stood as skeletal remnants of their former glory. The wind whistled mournfully through bare branches, carrying with it the acrid scent of decay and desperation. Where mighty trunks had once reached for the sky, only splintered stumps remained, their rings telling silent stories of centuries cut short.

The oceans, once alive with creatures darting through vibrant coral reefs, now stretched out in eerie stillness. Beneath the surface, there was an unsettling silence, interrupted only by the distant thud of a wave meeting the shore. The beaches, once scattered with shells and driftwood, stood bare, their former richness stripped away.

The Beast grew ever larger, its bulk now visible from orbit, a dark mass that seemed to pulse with malevolent hunger. It sprawled across continents, its flesh a writhing landscape of grotesque protrusions and swelling ridges. From space, it resembled a malignancy creeping across the planet, its tendrils reaching into every corner of the world.

But there was a twist to this nightmare, a cruel irony that made the situation all the more horrifying. The Beast's waste, a glowing substance that oozed from its pores and seeped into the ground, seemed to power the entire planet. It fueled the Floreans' technology, crackling through conduits and powering machines with a frightening efficiency. Their homes were lit by its sickly glow, casting long shadows that danced on walls like mocking specters of their impending doom.

Even more unsettling were the forms of life that this waste sustained. Strange, luminescent plants grew where the Beast had passed, their twisted stems and pulsating leaves feeding on its leavings. These alien flora glowed with an otherworldly light, creating forests of bioluminescence that were as beautiful as they were terrifying. Insects with translucent wings flitted between these plants, their bodies glowing with the same unnatural energy.

I watched a group of Florean children playing near a patch of these plants, their laughter echoing strangely in the strange light. Their skin seemed to shimmer as if the very essence of the Beast was seeping into their bodies. I couldn't help but wonder what this exposure was doing to them, how it was changing them on a level we couldn't see. The thought sent a chill down my spine, and I turned away, unable to bear the sight of their innocence in the face of such cosmic horror.

"A cruel irony," Creaniul explained, his voice bitter. "The very thing that will ultimately destroy us also allows us to live in comfort - for now."

As our departure date approached, the situation grew dire. The Beast's hunger seemed insatiable, and the Floreans were running out of offerings. The once-lush forests created by the monster's waste had been stripped bare, leaving only skeletal branches reaching desperately toward the sky. And fields, recently planted by the Floreans that had once burst from the soil, now lay barren, the soil cracked and lifeless.

We urged the Floreans to leave, to take as many as we could to safety, but they stood their ground. I still see Creaniul's face when he brought us their decision — an expression that held both fear and resignation, with a surprising glint of defiance.

"This is where we belong," Creaniul declared, a touch of pride rising in his voice, despite the weariness that clung to him. His once-glowing skin had lost its radiance, now pale and lifeless, yet his words carried strength. "Whatever comes, we will meet it here."

The other Floreans gathered around him, their delicate forms huddled together like reeds in a storm. Some wept silently, while others stood tall, chins raised in quiet dignity. Children clung to their parents' legs, wide-eyed and confused.

"It will devour you," Captain Ralius warned Creaniul.

"It promised it wouldn't."

"You cannot trust something driven by such hunger," came the Captain's response.

As the TradeStar's engines roared to life, the last thing I saw as we lifted off was the Beast, now large enough to wrap itself around the entire planet. Its massive form obscured the sky, a heaving shadow that swallowed all light in its path. The ground beneath the Floreans crumbled away, vanishing into the Beast's boundless hunger, as if the land itself was being erased piece by piece.

As we broke through the atmosphere, I watched in horror as entire continents vanished, swallowed whole by the creature. Rivers of molten rock burst forth where the planet's crust had been breached, briefly illuminating the Beast's grotesque form before being consumed as well.

The Floreans' final stand was lost to us in the chaos, but I imagined I could still see them - tiny pinpricks of light against the encroaching darkness, facing their end with a courage that left me humbled and heartbroken.

***

Seraphina and Kaelan sat in stunned silence as their grandfather finished his tale. The auroras outside seemed to pulse with a newfound intensity as if reflecting the gravity of the story.

"But Grandpa," Kaelan finally spoke, his voice small, "what happened to the Floreans? And the Beast?"

The old man sighed heavily, the burden of memory evident in his slumped shoulders. "We received reports that the

Beast continued to grow, consuming everything around it. First the Floreans, then the planet's crust, its core - until finally - "

"What happened, Grandpa?" Seraphina whispered, her eyes wide in horror.

"Until finally, there was - nothing. Where Aegis Terra once stood, there is now only empty space. A void where a world used to be."

Kaelan's voice was barely a whisper. "What do you mean there was nothing left?"

The old man's eyes grew distant. "When the last Florean was gone, when the last blade of grass had been swallowed, when there was no more rock or stone - the Beast, driven by a hunger that could never be satisfied, began to consume itself. And Aegis Terra? That jewel of creation? It became less than nothing. A black hole of emptiness that would make even God's eyes water."

The children sat in stunned silence, their eyes wide with horror at the tale their grandfather had spun. Seraphina, always the inquisitive one, broke the quiet first. "But Grandpa, how could the Beast be so - so selfish?"

The old man leaned forward, his shaking hands clasped tightly. "Ah, my dear, that's the crux of it. The Beast knew only hunger, you see. It cared not for the Floreans, nor for the planet itself. It used them, all of them, as mere fodder for its endless appetite."

Kaelan frowned, his young brow furrowed in concentration. "But the Floreans, they fed it willingly?"

"They did, lad. Out of fear, out of a misguided hope that they could appease it. But in doing so, they only made it stronger, more ravenous. The Beast grew and grew, consuming forests, oceans, entire continents. And the Floreans, in their desperation, kept feeding it, thinking each time would be the last."

Seraphina hugged her knees to her chest. "That's awful, Grandpa. Didn't they realize what was happening?"

"I suspect some did, my dear. But fear can blind us to the truth, even when it's staring us in the face. The Beast had become their entire world, you see. They couldn't imagine life without it, even as it devoured everything they held dear."

Seraphina reached out, taking her grandfather's hand. "But why tell us this story, Grandpa? It's so sad."

He squeezed her hand gently. "Because, my dears, it's a warning. About greed, about the dangers of feeding into the dark hunger of others. The Beast thought only of its next meal, never of those around it. And in the end, that shortsightedness destroyed everything – even itself."

Kaelan nodded solemnly. "So, we have to think about more than just ourselves?"

"Exactly, lad. We're all connected, you see. What we do affects others, affects our world. We must be mindful of that, always."

The children fell quiet, their minds whirling like the auroras beyond the window. Seraphina's fingers traced patterns on the cool glass, following the dance of colors in the sky. Kaelan's eyes were wide, reflecting the shimmering lights, but seeing something far beyond. They both felt it then, a weight settling on their small shoulders, heavy as planets and light as stardust.

"Grandpa," Seraphina whispered, her breath fogging the glass, "is that - is that where Aegis Terra was?" She pointed to a patch of darkness amidst the swirling colors and stars, a void that seemed to swallow the light around it.

The old man didn't answer right away. His gaze followed her finger, and for a moment, the children saw a flicker of something in his eyes - grief, perhaps, or regret. When he spoke, his voice was soft, barely audible above the constant whisper of Galadorn's winds.

"Perhaps, my dear. Perhaps."

In the Embrace of Darkness

The evening descends upon the world like a funeral pall, enveloping the landscape in a misty darkness that clings to the skin and seeps into the very marrow of the bones. The full moon looms high in the heavens, casting an eerie glow that illuminates the silhouette of a vast, foreboding mansion. Its windows, darkened eyes, watch silently as the night unfolds its mysteries. From within its shadowed halls, a figure emerges - a young woman, her form barely discernible against the encroaching gloom.

Her breath comes in ragged gasps as she flees, her feet pounding against the earth with a desperate urgency. Above her, crows perch upon the gnarled branches of ancient trees, their beady eyes following her flight with an unsettling intelligence. Their caws echo through the night, a chorus of ominous foreboding that seems to mock her frantic cries.

Where are you? Where are you, my love?

The thoughts tear through her mind, a lamentation that reverberates through the stillness, unanswered and unheeded. The young woman is a tempest of emotion, her heart a storm of longing and despair. Her mind is a tumult of memories, each one sharper and more painful than the last.

I remember the way you looked at me. Your eyes, a deep well of mystery and promise.

The caws of the crows, once mere whispers, now rise in a discordant crescendo, and her eyes, in frantic desperation, dart upward to meet their malevolent gaze.

And the sound of your voice - a melody that filled me with hope and dreams of a future - a future now shattered at my feet.

In her mind, she envisions him, gazing at her. He was an older man, a painter whose fame cast a long shadow over her life. She loved him with a fervor that consumed her, a passion that knew no bounds. Yet, he rejected her advances, his words a dagger to her heart.

I was not too young. Too young to understand your world, the darkness that dwelled within you.

His rejection was a wound that festered, a poison that seeped into her soul. She tried to forget him, to banish his memory from her mind, but it was a futile endeavor. His presence lingered, a ghost that haunted her every waking moment, a specter that visited her dreams with cruel regularity.

Her feet carry her through the mist, the landscape a blur of shadows and half-formed shapes. She is driven by a force she cannot name, a compulsion that propels her forward despite the fatigue that weighs heavily upon her limbs. Her destination is a place she knows all too well, a place of sorrow and finality.

There you are, my love. I've found you, at last.

At her feet, the earth lies cloaked in a wild tangle of grass and weeds, interrupted only by a solitary, unadorned stone that pours its sickly light over the scene, draping it in an otherworldly pallor. Shadows, long and gaunt, writhe upon the ground as if possessed by some malevolent spirit. She falls to her knees, her hands clawing at the dirt with frenzied desperation. Tears stream down her face, mingling with the soil as she digs, her fingers raw and bleeding.

Why did you abandon me? Why did you leave me wandering, adrift in this world?

Her mind drifts back to their last time together, the moment when her hopes were dashed upon the rocks of his indifference. She stood before him, her heart laid bare, her love a dancing flame that shone brightly in the darkness. But he turned away, his gaze distant and unfocused, as if he were seeing something beyond her, something she could never hope to understand.

In that instant, she grasped the harsh truth of her own insignificance, the crushing awareness that she was but a footnote in the grand narrative of his life. She watched him walk away, his silhouette swallowed by the shadows, leaving her alone with her shattered dreams.

Now, as she kneels before him, she feels the full measure of her loss. The earth beneath her hands is frigid and unyielding, an accursed coldness. With a feverish desperation, she continues to rend and tear at the soil, her fingers scraping the cold, indifferent ground in a futile attempt to bridge the chasm of her grief.

You cannot be gone forever.

Her heart, a vessel of torment, defies the grim pronouncement, ensnaring itself in the anguished hope that, despite the dark decree, he remains close to her.

I know you're here. Still with me.

The crows watch silently from their perches, their dark, ghostly shapes outlined against the moonlit sky. They bear witness to her sorrow, somber onlookers to the tragedy that plays out below their cold, unblinking eyes. Their presence serves as a cruel reminder of fate's inexorable hand - the relentless certainty that all existence must ultimately succumb to the relentless march of time and that all things must come to an end.

As the night wears on, her cries grow softer, her strength waning with each passing moment. The earth beneath her hands is a barrier she cannot hope to breach. Yet, she continues to dig, driven by a love that transcends the boundaries of mere mortal existence.

Exhaustion claims her, a relentless tide pulling her under. She sinks to the ground, her tears spilling onto the soil like a bitter rain. The moon, a spectral eye, watches her descent into despair and laughs, as the crows take flight, their wings beating a solemn requiem for the lost.

Are you happy, my love? My heart is shattered, wandering upon a sea of sorrow. The night enfolds me in its embrace, a cocoon of darkness that offers no comfort, no reprieve from the pain that consumes me. I am alone in a world that has lost its meaning, a world where love and loss are intertwined in an unending waltz of sorrow.

Curled upon the earth, she is a part of it, her fingers, like desperate roots, continue their slow, relentless clawing, searching for a wooden barrier.

I yearn to feel the grain of timber beneath my trembling fingertips, to tear at it with a possessed resolve, the way you tore away at my heart.

Her thoughts wander through a misty haze, tracing the gentle contours of her memories until at last, they settle upon a forlorn shore - the day of their first fateful encounter. That day, suffused with the haunting allure of promise and possibility, dawned with an otherworldly light.

Oh, I remember the whispers in the village, the talk of the famous painter who had taken residence in the grand mansion on the hill.

A small creature, a creeping horror, makes its way across her arm. She senses its presence before she sees it, a cold, deliberate movement against her skin. As moonlight kisses its shell, she observes its tiny journey, entranced. Then, just as quickly as it emerges, it disappears into the earth, leaving behind a trail of slimy indifference.

They said you needed a housekeeper, someone to tend to the sprawling estate and its neglected gardens. The thought stirred something deep within me, a chance to escape the drudgery of my impoverished life. So, I set out, walking the long road from the village and up the hill.

The mansion loomed large as she approached, its grandeur both intimidating and alluring. She stood before its imposing doors, her heart a wild drumbeat of anticipation and fear. When he answered her knock, she was struck by the intensity of his gaze, eyes that seemed to hold the secrets of the universe within their depths.

He listened to her words, her plea for work, and nodded with a quiet understanding.

Your voice was so rich as it echoed through the halls. You told me room and board, in exchange for keeping the place clean and helping with the gardens. Oh, my love, it was a lifeline, a promise of a new beginning, and I was so grateful for your offer. Do you remember the smile on my face as I accepted?

She puts her ear to the earth and thinks she hears a groan. She smiles.

The mansion was a labyrinth of shadows, a world unto itself, filled with the painter's creations - canvases that captured the beauty and despair of life in vivid strokes of color. She marveled at his talent, the way he could capture a fleeting moment and immortalize it in paint. She watched him work, his brush moving with a grace and precision that spoke of years of dedication and passion.

At first, I was just content to simply be near you, to bask in the glow of your genius. But love, that insidious creature, crept into my heart. I dared to hope, a foolish gamble against the odds. Your eyes held the universe, yet they saw me not. I wanted to be a canvas upon which your desires were painted. Yet you, a solitary figure, moved through the world with a detachment that chilled me. And so, I retreated into the shadows, a ghost in my own life, until -

The dim, flickering light of the atelier cast its spectral glow upon her, as she stood in the foreboding silence, her heart a maelstrom of dread and eager hope. The painter, a man whose fame cast a long shadow, sat before her, his eyes a deep well of mystery and promise. She watched him for countless hours, his brush moving with a grace that seemed to capture the very essence of life. Yet, in all that time, he never truly saw her.

That night it would be different. I would lay bare my soul, hoping to lure you into the depths of my love.

With fearful hands, she started the task of unfastening the buttons of her dress, each one a barrier between her and the world she yearned to so desperately inhabit. The fabric, like a shadowy veil, cascaded from her shoulders, gathering in mournful folds at her feet, whispering its lament as it surrendered to the cold floor.

Paint me, I implored. Capture me as you do the ephemeral splendor of the world.

Yet, it was not the ardent flame she had yearned for, but a mere ember, swiftly smothered by the icy weight of his indifference. He surveyed her with the same detached scrutiny he might bestow upon a lifeless still life, his fervor wholly devoted to the canvas and not to her fragile heart.

I stepped closer. See me, I begged you, a plea that just hung there between us. See me as I am, not as the world perceives me. But your eyes, those windows to the universe, remained distant, unfocused, as if they sought something beyond me, something I could never hope to understand. I felt the devastating weight of my insignificance, the realization that I was but a shadow in your life.

Turning away, she felt the searing sting of rejection, a venomous draught coursing through her veins, its bitterness unmatched by any other. Even as she gathered the remnants of her disheveled attire, the cruel embrace of fate ensured her return, for she was irresistibly drawn back to the man who held her heart ensnared, a hapless prisoner of love's cruel caprice.

She cradles her thoughts in a fleeting embrace. The moon's pallid light touches her with an icy hand, revealing the sharp contours of despair fixed upon her face. Her trembling fingers trace circles in the damp soil, a futile attempt to weave order from chaos. Her hair, a raven's wing, lay scattered about her like a discarded mourning veil.

When she releases her thoughts, an immense sadness grips her.

But all my dreams were dashed, shattered by your gentle yet firm rejection. You are too young, you told me. Too young to understand the world you inhabited, the darkness that dwelled within you. Your words were a knife to my heart, a wound that refused to heal.

As she draws her circles, they burrow deeper into the earth. The memory of that day lingers, a bittersweet reminder that shapes her thoughts. Her fingers persist in their slow, unyielding digging, propelled by a love that remained unyielding. She holds tightly to the hope that, in some way, she might find her way back to him.

Our story is not yet finished, my love.

The night deepens around her, and the crows return atop the trees, silent in their vigil. The moon, a cold and distant observer, casts its light through cloud wisps. For her, it is a reminder of the passage of time and the inevitability of fate. Her cries now gone are replaced by whispers. She is tired, her strength nearly spent, yet she cannot bring herself to stop.

You never understood, my love. A heart is a fragile thing, easily battered by the storms of grief and longing. There is no reprieve from the pain.

The night stretches endlessly, enveloping her in its thick darkness as she perseveres with her arduous task. Her fingers, raw and bloodied, tear into the earth, propelled by a fierce urgency to uncover the wooden barrier hidden beneath. Above, the crows stand watch, their sharp eyes reflecting a quiet understanding as they observe her labor.

Her eyelids, heavy as leaden shutters, struggle against the pull of sleep. Yet, through the fissures of slumber, a torrent of memories breaches the dam. New thoughts, those of regret, are a nightmare she cannot escape. Tears, insidious insects, crawl from their subterranean lairs, their silent march a mournful dirge upon her cheeks.

The anger. Oh, the anger. It gripped my soul with an iron fist. It was a madness born of rejection, a desire to possess you utterly. I watched you drink the wine, my heart a tumult of conflicting emotions - love and hatred, hope and despair.

She raises her hand to wipe away the tears, leaving streaks of dirt across her cheeks. She digs furiously now through the cold earth, as she is faced with the bitter truth.

Memories twist like vines around your mind, persistent reminders of what once was. I believed you could remain by my side indefinitely, that death would not sever our bond.

Her whispers to the night are a fragile thread of sound.

I carry that regret within me, a deep ache that colors everything I do.

Her fingertips scrape against something hard, and her heart leaps with conflicting emotions - anticipation intertwined with fear.

I am close now.

The thought fills her with a twisted sense of satisfaction, a belief that somehow, by reaching him, she can atone for her sins.

Now, as she digs through the earth, she is faced with the full measure of her folly. Her actions, born of desperation and madness, have left her alone, a ghost in her own life. The night blackens around her, the crows silent in their vigil, as if mourning the tragedy that has unfolded before them. Her body trembles with fatigue, yet she cannot bring herself to stop.

In the oppressive silence of the night, with her strength nearly spent, she at last reaches the wood. Kneeling, she brushes away the clinging earth with nervous hands, her heart a tumult of exhilaration and dread.

Soon, my love. Soon, I will be with you, again.

She stands on unsteady legs, her form a ghostly shadow against the moonlit grave, and reaches down with dirt-caked fingers, seeking the edges of the lid. Her fingertips find purchase, and with a final, desperate effort, she strains to lift it. The lid creaks ominously, a sound that shrieks through the stillness like a mournful dirge.

There you are, my love. Long have I missed you.

The sight of his decaying form strikes her soul with the force of a relentless hammer, casting her into a maelstrom of tumultuous emotions. She weeps, her tears carving pale trails through the grime that mars her once fair cheeks. Yet, amidst the grotesque display of death's inevitable victory, she feels a perverse sense of solace, a closeness to the one she long sought. With shaking hands, she brushes the dirt from her tattered dress, her movements methodical, almost worshipful, as she lowers herself beside him. She shifts his lifeless body with a tenderness reserved for the most sacred of relics.

The fetid stench of decay, a miasma thick enough to choke the living, envelops her like a veil. But instead of recoiling, she finds in it a strange balm, a bitter comfort that soothes her tormented soul. Her trembling hands reach up to grasp the lid. Slowly, with a solemnity befitting the act, she draws it down, sealing them both within the embrace of death's cold, unyielding grasp. The darkness is infinite, a void that swallows light and life alike. She closes her eyes.

Ah, the eternal silence of the tomb.

In this funereal chamber, beneath the weight of earth and stone, she discovers the peace that life so cruelly denied her. The storm that raged within her heart, a storm of sorrow and unfulfilled yearning, is finally quelled, stilled by the irrevocable finality of her choice.

She knew that in time, the soil, unsettled and pushed aside in uneven mounds, would gradually settle and flatten, lulled by the passage of the sun and moon. Each passing day would see the grave sink deeper into the embrace of the earth, the scar it left upon the land slowly healed, as though time itself sought to erase the memory of what lay beneath. Rains would descend, bringing with them the seeds of forgotten life, carried upon the winds from distant fields. Those seeds would find their home in the soft soil, and from the decay below, draw sustenance. Delicate tendrils would push forth, seeking the light, and tender shoots of green would emerge, timid at first, but growing in confidence as they stretched towards the heavens.

With a last breath, she whispers a final, broken farewell, her voice barely a whisper against the suffocating gloom, "Soon, my love - we shall be one in the dust - forever."

ABOUT THE AUTHOR

Philip Mazza is a novelist with a boundless imagination, captivating readers with the epic fantasy series *The Harrow Saga*. Born in New York in 1959, he earned a degree in Business from LeMoyne College and an MBA, later holding leadership roles in human resources and operations. Now a professor at the Madden School of Business and Economics, Philip dedicates his time to his students and writing. *The Quantum Gardener* is his seventh literary work. He and his wife enjoy travel and continue to live in upstate New York.

www.ingramcontent.com/pod-product-compliance
Lightning Source LLC
Chambersburg PA
CBHW030746030726
47497CB00001B/147